A N(

all the lost pieces

LARA MARTIN

This is a work of fiction. Similarities to real people, places, or events are entirely coincidental.

ALL THE LOST PIECES

First edition. February 16, 2023.

For my mom, who read the book and loved it,

but never got to see it published.

You fought bravely right to the end.

I love you.

I miss you every single day.

Chapter One

If Nina Abrahams hadn't been fired this morning, she never would have said yes. At least, that's what she told herself. Her face flushed with the humiliating memory: standing alone in front of Pablo's massive I'm-obviously-compensating-for-something desk and realizing no one had backed her, Pablo's smug face as he uttered the words his Napoleonic ego had been squirming to say for weeks, the sympathetic stares of her staff as she packed up her stuff, and the guilty absence of those who'd sworn to stand by her, but who'd evidently caved somewhere between vigorous nods in her attorney-general moment—*Pablo is stealing money from you, he's exploiting you, enough's enough, we shouldn't let him get away with it*—and the sobering reality of monthly bills that needed to be paid.

As if Mondays weren't bad enough.

As the credits for another *Grey's Anatomy* episode rolled onto the screen, Nina blew her nose, dug out the remote from under a throw pillow, and hit the Mute button. She checked the time: 5:00 p.m. After being thrown out of the restaurant, she'd spent the day stretched out on her couch, working her way through copious amounts of Coke and corn chips while she watched impossibly attractive doctors tear into each other and their patients.

Her phone rang, and she glanced at the screen: Lucas. Not Pablo, the Uruguayan chef turned restaurateur, admitting to a colossal mistake in firing her, begging her forgiveness and offering her and the rest of the staff at Mateo's Grill a threefold pay increase. That was Fantasy Number Two. Lucas had taken the number one spot years ago, and it had never changed.

Sitting upright, Nina cleared her throat of the residues of a crying jag. "Lucas," she answered lightly.

"So there's a charity fundraiser this Saturday," he said by way of greeting.

"No, no, and no," Nina said. And then, as though Lucas was hard of hearing, which she knew he was not, just hard on resolve, she said again, "Definitely, no."

"It's for charity."

"Still no."

"The tickets cost me five hundred dollars. Each."

She rolled her eyes, which only magnified her headache. That was a bodyguard for you. Trained to think of all the angles. "You can afford seven hundred."

"Think of the kids in Zambia," Lucas said. "They walk two hours every day to get fresh water. This will give them a tap right in their village."

She frowned at her phone. And at the man who called himself her friend on the other end of the line. "Low blow, Lucas."

"Did it work?" he asked hopefully. "Can you get someone to cover for you Saturday night?"

She'd been fired, so that wasn't an issue, but she wasn't ready to tell him. Not yet. She couldn't cope with the resulting lecture—and there most certainly would be a lecture filled with uninteresting words like "prudence" and "responsibility" and "discretion." Unlike the satisfying words she'd tossed at her ex-boss this morning: cretin, thief, bully.

"Saturday night?" she asked, considering. "You must be desperate."

"Desperate enough to continue begging, if that would help."

She laughed. And that was when she found herself saying yes.

Lucas gave a satisfied whoop. "Thank you. I owe you one."

Add it to the tally, she thought, suppressing a sigh.

Wedging the phone between her shoulder and ear, Nina stood and stretched out too many hours of lying curled around comfort food. Finding a Doritos snagged on her pajama top, she absently pulled it free and bit into it.

There was a charged silence. "What was that noise?" Lucas asked suspiciously.

She swallowed. Quickly. "Noise? What noise?"

"Are you eating chips?"

"What?"

"You are," Lucas accused. "You're eating chips! Doritos, I bet." She heard him give a loud sniff. "I can smell them."

"As if," Nina scoffed, and then groaned as she realized how neatly she'd fallen into his trap.

"What happened?" Lucas demanded.

"What makes you think something happened?"

"The last time you binged on junk food, that lowlife of the unmentionable name had just dumped you and you single-handedly upped Doritos's profit margin."

A half chuckle, half sob escaped her. "Objection to the word *dumped*," she said, and burst into tears.

"Nina Sarah Abrahams," Lucas said, drawing out her name in warning. "You better not be watching something sad and romantic."

She hiccupped out a "Talking to you...so not watching...at this very moment."

"Why do you do it?" he asked in exasperation. "Why do you torture yourself like this?"

"Meredith and Derek are never going to get it right!" she wailed.

"*Grey's Anatomy*? Seriously?" Lucas's sigh was heavy. "I'm coming over. You better not drink all the Coke."

#

Lucas lived in an apartment in the city, as did she. That was where the similarity ended, though. Lucas owned an expansive three-bedroom apartment in a trendy residential tower; she managed in a shabby one-bedroom in one of the city's dodgier areas. Lucas's building was

3

upscale, flashy, and boasted its own gym and indoor pool. Her building...well, at least it had an elevator and hot water.

They lived close enough so that whenever he was away on a job, she could water the herb pots he wouldn't give up on, collect his mail, and sneak in a few laps in the communal pool. And perhaps, now and then, open the drawers in his bedside cabinet and rummage through the contents. It was an urge she didn't indulge in too often, because the guilt trip afterward wasn't worth it. Besides, Lucas never left anything around worth finding. A few years ago, he'd been in charge of the protection detail of a prominent but now disgraced sports star. He'd learned from the mistakes of his client.

It would take Lucas roughly twenty minutes to drive to her place. Twenty minutes to splash her face, dab on a bit of makeup, and pick up the detritus of her six-hour pity party: corn chips scattered like grenade fragments, empty glasses and sodden tissues littering the carpet.

Nina sorted herself out first. Priority number one was brushing her teeth, because after consuming nearly a liter of soda, she could practically feel her molars growing cavities the size of craters.

After applying a quick coating of mascara, she ran a brush through her dark, copper-highlighted hair and tied it up in a high ponytail, aiming for the jaunty, sporty look. *See, look at me, still going for gold!* She was thankful for her coloring. Olive skin and dark eyes meant she didn't look washed out, even though inside she was hitting the spin cycle.

She stacked the dirty dishes in the dishwasher, vacuumed the carpet, and folded away the blanket she'd been buried in for most of the day. A quick glimpse of her reflection in the TV screen reminded her with a jolt that she was still in the comfort pajamas she'd put on as soon as she'd arrived home. She hurried to her bedroom to change, but halted abruptly.

What am I doing?

Her mind flicked to the makeup she'd applied, the frantic tidying up. She bit her lip. Why was she trying so hard to impress him? Nina didn't like this occasional detached glimpse of herself: a back wheel caught in a rut, revving herself up only to end up sinking deeper into the mud, making it so much harder to free herself.

Her intercom buzzed just as she remembered she possessed a spine. She picked up the entry phone. "Lucas?"

"Yep."

She pressed the button to let him into the building. A few minutes later, there was an impatient knock, and Nina drew back the bolts and opened the door. Lucas stood in the hallway, hands in the pockets of his black jacket, cheeks flushed from the crisp air.

Her chest ached at the sight of him. His tall, wide-shouldered build dominated her doorway. Even standing still, he carried himself with the assurance of a man who'd been trained to handle risky situations. She loved that confidence in him.

"You didn't check the peephole," he said.

She raised surprised eyes to his. "You can't know—"

"I know, Nina." One eyebrow lifted coolly. "What if I were some psycho stalker?"

She tilted her head to one side and made a show of looking him over: dark dress jeans, cashmere sweater under the designer jacket, Italian shoes. "A stalker dressed like he's stepped off the runway? Really?"

"Come on, Nina, evil comes dressed in all forms. You know that." After a pause, he said, "But those pj's are evil all on their own."

"Hey, it's Einstein! He rocks," she protested.

He winced. "Not on clothes. Never on clothes." He motioned to the doorway she was absently blocking. "Let me in before someone sees you."

"You mean, before someone sees *you* with me." With a sweeping gesture, she stepped aside, acknowledging on a sigh, "I know I need to be more careful. I'll check my peephole from now on."

"Promise?"

"Promise."

Lucas stepped inside, and she shut the door. Peeling off his jacket, he turned to face her, but didn't move from the entrance hall. That eyebrow lifted again. Nina was overcome by the urge to shave it.

"Forgetting something?" he asked.

She set her hands on her hips. "I have a trained and possibly armed bodyguard in my apartment. Why would I need to bolt my door?"

His gaze was steady. "For those times when that trained and currently unarmed security specialist is not around. Habits, Nina."

Yeah, annoying ones like nagging. "All right, Dad, locking us in," she said. "Locking us in so that when my hair straightener catches alight and the fire spreads and we're both unconscious from the heat and smoke, no one can open the door to rescue us."

Laughter flickered in his green eyes. "And the odds of that happening are?"

"Probably the same odds of a psycho stalker seeing me in my Einstein pj's and being overcome by murderous lust," Nina replied as she bolted the lock on her door, the one Lucas had installed the day she'd moved in.

Lucas followed her inside to the living room. She watched his eyes make a quick sweep of the area before moving over her in that same assessing mode: eyes red and swollen from crying—check. Pj's on alarmingly early in the evening—check. Female employing sarcasm to disguise the fact that she's hanging on by a thread—check.

Resentment rose up inside her, but before it could spill over, Lucas closed the distance between them and gathered her into a hug.

With her cheek pressed against his broad chest, his heart beating steadily in her ear, feeling the solid strength of his arms around her, Nina knew this was why she put up with his fault-finding protectiveness and the sometimes unbearable pain of platonic ignorance.

Her arms looped tightly around his back, and she closed her eyes and lost herself in the moment. *A good end to a really crappy day.* After a while, Lucas patted her shoulder blade. Cue received, she stepped back.

"Coke?" she asked.

"I'll help myself."

He poured himself a small measure of Coke and took a sip. He drank more in commiseration with her, Nina knew, than a desire for the sugary drink. Lucas was careful about what he put into his body. He had a training regimen that punished his body, but he typically didn't punish it further with junk food.

Resting a hip against the counter edge, Lucas eyed her over the rim of the glass. "What's going on?"

She tried to sound nonchalant, but couldn't help the crack in her voice when she blurted out, "Pablo fired me."

He straightened. "When?"

"This morning," she said, slumping onto a barstool. "Called me into his office and gave me the news. Told me I had to leave straight away."

"You got fired this morning," Lucas said, "and you were planning on calling me when?"

She mumbled, "Probably when I'd finished all the Doritos."

"Nina, this is...what?...the seventh job you've had—"

She held up an index finger, stopping him midsentence. "Not what I need from you right now, Lucas Wilson," she said. "If I wanted a lecture, I'd call my mother, who has a PhD in the field of Disappointing Daughter." And who wouldn't miss the opportunity to also bring up her daughter's sorry succession of short-term relationships. Another area of her life that lacked staying power and invited criticism.

Nina banged a fist on the counter. "C'mon, you know what I want."

Lucas pulled up a stool and straddled it, resting his forearms on the chair back. "Pablo is a short, rat-faced, selfish, greedy fraudster," he provided dutifully. "He doesn't deserve you. He never deserved you. Your talent was wasted in his poor excuse of a restaurant."

She smiled and said softly, "Thank you."

"You want me to rearrange his nose?"

"It would improve his face, but why give it to him for free? Let him pay to have it done."

Lucas was silent for a beat, as if weighing the impact of his next words. At last, he said, "You can't take on everyone, Nina. You can't fight every injustice. Your résumé can't handle it."

She stiffened. Of all the things she expected him to say, that was never on the list. Struggling to speak through the disappointment seeping into her, she said, "Pablo was filling out fake skills certificates for the waitstaff, all migrant workers, in return for exorbitant sums of money. He was bullying them, exploiting the fact that they're so desperate for permanent residency, they'll take whatever injustice he dishes out. What did you expect of me, Lucas? That I'd stay silent, keep my head down, make sure I was okay, and ignore the misery of everyone else?"

A pained grimace crossed Lucas's face. "All right, time to help your crusader conscience off the podium." His calm gaze didn't waver when he said evenly, "There are Pablos wherever you go. Little toads carving out their kingdoms on the backs of others. Too often, I'm protecting those toads. I'm required to put the lives of my men on the line for them." He raked his fingers through his hair, no doubt in an effort to stop them from shaking some sense into her. "Some fights you need to let go."

"I couldn't let this one go."

A mix of concern and frustration sharpened his voice. "You can never let any of them go. And it's costing you."

"Exactly, it's costing *me*, not *you*. Stop interfering."

When she saw the hurt in his face, remorse rolled over her. She was a horrible person. The moment Lucas had learned she was having a bad day, he'd come straight over. Her closest friend—*call it as it is, Nina*—was only trying to help, and here she was, sneaking sniper shots at him.

"Sorry," she whispered.

A beat of silence passed before Lucas said, "I'd be a poor friend if I wasn't honest with you."

"I know," she responded, "and that's a character trait of yours I really do appreciate, but right now, Lucas...right now, I'll take empathy over honesty."

His brow creased. "Uh, I believe that falls in the mysterious realm of female friendship."

"Hey, you badgered me into window-dressing duty for your charity function. It's only fair you bear the burden of sobbing-on-shoulder duty."

His eyes widened. "You're over the sobbing part, though. Right?"

"I'm sure I could squeeze out a few more tears," she said cheerfully.

"Don't exert yourself on my behalf."

She stretched her arms above her head. "Fortunately for you, I'm pretty much all cried out."

"My very expensive sweater thanks you. Any idea which restaurants you'll apply to?"

"I'll start looking tomorrow."

"You'll find something. You're the best front-of-house manager I know."

Her chin dropped to her chest while her finger glumly bullied a water droplet on the countertop. "Let's hope someone else recognizes that."

"Nina." The forceful way Lucas uttered her name had her head jerking up. Affection softened his features and caused her throat to tighten. "Your confidence has taken a knock, but don't you dare doubt yourself. One day, you'll own your own restaurant, you'll pay your workers a fair wage, and you'll run your place the way you want."

Nina could feel her cheeks coloring as embarrassment crept in, Lucas's rebuke hitting home and snapping her out of her funk. He was right. How many ways did she want Pablo the Toad to win here? Sitting up straighter, she smiled her thanks at him. "You're forgetting rave reviews from top food critics and the line of people queuing up outside for a table," she murmured, basking in the dream.

"That sounds more like it."

"I'll have to hire you as a bouncer."

"Nina, please. That word is never to be mentioned in my presence."

She laughed at the disdain in his voice. "Snob," she teased. She stretched out her legs, pointed and flexed her sock-clad feet. "What about you? You on assignment at the moment?"

He shook his head. "I'm out of the field this week."

"That explains the unshaven look you've got going."

He rubbed a hand over his stubble. "It'll be gone soon. A job's coming up out of state where we have to babysit a diplomatic delegation."

"Diplomats," she said. "Your favorite."

"At least they're one step up from rock stars."

"I can only imagine. So the terrorist threat is still high?"

"High enough for the government to want a visible display of security."

"When do you leave?" she asked.

"Sunday."

"How long?"

"Four days."

She nodded. Lucas was thirty years old and ran a successful close-protection agency. He had twelve people working for him, but he still opted to take on many of the high-profile jobs where he could sometimes be away for weeks at a time.

Lucas stood, rotated his shoulders. "Feeling better?"

"I believe I'm all done with wallowing." She got to her feet. "Lucas, I really appreciate you coming over."

He hooked an arm around her neck and planted a friendly kiss on her forehead. "Hey, you'd do the same for me. Buddies forever, remember?"

As if she could ever forget. When Lucas looked at her, it was through the lens of the past. A lens he couldn't seem to shake off. She'd first met Lucas when he'd been placed in her brother Ryan's class in first grade, where he and Ryan had hit it off immediately. Over the years, Lucas became a near-permanent presence in their home, shooting hoops with Ryan, conducting science experiments in the backyard, and blitzing through multiplication worksheets at their dining room table. And because Nina adored her brother, she had no choice but to form a cautious and slightly uneasy alliance with his best friend.

Her primary school years were defined by Lucas and Ryan doing their best to capitalize on her ingrained desire to please. They roped her in to be their target in paintball wars, the ball girl in their tennis matches, and the fielder tasked with retrieving the ball. And then she hit high school and wised up and said that fetching their own balls would be good practice in growing some.

11

Unfortunately, the moment she hit high school she also transitioned into full-nerd mode, her frizzy hair, spotty skin, and studiousness all radiation-warning signs to classmates with no interest in exposure to contamination. To add to her social quarantine, she'd been acutely self-conscious about her developing body, hiding it in shapeless clothing that got her stuck with the nickname *Bag Lady*.

Lucas and Ryan had no such problems in high school. The two of them grew into teenagers with an appealing blend of good looks, intelligence, and athleticism that slotted them into the popular group at school. Mercifully, Ryan went out of his way to include and protect her, and Lucas automatically adopted the role of Brother Number Two. A role he'd never moved on from.

"Want to stay and watch a movie?" she asked, trying to stifle a yawn. "No chick flick, I promise."

"You're hitting a sugar low," he said. "You should go to bed."

"All I need is a cup of coffee and I'll get my second wind."

"Tonight's out. I'm meeting Sally for dinner."

Right. Sally. Blonde, leggy, beautiful, Taekwondo instructor, hopeful contender for a weighted ring finger and oblivious destroyer of Fantasy Number One.

"Enjoy," Nina said brightly, tucking her disappointment away in small pieces to burn later in her bonfire of stupidity. Because she might not have her own restaurant or a husband or a luxurious apartment, but she did have the cold comfort of her pride. And there was no way she would ever let Lucas see how she hurt over him. "Where are you meeting her?"

"Lepilio's."

"Avoid the calamari. They always overcook it."

"Thanks for the tip."

"You could always invite Sally to the fundraiser," Nina suggested, unashamedly fishing as she walked him to the door.

Lucas shot her a look that said she should know better. "That would give Sally the impression we're in some sort of a relationship."

"Which you're not."

"No."

Alongside the rush of relief, there was a tug of pity for the woman. A minuscule tug, but still. "And you don't think Sally is already under that assumption?"

"No," he maintained, frowning, but she could see him warily circling that thought as he shrugged on his jacket. For a bodyguard trained to be observant, he was woefully blind when it came to matters of the heart. Exhibit A: Nina Sarah Abrahams.

"What's the dress code for Saturday?" she asked. "Smart casual?"

"Uh," Lucas said guiltily, opening her door and angling most of his body out, "the fundraiser is a black-tie gala. Knowing your closet, you probably need to shop for a dress."

"What? WHAT!" Nina yelled, but it was too late. Lucas had already shut the door and made his escape.

Chapter Two

The next morning, Nina took advantage of two unemployment perks: a late sleep-in and a leisurely shower. Afterward, she purged her pantry of any leftover Doritos. The smell alone was enough to make her gag. Vowing to never eat another corn chip as long as she lived, she made herself a mug of green tea chai and sat in front of her laptop to tackle her résumé. As much as she hated to admit it, Lucas was right. At twenty-nine, you weren't supposed to possess such an embarrassingly cluttered résumé. Even in an industry resigned to high staff turnover, she doubted many prospective employers would be impressed by what looked like serial job hopping. The absence of a reference letter from her last employer didn't help either. And there was no way that Pablo the Toad would give her one.

An hour later, with her employment history carefully edited and updated, Nina began the tedious online search for vacancies in restaurant management. In the middle of contacting yet another employment agency, it suddenly hit her. She had Pablo's e-mail address.

Oh, the power.

Oh, the line she'd be crossing.

She hesitated, but, really, this was too great an opportunity to pass up. Nina made herself another chai, returned to her laptop, and spent the next hour visiting the sites of clothing retailers, supermarket chains, and travel agencies and signing Pablo up for their promotional newsletters. Anytime there was the option to receive marketing communication from third parties, she happily ticked that box too, and tried not to think of all the laws she might be breaking.

At 11:30 a.m., she'd had enough. Enough of the cramped office space she'd carved for herself in the dining room. Enough of being petty and vindictive.

She was spinning lazy circles in her chair, mentally itemizing the contents of her fridge to see if she could whip up a Mexican omelet for lunch, when her phone blasted out *The Imperial March*. She groaned. Darth Vader's ringtone was reserved for one particular person.

"Hi, Mom."

"Nina, darling, I called the restaurant to chat with you before I left, and I heard the most distressing news. Tell me it's not true."

Hmm, what to do. "It's not true," she said, still spinning, giving in to the childish temptation.

"Oh, Nina, A Lie Is A Betrayal Of Who You Are."

Ah, a pearl of one of her mother's Capitalized Sayings, plucked from the murky sea of plagiarism everyone was dipping into. It had taken less than ten seconds. A new record. "It was a joke, Mom."

"Hmm. Not a very funny one. Anyway, some gentleman named Pablo told me he had to let you go because you were...oh, how did he put it?...difficult to work with."

Gentleman? Her mother was supposed to be an astute judge of character. And *difficult to work with*? Only because she wouldn't keep her mouth shut.

Quickly, Nina said, "I didn't know you were in town." *Deflect, deflect.* "Aren't you supposed to be in New York, kick-starting some big-cheese seminar?"

"I'm at the airport. My flight leaves in three hours."

"So life is still busy as a motivational speaker?"

"Inspirational speaker, darling. You know I try to do more than motivate. My goal is to inspire."

Inspire me to lose my breakfast, Nina thought, and immediately felt guilty. Cheryl wasn't a bad mother; she was simply a self-involved one.

"How about I drive over to the airport to see you?" Nina offered, her insomniac conscience prodding her to atone and suffer through the congested trip to the airport. "We can grab a cup of coffee, catch up on each other's lives."

"Sounds like a marvelous idea, it really does, but I have a massage booked before I board. Another time, perhaps."

"Okay." It wasn't okay. Truth be told, she could use a chicken-soup mother right now, not one jetting all over the world, helping other people get their lives on track and ignoring the derailing of her daughter's.

"Have you considered this could be a sign, Nina darling? A sign to look for a more challenging, a more...cerebral occupation?"

Nina stopped spinning. She was feeling nauseated. Hard to know whether it was all the chair swiveling or her mother's question. *Let it go, Nina.* But she'd never been any good at taking advice. Not her mother's. Not Lucas's. And certainly not her own. "Mom, being a restaurant manager is not just waitering with more money. Believe it or not, I do have to use my brain at work."

There was so much more she could say. *I'm on my feet twenty-four seven. My job requires me to be proficient in finance, administration, marketing, and sales. Since I'm dealing with suppliers, patrons, and staff members, I have to be an expert in people management and customer satisfaction.*

Nina didn't bother saying any of it, however. Psych 101: people hear what they want to hear.

"You could be so much more," her mother said. "You have so much potential. You could write a book on the hospitality industry, get onto a TV show, or become a restaurateur yourself."

So her mother's life story was now the blueprint for Nina's success. Cheryl Abrahams's bio, plumped up annually by her steroidal publicists, was well known: a beautiful young widow starts writing a blog about her grief journey and caring for two small children. The blog gains a surprising and growing number of followers, who connect with her raw out-there feelings and down-to-earth advice. The widow goes on to write an emotionally charged article for *Huffington Post*. The article goes viral, landing her a book deal and catapulting Cheryl Abrahams to a life of fame and fortune.

"Mom, your story's not mine. I'm pretty content with what I've achieved." The words limped out of her, and Nina was surprised she didn't choke on the big fat lie of them.

"Content?" Her mother gave a delicate snort. "Darling, Why Settle For The Moon When You Can Pursue Venus?"

"Because that would be classed as a suicide mission," Nina responded before she could stop herself.

"Only if you believe it to be. You know what I've always said, Nina. Where You See Obstacles, Others See Footholds To Climb The Mountain Of Success."

They'd jumped from space travel to mountaineering. And people paid money for this?

Nina rubbed her temples. She could feel a headache coming on. "At least I get to tell people what to do. Kind of like you."

Her mother was a motivational—correction, inspirational—speaker. She traveled the world telling people what to do with their money, their life, and their offspring. Cheryl Abrahams was a popular speaker on the TED Talk circuit and had recently hit half a million followers on Twitter. It was ironic, though, that when it came to her daughter, motivational too often morphed into criticism.

There was a sorrowful exhalation of air down the line. "If your father were alive..."

Nina's eyes watered. *Let's finish that sentence, Mom. If Dad were alive, he'd be at my restaurant every week, ordering a decaf macchiato and a spanakopita tart and telling me that if this was what I wanted to do with my life, then he wouldn't try to wake me from my dream.*

Nina blinked rapidly as the weight of a memory almost flattened her. She saw her skinny eight-year-old self waking up early on a Saturday morning, slipping on her cherry-blossom apron, donning her white chef's hat, and marching to her cubbyhouse in the back garden of her childhood home to set up her restaurant. She'd busy herself sweeping the floor, wiping down the three oddly matched tables and chairs, and placing freshly picked daisies in jam jars.

At 3:00 p.m., her restaurant opened. Her dad, home for the two-hour window when the restaurant closed between the lunch and dinner shift, would arrive in a smart suit and tie and fold his long legs under the small table, grinning his approval as she positioned a napkin on his lap. She'd wait, notebook in hand, while he solemnly studied the handwritten menu.

"Hmm, I'll have the chicken pie today, Ms. Nina."

"A fine choice, Mr. Abrahams."

And when she carefully served the mud pie garnished with clovers, her dad would loudly murmur his appreciation while stabbing the pie with his plastic fork.

"Best meal I've ever had," he'd proclaim, eyes twinkling, patting his tummy with a satisfied sigh.

Nina would beg her mother to join them in their Saturday ritual, but she was always too busy with chores and Pilates classes. She'd come once, at her father's uncharacteristically stern insistence, but from the moment she'd stooped, both literally and figuratively, to enter the restaurant cubby, she'd been so full of criticisms—helpful suggestions, she'd termed them—that Nina had never invited her again.

And her brother, Ryan... Well, what nine-year-old boy wanted to play at hospitality when basketball and backyard football beckoned?

So it became her special time with her dad, and Nina jealously guarded those Saturdays.

A year later, her dad was dead and Nina never set foot inside the cubby again. Not to collect her impressive collection of cooking utensils. Not even when a grieving Cheryl made an effort to dress up and ask for a reservation. I'm closed, Nina had said stubbornly, coldly, ignoring the crestfallen look on her mother's face.

Spiders and weeds slowly claimed the cubby, and two years after her dad's death, Cheryl hired a contractor to take it down.

"Well, Mom, Dad's not alive," Nina said now, dabbing her eyes.

"I know, darling. I know that more than anyone. But he wouldn't want to see you so...unfulfilled."

Nina's grip tightened on the phone. It was time to make that Mexican omelet.

"I have to go, Mom. Venus is calling. Enjoy New York."

#

An hour after the phone call with her mother, Nina was still pulsating with frustration. She'd cooked a huge omelet, but had only managed to eat some of it, putting the rest in the fridge for later. She needed an outlet. She could go for a walk, but it was raining. She should probably clean something. That usually helped. First, though, she needed to offload onto Tammy, who understood better than anyone the sometimes warped nature of family.

Nina sent her friend a text. *Argh! Mothers!*

She'd known Tammy since university days. Her first week at university, Nina had sat at a greasy cafeteria table opposite this tall, gorgeous redhead. Over spicy chicken tacos, she'd discovered that Tammy was enrolled in the same hospitality management course as her. The friendship had grown from there.

Over the course of numerous chocolate-fueled conversations, Nina would vent about Cheryl, and Tammy, in turn, would tell Nina about her childhood, how her parents had vetted her friends, banned her from parties, chosen all Tammy's outfits, and enforced

19

9:00 p.m. weekend curfews. Predictably, Tammy had rebelled at all the strictures, becoming an expert at lying and sneaking around.

Nina thought it ironic that in their effort to protect their daughter, Tammy's parents had instead raised the ultimate wild child.

A minute later, Tammy's response came through: *Directors! Actors! Makeup artists! Humanity!*

All right, then, looked like she wasn't the only one having a less-than-stellar day.

Nina typed: *Let's live on a remote island.*

Can't, no Starbucks. Tammy followed it up with a sad-face emoji. Then she texted: *Why don't you join me this Saturday?*

Alarm rocketed through Nina. As a stuntwoman, Tammy could work up to sixteen hours a day, but she played just as hard—and just as dangerous—in her downtime. Whatever she was proposing probably involved drink, drugs, or some sort of daredevil diversion. *Join you in what?*

Rock climbing.

Well, that would solve her frustration problem, Nina thought. You can't feel frustrated when you're dead.

Not this time, she typed. *Enjoy and try to stay alive.*

It looked like cleaning would have to do.

Chapter Three

Later that afternoon, Nina was on her knees scrubbing the shower when her cell phone beeped with a text from Lucas: *Where are you?*

Her thumb hovered over the keys, itching to reply, but she set down her phone and continued scrubbing. Good girl, she congratulated herself. No knee-jerk, I-have-no-life response time. After a couple of minutes, she texted back: *Home.*

I'm outside your building. Buzz me in.

Bother, Nina thought. Trust Lucas to ambush her like that, knowing she'd ignore the buzzer. She screwed up her nose at her phone. *Home,* she'd replied. Could she not have been more inventive? Added a little gloss? She was a Facebook user. She'd been projecting the lie of the perfect, smile-for-the-camera life for years.

She made the trek to the entry phone, debating her options. She didn't feel like contending with Lucas. Not so soon after dealing with her mother. She needed an excuse. A good one. And there it was, an idea in the form of a worn shoelace dangling from her shoe cabinet.

Hitting her palm on the entry button to let Lucas into the building, Nina hurried to her bedroom, digging in her closet for her one and only pair of black running tights (a birthday gift from Lucas, never used) and wriggling into them. She slipped on the sportiest T-shirt she could find and examined herself in the mirror. Something more was needed. Her gaze landed on the three teddy bears lined up on her dresser, childhood mementoes overdue for the charity shop. A year after the tights, Lucas had gifted her with a pack of three wrist sweatbands, another not-so-subtle hint to embark on a fitness regime. Not knowing what to do with such a useless present, she'd arranged the sweatbands on her bears in the classic hear-, see-, and do-no-evil poses.

Suddenly inspired, she grabbed the sweatband off the see-no-evil bear and slid it onto her wrist. Plucking her sneakers from the shoe cabinet, she was in the act of displaying them in a prominent position in the entrance hall when Lucas knocked at her door.

Swiftly scooping up her hair into a messy ponytail to complete her look, Nina opened the door and caught the surprise on Lucas's face as he eyed her outfit.

"Hi," she said, all perky and Fakebooky. "You just caught me. It's stopped raining, so I'm going for a run."

There was a brief, stunned silence. Then Lucas asked skeptically, "A run?"

"Yep. No time to chat."

"A run," Lucas repeated.

Holding on to the doorknob, Nina was starting to get annoyed. Her going for a run was not in the realm of the impossible. The improbable, sure, but give a person the benefit of the doubt. "I'm finally making good on that New Year's resolution."

"The same one you've had—and done nothing about—for the last three years?"

"The very one," Nina gritted out, keeping her hostess smile in place, although the effort was killing her. "You're missing the point, Lucas. The point is, I'm going running. Now. This very instant. It's what you've always nagged me to do, and now I'm doing it. You should be proud. And you definitely don't want to get in the way of this run because who knows when the urge will visit again. So, like I said, no time to chat."

She stopped, almost breathless with the effort of inventing on the fly.

Still standing in the hallway, Lucas was silent. Then he gave her the beginning of a smile, and a gleam lit up his eyes. *Uh-oh.* That half smile and the accompanying spark of mischief usually signaled trouble for her. And that was when she noticed what she should have seen the moment she opened her door. But she'd been so caught up masterminding her plan she hadn't paid attention to what Lucas was wearing: a tight-fitting, long-sleeved Nike top, shorts, and sneakers. Workout clothes. Her heart pumped out a sickening *undo, undo* beat.

"What a coincidence," Lucas drawled. "I was planning on heading to the gym after my visit here. I think I'll skip the gym and join you on your run."

"Oh, you don't want to miss your gym session."

"Oh, I most definitely do. Especially if it involves watching you run."

Her fingers, still wrapped around the doorknob, squeezed reflexively, her trapped mind picturing Lucas's handsome face imprinted there. "Come to think of it, Tammy might join me. And, well, you and she don't exactly get along." An understatement. Her two closest friends loathed each other.

"There's no way Tammy will run with you," Lucas said. "You'll never keep up."

Sadly true, Nina thought. Tammy trained five days a week, sometimes twice a day, pushing herself to ridiculous limits. Which was exactly how she lived her life.

Nina frowned suddenly, a thought occurring to her, a lone piece of driftwood in an ocean of disaster. "Wait a minute, why are you here?"

Lucas held up a manila envelope. "I wanted to give you this."

"What is it?"

"I'll tell you later."

"Let me guess," she said. "A job application form?"

Lucas gave a snort of laughter. "You need upper arm strength if you work for me. Your arms are still a work in progress."

"Mmm, like your brain?"

He laughed, and she smiled along with him. She wasn't serious about working for him. She wasn't capable of protecting other people when she'd done such a poor job of protecting herself from falling in love with her best friend.

She studied the envelope with interest. "It looks important."

"It is."

She brightened. "We can run another time. Let's go inside and open your mysterious envelope."

He shook his head, saying softly, "Time to make good on that New Year's resolution, Nina."

Yes, yes, she knew (thanks to Lucas) that her lack of physical activity meant she was at a higher risk for heart disease and strokes and other fun stuff, but she was also (privately) worried about her weight. She knew she had a reasonably good body. Time was still kind to her, but she couldn't rely on genetics and a fast metabolism forever. Working in the restaurant industry, a food enthusiast surrounded by food all day, she had to be especially careful.

She exhaled in defeat. "Okay, let me get a jacket."

Returning with a lightweight jacket, Nina noticed Lucas had placed the envelope on the hall table. Her curiosity was definitely roused. What was inside? And why did Lucas think it important enough for him to personally drop off?

"Ready?" Lucas asked.

"Not really," she said honestly.

His low laugh chased away some of her misgivings. "You'll be fine. Sore, but fine."

After shoving her feet into her sneakers, Nina locked her door, and they rode the elevator down in silence. They made their way through the lobby that always seemed to smell of marijuana and stepped outside into an icy wind. Shivering, Nina zipped up her jacket and tried to match Lucas's brisk walking pace.

"Where were you planning on running?" he asked.

"Um, wherever my legs take me."

Lucas smiled, shook his head. "Nina, honey, good runners plan their route. In the same way that motivated people plan their career path."

"Now you sound like my mother," she grumbled as they crossed the street. "Turning every moment into a life lesson slash recycled lecture."

"She called today, did she?"

"That she did."

"Feeling battered?"

"No more than usual."

Lucas squeezed her shoulder and led the way to the park, stopping at a flat, grassy patch. Only a handful of people were out in the park, mostly mothers looking cold and uncomfortable watching their children clamber over the play equipment under a relentless gray sky.

"Start stretching," Lucas advised, performing an impressive hamstring maneuver. "I don't want you straining anything."

Briefly distracted by the play of muscles on Lucas's thighs, Nina took a moment to admire the sight. Surely those legs were candidates to be one of the Seven Wonders of the Male World. Swallowing a sigh, she obediently bent forward and tried to touch her toes, her outstretched fingers barely making it past her kneecaps.

"Try picturing Doritos on the ground," Lucas suggested.

She couldn't help the flicker of a smile. "It would be more motivating picturing your pretty-boy face under my feet."

They slipped into the easy rhythm of good-natured bickering while Nina went through the motions of mimicking Lucas's warm-up routine.

"How'd it go with Sally last night?" she asked, loosening up her calves, thinking how much she needed a latte to loosen up some degree of enthusiasm for this farce of a run.

"We never made it to the main course. She walked out after the Halloumi starter."

Yes! "What happened?"

"You were right." He frowned, as if the notion was inconceivable. "Sally was looking at real estate listings and scoping out wedding venues."

"Told you. I suppose you set her straight."

"Had to."

"Sorry." *Not even the tiniest bit.*

He waved that away. "File thirteen. Moving on." He straightened. "Okay, enough warm-ups. Let's get started."

Nina fell into stride beside him as Lucas set off on a loop around the park, his pace steady and relaxed. For the first five minutes, she managed to keep up with him. Pride coursed through her. She could do this.

After ten minutes, she was starting to lag more and more behind. She shucked off her jacket, tying it around her waist. Her breath was coming in short, harsh bursts. A stitch jabbed her side.

"Sounds like a buffalo stampede back there," Lucas called over his shoulder, easing up his pace so he could jog alongside her. His breathing remained annoyingly steady. He looked like he could run all day.

"Just stick bamboo shoots under my fingernails," she managed to gasp between gulps of air. "It has to be less painful than this."

"C'mon, Nina, I'm practically walking here."

"Let's take out the 'practically,' then," she panted, slowing to a walk, hands on her hips.

Jogging in place, Lucas frowned. "It's been ten minutes. We're still warming up."

"This is a good start," she said. "We'll try for a longer run next time." *Like, next year.*

Now that breathing was no longer such a labor of pain, Nina spotted a trendy café she'd been meaning to try for a while now. The whitewashed former warehouse was surrounded by flower beds, and the people inside looked warm and cozy. What was the point of living in one of the coffee capitals of the world if you didn't take full advantage of it?

"You go ahead and finish your run," she said to Lucas suddenly. "I'll see you back at the apartment."

Lucas rolled his eyes. "Oh, please. I've known you for years. I can see right through you."

"It's like you said," she responded, grinning unapologetically. "Good runners plan their route."

#

The richness of a vanilla latte lingered on her tongue as Nina unlocked the door to her apartment and stepped inside, Lucas behind her. The first item to catch her eye was Lucas's envelope still lying on her hall table.

She picked up the envelope. "Moment of truth."

"Feed me first, please," Lucas begged. "All that nonrunning has made me hungry."

"There's leftover Mexican omelet in the fridge," she offered, heading to the kitchen and pouring them both a juice. "Help yourself."

He scrounged around in the fridge, pulled out a container, and scooped the contents onto a plate. "Want some?"

She grimaced. "I had some for lunch, and I'm still trying to hold it down."

After heating up the omelet in the microwave, they sat down at the kitchen counter. Nina slit open the envelope and drew out the piece of paper inside. She read it once, then twice, her jaw dropping.

"Lucas, what on earth?" She held up the glowing reference letter from Pablo, her disgruntled former employer, in disbelief. "How did you manage this? What did you do?"

Lucas cut into his omelet. "I stopped by Mateo's for a little talk with Pablo."

"Define 'talk.'"

"I brought along two of my men."

Nina clapped her hands in delight. "I want all the details."

Lucas stared longingly at the speared omelet on his fork.

"Food's not important right now," she said, even though she'd never in her life adhered to that statement. "Tell. Me. Everything."

And so he did. He told of how he'd roped in two of his biggest guys and the three of them had pitched up early that morning at Mateo's Grill, timing their arrival when Pablo was alone. They'd dressed the part, and Pablo had nearly wet himself at the show of three grim-faced, muscular heavies in dark glasses, combat boots, and prominent shoulder holsters. Lucas had done all the talking. Like all bullies, Pablo had caved when confronted with a bigger, meaner bully.

Nina was smiling so much, her cheeks ached. "I'm thinking I should be all feminist here and tell you this was a problem I could've handled myself, but the picture I have in my head is too good for objections."

Lucas dived into his omelet. "The guys had fun. My biggest worry was preventing them from having too much fun."

Nina toyed with her glass of juice. "So, uh, did you rearrange Pablo's nose?" she asked casually. A little hopefully.

Lucas's fork stopped in midair, and he looked at her without speaking.

She waved her question aside. "Just joking. Mostly. I don't know where that came from. Forget it." She downed her juice.

"You scare me sometimes."

ALL THE LOST PIECES

"I scare myself all the time," Nina admitted. "Seriously, though, Lucas, thank you for doing this."

He shrugged. "All in the name of keeping the toad plague under control." A slight smile played on his lips. "I admit I had fun too."

She smoothed down Pablo's reference letter. "This'll make it so much easier to look for a job." A lump formed in her throat. He'd done this for her. She was so overcome, it was a struggle to get the words out. "I can't believe you went to all this trouble."

At the quaver in her voice, Lucas froze. A second passed before he gave her shoulder an awkward pat. "Hey, come on, it's no biggie. This is what friends do for one another."

The lump dissolved. Of course. A friend helping out a friend. How...sweet. Now her lunch was so much closer to coming up. Why couldn't the universe work the way she wanted it to? She swallowed hard, blinking away her stupid, stupid tears that still hoped for something Lucas wasn't capable of giving. At least, not to her.

"Isn't it Francesca's birthday this Thursday?" she asked, not missing the relief his body language radiated at the dodging of an emotionally draining weep fest.

"Yep." Francesca was Lucas's older sister and loved to remind him of that fact as often as she could. "Ma's taking Frannie to this newly opened day spa. In a moment of insanity, I offered to look after Lexi for the day."

"Won't she be at school?"

"Thursday's report-writing day, apparently, so no school."

"Come on, it won't be so bad," Nina said, laughing at Lucas's expression. "You love your niece."

"I do, but I swear Lexi's a six-year-old shaman with her mother's sense of theatrics who has me wound around her little finger." A speculative gleam darkened Lucas's eyes. "What are you doing Thursday?"

"Contemplating my jobless existence."

29

"You could help me look after Lexi."

"What? No."

"Nina, please. Pretty please. I need you."

"So the big, bad bodyguard needs protection from his six-year-old niece?"

"He does."

She said yes, of course, because, hey, this was Lucas, but she also adored that little shaman and jumped at any opportunity to spend time with her.

After finishing his lunch, Lucas stacked his plate in the dishwasher. "I should get going. Thanks for lunch."

She walked him to the door. "Anytime."

"You got a dress yet for the gala on Saturday?"

"Not yet. What are you wearing? A suit?"

"Yep. Black tie, remember?"

Trying so very hard to forget.

Outside his work, it wasn't often she saw Lucas in a suit. Lucas's mother kept a scrapbook of newspaper clippings that she delighted in parading before guests, making Lucas groan out loud in embarrassment. The pages and pages of photos showed Lucas suited up and looking handsome and serious guarding A-list celebrities and prominent politicians.

"If I don't find anything I like, there's always my go-to black cocktail dress."

Lucas grimaced. "Please, no black," he said. "Everyone in the city wears black. All the time. It's like there's a mass funeral every day."

"Lucas—"

He kissed her cheek. "Surprise me."

Chapter Four

Nina moaned into her pillow. The threads of a hazy dream where she'd been awarded Restaurant Manager of the Year floated regretfully away as the insistent ringing penetrated her sleep. She moaned again. She'd forgotten to put her phone on silent last night. After a *Hell's Kitchen* marathon session (nothing like watching Monster Chef Gordon Ramsay utterly humiliate aspiring chefs to make a person feel better about her life), she'd been so tired, she'd barely remembered to brush her teeth before collapsing into bed.

Nina sat up and groped through the debris on her bedside table for her phone. Who would be presumptuous enough to call so early on a Wednesday morning? Didn't people know she was jobless? That she no longer had to wake up at... *Oh, crap.* Her eyes snapped open. What if it was one of the agencies she'd applied to?

Snatching up the phone, she cleared her throat and answered in what she hoped was an alert, professional tone. "Nina Abrahams speaking."

"Drop the managerial voice, sis," said Ryan. "I know you were drooling on your pillow a few seconds ago."

Nina pushed aside a hairbrush, lip balm, and Anthony Bourdain's *Kitchen Confidential*, which she was rereading for the third time, to squint at her digital clock. "Ryan, it's nine in the morning!"

"Good to see all my math tutoring wasn't wasted."

Holding the phone to her ear, she burrowed back into bed. "Remember when you and Lucas taught me how to take down a potential attacker? Well, come on over, evil brother, and I'll be happy to demonstrate that training wasn't wasted either."

His laugh vibrated in her ear. "Shall I wait while you drink your morning cup of coffee and transform into a human?"

She grumbled, "I can't be bothered to get up."

"You should just set up an IV line. It'll be easier."

She yawned. "Is there a reason for this call? Other than to harass me?"

"Spoilsport, cutting short my fun," Ryan said. "Yeah, there's a reason. Dinner at our place Friday. Seven o'clock."

"Friday," Nina repeated, frowning at a water stain on her ceiling. "It's late notice. Who cancelled?"

"Such a lack of confidence, sis. Nobody canceled. It's called spontaneity."

Nina snuggled even farther under her comforter, drowsiness tugging at her eyelids. "I don't know," she mumbled. "I'll have to check my calendar."

"By all means, check the calendar of the unemployed," he said slyly.

Annoyance chased away any hope of slipping back to sleep. "How'd you find out?"

There was only maddening silence on the other end of the line.

"I know it wasn't Lucas who blabbed," Nina said. "He mentally signs an NDA before every conversation."

Ryan said, "Sibling telepathy."

"Oh, please, that's never been true for us. We don't even look alike." She'd inherited her father's dark coloring, while Ryan got Cheryl's blonde, blue-eyed genes. And, it seemed, the weakness for familial gossip. "When did Mom phone you?"

"Last night."

Nina closed her eyes. "Our twisted family grapevine."

"She's concerned."

"Concerned." The word left an alien taste in her mouth. "Interesting interpretation. My take was interfering, patronizing—"

"You're sipping a bitter brew," Ryan warned gently. "Like it or not, she gave birth to you."

The rebuke cut her, as he'd intended. "You're right. Sorry." *Sorry I can't share my feelings with a sibling who's always been more of a Mommy's boy than a brother.* But she heard truth in his words. Ever since she'd finished reading *A Man Called Ove,* she'd harbored a secret terror of ending up the female version of an embittered Ove, spitting vitriol about her mother and life to anyone who would listen.

"Apology accepted," said Ryan.

Nina opened her eyes. The water stain looked pretty bad. She should alert her rental agent before the damage spread, before the ceiling became so full of mold and rot, it was irreparable.

"Hey, you there?"

Averting her eyes from the damaged ceiling, Nina said lightly, "Still here. And still convinced Dad incubated me for nine months."

Laughter tinged Ryan's voice. "Yeah, you're a carbon copy of Dad. Even the fact that you landed up in hospitality, just like him."

Just like you wanted to, Nina itched to say, but didn't because it was an old argument between them, one she didn't want to resurrect right now. It still stung to remember how her brother, fresh out of school and eyes shiny with dreams, had caved under the pressure of Cheryl's fiscal logic and tearful pleadings and put aside his first career choice—to become a certified cicerone—to opt instead for the comfortable path of a financial accountant.

Nina tightened her grip on the phone. What was that Chinese proverb? Something about the first generation planting the trees and the next generation living in the shade. A real warm-the-heart proverb, except Mom's tree blocked out the sun with roots that sucked up all the water so no grass could grow around it and...oh, blast it, hello, Mrs. Ove! She bit her lip. She missed her dad unbearably.

With uncharacteristic intuition, Ryan said in a low voice, "I miss him too, you know."

She swallowed past the grief clogging her throat. "I know."

"Want to, uh, talk about it?"

She couldn't get the word out fast enough. "No."

"Okay." She could hear his exhalation of relief through the phone. "How are you for money?"

"I'm fine."

"Because if you're stuck, I could lend—"

"Ry, I'm okay," she said firmly. "But thanks for the offer. I'll keep it in mind, I promise."

"Yeah, anytime, sis." There was still the hint of worry in his voice, but she could hear the effort he was making to trust her to stand on her own.

"So are you coming?" Ryan asked. "Lucas is a yes. It'll be just the four of us."

Nina said, "I'll come if you take down my photo."

"What! No way," Ryan protested. "Your photo stays in the entrance hall."

"Ryan, it's the first thing people"—her mind went to one person in particular—"see when they enter your house. Don't you think I've been punished enough?"

"Four years. Still another two to go."

She let out a long-suffering sigh. Ryan had never forgiven her for what she'd said to him when she was seven. He still had that whole eye-for-an-eye thing burning inside him. The year she turned seventeen, survival instinct had dictated she destroy any photos, digital or printed, that Ryan might one day use as ammunition against her. There weren't too many. Much to her mother's annoyance, Nina had mastered the art of avoiding having her picture taken, lowering her head right before the click. What rotten luck that two years ago, Cheryl had snorted the KonMari Method drug, and in the process of following the Japanese guru's decluttering instructions, she'd found the one printed photo Nina hadn't managed to get rid of. Even worse, Ryan got hold of it before she did.

She said now, "Seriously, Ry, come on—"

"I'm not taking it down."

Nina drummed her fingers on her knee, wishing it was his head she could drum some sense into. "A compromise, then. Could you put the photo somewhere else? Anywhere but the entrance hall."

There was a brief silence, finally followed by an ungracious "All right, I'll move it."

"Good," she breathed out, careful to keep the triumph from her voice. "I'll see you Friday at seven."

Chapter Five

Nina stood in the shade of a towering tree outside Lucas's childhood home, memories assailing her of backyard barbecues, Friday-night movie marathons, and bike rides down quiet, leafy streets where gorgeous Victorian homes bumped up against modern McMansions. She remembered Saturdays spent in the local shopping village exploring its eclectic mix of specialist food shops and assorted eateries. Come to think of it, Nina thought, that was probably the start of her foodie fixation.

The wind picked up, carrying the smell of rain and freshly mowed grass in its chilly blasts. A quick check of the weather app on her phone this morning had confirmed that Thursday's cold and rainy weather was set for the rest of the day. Fortunately, most of what Lucas had planned for today was indoors.

Pulling her jacket snugly around her, Nina hurried past Lucas's Range Rover in the driveway, her eyes flicking to the basketball hoop still suspended over the garage door, waiting for the next generation of kids to top up the memories of Ryan and Lucas practicing their jump shots.

Standing in the shelter of the front porch, Nina rang the doorbell.

"Nina!" Through the frosted glass panes of the front door, she glimpsed the shadow of a small body hurtling down the hallway. "Open, Grandma, open!"

Nina had to laugh. Lucas's niece was clearly excited to see her. The door opened, and Lexi flung herself at Nina's denim-clad legs.

Nina scooped up the curly-haired girl and held her close. "Lexi Llama, did you eat stones for breakfast? Why are you so heavy?"

"I'm growing," Lexi informed her with satisfaction, twining her arms around Nina's neck.

From somewhere inside the house, Francesca yelled, "Give my girl a fat complex, why don't you?"

Nina rolled her eyes at Lucas's older sister. "You're the one giving her a complex," she said, loud enough to be heard. "I'm trying to give her a sense of humor."

Holding open the front door, Christina said, "My daughter's sense of humor disappears whenever there's any mention of weight." At the sight of Lucas's mother smiling warmly at her, happiness tumbled through Nina. "You look lovely, Nina. As always."

Still carrying Lexi, Nina stepped into the house and into Christina's welcoming embrace. Nina breathed in a mix of Chanel and Bolognese, her signature scent. Nina remembered the first time she'd tagged along with Ryan to the Wilson household and experienced one of Christina Wilson's enveloping hugs. She'd formed a sentimental attachment to the scent—and the person wearing it—ever since.

Lucas's mother took a step back, and Nina was able to get her first proper look at her. It had been months since they'd caught up, and Nina was dismayed to note the brutal stamp of age in the deep creases marking her skin, the slight tremble in her hands, and the now-fully gray cap of hair. But kindness was etched in every fold of her face, and her brown eyes still twinkled with mischief.

Nina pulled out a smile. "You're looking extra snazzy today, Mrs. Wilson."

"Mrs. Wilson?" Lucas's mother narrowed her eyes. "Who is this person? You're not in school anymore, Nina. You're"—the next bit was said in a whisper—"*nearly thirty*. Call me Christina! How many times have I told you this?"

"Many times," Nina replied, as she always did. "But it still feels strange. I'll have to come round more often to practice."

"You're welcome here anytime," Christina said. "You know you're like a daughter to me." Raising her voice, she added, "After my one and only beautiful daughter, of course."

Right on cue, Francesca shouted, "I should hope so, Ma."

Lexi wiggled in Nina's arms. "Close the door, Grandma. The cold's sneaking in."

"Lexi's right." Christina hustled them away from the entrance and shut the door, leading the way to the living room.

"You look pretty today, Nina," Lexi whispered in her ear.

"Thank you." The light touch of mascara, blush, and lipstick had to account for the pretty, Nina thought, not the worn denims, oversized jacket, and battered Converse sneakers she had on. No point in dressing up when you were looking after a six-year-old for the day.

"Where's the real beauty queen?" Nina asked Lexi, who dissolved into giggles, her breath hot and sweet on Nina's neck.

Oh, man, she loved this girl to bits. Lucas's niece was all bouncy mischievousness, her milky-white skin and inky dark eyes sucking you into the magical innocence of a child's outlook on the world.

"Mama's in the kitchen," Lexi said. "She's talking to Uncle Lucas."

Talking, hah! Lecturing, more likely. Francesca was two years older than Lucas and liked to lord it over him. As a teenager, Nina had always been a little intimidated by Lucas's older sister. For the most part, Francesca had ignored her, but Nina remembered sporadic moments of kindness: Francesca teaching her to braid her hair, mixing together a banana-and-honey face mask when Nina had one particularly bad skin breakout, and helping her shop for an outfit for her first date with sweaty-palms Joey.

"Can I show you what I builded, Nina?" Lexi asked.

"Sure."

Lexi squirmed out of Nina's arms and skipped to the center of the living room. The room was Christina's space, overrun with the dog figurines she loved to collect. Trying to ignore the lifeless stares of what seemed to be hundreds of canines perched in various poses around her, Nina crouched beside Lexi and admired the sprawling, lopsided LEGO farmhouse taking up the coffee table. "Great job, Lexi."

"Grandpa helped," Lexi said, "but I put the animals in their houses."

Lexi plunged her hands into the giant container of LEGO pieces beside her and recklessly added to the farmhouse roof. Nina smiled. There were no annoying inconveniences like building codes when you were a child.

Leaving her to it, Nina stood and nearly collided with Lucas, who had come up behind her.

"Easy," he said, reaching out a hand to steady her.

She stared up into green eyes only a breath away from hers.

"Hi," she said.

"Hello yourself." He leaned in to kiss her cheek, saying softly, "You're looking a little stiff. Feeling the effects of the run?"

"Unfortunately."

"Mission accomplished, then," he declared with a grin, looking way too delectable in cargo pants and a sweater that perfectly outlined his broad shoulders. "Here, let me take your jacket."

"Thanks." She turned around, and he helped her slip out of her jacket, his fingertips skimming the nape of her neck. Pleasure coursed through her at his touch.

"Nina, you look funny," observed Lexi sharply from her vantage point on the floor.

Nina felt her face flame. "Do I? Oh, I was just, um, daydreaming." No way on this green earth was she explaining the ins and outs of fantasizing to a child. She turned to Lucas. "All set for today?"

"All sorted," he said. "I appreciate you helping me out. Again."

She raised an eyebrow. "Hmm, twice in one week."

"Not that you're counting."

"Not that I am."

A corner of his mouth curved. "This is going to come back and bite me, isn't it?"

"A great big chunk," Nina agreed. "Who knows when I'll cash in?" She pretended to think. "Perhaps when I finally sign up for those samba classes, you can come along as my partner."

She gave in to a wild dance move she'd seen in one of the *Step Up* movies, causing Lexi to shriek in delight and Francesca to whoop from the kitchen, "You go, girl!"

Lucas's face was the picture of appalled dismay. *A dance class!* He loathed dancing. Probably because he was so awful at it.

Nina struggled to hold back a grin. Power was so much fun. She could understand why politicians were so reluctant to give it up.

Reclaiming a bit of serious, she touched Lucas's arm and said quietly, "I'm just teasing, Lucas. You don't owe me anything. That reference letter you strong-armed out of Pablo... I can never thank you enough for that."

Lucas shook his head. "No need to thank me. My...discussion with your idiot ex-boss was pure pleasure."

Nina glanced over at Francesca in the kitchen. "I better say hello to the birthday lady."

"About time," Francesca retorted, handing over the wooden spoon to Christina, who took Francesca's place in front of a large pot of what smelled like minestrone soup.

"Happy birthday, Frannie," Nina said as Francesca kissed her on the cheek. "You look amazing."

"Thank you, sweetie." She put on a cute little face scrunch. "When you're in the beauty industry you're obliged to look the part."

And Francesca, who'd always been a stunner, had no trouble looking and playing her part to the hilt. She wore her glossy black hair past her shoulders so that it flew impressively around her when she indulged in one of her dramatic outbursts, and her curvy figure still drew appreciative stares.

As a teenager, Lucas had his work cut out for him protecting his older sister from all the love-struck fools following her around. Francesca often joked that she was responsible for her brother's first foray into bodyguard duty. That duty, however, officially ended when Francesca turned twenty-two and fell madly in love with a professional race car driver. On her wedding day, Lucas announced that her good looks were now her husband Alberto's problem. The fact that Alberto was Italian and outmatched Francesca in the drama department became everyone else's problem at family gatherings.

Nina dug into her handbag and handed Francesca an envelope.

Francesca ripped it open. "Nina!" she squealed.

"What is it?" Christina asked.

"A voucher for Marian's. I have literally been *dying* to eat there."

Lucas flicked a glance at Nina. "It fascinates me how you always think in terms of food."

"And where does your mind wander to, Lukie?" asked Francesca archly before pulling Nina into a perfume-drenched embrace. "So generous, Nina. Thank you. As soon as Alberto is back from touring Europe, we're off to Marian's."

"So Alberto's still racing on the international stage?" Nina asked.

Francesca nodded. "My man is still chasing the checkered flag."

"We're all savoring the peace and quiet," Lucas admitted, deftly sidestepping Francesca's right hook.

"Be nice to your sister on her birthday," Christina ordered.

"Yes, Ma. One day out of three hundred and sixty-five shouldn't be too difficult." Lucas looped an arm around Francesca's shoulders and pulled her close. "I don't get why you're choosing to spend your birthday at a beauty spa," he said to her. "You're at a spa every day for work."

"Yes, but now it's my turn to be pampered. Plus, I get to check out the competition." Francesca nudged Lucas in the direction of the kitchen. "The birthday lady would like a cappuccino before she leaves."

"Coming up." Lucas stationed himself in front of the coffee machine. "Your usual latte?" he asked Nina.

"Yes, please."

Christina shook her head. "Nothing for me."

"Hot chocolate!" Lexi demanded from the floor. "Please, Uncle," she swiftly added when Francesca raised her eyebrows.

"One hot chocolate for the princess." Lucas poured milk into the frother. "Can someone check if Dad wants another espresso?"

"I'll go," Nina offered, heading for the TV room, Colton Wilson's favorite hideaway.

Francesca stayed her with a hand on her arm. "Pops!" she hollered. "You up for another coffee?"

Lucas winced. "Frannie, it amazes me that your voice hasn't softened with marriage or motherhood. I guess I'll have to hold out for menopause."

Francesca's dark eyes flashed, and Nina stifled a giggle. Lucas was one of the few family members who didn't tiptoe around his sister. Francesca, for her part, was so accustomed to men falling all over themselves for her, her husband and father included, that she was always slightly bewildered by Lucas, who remained annoyingly unmoved by her beauty and tears and temper.

"Aren't you the comic, Lukie?" retorted Francesca, shooting out a hand to clip him on the back of the head, Lucas not able to duck in time.

Nina loved the warm, happy chaos of the Wilson home, the air invariably rich with the scent of whatever was bubbling on the stove or baking in the oven. The moment you crossed the threshold you were surrounded by noise and laughter and banter. Nina felt a jab of deep sadness thinking of her own childhood home and its atmosphere of cool judgment and impossible expectations.

"Pops!" Francesca shouted again.

"Your father can't hear you," Christina said to Francesca, dipping a spoon into the soup to taste. "He's losing his hearing, remember?"

"No worries. I'll ask Mr. Wilson...uh, Colton," Nina amended quickly at Christina's meaningful look, "if he wants another coffee. I'd like to say hello anyway."

Nina accepted her latte from Lucas and made her way to the TV room, discreetly scooping up her handbag along the way. She found Lucas's father resting in his leather recliner, tucked into a flannel blanket and watching what looked like a World War II documentary on the TV.

"Hi, Mr. Wilson."

"Nina." He pressed Pause on the remote, and Nina leaned down to kiss his cheek, taking in the additional lines on his handsome face, the watery sheen to the green eyes Lucas had inherited. He didn't want another coffee, and Nina let Lucas know before returning to Colton's side.

In a low voice, he said, "If you want to keep calling me Mr. Wilson, that's fine by me. Mr. Wilson makes me feel important."

"Wait," Nina said in confusion. "You heard what we were saying?"

"There's nothing wrong with my hearing," he admitted with a half smile, "but if the rest of the family think I'm slightly deaf, well, it has its advantages."

She chuckled into her coffee. "Aren't you the sneaky one?" she said admiringly. "Looking forward to a quiet day at home?"

"I've been looking forward to it all week," he confided. "Are you and Lucas taking Lexi to one of those indoor play centers?"

"Yes."

"Very brave of you," he murmured, setting off a niggle of alarm that Nina tried to wash away with a mouthful of coffee. "Tell me, Nina, what's Christina cooking for me?"

"Minestrone soup." When his face fell, she said gently, "She's worried about your cholesterol."

He gave a doleful nod. "One small scare and I lose all my little pleasures."

"Not all of them." Nina checked the doorway before reaching into her handbag and pulling out a box of Turkish delight.

Colton Wilson's eyes lit up. "They're my favorite."

"I know."

She handed him the box, and he clutched it to his chest, the way a capsized passenger would hold on to a life buoy.

"You've made an old man very happy."

A second later, Christina came bustling into the room, and the box of Turkish delight disappeared under the blanket. "Colton, there's minestrone soup on the stove top and fresh orange juice in the fridge. If you want dessert, grab some fruit."

"Will do. Thank you, my dear."

Christina kissed his forehead. "I'll see you later."

"See you later," he echoed, managing to slip Nina a wink before she accompanied Christina out of the TV room.

They finished up their coffees, and Francesca called, "Time to go, Lexi."

Lexi jumped up and headed straight to Lucas, who was standing at the front door, pulling on his jacket. She held up her arms, and Lucas obligingly picked her up, using his thumb to wipe off her milk mustache.

She snuggled against his chest. "Tell me a scary story, Uncle Lucas," she begged.

"A scary story," he murmured, opening the front door. "Let's see. Once upon a time, Grandma SoftHeart decided to take Queen

Spoiled-a-Lot to a faraway kingdom called, uh, Waxy Land. Terrible tortures existed in this secretive place, like potions that peeled a layer of skin off your face and..."

"Lucas!" Christina scolded. "Lexi won't sleep tonight."

Lucas examined the laughing face of his niece. "She doesn't look too traumatized, Ma."

Francesca let out a reluctant chuckle. "I'll admit some of the back waxes we do are pretty scary. And if there's one more request for a trimming of pubic—"

"What's pubic, Mama?"

Francesca froze, staring mutely at her daughter.

"Guess what, Lexi?" Nina said brightly. "Uncle Lucas is buying you ice cream today!"

"Ice cream! Yay!" cried Lexi, cupping Lucas's jaw in her small hands and giving him a lip-smacking kiss on the cheek.

"Sugar high. Yay," Lucas mumbled through distorted lips as Lexi squeezed and stretched his skin like it was Play-Doh.

Nina picked up Lexi's backpack, and Francesca whispered a fervent "thank you."

"No problem."

Lucas carried Lexi over to his car, sheltering her as best as he could from the light spattering of cold rain. Nina hurried to open the back door and he buckled Lexi into her car seat.

"Lukie, you take care of my granddaughter," Christina ordered, climbing into Francesca's red sports car.

"Ma, it's my job to watch over people."

"Yes, but no one, not even a politician, is as sneaky as a six-year-old child."

#

The noise was at a level Nina had never encountered before. Children swarmed all around them, screaming, crying, laughing, begging...oh, sweet George, the begging for one more lollipop, one more cookie, one more ride on the coin-sucking carousel positioned strategically in the middle of the play center.

"My butt's numb," Nina said, shifting uncomfortably on the hard chrome chair.

Lucas groaned agreement. "I lost feeling there ages ago."

It had taken all Lucas's skill to secure a table in the center's café area, which afforded them a good view of Lexi's bobbing figure amid the play equipment. The rain had herded what felt like hundreds of desperate parents into the center, happily paying the cover charge so that their cabin-fevered children could burn off energy clambering over climbing frames, going down gigantic slides, and bouncing on the jumping castles.

"Watch me, Uncle Lucas!" shrieked Lexi. "Look, Nina, look!"

They both gave a weary wave of acknowledgment.

"I don't get it," Lucas said, white-faced. "Why isn't she tired? It's been three hours. Surely she's had enough."

"It's the ice cream." Nina stifled another yawn. "It's given her an unlimited energy store."

"As well as a complete personality change," Lucas muttered.

They watched a sweat-sticky Lexi come bounding up to their table, grab her pink water bottle, and begin gulping.

"You ready to go, Lexi?" asked Lucas.

"No!" she screamed. "Not yet!"

"You must be tired," Nina pointed out.

"Not tired! Not! Not! Not!"

Oh, where was that sweet, gentle girl who had cuddled in her arms earlier?

"Lexi," Lucas said in a warning tone.

"Don't want to go!"

Lucas rubbed the back of his neck. It was a familiar gesture, one Nina knew he used when he needed to calm himself down. "So you don't want to go back to Grandma's house and watch *Frozen*?"

Lexi hesitated, her expression torn. Nina held her breath. At last, Lexi held up a hand, fingers splayed. "Five more minutes, Uncle Lucas."

Lucas raised his eyebrows.

"Please," she added.

He narrowed his eyes at her. "No more shouting."

She shook her head solemnly. "No more shouting."

"All right, five more minutes."

Grinning, Lexi skipped off, and Nina nudged him with her shoulder. "You big softie."

He grimaced. "It's those eyes."

"How many times has she watched *Frozen*?"

"More times than what is probably healthy, but we're desperate here."

A couple of minutes later, an angry-looking mother stalked up to their table, towing a wailing ginger-haired boy.

"That your kid?" she demanded, pointing an accusatory finger at Lexi, who was trailing the mother.

Lucas winked at Lexi. "She's way too beautiful to be my child."

The woman slitted her eyes. "Are you responsible for her?"

"Yep," Lucas answered cheerfully.

"Well, she tackled my poor little Eddie around the waist and threw him to the ground."

Nina studied the sniveling, not-so-little Eddie, who looked about two years older than Lexi.

"Did you tackle Eddie?" Lucas asked a defiant-looking Lexi.

Her small hands fisted at her sides. "Yes."

"Why'd you tackle him?" Lucas asked Lexi mildly.

"It doesn't matter why," the woman snapped. "That girl resorted to physical violence. That's all that matters."

"Give her a chance to explain," Nina said. "Why'd you tackle him, Lexi?"

Lexi glared at Eddie. "He was mean to a girl on the jumping castle. He said she couldn't play because she was a stupid girl and he made her get off. I told him he shouldn't say that because it's mean, and he said I should keep my mouth shut because I'm also a stupid girl and he's gonna make me get off. That made me super mad, so I pushed him."

The woman pulled Eddie protectively to her side. "You see, straight from her mouth, what she did to my boy."

Lucas turned to his niece. "Next time this happens, Lexi, I want you to do better."

Lexi stuck out her bottom lip mutinously.

"Next time," Lucas said, "when you tackle him, go for the legs. You'll bring him down faster."

The woman's mouth dropped open. "Are you serious? What kind of caregiver are you?"

"The kind who applauds a child when she stands up to bullies."

Muttering something they couldn't make out, the woman stormed away, dragging her boy with her.

Lexi threw herself into Lucas's arms, and he picked her up and held her tight. "Ready to leave now, princess?" he asked her.

She nodded, her face buried in his neck.

Oh, man, Lucas would make an amazing father, Nina thought as they headed for the exit. She pictured a solemn little boy with Lucas's self-confidence and a mischievous girl with his dimple. Perhaps they'd inherit her dark hair and cheekbones, but Nina hoped they'd both get Lucas's green eyes.

Abruptly, Nina stopped walking, aware of where she'd inserted herself in this idyllic picture. Time to exit not just the play center, but this dangerous train of thought. Time to head to the Wilson house so Lucas and Lexi could fall asleep on the couch in front of *Frozen* and she could head home and swear off playing at mommy and daddy with her best friend.

Chapter Six

Friday came around more quickly than she expected. Nina parked her Prius outside her brother's suburban home, a painful forty-minute drive from the city, and walked up the gravel path to ring the doorbell. Shifting the weight of the bowl in her hands, she noticed a new addition to the front porch—a ceramic *Bless This Home* plaque on the brick wall. She couldn't help her smirk. Her footloose brother had been well and truly tamed.

Olivia answered the door, genuine pleasure lighting up her face. "I'm so glad you could make it. I believe it was touch and go for a while."

"It was, but your cooking outweighs the defects in my brother's personality."

"Hah. I'll be sure to tell him that."

They shared a smile. Nina got on surprisingly well with her sister-in-law, considering they were opposites in so many ways. Olivia, the product of a military home and therefore a rabid follower of rules and of ordering her days like an army general, despaired of Nina's loose approach to authority and of letting her days unfold unscripted.

Any kind of friendship between them should have been impossible, but they managed to make it work, which Nina attributed to three factors: Olivia shared her passion for all things culinary, she unabashedly loved Ryan, and she wasn't averse to mimicking the same surreptitious eye roll when her mother-in-law doled out her Capitalized Crud. It was the third factor that cinched their transition from sisters-in-law to sisters-in-arms.

"You look good," Olivia said warmly.

Nina smiled. "Thanks." No need to state she'd put in extra effort with her appearance tonight, wearing tight denims, knee-high boots and a formfitting burgundy sweater. She'd used heated rollers on her hair, and it fell down her back in soft dark waves.

"Hey, sis, you made it."

Ryan came up behind his wife and lifted aside the shiny curtain of strawberry-blonde hair to place an affectionate kiss on her neck.

A blush colored Olivia's cheeks. "Sweetheart, not now."

Ryan leisurely straightened. "You're right, Liv. Not in front of the little one."

"I think Liv's more concerned I learn from an expert, not an amateur," Nina retorted.

Grinning, Olivia shook her head. "Don't involve me in your war of words, you two."

Ryan peered suspiciously at the foil-covered bowl in Nina's hands. "You brought your specialty salad?"

"Yes, boss, like you asked." Nina held up her bowl of mixed greens, grilled chicken breast, blue cheese, avocado, tomatoes, and quinoa, a sealed jug of raspberry walnut vinaigrette balanced on top.

He frowned. "There's only one bowl. Did you make a separate dish for me—without the tomatoes?"

"Yes, Ry, I went to that level of inconvenience because of your irrational aversion to tomatoes."

"Nothing irrational about it. Spawn of the deep, tomatoes are." He made an exaggerated gagging sound. "What did you replace the tomatoes with?"

"Arsenic."

Olivia laughed, and Ryan flashed Nina an appreciative grin.

"Dried cranberries," Nina said. "Your bowl's in the car."

"You know I love you, right?"

She dropped her car keys into his open palm. "Yeah, I know. Our family just has strange ways of showing that love."

"Uh-huh." Ryan looked over her shoulder, and a broad smile split his face. Other than Olivia, Nina knew of only one person who could cause her brother to light up like that.

Preparing herself, Nina turned to see Lucas strolling up the path. He was dressed casually in denims and a sports jacket, carrying a bulging shopping bag. Her stomach responded before her mouth could, giving a little flip.

"Buddy," Ryan said in greeting, pumping Lucas's hand. Olivia stepped forward to envelop him in a hug.

"Lucas, hi," Nina said when she found her voice, holding her bowl like a barrier.

"Hey, Nina." His face creased into a smile, and he leaned in to kiss her cheek. She smelled sun and spice, a heady fragrance. "You still stiff and sore from Tuesday?"

"What happened Tuesday?" Olivia asked.

Nina said, "I went for a run with Lucas."

Ryan's jaw dropped. "My little sister went for a run? Who was chasing you?"

"I'd hardly call that a run, Nina," Lucas said.

"It was a run!" Nina insisted. When Ryan gave a stifled chuckle, she glared at him and said, "Why don't you *run* along to my car and fetch your tomato-free salad?"

"Fido's on his way, sister dear." Ryan looped her keys around his index finger, singing "Run, Baby, Run" as he set off down the path.

Olivia affectionately tucked her arm into Lucas's. "Why isn't there a Mrs. Wilson on the horizon? What's going on?"

A look of alarm crossed Lucas's face. He tried to extricate his arm, but Olivia, swimming with military genes, held on tight. "Hey, why aren't you interrogating Nina?" he complained. "She's as spouseless as I am."

"Glad to see you've got my back," Nina muttered.

Olivia never took her eyes off Lucas. "I thought I'd tackle you first."

"Leave him alone, Liv," Ryan yelled.

Nina rolled her eyes. As if that would in any way shut down Olivia, who'd been trained by her father to ignore unwelcome tactical advice. Olivia continued her grilling of Lucas as they stepped into the heated air of the entrance hall. Nina's gaze automatically went to the space on the wall where Ryan exhibited her photo. Relief washed through her when she glimpsed the bare wall. He'd made good on his promise and removed it.

She was feeling so grateful, she decided to rescue Lucas, who was looking increasingly hunted under Olivia's onslaught. "What's in the shopping bag?" she asked him.

"Ryan's put me on drink duty," Lucas answered hurriedly, almost groveling at her feet in gratitude. "These are ingredients for a kombucha cocktail."

Olivia wrinkled her nose and was distracted enough to ask, "Kombucha? Isn't that the weird fermented drink with the jellyfish thing floating in it?"

"Yep, my kombucha has a SCOBY." At Olivia's expression of horror, Lucas said with relish, "You know what SCOBY stands for, right? A symbiotic colony of bacteria and yeast." He faked an apologetic smile. "Oh, and I didn't bring a strainer."

Leaving Lucas to his revenge, Nina deposited her salad bowl on the entrance table, slipped out of her coat, and was hanging it up when Ryan came breezing in carrying his salad. "Hey, why are we congregating here? Appetizers are already laid out, and I'm starving."

They followed Ryan through to the dining room. The six-seater table had been set perfectly, cutlery in infantry lines, napkins like deployed parachutes over cocktail glasses, an antipasto platter and crusty ciabatta bread flanked by dipping bowls of olive oil and balsamic vinegar in the center of the table.

Nina's stomach growled. She'd skipped lunch in anticipation of dinner. As Olivia took the salad bowl from her, Nina caught Ryan staring at her, his eyes alight with what looked like...excitement. The hairs rose on the back of her neck. What was he up to? She'd seen that look in his eyes before—the time he'd hacked the hair off all her Collector Edition Barbies. Frowning, she searched the room. And then, stomach plummeting, she saw it.

Ryan had honored his promise and moved her photo from the entrance hall. He'd moved it to pride of place above the gas fireplace in the dining room. Her face would be staring at everyone while they ate dinner. Worst of all, they would be staring at her. Staring at her frizzy-haired, teenaged face wearing orthodontic headgear that had her resembling an alien in a sci-fi movie.

Fuming, she turned on her brother. "Seriously, Ryan! This is the level of immaturity you've sunk to? Take down that picture. Now!"

Ryan folded his arms. "Nina, you seem to be forgetting *why* I have that photo on my wall."

"Oh, come on, it happened eons ago," she said dismissively. "And I was trying to be helpful."

"Helpful!" Ryan spluttered on the word. "You had me dabbing John Thomas with toilet paper after I'd taken a leak."

Olivia pressed her lips together. Lucas looked away swiftly, his shoulders shaking. Nina wanted to laugh herself, but didn't dare. Ryan was the only one who never laughed at the memory of her seven-year-old self instructing her older brother in the proper way to clean himself after he'd "tinkled." Ryan typically never listened to her, but this time, for some unfathomable reason, he'd bowed to the authority in her voice and obediently followed her instructions. Soon after, Lucas (and unfortunately a number of other boys) had caught him using toilet paper to clean up and, amid much ribbing, he'd been given the "Hey, buddy, boys shake, never dab" talk. Ryan had been so mortified, he'd never fully forgiven her. For as long as she could remember, he'd been looking for a way to get back at her. Two years ago—*thank you, Mother*—he'd found it.

"How was I supposed to know boys didn't do that?" Nina protested now. "It seemed more hygienic."

"Hygienic!" Ryan was working himself up, regressing impressively right before her eyes to that eight-year-old boy.

"Nina, stop talking," Lucas ordered. He clamped a hand on Ryan's shoulder. "Ry, I'm not sure I'll have much of an appetite with Terminator eyeballing us throughout dinner."

Terminator. Oh, that was just perfect. Lucas was a regular visitor to her brother's home, that photo confronting him every time he crossed the threshold. Jungian analysts would have a field day with that one. And yes, she was sure it was one of the reasons Lucas never seemed to look beyond the girl in braces to the woman she was now.

"I agree with Lucas." Olivia set down Nina's salad bowl on the server, and her blue eyes skewered Ryan. "Sweetheart, take it down."

Seeming to realize he was outnumbered, Ryan complied, grumbling to himself as he yanked open a drawer and tossed the framed photo inside. Nina made a mental note to destroy it the moment his back was turned. She caught Lucas's gaze. *Thank you,* she mouthed. He winked at her.

Olivia eyed Lucas's shopping bag. "Do those ingredients need to be refrigerated?" she asked, in the tone one might ask, *Does that lice-ridden teddy need to be incinerated?*

"Yeah." Lucas waited a beat, then offered casually, "Or I can make the kombucha cocktail now."

Olivia took the bag from him. "Let's wait," she said, adding under her breath, "Let's wait until corruption no longer exists in government."

The second she disappeared into the kitchen, Lucas used an index finger to casually knock crooked a framed oil painting of the Eiffel Tower that hung above the dining room server.

Ryan shook his head. "You want the wrath of Patton to come down on you?"

"Just keeping Liv on her toes," Lucas replied. "I'm waiting for the day she won't notice."

Ryan snorted. "She could be eighty and on the waiting list for cataract surgery and she'd still notice."

Ryan opened a 2009 Bordeaux, and Olivia returned to the dining room with a bowl of homemade hummus and a platter of portobello mushrooms stuffed with gorgonzola and spinach. She placed the food on the table and immediately walked over to the painting to right it, leveling Lucas a pointed look.

Ryan chuckled. "That's my wife."

They sat down to eat, and conversation flowed fast and easy around the table as they slathered hummus on the bread and helped themselves to mushrooms and antipasto. Olivia, as a kindergarten teacher, had a seemingly endless supply of horror tales of out-of-control five-year-olds.

Lucas grimaced. "I'll take a rock star over one of those any day."

"Give me an egomaniacal chef," Nina added.

"What about a starched shirt divulging all the details of his prostate exam?" Ryan put in.

Nina laughed, Lucas gave a pained wince, and Olivia shoulder-bumped Ryan, saying, "Okay, hubby, you win."

After they finished the appetizers, Olivia and Ryan brought out the main course—a two-cheese gnocchi paired with Nina's salad. Lucas uncorked a second bottle of wine, while Ryan stuck to his beloved beer.

Nina shared the story of Lucas's intimidation of Pablo, and Ryan laughed so hard, he snorted beer down the front of his *Walking Dead* T-shirt, causing Olivia to fist pump the air, saying she'd been desperate for a reason to throw that shirt away.

ALL THE LOST PIECES

Buffeted by the lighthearted banter and tempered sarcasm, Nina felt suffused in warmth and familiarity. These were her people, she thought on the mellow wave of a wine gulp. They had your back. They loved you even when you were at your unemployed worst. They refilled your wineglass when you were running low.

Listening to Lucas tell the story of an anonymous C-lister client whose ego was so supersized, he'd rejected one of Lucas's bodyguards because he didn't look good enough in a Dolce & Gabbana suit, Nina was acutely aware of Lucas's arm brushing hers, the way his whole body vibrated with the rich abandonment of his laugh, the intimacy warming his eyes whenever he looked at her. Her heart throbbed with all the self-destructive love she felt for him.

After the gnocchi was demolished, Lucas stood and stretched. "Time to make my kombucha cocktail."

"No alcohol for me," Olivia said. "I'm fighting a headache."

"I'll make you a separate one without the vodka."

"I don't want to put you out."

"It's no trouble at all. In fact, it'll be my pleasure to watch you drink it."

Ryan stood too. "Stop torturing my wife. The rules for drink dares don't apply to her."

Olivia smiled triumphantly in the face of Lucas's disappointment.

"Fighting a headache, huh?" Nina asked Olivia.

Olivia nodded, not quite meeting her eyes.

Nina could commiserate. She was battling heartache and experimenting with wine as a cure. So far, the Bordeaux was in no way helping to dull the ache, but the night was young and the second bottle still three-quarters full. She propped her chin up in the palm of her hand, her gaze following Lucas as he and Ryan cleared the table and carried the plates to the kitchen. Wow, Lucas really was handsome. He'd always been good-looking but, like wine and whiskey, he seemed to improve with age.

A sudden, sharp pain in her ankle jerked her upright in her chair. "*Ow!* What on earth?" Shocked, Nina glared at Olivia. "Why'd you kick me?"

Olivia hissed, "Because you're going all gooey eyed over Lucas."

"Am not."

"Nina!" Olivia barked.

"Okay, fine, I am," she admitted, because you didn't mess with Olivia when she used her father's military bark. "I can't help it."

"Yes, you can," Olivia retorted, her frustration showing. "Come on, where's your pride?"

"Waiting for me in my empty bed. And you know what, my happily married friend? I'm sick of sharing a bed with that cold, unfeeling cow."

"Oh, Nina..." Olivia trailed off helplessly.

Nina drained the rest of her wine and stared bleakly into her empty glass. "I love him," she whispered.

"Then tell him," Olivia urged, not for the first time.

"I can't." Because once you know something, you can't unknow it. If she told Lucas how she felt and he didn't love her in the same way, his awareness of her feelings for him would always be this massive, mortifying wall between them. They would never get past it.

Olivia's face was soft with sympathy. "Okay, then, but try to go easy on the wine and the ga-ga eyes. I'm sure Lucas will realize he loves you in his own time."

Yeah, like on his deathbed, Nina thought, and a fat lot of good it will do me then. She sighed. A few years ago, Olivia had picked up on Nina's more-than-sisterly feelings for Lucas. She'd sworn to keep Nina's secret, even from her husband. *Especially* from her husband, Nina thought, shuddering to think what Ryan would do with that kind of ammunition. It would be a nuclear weapon in his hands. Thankfully, though, in the age-old way of most brothers, Ryan remained blissfully oblivious.

Lucas and Ryan returned with the drinks. Nina stared dubiously at the sickly green liquid in each glass. "I think you've invented a new shade of green. What's in there?"

Lucas handed her a glass. "A mixologist doesn't divulge his secrets."

Scrunching up her nose, Nina tried a cautious sip. "Hmm, thankfully, the taste doesn't match the color." She took another sip. "Not bad. I taste ginger and lemon. Also mint." She turned to Olivia and held out her drink. "Give it a go."

Olivia's face paled. Clapping a hand over her mouth, she mumbled a hasty "excuse me" before jumping up with a backward scrape of her chair and fleeing the dining room. A couple of seconds later, they could hear her retching in the guest bathroom.

Nina got to her feet. "Should I go after her?"

Ryan hesitated, then shook his head. "Nah, she hates anyone seeing her vomit."

A grin played on Lucas's lips. "You have something to tell us, buddy?"

Ryan froze, his cocktail halfway to his mouth. "Uh, no."

Lucas's grin widened, and he ticked off the points on his fingers. "Liv's not drinking alcohol, she's nauseous, and you've invited both Nina and me over for what appears to be a celebratory dinner."

"Uh..." Ryan shot a desperate glance toward the bathroom, where Liv was still making noises like she was ejecting one of her lungs.

Nina gaped at her brother, absorbing his simultaneously trapped and triumphant expression. "Liv's pregnant!"

Olivia reappeared at the entrance to the dining room, leaning against the wall, one hand over her mouth, the other splayed on her stomach. "I had a feeling one of us would give it away," she said weakly. "I was saving the news for dessert. I'd baked and frosted a chocolate cake in the shape of a rattle."

Ryan went to stand at her side, tenderness softening his face. "You okay?"

Olivia nodded. "Over the worst of it, I hope."

"You guys are having a baby," Nina said, struggling to get the words out past the sudden constriction in her throat. She was happy for them. She was. Never mind that her sister-in-law was pregnant and Nina wasn't even married. Or engaged. Or in a steady relationship. Or in any kind of relationship, for that matter. Never mind all those unimportant details.

Lucas hugged Olivia and slapped Ryan on the back, offering his congratulations, a broad grin splitting his face.

Seeing Lucas's reaction to their news, his open and unreserved happiness, was the shaming nudge Nina needed. Stomping on her selfish heart, she embraced Olivia tightly. "I'm so pleased for you."

Olivia gripped her hand. "Nina, I want you there."

"There?" she repeated, the wine slowing down her connection points.

"At the birth. You and Ry."

Both touched and appalled, Nina groped for the right words. "Liv, I don't know..."

Olivia's grip tightened. "Please! I need a woman there with me, and not just a nurse. I want it to be you."

Tears pricked Nina's eyes. Like her, Olivia had lost a parent young. In Olivia's case, she'd been eleven when her mother was diagnosed with breast cancer, dying six months later. Liv was an only child and her dad had never remarried.

"Wow, Liv, that's..." What? An honor? A punishment? Nina swallowed. She thought of every movie she'd watched of someone giving birth. There was always blood and gore and screaming. Lots of screaming. She stared into Olivia's pleading eyes. "Of course I'll be there," she managed.

Relief filled Olivia's face. "Thank you!"

Nina turned to her brother and hugged him. "Congrats, Ry. You'll be a great father, just like Dad."

"Thanks, sis."

"How many weeks?" Lucas asked Olivia.

"Thirteen. We wanted to get past the twelve-week mark before telling anyone."

"Thirteen weeks." Nina gave a loud and violent sniff. "You guys made a baby together. I'm trying not to think about that part too much, but I want to put it out there that I still love you both."

"Love you too," Ryan said, grinning, and Olivia echoed his words. They exchanged one of those annoying you-can-only-decode-this-if-you're-married-to-me looks.

Nina bent at the waist, peered at Olivia's stomach, and shouted, "Your awesome aunt loves you, little baby!"

"I'm thinking the awesome aunt won't be able to teach the baby to hold her liquor when she comes of age," said Lucas with a laugh, steadying her with a firm hand on her arm when she stumbled slightly.

"She?" said Ryan. "It could be a 'he' in there."

Nina squinted at Ryan. "Hey, evil sibling, you know what? You're actually okay looking when you're all blurry like this."

"Oh, boy," said Ryan with his patented big-brother look. "Spare bedroom for you tonight."

And doesn't that just sum up my life, Nina thought.

Chapter Seven

Nina looked good. Her bedroom mirror confirmed it. The mirror she couldn't help gazing into every five minutes, as if the person staring back at her was a source of endless, delightful surprise. No doubt about it, she'd put enormous effort into her appearance for tonight's fundraiser. Her budget wouldn't stretch to having her makeup professionally done and Francesca was holed up in bed with a debilitating migraine, so this afternoon, Nina had wandered into a department store and charmed a salesperson at a makeup counter into giving her a free makeover. She had to resist the pressure at the end to buy the products, but apart from the slash of heavy red lipstick (which she'd wiped off as soon as she got home) she was pleased with the result. Smoky eye shadow brought out her dark eyes and her skin looked healthy and glowing, thanks to the mysterious application of all sorts of primers and bronzers. Diamond studs—castoffs from her mother who collected jewelry like candy—glittered on her ears.

Since her hairdressing skills were limited to heated rollers and basic French braids, Nina had sought the help of one of the servers at Mateo's Grill, who was also moonlighting as a trainee hairdresser. He'd been so remorseful of his silence in the face of her standoff with Pablo that when she'd asked him to style her hair, he'd fallen over himself at the chance to make it up to her. Earlier today, he'd spent the best part of an hour arranging her long hair into an artful chignon. The look was understated elegance.

The crowning achievement, though, was her dress. She'd set aside the whole of Friday to shop for a dress with the sole aim of provoking Lucas to slack-jawed admiration and perhaps a lightning-bolt realization of *Whoa, Nina, it's you I love. It's always been you.*

In pursuit of that goal, she'd skirted the tourist grid and wandered into the city's hidden laneways. She'd finally found what she was looking for at a small stylish boutique—a rich scarlet dress that hugged her body, showing off her curves and complementing her dark hair and eyes. The best part about the dress was the back. There was none.

Although she'd sooner bite off her tongue than admit it to Lucas, she was looking forward to tonight. After nearly a week at home, the monotony was starting to drive her crazy. At first, Nina had reveled in all the free time. She'd caught up on some of the TV shows the Twitterverse was raving about. She'd read two of the latest bestsellers from the library. For so many years, her evenings had been taken up with work. Suddenly having her nights free was a revelation.

After a couple of days, though, she was bored. She could only watch so much TV before the story lines all blurred in her mind. It was the same with books. When she opened a novel, she couldn't help thinking, *Why am I reading about other people's lives and doing so little with my own?*

What did other people *do* in their spare time? Clubbing? Book clubs? Both activities worked better with friends, and hers had mostly fallen by the wayside. This, Nina realized with some degree of consternation, was what happened when you continually said you couldn't go out because you had to work and then somehow failed to notice when your friends finally stopped asking. Only Tammy was still hanging in there, possibly because her work life was equally hectic.

Maybe she should take up a hobby, Nina thought. Lots of people had hobbies. But the only hobby that interested her was food—buying, cooking, serving, and consuming it. Yet food was also her work, so technically would she be working and not...hobbying?

Nina popped another aspirin to chase away her lingering headache, not helped by all this angsty self-examination, and checked the time on her bedside clock: 6:10 p.m. The fundraiser started at seven, and she'd been ready since five. Another rung down the ladder of pathetic.

At least it looked more promising on the job front. Now that she had Pablo's reference letter, she'd sent her résumé to a number of employment agencies and restaurants on her wish list. Only one restaurant had responded to her, and she had an interview with them next week. Despite the poor response, she was feeling hopeful she'd land a job soon. Hopeful and a little desperate. Utilities, rent, car insurance... It was like an unstoppable tidal wave coming her way.

Uh-uh, stop right there. She was no longer supposed to think in terms of overwhelming tidal waves. Last night, tossing and turning in Ryan's guest bed, she'd decided to rip out a page from her mother's life manual and focus more on the positives in her life. Granted, it was a wine-hazed vow, but there was wisdom there, and now would be a good time to apply some of it.

To start with, in roughly six months' time, she'd be an aunt. That was a fairly big positive. She could get her baby fix whenever she wanted, but she wouldn't have to deal with stretch marks or sleepless nights or volcanic nappy explosions. Nina racked her brain for another positive. Oh, this one should be at the top of her list. In the early hours of the morning, she'd snuck downstairs, retrieved her Terminator photo, and had herself a little ceremonial burning. Sure, Ryan was mad at her right now, peeved he'd been denied his future punitive two years, but Olivia couldn't wipe the smile from her face and had already put up a decorative plaque of fun house rules in the entrance hall where Nina's photo had been.

At 6:20 p.m., her buzzer sounded, and she let Lucas into the building. Her heart was beating way too fast, which was silly. She'd been out with Lucas many times before. He'd seen her dressed up, and he'd also seen her in ratty sweats with a monstrous cold sore like an incubating alien egg on her lip. But he'd never seen her like this.

Don't hope for too much, her inner voice cautioned, but it was drowned out by the knock on her door. She took a deep breath, remembered at the last second to check the peephole—yep, that looked like Lucas's Adam's apple—and opened the door.

Warmth flashed through her at the sight of Lucas looking seriously cool in a classically tailored suit the color of charcoal, an overcoat draped over one arm. He was still hanging on to his stubble, and she liked the more rugged look on him. His brown hair fell naturally into a short-cropped style that framed a strong face with no need of bronzers or primers. In the genetics lottery, Lucas had drawn the winning ticket.

"Hi," she greeted him.

His gaze wandered over her, and she watched him flinch. "You'll be cold in that," he said at last.

She shut the door in his face, seeing shock flash across his features before the door closed.

"Nina? What the heck?" His voice came out muffled and confused on the other side of the door.

She exhaled slowly, striving for calm. She hadn't spent hundreds of dollars she didn't have to be given a weather report. "Let's try that again, Lucas."

She waited five seconds before opening the door and standing there with one impatient hand on her hip, ready to fling the door back in his face if there was a repeat of his...*hmm, what to call it*...stupidity.

Looking like he'd been dropped into land-mine territory, Lucas cleared his throat and chose his next words carefully. "That's quite a dress, Nina. You look...cute."

Cute. Everything inside her shriveled in abject misery. Cute was when your dog brought back your tennis ball all covered in drool and grass shavings and dropped it at your feet. Spielberg's E.T. was cute. She'd had to endure being described as cute all through high school, when it still had that whole ugly-but-interesting stigma attached to it. In Lucas's eyes, cute kept her in a box clearly labeled *good friend*.

She dug her nails into her hip. Sometimes she'd like to stuff him in a box, stamp *heartache* on top, and archive the entire lot to the back of her closet. Out of sight, out of mind, as the saying went.

She wished, for the thousandth time, that that night had never happened. The night where everything had changed, where she'd fallen so hard and so unexpectedly for Lucas.

Before that pivotal night, she'd been so focused on surviving high school and coming to terms with her maturing body, she'd never really looked upon Lucas as boyfriend material. He was her brother's best friend, annoying most of the time, mildly amusing some of the time, and just...there all the time. A tall, gangly, quiet presence in their lives.

Then he and Ryan hit sixteen and started hanging out at the gym, slowly putting on muscle, their shoulders broadening and their voices deepening. Their minds... Well, frankly, not much growth was happening there, besides an obsessive and maddening interest in all things female. A category Nina didn't fall into, according to them. They typically treated her like some sort of sexless being, and she cheerfully returned the favor. The three of them had a tolerable system that operated in the way most families did, strong connections tied up in casual intimacy, annoying quirks, and fierce loyalty.

Until the night of the house party.

But Nina didn't want to think about that night. Not now. Not when she was wearing such a gorgeous dress. She didn't want that night in this moment.

Lucas jangled his car keys. "You ready to go?"

"Yes." Her hand had a mind of its own and brushed an imaginary piece of lint off his suit as she gave in to the overwhelming desire to touch him.

"It's cold outside. You'll need a jacket."

What is it with him and the weather? She held up a sheer black cardigan. "Sorted."

He frowned. "It's impractical."

"But it's pretty."

He sighed, loud and deep. "How do I argue with that logic?"

She retrieved her clutch and stepped into the hallway. Lucas put a courteous hand to her back, and her breath caught as his fingers grazed her bare skin, stirring a shiver that sent aftershocks zinging through her body. It was so unfair, the effect Lucas had on her with simply a touch or a look. But when she went all out with her appearance, he displayed an immunity she couldn't sneak past. How irritating.

Then Lucas snatched his hand from her back as though it burnt him.

Oh.

Oh, yes.

A quick sideways glance showed the almost comical widening of his eyes at the sight of her dress dipping to the curve of her spine, exposing her bare back—exfoliated, moisturized, and tanned. A thrilling satisfaction stole over her.

Yes, Lucas, BUDDY, *I'm no longer that brace-toting, frizzy-haired teenager you remember. Look and see the real me. The me who discarded her braces, who learned to embrace her body rather than hide it, who discovered the wonder of a hair straightener, and who has been in love with you and paying the price for too many years.*

"You like?" she asked provocatively.

"I'd like more dress," he responded as they set off in the direction of the elevator, Lucas keeping his eyes rigidly ahead. "Did they run out of material?"

"Such wit, Lucas." She made a sweeping gesture that took in her dress. "You said to surprise you."

"Not at the level of a coronary," he muttered. "I hope it came with a discount."

She raised her eyes to the ceiling. "It's like Ryan inhabits that body with you."

"You're fortunate big brother's not here."

Nina snapped her fingers in front of his face. "Twenty-nine," she reminded him. "Not in high school anymore. Capable of making my own decisions. Picking out my own clothes." She paused, then added meaningfully, "Declining a certain charity event."

Lucas put an arm out to hold open the elevator door for her. "I'm giving in to blackmail, but I'm still not comfortable."

"Comfort yourself with this, then," she retorted as she swept past him into the elevator. "At least it's the back of the dress that's missing and not the front."

If she couldn't have the happy ending, Nina thought, she could at least have the final word.

Chapter Eight

Within ten minutes of their arrival at the charity gala, Nina had to fend off a Gucci-dressed blonde who had her shark eyes fixed on Lucas, smelling matrimonial blood. Nina's whispered aside—*you're welcome to him, but you should know he's impotent and he wears a wig*—got rid of the blonde quickly enough, but the damage to her confidence had been done. Alone, in her apartment, she'd been so pleased with her appearance, but here in the foyer of one of the city's grandest hotels, she was up against twenty-year-olds with gravity-defying breast implants, dazzling porcelain veneers, and Salvatore Ferragamo peep toes.

Thankful for a floor-length gown concealing her discounted what-brand-was-that-again heels, Nina nervously opened and closed the clasp on her clutch.

Lucas placed his hand over hers, stilling her fidgeting. "Relax, Nina," he murmured in her ear. "We're here to enjoy ourselves."

"I need a little something to help me with that." She intercepted a passing server carrying a tray of complimentary shooters, grabbing and downing one before Lucas could say a word.

"Not wasting any time, are we?"

"You know the drill, bodyguard."

He sighed. "When will we be old enough to leave behind childhood dares?"

Nina opened her mouth, and he narrowed his eyes at her. "Don't you dare make chicken noises here." She shut her mouth with a snap, and Lucas picked up a shot glass and tossed back the contents.

A smile twitched her lips. The whole drink dare thing had started nearly fifteen years ago with Lucas and Ryan paging through the *Guinness World Records* and coming across an entry where a man had drunk a liter of lemon juice in a record number of seconds.

"Easy!" the two boys had boasted simultaneously.

"Bet you couldn't drink even one glass of lemon juice," Nina retorted.

"I'll take that bet," Lucas said, adding challengingly, "Bet you can't."

And so, in the interests of science and one-upmanship, they raided the neighbor's lemon tree and hijacked the kitchen counter to take turns manually squeezing what felt like a never-ending pile of lemons. Ryan poured the juice into three glasses, Nina scrounged around for straws, and on the count of three, they screwed up their eyes and started sucking. Her tongue still curled in remembered agony at the excruciating sourness. After the first sip, she was tempted to call it quits. Only the thought of the boys holding that card over her for the rest of her life kept her going. It was no doubt the same motivation spurring on Lucas and Ryan. The three of them sputtered and gasped their way to the bottom of their glasses, suffering through painful mouth ulcers and stinging toilet sessions for days afterward.

A new tradition was born, and the years after that were marked by peanut butter smoothies you could safely tip upside down, green frappes holding half the garden, and liquor milk shakes that robbed you of the ability to form a coherent sentence. Although the nature of the drinks changed, the deal remained the same: whenever one of them drank any kind of concoction, tame or boundary pushing, the other two had to follow.

Nina could feel an unexpected sting in her eyes at the onslaught of memories. She blinked. Perhaps another drink would take away the sting. Her fingers fluttered at her side as she eyed out another shooter.

"Easy does it." Lucas dismissed the hovering server with a look. "Let's pace ourselves."

"Good idea. I estimate twenty paces to the nearest exit."

"Such wit, Nina," he mimicked, steering her away from the double-door entrance and its intermittent blasts of cold air. "Marking the exits is my job."

They joined the air-kissing, accessorized crowd of glamorous couples in animated conversations making their way slowly through the foyer into the ballroom. According to Lucas, the charity organizers were known for their often outlandish and controversial takes on traditional galas. It was one of the reasons their overpriced tickets were snapped up so quickly.

Nina tried not to gawk at the mix of celebrities and VIP guests in the crowd. She tried to play it as cool as Lucas, who looked unfazed by all the famous faces surrounding them. She whispered, "I want to ask for autographs."

"Don't," was all Lucas said.

Sucking in an awestruck breath, she pressed a hand to her chest. "There's that judge from *Dancing with the Stars*, Lucas!"

He spared a brief glance. "Yep."

"How do you do it?" she asked, frowning. "How do you remain so blasé surrounded by all these superstars?"

He shrugged. "Because I've seen them before stylists and makeup artists have worked their magic on them. They're just people, Nina."

"Spin that for someone else," she scoffed. "They're household names." Her voice rose. "I want to be a name someday. A celebrity restaurant owner."

A corner of his mouth turned up. "You're making quite a name for yourself right now."

Her reply fizzled out into a gasp as they stepped into the ballroom.

"Wow," she breathed. "Just...wow."

Everything—the low lighting bathing each table in a warm glow, the elaborate table centerpieces, the dressed-up waitstaff—added up to a vision that Nina had only ever glimpsed on TV. The reality was even more spectacular.

While Lucas consulted a hostess to find out where they were seated, Nina's gaze continued to roam. It struck her how many couples were holding hands. It was such a proprietary, intimate act, one she missed so much, that sensation of warm, strong male fingers entwining with hers. She stared at Lucas's arm hanging loosely at his side. He'd never held her hand. Hand-holding was the official stamp of a couple, and Lucas had never seen the two of them in that light.

They followed the hostess to their allocated table. Nina expected it to be on the periphery of the ballroom, away from the cluster of VIP tables close to the stage, but to her surprise, the hostess led them to a table right in the front. Since when had Lucas attained this kind of VIP status? She knew he was successful, but she'd had no idea he had a standing that grouped him with media personalities and prominent politicians.

They were the first to arrive at their eight-seater table. Lucas pulled out a chair for her. She remained standing.

"Maybe I should ask for *your* autograph," she said. "Do you have a wildly popular YouTube channel I don't know about?"

He leveled a look at her. "Do I look like a YouTuber?"

She tapped her chin, giving the question serious weight simply for the pleasure of annoying him. "Well, you look good enough to build a strong female fan base, but on second thought, to be an internet sensation, your face would have to show emotion, and I know how difficult that is for you."

"Remind me again why I asked you to accompany me to this function?"

A beautiful question underscored by a trip wire. Nina had her answer all ready, but there was no chance to voice it.

"Lucas Wilson, my personal wingman," said a gravelly voice belonging to an imposing man with a paunch that tortured the seams of his Italian suit. "It's good to see you again."

"Senator Scamp," Lucas acknowledged, shaking the man's outstretched hand. "I see you're still playing *World of Warcraft*."

The senator leaned in conspiratorially. "It's sometimes safer navigating the world of Draenor than the corridors of politics." He clapped Lucas on the shoulder. "A little PR bird tweeted you were going to be here tonight. I requested you at my table in case someone decides to take a shot at me again."

"Again?" Nina turned questioning eyes on Lucas, who wore the inscrutable look he'd mastered early on in his profession. One that brought out the snippy side of her tongue. Anything to provoke a reaction.

Ignoring her question, Lucas introduced her to the senator, who shook her hand and said formally, "It's an honor to meet a friend of the man who saved my life."

"That must be quite a story, Senator," she said, taking her seat.

Lucas sat too. "Not a very interesting one."

"Only when you tell it," she replied sweetly.

Scamp boomed out a hoarse laugh, and Nina didn't miss the wink he directed at Lucas. Fortunately, while Lucas was all reticence, the senator was all talk. He pulled up a chair next to her and huddled the three of them together as though their table was a campfire. This was a story he clearly relished telling.

"So four years ago, there I was, rising up the political ranks and targeting global crime syndicates engaged in drug trafficking and money laundering. My campaign attracted the attention of a powerful crime syndicate, and I started receiving death threats. I hired Lucas here to protect me." He paused, and Nina couldn't help thinking the senator could give her mother a run for her money in the drama department. "I'd just finished a late-night meeting, and

Lucas was walking me to my car, when someone took a shot at me. Lucas pushed me aside and took a bullet in the shoulder."

Nina stiffened in her seat. What the heck? Lucas had been shot? *Shot!*

Seeing her reaction, Lucas grimaced. "Exactly why I never told you."

"Lucas!"

"Four years ago," he reminded her, touching her arm. "The scar's barely visible."

"Apologies, Lucas," the senator interrupted. "It looks like my mouth is putting me on a hit list again." He turned to Nina. "Don't take it out on him, my dear. He was doing what he does best. Protecting people. In this case, you."

Protecting was starting to feel uncomfortably like swaddling, Nina thought, pointedly removing her arm out of Lucas's reach.

"It appears I'm in the hot seat," Lucas said ruefully. "Nina..."

She gave a slight shake of her head. Not now, not yet. This felt big. Or maybe she was making it into something bigger than it actually was. She knew that in Lucas's line of work, confidentiality agreements were everything, but this had been about *him*. He'd been shot, and he'd kept it from her. Her chest felt tight. She could feel Lucas's eyes on her, but it was too soon. Forgiveness wasn't a fast-food meal; it was a dish that needed to simmer awhile.

He sighed, a sigh that said he knew her well enough to give her the space she needed. He turned to Scamp. "What about you, Senator? You annoying any more trigger-happy crime lords?"

"My boy, I'm always annoying someone. It comes with the territory. These days, though, I fear telephoto lenses more than bullets." Scamp's gaze circled the ballroom. "Excuse me, I see someone I need to speak to about an asinine bill he's trying to get passed."

Nina was the first to break the silence left in the senator's wake. "Any other secrets, Lucas? Like amputated toes from a torture session? Or a wife stashed away somewhere?"

"All my toes are accounted for, and I'm too busy getting shot to find a wife," he deadpanned.

"Not funny."

"There's a lot I don't tell you," he said carefully. "For good reason. You'd worry too much, and I don't want you worrying." He reached for her hand, holding on when she tried to pull away. "But I should've told you about this."

"Yes, you should've."

Their eyes connected. She had her secrets too. She could choose to nurse this and allow her resentment to spoil the evening, or she could act like an, *ugh*, good friend and move on. No doubt her mother had some shoplifted saying to shine a haloed light on this situation.

Nina huffed out a breath. It took effort, but she dug up a smile. Years of working as a front-of-house manager and dealing with difficult diners (*the ice cream's too cold, could you warm it up?*) had given her plenty of hard-knock experience in swallowing her feelings.

Lucas's mouth quirked, acknowledging her effort. "That's my Nina."

If only. "Any other times you've been injured while working?"

He squeezed her fingers. "C'mon, Nina, let's talk about something more important than work hazards." He let go of her hand to open up a silver-embossed menu. "Let's talk about...mmmm...sesame-crusted scallops, braised pork sliders, and roasted cauliflower wedges, mascarpone pancakes with parsley sorbet..."

"Parsley sorbet! No way." She peered over Lucas's arm and read aloud, "Parsley sorbet with frozen crystallized parsley leaves. The combination of textures should be fantastic!" She caught the hint of a smile on his lips. "Not fair, Lucas," she complained, giving his arm a playful thump. "I shouldn't be this easy."

"Only to those who know your weakness."

Still scanning the menu, she let out a gasp. "I don't believe it. Roland Sollberger is in charge of tonight's food."

"Is he the chef you're always going on about?"

"He's the rock star of celebrity chefs." She punched the air. "I haven't had the opportunity yet to taste his food. This'll be the most exciting part of the evening."

"Thanks, Nina. My ego will one day recover."

She laughed. Others joined their table, the lights dimmed, the emcee—Aidan Mann, a popular talk show host—stepped onto the stage and the entertainment lineup began.

From the moment Lucas had asked her to the charity gala, Nina had mentally prepped herself for a dull and drawn-out evening, but the combination of Lucas's presence and culinary creations that exploded like flavor bombs in her mouth eased one of the more painful aspects of the night: the obligatory small talk with old-money philanthropists seated at their table. In between the live auction and stirring video presentation on the importance of clean water in a Zambian village, she and Lucas shared a few laughs with the senator, but Scamp was in lobbying mode and played musical chairs for much of the time.

She was halfway through a strawberry daiquiri when the announcement came. "Ladies and gentlemen, your attention, please. We need ten ladies from the audience up here on the stage."

Feeling vaguely sorry for the women who'd be subjected to whatever shock stunt the organizers had planned, Nina was contemplating a bathroom break when she heard the senator's raspy voice declare in her ear, "Young lady, you need to get up there."

Chapter Nine

Before Nina could take in what was happening, her daiquiri was plucked from her hand, she was pulled to her feet and strange hands were propelling her toward the stage. What on earth? No way, not in this lifetime was she getting up there, but she couldn't seem to stop her momentum. Scamp had too many enthusiastic coconspirators. Nina cast a frantic glance at Lucas, who responded with a what-can-I-do shrug. Cold panic settled in her chest.

"Come on up, ladies," Aidan called from the stage. "Don't be shy."

Shy couldn't even begin to cover her feelings. *Mortified* was more like it. She was going to kill Lucas for this.

At the foot of the steps to the stage, Nina made a last-ditch attempt to escape back to the anonymity of her table, but a redhead with one designer heel on the first step forcefully linked her arm in Nina's and muttered, "I'm not walking up there by myself. If I have to do this, so do you."

"Let go of my arm," Nina hissed.

"Not a chance. Nice dress, by the way."

Nina debated jerking her arm free, but the sudden image of the redhead toppling to the floor and everyone in the room staring openmouthed at the bully who'd pushed her gave her pause. Gritting her teeth, she and the redhead climbed the steps up to the stage, where Aidan herded and cajoled them, together with the rest of the ladies, into a semicircle facing the audience.

"A round of applause, please, for these ten brave ladies," Aidan boomed.

Standing in the middle of the semicircle, listening to the wave of applause, Nina felt her skin prickle with the feeling of hundreds of eyes on her.

Aidan faced the crowd. "Ladies and gentlemen, I have ten sealed envelopes in my hand." He held them up. "Each of these ten lovely ladies will receive one. Nine of the envelopes contain a blank piece of paper, but inside one of them is a slip of paper with this magical number: four thousand dollars." There were the appropriate *oohs* and *aahs* from the audience, and Aidan made a big show of handing out the envelopes.

Nina held tightly on to hers, dimly hearing Aidan name a giant tech corporation sponsoring the prize. Hope fluttered inside her. She'd won the odd restaurant voucher and free drink, but never anything big. And four thousand dollars was big. Her imagination was spinning out a list of what she could do with that money, even as caution, often the smallest voice in her head, tried to make itself heard.

"But there's a catch, ladies and gentlemen," Aidan continued, pulling Nina out of her Alaska cruise dream. "The catch is that the guys get to play as well." A chorus of deep male cheers erupted from the onlookers. "This is how it'll work. Gentlemen, I get to pick one of you, and you get to come up here and pick one of these lovely ladies."

Nina's eyes widened, her uneasiness growing. *What?* It sounded like high school all over again.

Her gaze flew past Aidan to Lucas's tall form sitting rigidly in his seat. He looked as unhappy as she felt. She pulled her attention away from him and used her envelope to fan her flushed face. Aidan frowned at her. Nina lowered her hand. Right. Lovely ladies weren't supposed to sweat.

"If you're the lucky man who chooses the lady holding the four-thousand-dollar envelope, you get half," Aidan said. "That's right, she has to share the prize money. Two thousand dollars for each of you."

Down to two, Nina thought. It was still a lot of money. If she won, she should opt for the wisest course and earmark it all for rent. Take a bit of the financial edge off. It would be a change, acting wisely.

"Okay, gentlemen, get those hands up."

Hands shot up in the audience. With a showman's flair, Aidan pointed to a middle-aged man with a thick goatee. Smiling broadly, the man accepted the congratulatory cheers from his companions and made his way onto the stage.

Aidan motioned him closer. "What's your name, sir?"

"David."

"And what would you do with two thousand dollars, David?"

"I'd probably take the family to Belles Âmes," he answered, naming one of the city's most expensive restaurants.

Nina's pulse quickened. A man after her own stomach. She'd always wanted to eat there. If she won, she could treat herself and Lucas to Belles Âmes's experimental ten-course degustation experience. When you landed a windfall, she rationalized, rarefied dining eclipsed rent. Always.

"Someone's scoring points with the wife," Aidan observed, prompting appreciative laughter from the crowd. "Okay, David, will you be our fortune-favored first? Which of these lovely ladies will you pick?"

David tilted his head to one side as he inspected each lady in turn. The ballroom echoed with the sound of a drumroll. David was in no hurry, teasing out his moment of fame.

Nina fought to keep her smile in place and her feet from fleeing. This whole stunt had the air of a cattle market. And why was it only women on display? Why not have men standing here like farcical mannequins and women doing the choosing? This was wrong on so many levels. Really, she should walk away on a principled burst of feminist outrage, but the shameless capitalist in her wanted that money.

David picked the redhead. No surprise. She was stunning, an ethereal vision in an almost transparent gown. Along with everyone else in the room, Nina held her breath as Aidan encouraged her to open her envelope. With David standing next to her, she pulled out the slip of paper and stared at it. She turned it over. It was blank on both sides. Disappointment clouded her face, spilling over onto David's. Nina's heart swelled with relief. Yes, she still had a chance!

The two were escorted off the stage and Aidan picked the next guy. And the next and the next. As they came up onto the stage, one after the other, no one chose her. No one even hesitated over her. Clutching her envelope, Nina watched the other ladies preen and giggle as, one by one, they were chosen. She stood tall and kept smiling, while inwardly cursing Lucas for inviting her and cursing herself for accepting the invite. Her only consolation was that none of the chosen ladies possessed the winning envelope.

Ten minutes later, there were three of them left on the stage. Aidan skillfully drew out the tension, stirring up the crowd who were sounding more and more inebriated as the show dragged on.

Nina chanced a look at Lucas, who was staring straight at her. He mouthed something that she thought was *sorry*, but she wasn't sure.

She broke eye contact with him when Aidan called out, "That gentleman over there. Yes, sir, I'm looking at you. Up you come."

A man wearing tight pants and a shirt with the top two buttons undone, displaying a gold medallion and a scary amount of chest hair, approached the stage.

Nina watched him swagger over to Aidan. *Oh, you are just a horrible walking cliché, and I think I can see lice in that chest hair, but please, please pick me so I can get off this stage and make my way home.*

Aidan and the man—Hector—exchanged the usual meaningless banter. Nina was too tense to take it in.

The drumroll started up, and the moment of selection came. Hector wet his lips and stared at the brunette on the far left, his gaze raking over her in an insolent once-over. Nina dug her nails into her palms, crushing her envelope. Obviously enjoying himself, Hector's eyes traveled to the glossy blonde next to Nina.

Aidan shifted uneasily, the discomfort showing on his face as he realized the mistake he'd made in his candidate choice. Finally, Hector stared at Nina. She held his gaze. And chanted silently, *Hairy Hector, Horrible Hector, Hang Hector.*

Out of nowhere, Nina thought of Tammy, tried to imagine her friend spotlit on the stage like this. Tammy would verbally tear Hector apart. She'd tear the whole show apart, she was that fearless.

Nina looked away from Hector and locked eyes with Lucas. How could he be okay with this? But one look at him—at the furious line of his mouth and his fisted hands—showed her he wasn't. As their eyes connected, Lucas half rose out of his chair, but Nina gave a quick, slight shake of her head. This was something she had to handle. His eyes fought to hold hers, but she dragged her gaze away.

Two seconds later, Hector picked the blonde. She tore open her envelope and drew out a blank paper. With great satisfaction, Nina watched Hector's face mottle in angry disappointment. Aidan swiftly hustled Hector and the blonde off the stage.

Only two of them left now, Nina thought. The brunette with a butterfly tat on her neck flicked Nina a nervous smile and reached for her hand as if they were at a Miss Universe pageant. Nina didn't have a smile in her right now, and she tolerated the damp handholding only because the room was hushed and all eyes were on them.

Aidan played it safe this time and picked a bespectacled man in a conservative suit, banker stamped all over him. Nina wasn't surprised when the banker gave her a polite smile and picked the tatted brunette. As the three of them gathered around the envelope, Nina marked the time with a kind of numb resignation, counting down the seconds until she could exit this horror show.

She was the only one who hadn't been picked. That was all her mind could comprehend. So much for focusing on the positives in her life. There wasn't a positive affirmation left in her.

She jumped as Aidan threw an arm around her shoulders. Her heart stalled as the realization hit her that the brunette and the banker were no longer on the stage.

Aidan beamed at her, urging her to open her envelope, his voice sounding faraway and surreal. There was a roaring in her head. Or maybe it was the roaring of the crowd. She didn't know. What she did know was that she'd ripped open her crumpled envelope and her shaking hands were holding a piece of paper with $4,000 blurred in front of her. Aidan grabbed her wrist and held up her arm in victory. Thunderous applause and cheers washed over her.

It was one of the most humiliating moments of her life: no one had picked her.

It was also her most triumphant: she was the last one left, so she didn't have to share. She'd won the whole lot. Four thousand dollars.

Chapter Ten

Lucas was waiting for her at the bottom of the stage steps. He'd taken off his jacket, and his green eyes were watching her steadily as she wobbled her way off the stage and half fell, half launched herself into his arms. He held her tightly, not saying anything, his solid and steadfast presence the infusion of strength she needed. Nina closed her eyes, feeling simultaneously drained and exhilarated as her body came to terms with everything that had happened up there on the stage.

And then Lucas whispered in her ear, "You would've been my first choice."

She pulled back to look at him. She saw the usual intelligence and fearlessness blazing in his eyes, but whatever else he was feeling was carefully masked. Once, she could've summed up in a glance whatever emotion flared up inside him—anger when Ryan kissed the girl he had a crush on, disappointment when his drone project failed to make the national science fair, devastation when a school friend shot himself. But once they'd left school behind, she'd also left behind the ability to read him.

You would've been my first choice. As the murmur of conversations rumbled around them like static on a radio, she finally got it. A pity pick. She looked away and made to brush aside his statement with a lighthearted comment, but he moved his hands from her back to grip her arms and said firmly, "Nina." She lifted her eyes to meet his, and he said quietly, emphasizing each word, "I would have chosen you."

She was stunned into silence. What was he saying? The fear of misreading him trembled through her. Was there an underlying message there, one he couldn't bring himself to reveal? She thought of all those years of bodyguard duty, of operating under the directive *speak when spoken to* and how the habit of staying silent and unobtrusive might have reflexively spilled over into his private life.

Confused, she simply nodded. For an instant, she glimpsed something work in his face as though he was on the verge of saying something more, but then she heard Senator Scamp call her name as he barreled toward them, and the moment was lost.

Scamp offered his congratulations. Swept up in the force of his personality, Nina allowed herself to be towed away to meet "lobotomized voters, but major movers and shakers." She floated through the next hour in a happy daze, still reeling from the unexpected turn of events. There was no chance to continue her conversation with Lucas. Constant interruptions by strangers congratulating her on her win saw to that. And for the sake of her sanity, she'd already relegated Lucas's statement *I would have chosen you* to the familiar territory of friendship.

In a quiet moment, when they were the only two at their table, Nina offered to share the prize money with him, but Lucas cut her off with a shake of his head. "Nina, it's all yours."

A local act took over the stage, pounding out their catchy songs and luring a few brave souls onto the dance floor. Lucas didn't do the dance thing, and there was no way Nina was participating in anything more tonight that might warrant eyes on her.

"You ready to leave?" Lucas asked.

"More than ready." She got to her feet, picked up her clutch. "I need to go to the ladies' room, then I'll meet you at the organizer's office." A briskly efficient PR lady had approached her earlier this evening to say they'd sort out all the nitty-gritty details of the prize money once she was ready to leave.

Lucas nodded. Nina noticed she wasn't the only pair of female eyes tracking him as he threaded his way through the crowd, stopping to say his goodbyes to Scamp.

Nina headed down a long hallway to the ladies' room. She did her thing, washed her hands, stared at herself in the mirror. It was nearly eleven, her crash time, but she was still riding the high of her win. It showed in her flushed cheeks and too-bright eyes and the smile she couldn't keep from her lips.

Lost in her thoughts, she was making her way back down the hallway when Hector stepped out from an alcove, intercepting her with an outstretched arm and a blast of whiskey breath that had her recoiling.

"So you had the winning envelope," he slurred, swaying a little. "Who would've thought?"

"Obviously not you," she replied, not above a little payback for the man's stage antics.

Hector frowned. Yep, he knew he'd been insulted, but from the confusion on his face, he was still working out exactly how.

Nina tried to step past him, but he lurched in front of her, blocking her way.

"I should've picked you," he said, eyes glassy with drink and resentment. "I would have two thou right now. Instead, I got nothing."

She eyed the gold medallion lost in the forest of chest hair. "I'm sure two thousand is petty cash for you."

"Six months ago, yeah. But now I got debts. What about it, babe? Feel like sharing?"

So many, many retorts to choose from. She had to swallow them all. A rebuttal would be too cruel, like hitting a man in a coma. How did a guy with such...limited intelligence make the grade to a black-tie function like this?

"Everything okay here, Nina?" Lucas asked, coming up behind Hector to stand next to her. His eyes moved from her to Hector, assessing the situation. There was an edge to his voice and a hardness to his face that took her by surprise.

"Everything's fine," she said quickly. "Hector was just complimenting me on my win."

Hector scowled. "No, I wasn't."

Limited intelligence. Really, she'd been overly generous.

Turning to Lucas, she placed a hand on his arm. "It's been a long evening. Let's go."

Catching a glimpse of her bare back, Hector sneered, "Babe, if you'd showed me the back of your dress and not your face up on that stage, I would've chosen differently."

Astonishment froze Nina in place. She could blame the alcohol, but she'd listened to a talk once where a speaker had said that there was nothing that comes out of the mouth of a drunk that wasn't there in his heart in the first place. Going with that theory, a sober Hector would still be a mean Hector. Alcohol had simply loosened the leash on the brute within.

But even the words of a vain, stupid brute could hurt.

Before she had a chance to react, Lucas stepped between her and Hector, getting in his face, and jabbing at his throat with the extended fingers of his right hand. Hector gasped in pain and doubled over. It happened so quickly, the unexpected violence of Lucas's reaction caught her completely off guard.

"You'll be okay," Lucas said calmly to a wide-eyed and wheezing Hector. He helped him slide into a sitting position against the wall. "Your breath will come back in a minute. You can use that minute to think about finding a brain cell before opening your mouth."

Still rooted to the spot, Nina stared openmouthed at the now blissfully mute Hector slumped on the glossy checkered tiles in the middle of a hotel hallway. Cupping her elbow, Lucas tugged her away, and she automatically fell into step beside him, unable to help one last look over her shoulder.

"Should we call a doctor?" she asked.

"You know offhand the number of a neurosurgeon?"

A laugh bubbled up inside her. "I thought a bodyguard was not to engage."

"A *security specialist* has no choice when a person's a hazard to himself and to others." He let go of her elbow, but kept her close to his side. "Let's get you and this dangerous dress home."

#

The chill in the night air sucked the breath out of Nina's lungs. She stood shivering on the sidewalk outside the brightly lit entrance of the hotel, staring at the darkened windows of the office building across the street and already missing the warmth of the hotel ballroom. Her very pretty and very impractical black cardigan was proving a completely useless barrier against the cold.

At her side, Lucas glanced at her, shook his head and took off his overcoat without a word.

"No, you need it," she protested, teeth chattering.

Lucas held out his coat. "Put it on."

Nina hesitated for all of five seconds before she gave in and slipped her arms into the sleeves. The coat dwarfed her, but she didn't mind. She was warm and wrapped up in Lucas's body heat.

"I should've listened to you," she mumbled. "About the cardigan."

Lucas cupped a hand to his ear. "I'm not sure I heard you right."

"You heard me."

He shivered dramatically. "Hypothermia has probably affected my hearing."

She rolled her eyes. "What a pity it didn't get your tongue."

A smile touched his lips as he patiently waited her out.

Shuffling her feet, she sighed and gave in. "I should've listened to you. You were right. I was wrong."

His smile widened in victory. "I've waited years to hear those words."

She poked him with her elbow. "It might be years before you hear them again."

His smile stayed. "Somehow, I don't think so."

He offered her the crook of his arm, and she took it. They set off down the street, leaving behind the last of the charity gala guests trickling out of the hotel. Ahead of them loomed a lonely stretch of empty office buildings and shuttered cafés, street lamps leaking jaundiced light on to the asphalt. It always amazed Nina how, at the setting of the sun, a bustling financial district transformed itself into an eerily quiet ghost town.

Typically, she loved walking the city's streets, loved the mix of gothic architecture and futuristic glass skyscrapers. There was a vibe to the city that her mother often said reminded her a little of New York City's buzz. But there was no sense of that now, she thought, pulling Lucas's coat more closely around her. Instead, the area had the look of an old woman staggering out of a candlelit room to reveal the ravages of a life lived long and hard. Ravages that showed in the cigarette butts strewn on the cracked sidewalk like bullet casings, graffiti tags marking concrete surfaces, and the smell of urine hitting her from dark doorways.

"Tired?" Lucas asked.

"Yes." It was an absent-minded reply, but she realized all at once it was the truth. She was mentally and physically flatlining.

The corners of his mouth twitched. "I was wondering when the adrenaline of your win would wear off."

"It's worn off," she confirmed, yawning. It had taken longer than she'd anticipated tying up the banking details with regard to her prize money. According to the PR lady, the money should be in her account sometime next week.

"When did you say your job interview was again?" Lucas asked.

"Next week, Thursday." She'd secured an interview at Ariadne, a Michelin one-star restaurant in the city. That nudged her memory, and she turned to him excitedly. "Up there on that stage, that David guy gave me an idea. I promised myself if I won, I'd take you to Belles Âmes. Tick off one item on my bucket list. How about it? You keen?"

Lucas remained silent. Even at the best of times, he wasn't the most talkative individual, but this silence was odd, even for him. She tried to catch his eye. "What's wrong? Have you eaten there before and not enjoyed it?"

"I've never eaten there," he replied, still not looking at her.

She frowned in confusion. "I didn't think so."

What is going on? She quickened her pace to keep up with him, suddenly flustered by an unnerving revelation. Maybe money was the issue. Lucas had all the trappings of a flashy lifestyle—expensive clothes, fancy car, the latest gadgets, luxury apartment—but he wouldn't be the first prideful fool hiding massive debt behind the bling.

She jammed her hands into Lucas's coat pockets and considered the most tactful way to broach this. You'd think living and breathing hospitality air for too many years to count would've given her an edge in diplomacy, but tact had never been her strong point. Sometimes, confronted with the snide complaints of a you-will-never-please-me diner, there rose inside her a wild impulse to mimic the autocracy of a chef like Nico Ladenis, who'd cultivated a spectacular reputation for throwing diners out of his restaurant if they dared to ask for salt. Nobody knew how many times she'd had to smile and bite her tongue to keep from forming words that could sink her professional reputation. Restaurant managers weren't given the same level of indulgent leeway as chefs. Which she'd learned to her cost.

Lucas, however, wasn't a customer. He was someone she'd known for too many years to worry about treading delicately. "Is it the cost?" she asked straight out. "Because I'm paying."

"It's not the cost," he said gruffly.

"So you're not in massive debt?" she asked, just to clarify.

His steps faltered slightly, and he turned to her with an astounded expression. "Of course not! Why would you think that?"

"Why would I?" she echoed, throwing her hands in the air. "Your weird silence, for one. My imagination's working overtime because your mouth is not."

They reached the entrance to the underground car park. Nina's heels tapped out her irritation on the narrow pedestrian walkway as she marched past the exit boom, following the walkway as it wound its way to the first level, where Lucas was parked.

Lucas touched her arm in a conciliatory gesture. "Don't be mad."

"Don't make me mad. Just say yes. Let me treat you."

Again that maddening, mystifying silence. Oh, really, enough was enough. Her only thought now was to climb into bed and sleep for nine hours straight.

"Why don't we eat somewhere else?" Lucas suggested. "Somewhere other than Belles Âmes?"

It was her turn to be astounded. "What! Why? No one in their right mind would say no to Belles Âmes."

Unless...unless they had a valid reason for saying no. A reason named Nina Clueless Abrahams. Embarrassment burned a blistering path across her skin. Heart pounding, she turned to face him. "What's going on here, Lucas? What aren't you telling me?"

Seeing the expression on his face, an unsettling combination of discomfort and apology, Nina had the sensation she was standing on the friable edge of a sinkhole, that his answer would change everything. On her tongue were the words, "Let's forget Belles Âmes, let's go somewhere else," but she was too late.

Lucas said, "Nina, I've never been to Belles Âmes because that's where I plan to ask the woman I love to marry me."

His declaration robbed her of all air, and she couldn't breathe.

"I haven't found her yet," he continued, "the woman I want to spend the rest of my life with, but I'm saving Belles Âmes for that experience. That's why I can't go with you."

No potential fiancée, but no feeling of relief either. She took an involuntary step back, but it couldn't save her from falling into the sinkhole, into the utter blackness of it, and there was no hopeful root to grab on to. Only the surreal and incongruous thought, *What a memorable place for a marriage proposal.* Who wouldn't want to be proposed to on the top floor of the city's most iconic tower? Who wouldn't say yes when faced with sweeping and dramatic views of the city's skyline? An expensive and elite restaurant signifying a treasured and exclusive relationship. The metaphors in that mental picture were killing her.

"Nina." Lucas's voice seemed to echo from a long tunnel. "Hey, are you okay?"

No, she was most certainly not okay. She was suddenly so tired of living this lie. Of pretending to be the friend she wasn't. If Lucas had shared this news with Ryan, her brother would no doubt slap Lucas on the back and say admiringly, "Great idea, buddy." The response of a true friend. At the moment, the only person Nina wanted to slap was herself.

"Nina?"

She held up a hand. "I need a moment. Please."

She couldn't do this anymore. She'd become what she'd vowed never to be. A tired cliché. The loser in a knock-down fight her heart had dragged her into. She'd been in love with Lucas since she was eighteen. That was, what? Her math-impaired brain did a fumbling calculation...eleven years! Eleven years of waiting on the sidelines for Lucas, despite his obviously flawed peripheral vision, to fall in love with her. Eleven years of venturing out on dates and dipping a tentative toe into the relationship pool, but never seriously immersing herself because she was always comparing every man to Lucas.

How pathetic, rebuked her internal critic savagely.

She wanted to crumple under the force of her own stupidity, *but* (and oh, how she was clinging to that pride-salvaging, life-saving *but*) tonight had proven she was a winner. A four-thousand-dollar winner. It was time to start acting like one.

Striving for an offhand tone, she said, "So no Belles Âmes."

Lucas was watching her intently. "You seem upset by the idea."

"Upset? Me?"

"Yes, you."

Nina summoned what she prayed would pass for a smile. "Okay, maybe a little. You know me, I love my food, and you've just deprived me of the ultimate foodie experience."

Lucas frowned. "Nina—"

She said quickly, "It's a good thing we're not going, because I should probably be wise here and save my money."

"Is everything okay?" he asked carefully. "I feel like I'm missing something here."

She faked a yawn. "I'm tired, Lucas, that's all, and the only thing I'm missing is my bed. I'd really like to go home now."

Chapter Eleven

Nina woke up Sunday morning with Lucas's words—*I haven't found her yet, the woman I want to spend the rest of my life with*—front and center in her mind. She shut her eyes, opened them again, trying to restart her day. Those stupid, heartbreaking words had already robbed her of sleep; they were not going to steal her day as well. The only way to stop that from happening, she told herself, was to keep busy.

She spent the morning cleaning her apartment and thinking about the interview lined up for Thursday, an interview she still couldn't believe she'd managed to land for a front-of-house position at Ariadne. Her minimal fine dining experience, though, meant her chances of landing the job were slim.

There was still no response from the other restaurants and agencies she'd sent her résumé to, but as she sat in front of her laptop with a cup of chamomile tea, she reminded herself there was still time. The prize money from the charity gala should be in her account in a couple of days, and she'd use some of that money to tide her over.

Her phone rang. Nina didn't recognize the number on the screen. It could be one of the agencies trying to get hold of her. Would they call on a Sunday? If someone possessed her work ethic, yes. A tiny flare of hope lit up inside her.

"Nina Abrahams speaking."

"Nina, darling."

"Mom," she responded with a sink of disappointment in her belly, wondering why there'd been no Darth Vader ringtone to warn her. The inevitable flood of guilt followed, because what daughter is disappointed to hear her mother on the other end of the line? This'll come back to bite me one day, Nina thought on a wave of superstitious dread, already picturing a future where her own children would irritably screen her calls. "This isn't your number."

"My phone's charging somewhere," Cheryl explained over the faint buzz of background noise. "I'm calling from Darryl's phone."

Darryl? Who was Darryl? No, don't ask. "How's New York?"

"Oh, it's fabulous here. You know how much I love this city. Paris is still my favorite, of course, but there's a vibrancy to New York that I fall more in love with every time I'm here."

New York. Savoring one of Daniel Humm's playful dishes at Eleven Madison Park, sipping a kumquat mojito while she celebrity spotted at The Mark, soaking up the food and atmosphere at cult chef David Chang's Momofuku Ko. Her saliva glands were already planning a trip.

"Darryl's showing me all these hidden gems in New York," Cheryl continued. "We're having so much fun."

Darryl again. She knew her mother was dying for Nina to ask about him. She asked, "How's the seminar going?"

"Sold out," Cheryl admitted delightedly. "Darryl says he's never seen anything like it."

Oh, good grief. It was sometimes easier to just give in. "Who's Darryl, Mom?"

"An absolute darling of a man," her mother gushed. "He runs a highly sought-after event management business. We crossed paths a couple of years ago, but he was married—an absolute no-go in my book. But now he's divorced and, well, sparks are flying."

Nina suppressed a sigh. Cheryl was a relationship junkie, falling in love with men who were initially drawn to her intellect, success, and strong personality, but who, over time, became threatened by the very qualities that attracted them in the first place.

"I'm happy for you, Mom," Nina said. "I hope this thing with Darryl works out."

"Oh, darling, hope alone achieves nothing. Hope Plus Action Makes Things Happen."

"Mmm-hmm," Nina murmured, wondering what action she could take to make this phone call end. Her mother was right. Hope alone wasn't cutting it.

When Nina heard Cheryl pointedly clearing her throat a second later, she realized they'd come to the real purpose of the call. "Do you remember Lisa? Skinny blonde, penthouse in the city, husband in banking, two children in play therapy?" Nina didn't remember Lisa, but she mumbled something, and Cheryl said, "Lisa was present at a certain charity event last night. A charity event I believe you attended with Lucas."

"You know, Mom, if motivational speaking stops working out for you, you might want to consider launching your own WikiLeaks."

That earned her an irritated huff of air. "I have friends, hardly informants. Anyway, Lisa told me everything that happened last night. The whole terrible story."

Nina frowned. "The terrible story that ended with me winning four thousand dollars?"

"Yes, exactly," her mother put in eagerly. "It's a story loaded with meaning: an average, unremarkable woman is upstaged by all the other beautiful women there. In front of everyone, she's rejected again and again, but what happens? The loser ultimately becomes the winner. What a message!"

What a summary. Nina closed her eyes. Her ego was feeling way too fragile right now. "It was just dumb luck," she said at last. "There's no message there."

"On the contrary, darling, what happened to you is an inspiring illustration of perseverance on your part, and on the part of your short-sighted audience, an exhortation to look beyond the surface to find your winning partner. This is a story which could benefit so many people. And you know the best part of it?"

"I can't imagine."

"The best part is, I want *you* to share this story. Up on stage with me as part of a new self-esteem seminar I'm putting together."

It took Nina a while to find her voice. "I'm sorry. What?"

"I know, I'm at a loss for words too! This'll be the first time you and I will work together. I'm considering calling the segment, 'You Are More Than What You See In The Mirror.' What do you think?"

Well, Mom, I'm thinking that college courses are mandatory for professions dealing with a person's physical or mental health, but what about a mandatory course for parents, who are entrusted with the physical and mental health of their offspring?

"You're asking me to relive last night's experience again and again in front of an auditorium full of strangers," Nina said. "Going through it once was bad enough."

"Darling, you know what they say: strangers are simply friends you haven't met yet."

"No. Absolutely not."

"But think of the thousands of people out there who could benefit from your story."

"What about the one person, who just happens to be your daughter, who would die every time she told that story?"

"Don't be so dramatic. If our tragic or embarrassing experiences hold the potential to help others, isn't it worth it in the end?"

"I'm sorry, Mom, I'm not doing it."

"Nina."

"No."

A sigh drifted down the line. "I'll simply have to relate the whole episode without you." Another martyred sigh. "It won't have the same impact."

"Whatever, Mom. Go ahead and use the story. Embellish away. It should be second nature by now." Her tone was peevish, but she didn't care. Nina knew that she and Ry were featured heavily in her mother's talks, sometimes positively, mostly negatively. It was one of the reasons she never listened to any of Cheryl's podcasts, read any of her articles, and kept her tell-all book buried under a stack of dated cookbooks.

"Don't make me out to be the bad person here," her mother said softly. "This was a way for us to spend time together. With my schedule and your long work hours, we hardly see one another. I miss you. I know I don't say it often enough, but I do. And I thought working together like this would be a wonderful opportunity for us to bond."

Guilt burned the back of her throat. "I can't do it."

A heavy silence fell, her mother's injured feelings carrying clearly across the connection. After a few more minutes of painful conversation, Nina ended the call. Her apartment felt suddenly suffocating, the walls closing in on her. Jumping to her feet, she jerked open the sliding door to her tiny balcony and carried her tea outside. She leaned against the railing and stared at all the bundled-up tourists strolling past wind-bent trees to get to where they needed to be. She felt tired just watching all that energy and purpose on the streets below. She closed her eyes, wrestling shut the familiar mental door on her mother, but unable to stop her mind from trawling through the conversation with Lucas last night, replaying, regretting, rewriting.

Her mother she could handle, she told herself. Dealing with her was well-known territory, the hurt an old wound you became accustomed to living with. But Lucas... That was a whole new level of anguish.

She went back inside, poured the remains of her tea down the sink and stood in the kitchen that two hours earlier she'd scrubbed and bleached to within an inch of its sterile life. At least there was the consolation that one part of her life was shiny and bright right now.

The day loomed ahead, long and empty. One step at a time, she told herself dully. First, a shower. She stood under the spray for a long time, letting the hot water wash over her, letting the tears come. It shouldn't hurt this much. She hadn't expected it to hurt this much. She was overwhelmed by how rootless and alone she felt. She'd lost her job and the hope of her best friend falling in love with her. Her brother and his wife were having a baby and tightening their circle. Her mother... Well, who needed a daughter you struggled to understand when you had your fawning fans who understood you.

Nina stepped out of the shower and into baggy sweatpants and an old hoodie. She didn't like this version of herself, this sad, sorry woman drowning in self-pity.

You have so much, she told herself as she dumped a laundry load of whites into the washing machine. You have a family (however dysfunctional), a roof over your head (never mind she was throwing money away on a rental), good health (no sign yet of the varicose veins endemic in her line of work), and four thousand dollars (still awaiting the bank transfer). No more wallowing, she told herself sternly. Get a grip. Buck up. Find the bright side. But the tears still streamed stupidly down her cheeks as she pictured herself running for the rest of her life on the pathetic treadmill called *I can't get over being in love with my best friend*.

That was the crux of it, Nina concluded. How do you stop yourself from loving someone? How do you suddenly switch off those feelings?

She thought of everything she and Lucas had shared over the years, the thousands of incidents that made up their history together. Maybe that was the problem. Their past was so entwined, their memories so entangled, that they dragged her back whenever she wanted to move forward.

Chapter Twelve

Eleven years ago, Nina had no premonition that accepting an invitation to a house party would change her life. It surprised her now how many things her eighteen-year-old self hadn't known back then. For starters, she hadn't realized that the first year of university is regarded as one of the most dangerous times for young women. She hadn't known that the prefrontal cortex, a section of the brain that governs impulses and emotions, isn't fully developed until a person hits midtwenties. What she did know now, though, was that some people are just plain evil. No blaming an underdeveloped prefrontal cortex.

The invitation to the house party had come through Tammy, who had an uncanny knack for securing invites to all the cool parties.

"Rich hosts, huge house, tons of students," said Tammy as they claimed a spot on the campus lawn between classes to soak up the sun. It was an unseasonably hot afternoon and the lawn was dotted with students wanting to make the most of the good weather. Tammy slipped off her sandals and stretched out on her back, hiking up her short skirt so she could tan her long legs. "It'll be fun."

"Fun?" repeated Nina, pillowing her head on her backpack. "Drinking games and cheap vodka and watching jocks upchuck into potted plants?"

Tammy levered herself up on her elbows. Nina watched passersby, male and female, gawk at this gorgeous redhead lying about on the grass like she was in a Calvin Klein shoot. By now, Nina was used to the stares Tammy generated, but she was still sometimes caught off guard by the sensuousness that wrapped around her friend like an exotic shawl.

Tammy arched an eyebrow at Nina. "You have anything better to do this Friday?"

"Does a Tom Cruise movie marathon count?"

"Not for a Friday, my little homebody. Come on, Nina, say you'll be my plus one." She squinted mischievously up at her. "There's guaranteed to be some really hot guys at the party. H-O-T, my friend."

"D-E-E-P, Tammy."

Tammy gave a flippant shrug. "Let's leave deep to the philosophy students. Are you in or out?"

"In," Nina relented on a sigh. In truth, she was secretly excited.

"What about your mom?" Tammy asked. "Will she be cool with you going?"

"Mother Dearest is on a motivational speaking tour in Toronto for the next two weeks."

"So my friend has no keeper."

"Mom's put Ryan in charge." Nina grimaced. "Trust me, he's taken to his role as surrogate father with great enthusiasm."

Tammy made a *pfff* sound. "I have a father with Ukrainian blood. *Overprotective* is the language of my family." She stretched languidly. "I can handle your brother. He's a man, after all."

#

"House party?" Ryan muted the basketball game on the TV and narrowed his eyes at her. "You know what goes on at these parties?"

Sitting cross-legged on the armchair opposite him, Nina pretended to think the question over. "People having fun." She mock widened her eyes at him. "No, Ry, no! Not fun!"

"Rag me all you want, but some guy's idea of fun might not be yours."

"I'm eighteen, Ry!" she pointed out in frustration.

"But still living at home and therefore under Mom's rules."

And breaking Mom's rules meant her spending allowance would be taken away. "I'm not going alone," she said to him. "I'm going with Tammy."

Lucas, wearing his Joey's Pizza work shirt, wandered into the living room, munching on an apple. He'd taken on a part-time job at a takeaway pizza joint and was hanging out at their place before heading into work.

"Who's Tammy?" Lucas asked.

"She's a friend I met in class. I'm sure I've mentioned her to you guys."

Ryan frowned. "Nope, don't think you have."

And you would be right, brother dear. For good reason, I've kept quiet about her.

Lucas flopped down on the couch next to Ryan, unconsciously joining forces with her brother. "Is she reliable, this Tammy?"

Nina thought of Tammy's habit of dozing in classes and skipping tutorials. "Of course she's reliable."

Ryan grunted, looking skeptical.

Nina sneaked a glance at her watch: four hours before Tammy was due to arrive. Nina had waited until Friday before broaching the subject of the house party with her brother, not wanting to give him too much time to think about it. She'd also waited until Ryan had eaten an entire spicy pork pizza and was sitting in a mellow food coma on the couch. As she'd told Tammy, Ryan was a tough sell. Ever since their dad died, he'd assumed the role of her protector. Working in her favor, though, was the fact that Ryan's girlfriend was coming over tonight to watch a movie. Nina was hoping she'd be the third wheel he'd be keen to get rid of.

"Ry, I really want to go. I'll be careful, I promise. Tammy and I will look out for one another."

Ryan turned to Lucas. "What do you think?"

Lucas tossed his apple core in the trash. "I don't know. I'm thinking *American Pie, Animal House, Old School*," he said, referring to movies of house parties gone wild.

"Lucas!" Nina threw a cushion at him. "As if real life is like that."

"You're right," Lucas shot back. "Real life is worse."

"I'll make you a deal," Ryan said finally. "It's a yes for now, but if I don't like the look of this Tammy, if I'm uncomfortable with her in any way, that's it, you're not going."

Nina nodded, but her heart sank. Ryan would take one look at Tammy and that would be it. A firm and decisive no.

#

Four hours later, Nina nervously twisted her fingers together as she heard Tammy's car pull into the driveway. Oh, please, let Ryan by some miracle approve of Tammy. She didn't want to be all dressed up for an evening at home with her brother and his girlfriend of the moment. And she was dressed up. Even Lucas had raised a surprised eyebrow at her appearance tonight. Black lace fringe top and tight denims, accessorized with a long chevron necklace and gold hoop earrings. She had on slightly more makeup than usual, and her dark hair hung slick and straight over her shoulders.

Ryan opened the door. Nina stood slightly behind him, which was just as well because he couldn't see her jaw drop at the sight of Tammy standing on their front porch looking nothing like the Tammy she knew. She wore a conservative gingham wrap dress and her red hair was tamed into a tight ponytail. Even her makeup was muted. Black horn-rimmed glasses Nina had never seen before framed her blue eyes which were staring in wide-eyed innocence at Ryan.

"Hi, I'm Tammy. You must be Nina's brother, Ryan," said Tammy demurely. "Nina's spoken so highly of you."

Ryan shot Nina a look of disbelief. "She has?"

Recovering, Nina said, "I had to dig really deep."

With Ryan's attention briefly diverted, Tammy winked at her.

Unbelievable, Nina thought. This woman was both magnificent and scary.

Ryan shook the long-fingered hand Tammy held out and offered a broad smile. "Good to meet you, Tammy."

The two of them chatted for a few more minutes, mostly about his course (financial accounting, boring) and her family (only child, but how she would love a brother like him). Nina stood there in silence, watching Ryan fall without question for Tammy's act. At one point in the conversation, Ryan looked over at her and nodded, and Nina knew he'd just given his tacit approval to the house party. Elation, that's what she should be feeling, Nina thought, but instead, she felt strangely unsettled. She wondered if Lucas, who'd left for work half an hour before Tammy's arrival, would've been just as taken with Tammy or if he'd have seen right through her.

At last, Ryan cleared his throat, and Nina braced herself for The Lecture, which he duly delivered. No leaving your drink unattended, no letting a guy buy you a drink, and no taking a sip from anyone else's drink.

"Come to think of it," Ryan added with a scowl, "there should probably be no drinking at all."

"Thanks, Ry," Nina said. "We get it."

Ryan gave Tammy his cell number, making her promise to text him if there was any trouble. It seemed a good moment to leave. Before Tammy overplayed her hand and before Ryan's suspicions were stirred.

Once they were in the car, Tammy grinned triumphantly. "That was easy."

"Look at you," Nina said, doing just that. "I can't believe how you transformed yourself."

"Living with a paranoid father has given me plenty of practice," Tammy said. "Your brother's pretty hot, by the way."

Nina winced. "We're not going there, Tammy."

"Just saying."

A couple of streets away from Nina's house, Tammy pulled over and cut the engine.

Nina frowned. "Why are we stopping?"

"You don't think I'm going to the party dressed like this?" Tammy asked, gesturing to herself.

Nina opened her mouth, closed it. Well, yes, she had been thinking that.

"Oh, naive one, there's so much I need to teach you." Unbuckling her seat belt, she wriggled out of her wrap dress and tossed it onto the back seat.

Nina's eyes widened at the sight of Tammy in a tiny black bikini. "What are you doing?"

"Entry is free if you're in a bikini," Tammy explained. "Otherwise, it's a ten-dollar cover charge."

"How come I'm only hearing about this now?"

"Because I knew you'd chicken out." She plucked a red bikini from a beach bag. "Here's yours. It should fit, and red will suit your coloring."

Nina could feel her face heating up. "Tammy, there's no way I'm going to a party in a bikini. I'd rather pay the ten dollars."

Tammy looked her up and down. "I recommend the bikini."

"No way."

Tammy stared at her for a second, then shrugged. "Suit yourself." The expression on her face said, *conservative prude*.

Nina shifted uncomfortably in her seat. Every now and then, she observed these flashes of cruelty in her friend, but this was her first time on the receiving end.

Tammy took off her just-for-show glasses and pulled out her hair tie, her long red hair tumbling over her shoulders. She unzipped a giant cosmetics bag, flipped the interior light, and began applying glittery eye shadow, a bold, red lipstick, and heavy black eyeliner to create a classic cat eye.

"Tammy, I don't know about this."

"Relax, it's okay." Smiling, she pulled out into the street and accelerated into the growing darkness. "You're about to have the time of your life."

#

"Partay!" a guy yelled in her ear.

Excitement and nerves fluttered in Nina's stomach as she and Tammy weaved their way across the living room crowded with students dancing or talking while they tipped back plastic cups. There was a skinny blonde in a string bikini dancing on a coffee table who seemed to have swallowed a little too much of whatever was in those cups. No staring, Nina told herself. Act cool.

Tammy stopped to chat to a cluster of bachelor of business students she knew. All guys. All clutching plastic cups. And all noticing, with a kind of comical horror, that she and Tammy were empty-handed.

"Unacceptable, ladies," cried a thin guy with a hooked nose. "We need to fix this."

"I'll come with you, Ben," Tammy said.

Ben put on a wounded expression. "You don't trust me?"

"I don't trust anyone with a Y chromosome," Tammy retorted.

Nina watched as he and Tammy made their way over to a giant cooler. Tammy dipped two cups inside and returned to offer one to Nina. "Jungle juice is a rite of passage, my friend. Right, boys?"

"Right!" they all cheered.

Tammy raised her cup in a toasting gesture. "To new experiences." She leaned over to whisper in Nina's ear, "Sip it slowly. And I mean slowly."

Nina took a cautious sip of the cocktail and instantly felt the buzz. A buzz that blended with the thumping techno-music and loud conversations swirling around her.

"Yo, Tammy," called out a burly guy with glazed-looking eyes. "You wanna dance?"

"Oh, yeah."

He grinned.

"But not with you."

Scowling, he muttered, "Blast it, Tammy, but you're a man-eater."

"Guess you're safe, then, Mikey."

Nina hid a wince behind her cup and watched Mikey make a bad-tempered retreat. She let her gaze do a slow sweep of the room, taking it all in, the press of gyrating bodies, the smell of sweat and beer, the stickiness of the laminated floor beneath her sandaled feet. She took another small sip of her drink, and her gaze collided with a pair of blue eyes staring straight at her. Blue eyes that belonged to a startlingly good-looking guy with the broad-shouldered, muscular build of a committed football player.

Nina's pulse spiked, and she looked away. Calm down, she told herself. He was probably checking out all the women here. His gaze just happened to land on one who was fully dressed. She waited a couple of seconds, then looked his way again. He was still watching her, a ghost of a smile playing on his lips.

"Steve Morton," Tammy said in her ear. "Trouble."

"Why's he trouble?"

"Someone that good-looking can only be trouble."

Nina muffled a laugh. That was rich coming from Tammy. Nina turned to face her friend. "See you later."

"Oh, come on, seriously? The first guy who notices you?"

"Yes, but look at him."

"It's your heart," Tammy said with a negligent shrug, crooking a finger at one of the business students, who followed her adoringly onto the dance floor.

Nina made eye contact with Steve Morton again and gave him a hesitant smile. His lips curved into a slow grin, and he pushed off the wall and threaded his way through the dancing throng to her. The knot of excitement in her stomach twisted tighter, and she tried to untangle it with another swallow of her drink.

He stopped in front of her. "You obviously noticed I couldn't take my eyes off you."

She cringed a little at his come-on line. "I'm Nina."

"Steve."

To her amazement, Steve spent the next hour chatting to her. She discovered he was a second-year student studying sports science. He asked her questions and appeared interested in her answers. His attention was wholly fixed on her. Not on any of the other beautiful, confident, scantily dressed female students circulating the room. He wasn't waiting for someone better to come along. He was choosing to be with her. The thrill of it consumed her.

Steve introduced her to his friends, and while Nina thought that Steve was charming, she didn't like his friends, inwardly recoiling from their collective creepiness. They all had a sort of leering look about them, like they knew something she didn't.

The music changed, a slow rock ballad stealing through the speakers. Steve set her drink down, took her hand in his and guided her to a less crowded space on the dance floor. Drawing her close to him, he rested his hands lightly on her hips, and then they were slow dancing, his face inches from hers.

"You're so pretty, Nina," he whispered.

"You're not too bad yourself," she dared to say.

Steve smiled, and his hand drifted to the small of her back. When it traveled a little lower, she stiffened, and he immediately returned his hand to the curve of her spine. His consideration of her feelings sent a rush of warmth through her.

Another ballad came on. Nina shivered with the pleasure of Steve's body pressed up tight against hers. She couldn't stop staring at his lips, and he finally ended her torment when he leaned in and kissed her. He knew exactly what he was doing, and Nina allowed herself to be swept away.

Minutes later, he lifted his lips from hers. "There's not much privacy here," he murmured. "Why don't we go outside, get some air?"

She hesitated.

His thumb caressed her cheekbone. "I don't want an audience while I'm kissing you."

She didn't want an audience either. "I could do with some fresh air," she said finally.

Smiling his approval at her, Steve linked his fingers with hers and guided her off the dance floor.

Tammy stopped them at the French doors leading out to the back garden. "Going somewhere, Morton?"

Steve raised his eyebrows and turned to Nina. "Do you know this beautiful door guard?"

"Uh, yes, I do. Steve, this is Tammy."

"How about we catch up with you later, Tammy," Steve said smoothly. "Right now, Nina needs some air."

Tammy snorted. "Plenty of oxygen inside."

Annoyance crossed Steve's face. "Well, you and your overprotective ego seem to be taking up most of it."

Nina was startled to hear the edge in his voice. She broke in quickly. "Tammy, it's okay."

Tammy's gaze, however, was fastened on Steve. "I'm stepping in something here, Morton, and it smells a lot like the crap coming from your mouth."

"What's this all about, Tammy?" Steve asked slowly. "Are you jealous?"

Tammy rolled her eyes. "And you say I've got an ego. How about, I just don't trust you, Moron...oh, apologies, Morton."

"Okay, that's enough." Nina glared at Tammy, furious with her for interfering like this, for popping the euphoric bubble she'd been floating in ever since Steve had kissed her. "We're going outside."

"I'll come with you," Tammy said.

"No," Nina said forcefully. "No, you won't."

Tammy held her gaze for several heartbeats, and Nina wondered if indeed she was jealous. Jealous that Steve had chosen her and not Tammy.

"Have it your way, then," Tammy said quietly, and disappeared into the crowd.

Still holding her hand, Steve pushed open the French doors and led Nina down the steps and onto a gravel path that wound through an extensive shadowed garden. They walked in silence for a while, past knots of people drinking and making out. Nina barely noticed them, still fuming in disbelief over Tammy's behavior.

"That's an interesting friend you've got there," Steve said at last.

Nina kicked at the gravel beneath her feet. "If you don't mind, I'd rather not talk about Tammy."

"I don't mind at all." They walked for another couple of minutes and then he tugged her off the path, down the sloped lawn and behind a giant tree, pressing her up against its trunk. He murmured against her lips, "I'd rather continue where we left off."

But Tammy's attitude had broken her mood, and when Steve pressed his mouth against hers, Nina turned her head away. "I'm sorry, I need a moment. I'm trying to get over what we're not talking about."

He nuzzled her neck. "I know a sure way to help you get over it."

Nina forced a smile. "I'd rather talk for a while."

"No worries." His hand stroked her collarbone. "Let's talk and play."

Her smile slipped a little. "Steve, I told you I'm not in the mood anymore." She tried to wriggle out of her trapped position against the tree. "Actually, I'd like to go back now."

He tightened his hold on her, excitement rolling off him. "We just got here."

Her breath caught in her throat. She had the strongest feeling she'd made a monumental mistake coming out here with him. "Steve, please." She pushed against his chest, trying to extricate herself.

He licked his lips. "So Nina wants to play rough." His voice lowered to a whisper. "Oh, baby, you're going to love what I'm going to do to you."

Nina flinched at his words and the lie in his eyes. She wasn't going to love it, and he knew it. The most frightening part was that this seemed to fuel his excitement even more.

Instinct took over, and she fought him frantically. But despite her desperation, she was no match for his strength, for his hands that were suddenly everywhere, hurting her. She tried to scream, but he clamped a sweaty palm over her mouth.

"Get away from her."

Nina knew that voice. Even through her pain and panic, she knew that voice.

Lucas.

Oh, thank you, thank you, thank you.

Abruptly, Steve was yanked off her. And there was Lucas as she'd never seen him before, shoulders bunched, face hard and full of rage. He punched Steve in the face, surprise and fury on his side, backed up by two years of weight lifting with Ryan. Steve staggered, his head snapping back from the force of the blow. Lucas didn't let up, hitting him again and again. Only when Steve lay moaning and whimpering on the ground, his face a bloodied mess, did Lucas finally stop, his chest heaving.

He knelt beside her. "Nina. Hey, honey." She hadn't realized she'd slid to the ground, her back still against the tree, knees pulled up to her chest. Lucas's eyes traveled over her, his jaw tightening when he saw her clutching her ripped top. "Are you okay? Did that son of a...?"

She shook her head, her breath hitching on a sob, the realization of what had almost happened crashing over her.

"It's all right," Lucas said softly. "You're in shock. I want you to look at me and take slow, deep breaths."

Dimly, she registered that every inch of her was trembling, that her throat was working convulsively, but no words were coming out.

Lucas's hands rested gently on her shoulders. "Nina, look at me. It's okay. I'm here."

Yes, he was. By some miracle, he was here when she needed him most.

But Lucas was supposed to be working tonight. How had he known she was in trouble? That Steve was going to...

A burning shame rose in her chest. "Please take me home," she finally managed to whisper.

The next instant, she was in his arms and he was carrying her across the garden, away from the house and the curious stares and the whispers, carrying her to his car double-parked at a crazy angle in the street.

Much later, sitting on the sofa at home and wrapped up in a blanket with Ryan and Lucas on either side of her, urging her to drink a cup of tea she suspected was laced with a sedative, Nina heard from Lucas that three male students on their way to the house party had entered the pizza joint where Lucas was working. While waiting for their pizzas, they'd drunkenly boasted about a second-year college guy at the party, whose MO was to target naive first-year female students, get them wasted, and then rape them. They would either be too drunk to remember the incident, or too ashamed to report it.

Lucas confessed that as he'd listened to their awful boasting, a sick feeling in his gut had all but screamed that Nina would be this guy's target tonight. Abandoning their half-made pizzas, he'd jumped into his car and raced to the party. The moment he'd pulled up to the house, he'd received a call from Ryan saying that Tammy had messaged him with the news that Nina was outside with a guy she didn't trust. Ryan was on his way to the house party, but he knew Lucas was closer.

So many things changed for all of them as a result of that night, Nina thought. But the greatest change lay secretly and devastatingly inside her: she'd fallen in love with her best friend.

Chapter Thirteen

Nina's heel caught in a sidewalk crack, and she stumbled slightly, catching herself before she fell. She was late. And the worst kind of late because it was the job interview at Ariadne. Everyone knew (her hospitality-trained psyche most of all) that tardiness meant you'd forfeited the job before you'd even stepped into the interview room. Your excuse didn't matter. In her case, her temperamental car wouldn't start. What rotten timing that the four thousand dollars would only be in her account tomorrow, because if she had the money, she'd have hailed a cab.

Nina hurried down the street, dodging tourists holding up selfie sticks like quivering antennae. She spotted the marqueed entrance to Ariadne up ahead. Nerves turned her already-queasy stomach into a churning mess. She'd read everything she could lay her hands on regarding Ariadne. She'd even depleted the last bit of money in her account to eat there Monday night, wanting to experience the restaurant firsthand. Any kind of edge she could get to secure the position of Ariadne's front-of-house manager.

Pushing her way through the crowd, Nina fought to hold back tears of frustration. All the time and research she'd expended in preparation for this interview and she'd been let down by her car, an empty bank account, and her own poor planning. She bit down hard on her lip. To borrow a bastardized saying of her mother's, *It Is What It Is So Don't Torment Yourself With The What-Ifs.*

Her mother. Nina didn't want to think about her right now. Thanks to Ryan's big mouth, Cheryl had sent a text this morning: *So excited for your job interview at Ariadne! A Michelin 1-star restaurant! Wow. Make me proud.*

So Cheryl wanted her to leave the hospitality world except when it was inhabited by Martin Feenstra. Apparently, he was Nina's step up to a bigger and better life. The hypocrisy of it made her want to kick something.

Juggling her coat, handbag, and feeble excuses, Nina shouldered open Ariadne's heavy glass door.

Inside, the restaurant was moodily lit and hushed. She loved that between-services hush, the narcotic quiet before the 6:00 p.m. dinner rush. Through an open doorway, she glimpsed the silhouettes of kitchen staff moving back and forth in the kitchen, heard the clink of cutlery, the *thunk-thunk* of a knife punishing a chopping board, a grill firing up, musicians tuning their instruments for their impending performance.

At one of the tables in the center of the dining room sat a lean man sporting black-rimmed hipster glasses and a salt-and-pepper goatee. Nina knew who he was. Martin Feenstra, the exacting and infamous owner of Ariadne. She'd done her research on him as well. Possessor of two ex-wives and, according to restaurant gossip blogs, a soon-to-be third. An aficionado of Greek mythology (hence, Ariadne) and partial to consuming bottles of d'Meure Pinot Noir late into the night, unleashing an outsize temper and compromising hot tub photos (hence, impending divorce number three).

As she approached his table, Nina smoothed down her hair and took a you-can-survive-this breath of the restaurant's overheated air. "Mr. Feenstra, I apologize. My car—"

"Stop." She stopped. Speaking. Blinking. Breathing. He asked, "Ms. Abrahams, would you go to my wallet and steal five dollars?"

Nina froze. The question felt like an opening salvo in a battle she hadn't realized she was caught up in. "I'm not sure I understand."

He briefly closed his eyes. "If I have to repeat or explain anything, you can leave the way you came in."

The rebuke caused her already flushed skin to heat up even more. "No," she answered, adding quickly, "No, I, ah, I wouldn't steal five dollars from your wallet."

"I'm gratified to hear it," Martin Feenstra said, "but you're stealing five minutes of my time because you're late."

The steel teeth of his trap closed around her work ethic. He was right. Five minutes might as well be fifteen. Her one and only job interview and she'd blown it. Never mind how professional she looked in her cream blouse, dark trousers and sensible heels, soul sister to his dark blue blazer and pastel shirt. In Martin Feenstra's disinterested eyes, she might as well be wearing a streetwalker Lycra mini dress and fishnet stockings. There was no way he'd pick her to be his restaurant manager now.

She squared her shoulders, one hand gripping the back of the chair he hadn't invited her to sit in. "I apologize for my tardiness and for wasting your time," she said in a low voice, but he was no longer looking at her, already shuffling through the stack of papers on his table, no doubt résumés from punctual job applicants.

Nina hitched her handbag on her shoulder and turned to leave, but something about the fact that her apology wasn't worth one precious second of his attention got to her. Stepping impetuously into an I-couldn't-give-a-stuff moment, she blurted out, "Ariadne's received some unexpectedly bad reviews lately. My take after eating here Monday night? There was a three-minute wait before I was greeted, a ten-minute wait for the bill, and your manager didn't come near my table the entire time."

Martin Feenstra's hands stilled on his papers. He said slowly, incredulously, "You dare talk to me about bad reviews when you're unable to arrive on time for a job interview?"

Nina took a small step back from the fury that lit up his dark eyes. The urge to turn and run almost overwhelmed her. He was right. How dare she? What had she been thinking?

"I...of course, I wouldn't..."

As if from a distance, she heard herself grovel. *Really, Nina, this is your exit? A whimper instead of the proverbial bang?*

She straightened her spine. "I might have no experience in how to fix my car that wouldn't start, Mr. Feenstra, but I know restaurants. I know how to run them, and I know what distinguishes good from great." His eyes narrowed, and she qualified hastily, "As I'm sure you do, but you're overseeing the big picture, and when every detail counts, it's up to your manager to catch them for you."

For an excruciating minute, Martin Feenstra simply stared at her. Then he asked, "What did you think of the food at Ariadne?"

Nina's heart gave an elated leap. He was either playing with her or genuinely interested in her answer. But at least he was talking to her. At least he hadn't kicked her opinionated butt out of his restaurant.

The lie—*the food was amazing*—fluttered inside her. Should she play it safe?

Martin let out an impatient sigh.

Nina said, "I couldn't smell the food when I walked into Ariadne. My whole dining experience felt overintellectualized. In all the innovation and ego on my plate, it felt like Ariadne had lost something. Like she'd lost the honest, primal, sensual pleasure of eating."

She'd certainly lost her mind, Nina thought, telling Ariadne's renowned owner that his restaurant wasn't up to scratch. Lucas would either kill her or applaud her. On second thought, she might not tell him. She might not tell anyone about this encounter. She'd simply shove it to the furthest corners of her mind, those dark places she tried never to revisit.

Martin tapped an elegant finger on his pile of papers. "You might not be aware that my chef has studied at Le Cordon Bleu in Paris and worked in Italy and London, training with many of the world's leading chefs."

Nina's gaze shifted from his finger to his face. "I'm aware of his background."

"Yet it hasn't stopped you from voicing your opinion." He held her gaze for a long time. Her calf was starting to cramp when she saw his lips move, as though toying with the idea of a smile. "Are you always this outspoken?"

"Never with restaurant patrons, but when it comes to colleagues and employers, yes." She gave a rueful shrug. "To my detriment most of the time, but at least you'll always know where you stand with me."

He said reflectively, "It's been a long time since anyone's spoken so candidly to me. It's both annoying and refreshing." He took a sip from the glass of wine on his table, in no great hurry to say anything, watching her carefully.

Don't fidget, Nina told herself, don't look away, don't rush to fill the silence. Everything is a test with this man.

"Tell me, Ms. Abrahams, do I want two Michelin stars?"

Yes was the most obvious answer, one that came so close to tripping off her tongue, but Martin Feenstra was anything but obvious. She made herself take a second to think it through. And then she got it. Oh, the craftiness of the man. He'd seen that her first response was an impulsive, impassioned outburst, and now he was testing her cerebral capability, the very capability for which she'd just criticized his restaurant.

"Ms. Abrahams?"

She swallowed. She was taking such a chance here. "Your reputation would like to see a two-star Ariadne, but the businessman in you is wary of two Michelin stars."

"Why?"

"The pressure and expectations of two stars will push up your food and wage costs. At the same time, your guests become more demanding and more critical."

Martin pointed to the only other chair at his table. "Sit."

Nina collapsed in the seat across from him and slipped her handbag off her shoulder. Her parched mouth longed for a sip of the wine he wasn't sharing.

"I don't agree with you on Ariadne's dining experience, but I admire your candor." He adjusted his glasses. "A quality that almost makes up for your tardiness."

More hoops to jump through, she thought, unsurprised. She folded her hands in her lap and waited.

"To secure this position, you'll have to answer every single one of my questions correctly."

Well, this was familiar territory. She'd grown up with loaded questions served as appetizers to any main meal of acceptance and approval. She nodded. "All right."

"Name the greatest challenge in hospitality today."

"Labor." So he was starting easy, like a cat playing with its prey.

"How do patrons first taste a chef's creation?"

"With their eyes."

"What quality is essential in a server?"

Nina hesitated. A tricky question, one with many possible answers. She finally settled on, "The ability to read a table."

He frowned. "Explain."

"Servers should be able to pick up on various cues and respond accordingly. Is this a couple celebrating their engagement or two executives about to close a deal? Do diners want to engage in conversation, have someone share their news, or do they want to be left alone? I guess servers are a little like psychologists in that sense."

The frown stayed and that telltale finger resumed its dissatisfied tap on the stack of papers.

Nina stiffened, reviewing her response. It was the correct answer, she knew it was, but clearly not the one he wanted. She said quickly, "Obviously, an essential quality in a server is the ability to make every guest feel as if he or she is the most important person in the room."

She managed a smile, stretched out a mental hand for an ego stroke. "I assume you're not looking for the most obvious answer, though."

The finger stopped tapping, and he gave a small nod of approval. *An essential quality for a front-of-house manager? The ability to bluff your way out of any sticky situation.* Her shoulders loosened a little, and she settled more comfortably into her seat.

Martin sipped his wine. "Who are a restaurant's greatest marketers?"

"Its guests."

"True or false: every restaurateur wants satisfied employees."

"False. Engaged or passionate employees are better."

"Why?"

"They're not just thinking of their own satisfaction. They're hungry to learn and passionate about the restaurant in which they work."

He finished his wine and gently set the glass on the table. "Tell me a joke."

She didn't register the question at first. When it did penetrate, she stared at him in confusion, not sure she'd heard him correctly. He wanted her to do *what*?

He raised an eyebrow, but didn't repeat the question. As he'd stated, he wasn't a man in the habit of repeating things.

Under the table, Nina's fingers twisted together in her lap. A joke? Her mind was blank.

One day, a young woman who doesn't feel so young walks into an upscale restaurant. She's so nervous and hopeful it's frankly embarrassing. It's been her dream for as long as she can remember to work in a restaurant exactly like this one. But as she sits at the beautifully set table opposite the beautifully groomed owner, she's no longer sure she wants to put up with all the pretentious crap that will come with working there. Ha! Ha! Ha! The joke's on her.

Nina was so blindsided by the unbidden mental picture that for a second or two, she couldn't breathe. Where had that come from? And what on earth did she want to do with it?

Nothing, she thought hastily, absolutely nothing. It was a traitorous little worm of a synapse wriggling its doubt and discontent in her head. She'd squash it under the practical heel of her five-year career plan, the one Lucas had encouraged her to come up with.

She realized Martin Feenstra was still gazing at her expectantly. The only jokes she could think of were ones Ryan had told her over the years, and they were all awful.

Martin cleared his throat.

Nina knew that sound, had used it herself on occasion, the throat-clearing prelude to a brutal and effective *thank you for your time, you know your way out.*

She hated being put on the spot almost as much as Ryan hated tomatoes. *Tomatoes!*

The words tumbled out of her. "One day, three tomatoes are walking down the street...a daddy tomato, a mommy tomato, and a little baby tomato. Baby tomato begins to lag behind, making daddy tomato angry. He strides over to baby tomato and squashes him and says 'ketchup.'"

A short silence fell when she finished.

"You tell it almost as well as Uma Thurman," he said.

She swallowed. "*Pulp Fiction*'s a favorite of mine."

He gave a thin smile. "Finally, we agree on something."

He leaned back in his chair and scrutinized her. The minutes before he spoke again seemed to last forever.

"The staff at Ariadne are a family, a tribe," he finally said. "They eat, drink, work, and essentially live together twelve hours a day. For our guests, Ariadne is their shelter from the storms of life. Here, they're pampered, their senses stirred, their taste buds awakened."

Relief flooded her. Nina recognized this speech too, or a variation of it. The prelude to the announcement *congratulations, you've got the job.* She wasn't sure at what point he'd caught a glimpse of whatever it was he was looking for in her, that nugget of charm and charisma that had finally tipped the scales in her favor.

While Martin Feenstra spoke, Nina tried to concentrate on what he was saying, but her attention kept getting snagged by all the expensive trappings of a fine dining experience, by an owner who she knew was going to be an unrelenting, jabbing thorn in her side. And she thought, do I really want this? Do I want a prestigious restaurant on my résumé that much?

Think how pleased Mother would be if you accepted a position at Ariadne. Think how proud she'd be telling everyone her daughter was the acolyte of Martin Feenstra.

Nina gritted her teeth. It was aggravating sharing her body with a child who fed off approval, a needy thing she'd tried to erase countless times over the years, but it was unkillable, always resurrecting itself.

Nina tried to envision herself working at Ariadne, juggling tables and temperaments, greeting moneyed guests poor in manners, dealing with an ego-driven chef, terrified line cooks, and a revolving door of fresh-faced servers. It wasn't excitement skimming the surface of her skin, but dread.

You need this job, she reminded herself. You need the money.

As if he could read her mind, Martin subjected her to a sharp look. "When you work for me, there's no such thing as a normal life with normal working hours. I got to where I am today by working hard, by living on food scraps and in a disgusting hovel of an apartment because I knew what I wanted and was prepared to endure anything to get it. Do you have the same dedication and drive, Ms. Abrahams?"

The word *yes* stopped in her throat. Did she? Waking up every day at 5:30 a.m. for a 7:00 a.m. start, a snatched break when the restaurant closed after lunch to shop/shower/sleep, back for dinner service, home at midnight, sleep for five hours, only to wake up so she could step onto that spinning hamster wheel again the next day and the next and the next. All the while watching other people eat, drink, socialize, and live life.

She loved this industry with all its flaws and quirks and insane hours and adrenaline-charged pressure, but did she love it to the degree she once did? To the degree Martin Feenstra did?

No, she decided in a painful burst of honesty. No, she didn't. Yes, she was prepared to work hard and give it her best, but she wasn't prepared to give it her all, not at the expense of everything and everyone else. Not anymore.

Something loosened in her chest, a life-changing epiphany or one of the worst mistakes of her life.

"Ms. Abrahams?"

Nina cleared her throat. "Thank you for your time, Mr. Feenstra. I'm sorry to have wasted it, but you need to look elsewhere for a front-of-house manager."

Chapter Fourteen

Nina stumbled out of the hushed shadows of Ariadne and into the lukewarm light of a fading day. She stood stranded on the sidewalk in the surround sound of urban bustle: suited commuters talking loudly into their phones, tourists chattering away in languages Nina couldn't identify, angry horn blasts of vehicles trapped in rush hour traffic. She put a hand to her stomach and bent forward slightly, feeling physically sick. What had she done?

The events of the last twenty-five minutes whirled through her. It was like watching a horror movie, one where you're screaming at the screen, *No, you stupid woman! What are you thinking, going down alone into the basement where a serial killer with an axe is waiting for you?*

Nina straightened, her stomach still turbulent, wishing that life had gifted her with a rewind button, where she'd walk into Ariadne on time, breeze through the interview, and graciously accept the position. Of course, there was always the swallow-your-pride button where she could grovel at Martin Feenstra's polished shoes, confess her momentary insanity, and beg for another chance.

No, thought Nina, squaring her shoulders, that was an unappealing button, one she rarely pressed. She began walking in the direction of the bus stop, picking up her pace in case she gave in to the temptation to press it. There were good reasons for declining Martin Feenstra's offer. For the life of her, she couldn't recall any of them right now, but at the time, they'd made sense. Follow your gut, Lucas always said, and that was exactly what she'd done. She just hoped her gut knew what it was doing.

She took a seat on the bus and started making a mental list of everything she needed to do. First on the list was putting out feelers to other restaurants in the area and chasing up the agencies who'd received her résumé. Next up was letting everyone know she hadn't accepted the job at Ariadne. By everyone, she meant Olivia, Ryan, Lucas, and...Nina almost groaned out loud...her mother. What had possessed her to tell so many people about the interview? What had she been thinking? She decided to bump that action point to the very bottom of her to-do list.

Swaying with the motion of the bus, Nina breathed through her mouth as too many people around her sweated out their lunch through their pores. To distract herself, she dug out her phone and clicked on her mail icon. After such an awful morning, surely there was one piece of good news sitting in her inbox to redress the balance of the day. She had one new e-mail. It was a message from her landlord stating he was selling the apartment and she had until the end of the month—just over two weeks—to find a new place.

Breathe, Nina reminded herself. Just. Keep. Breathing.

Dropping her phone into her bag, she stared blankly at the dandruff-spotted shoulder of the man in the seat in front of her as her brain tried to process the news. People moved all the time. It was a part of life, like death and taxes, and there was no reason to feel so overwhelmed, but it took money to move, and Nina thought of four thousand lovely crisp dollars being sucked up into the vacuum cleaner of incidental removal costs.

In the middle of that cheery thought, she caught the whiff of someone's liquid lunch, and that unpleasant whiff sparked an excellent idea. Now jumping to the top of her list was that bottle of Merlot tucked away in her pantry. Nothing like two or three glasses of red to wash away the day's mistakes. But she wouldn't drink alone. She'd spent enough time moping alone in her apartment. This time, she'd invite a friend to commiserate with her.

#

Tammy took a slug of her wine. "Let me get this straight. You looked Mister Bigshot Bonehead in the eye and said no. Impressive." She tapped her glass against Nina's. "Here's to a new fearless you."

"I don't know about that." Nina tucked her legs underneath her, played with her wine glass. "All I know is you're looking at an unemployed me right now."

"If we're going with the negative vibe, don't forget potentially homeless as well."

"Well, aren't you full of encouragement?"

"You know, you could stay with me."

"I could," Nina said slowly, thinking about it, but somehow the idea made her uneasy. "Let's see how it goes."

They sat on opposite ends of the three-seater couch in Nina's living room, two floor lamps bathing the room in a warm glow. A massive bowl of cheese-flavored popcorn was perched between them. The Merlot stood sentry on the coffee table, amid the remnants of their Thai takeaway, which Tammy had paid for, along with a box of imported chocolates.

"What's Cheryl's take on this?" Tammy asked, absently braiding her long red hair, which, when she was working, disappeared under a wig.

"I haven't told her yet."

Tammy looked around the room. "I'm sure fearless Nina was here a second ago."

"Give me a chance. The interview only happened today."

"You've told *me* all about it," Tammy continued relentlessly.

"Yes," Nina muttered. "Much to my regret."

Tammy grinned. "What I live for. To cause regret."

Struck by a sudden thought, Nina said, "Hey, wait a minute, I can be fearless. I stood up to Pablo when he was exploiting the staff at Mateo's."

"Yeah, you're fearless when you're someone else's champion, my friend, but too mouse quiet when it comes to advocating for yourself."

Nina scooped up a handful of popcorn, rolled her eyes. "So you and Lucas tell me. All the time."

Tammy grimaced and gestured to her glass of wine. "At least wait until I've had another two of these before lumping my name with his."

"You know, you mock him, but the two of you are weirdly similar."

"So you tell me," Tammy countered. "All the time."

Nina smiled. "Touché. But the truth still holds."

"Maybe," Tammy allowed after a moment. "Except for the fact that I'd beat him hands down in a fight."

Only because Lucas, always the gentleman, would hold back, Nina thought, chewing her popcorn, but Tammy would fight like she lived: no holds barred. An attitude that served her friend well in her career as a stuntwoman when she was jumping out of helicopters, abseiling down buildings or whatever other crazy activity the stunt coordinator had her doing.

"I have my inevitable fights with suppliers and staff," Nina said, "but at least they're not physical." She frowned. "Although when it comes to certain diners, I confess I come close to clouting them over the head."

"Instead, you paste a smile on your face and take their grief."

Nina nodded. "Most of the time, yes."

"Exactly why I abandoned the idea of working in hospitality."

About eight months into the course, Nina remembered, Tammy had quit. She had no issue with the long hours and aching feet and the sometimes tedious nature of the work, but it was clear early on that her volatile personality wouldn't put up with difficult customer demands. She'd sooner tip a plate of food into a lap rather than swallow the acid edge of her tongue and try to smooth things over. Which, come to think of it, pretty much ruled out any customer service line of work for her.

"What about the film industry?" Nina asked. "There must be plenty of difficult people there."

"We're overrun with them," Tammy agreed, "but when you have no problem setting yourself on fire for a stunt, people don't tend to mess with you."

"People don't tend to mess with Lucas either," Nina said, recalling his not-so-friendly encounter with Pablo. "Which reminds me, you won't believe what Lucas said to me after the gala..."

Gagging, Tammy put a finger gun to her head. "Not interested."

Nina swept a hand in the direction of the wine and chocolates. "But that's one of the reasons why you're here."

Tammy groaned. "I don't want to talk about Lucas."

"Hey, when you're on a shoot, you're away for sometimes six months," Nina said. "This is our chance to catch up."

"But do we want to waste this precious time talking about *him*?"

"Yes, because I have to hear all the details of your love life."

Tammy drained the last of her wine. "But at least in my lust life—never the other *l* word, please—the names change. At least I offer you variety, my friend."

Nina grabbed the backup bottle of red and topped up Tammy's glass and her own, thinking about that. How was Tammy's succession of boyfriends healthier than her own obsession with Lucas? Tammy certainly didn't appear any happier for her revolving bedroom door. There was still that empty look that more and more often crept into her eyes, the coke she inhaled on her off days, the stunts she took on that no one else would touch, the alarming number of extreme sports she indulged in.

She's feeding off her own destruction, Lucas had said once, one of the many reasons he remained wary of her friendship with

Tammy, worried that some of that destructiveness would spill over onto her.

Nina returned the bottle to the table. "Fine, no more talk of Lucas. Let's trash-talk Martin Feenstra instead."

"You know what, I've changed my mind," Tammy announced, straightening from her wine-doused slump. "Let's talk about Lucas."

Nina's skin prickled. The expression on Tammy's face suggested she didn't care how far she pushed this. "Actually, you're right, we talk about Lucas way too much," she said hastily. "Let's move on to something else. Like the last famous actor you doubled for."

"Nicole Kidman. Nice deflection, but moving on."

"What? No way. *Nicole Kidman*?"

"She's lovely, and the movie was a blast." Tammy waved that away. "You insisted we talk about Lucas, so let's do it."

Nina set down her wineglass. "I have a feeling I'm not going to like what you're about to say."

"Probably not." Tammy locked eyes with her. "It's not too hard to get why you're in love with him. Yes, he's hot and successful and intelligent. Yes, he's no doubt great in bed, but he's not into you, Nina. He never has been. And probably never will be."

Nina could feel the flush of a well-deserved rebuke heating her cheeks. "Wow, no one can accuse you of Hallmark-card sentimentality."

"You know me, I tell it like I see it."

"I really hate how you see it," Nina admitted, feeling the prick of tears, "but I think you're right."

Tammy's lips tightened. "Don't you dare cry."

"I'm trying not to," Nina whispered.

Tammy pointed her wineglass at her. "Not one tear, Nina Abrahams. Do you hear me? That man is not worth it."

Nina nodded and blinked back her tears.

Tammy selected a chocolate and tossed it her way. Nina caught it one-handed. The chocolate was one of those layered nut ones, a flavor they both loved and one they usually rock-paper-scissored for. Nina recognized the gesture for what it was—a peace offering.

"You need the distraction of another man," Tammy stated.

"No, I don't."

"Yes, you do. Dating someone is the best way to get over Lucas."

"I've tried that. Numerous times. It hasn't worked."

"You dated the wrong men, that's why." Tammy selected another chocolate. "I know a cousin of a friend."

Nina laughed. "You must have done stunt work for *The Sopranos* at one time."

"He's cute and single and in a steady job. Totally the type I steer clear of, but I know that whole Volvo-driving, I-fill-in-my-tax-return persona appeals to you."

The woman was relentless, Nina thought, touched and irritated at the same time. No wonder Tammy thrived as a stunt performer. Her I-don't-know-when-to-quit personality landed her some of the best stunts, and, as Tammy pointed out, the more dangerous the stunt, the more she got paid.

It just sucked, though, when you were on the receiving end of all that dogged determination.

"Let me think about it," Nina hedged.

"Nina..."

"I *promise* I'll consider it."

Tammy's phone buzzed on the table with a text message. She picked it up and glanced at the screen. "I have to make a call," she said, not looking up from her phone as she disentangled herself from the couch and disappeared into the bathroom.

When Tammy reappeared ten minutes later and flopped back down onto the couch, Nina asked, "Everything okay?"

"Yeah. It's all good."

Nina held back a grimace. If ever there was a phrase she hated, it was that one. *All good.* Way too many people hid their monsters behind that insipid response, exactly what Tammy was doing now.

Too mellowed by the wine to call her on it, Nina brought up the one subject guaranteed to loosen Tammy's tongue. "You working at the moment?"

"Nope. I'm on a break. The last couple of months have been pretty intense."

While Tammy spoke about wrapping up a complicated fight scene that took weeks to practice and get right, Nina couldn't help but feel that Tammy was saying all the right words, but her thoughts were off somewhere else.

"How long is your break?" Nina asked.

"Three weeks. I'm leaving for Italy this weekend, trying my hand at paragliding over the Alps with a few colleagues."

Nina took a deep gulp of her wine. Tammy's exploits always agitated a restless feeling inside her, as if she should be pursuing something more with her life, risking more.

"We should do this again," Tammy said, as though reading her mind. "When I hear how crap your life is, I feel so much better about my own."

Nina blinked, caught off guard. Tammy and her whiplash mood swings. Anything could trigger them—a bad day at work, a breakup, a phone call. It shouldn't faze her, not after all these years, but, *really,* those barbs still pricked. "Glad to oblige," she eventually managed. "It must be why we're still friends."

"Nah, what happened with Steve Morton that night bonded us for life."

Just the mention of his name, and it was like something slimy had crawled up her spine. Nina kept her eyes on the rain pelting her living room window. It was better than staring at Tammy when she was in a mood Nina couldn't read. It had surfaced again, that flash of cruelty Tammy kept contained most of the time, but every now and then was let loose. Nina could never quite work out whether the unleashing was deliberate or unintentional.

"Oh, heck, I'm sorry." Abandoning her wineglass, Tammy scooted across the couch and laid her head on Nina's shoulder. "That was a rotten thing to say, and I'm a rotten friend for saying it. Forgive me?"

"What's going on, Tammy?" Nina asked. "Why won't you talk to me?"

She couldn't shake the feeling that something was going on with her friend. Tammy was either pushing her away or smothering her with her clinginess. There seemed to be this angry core to Tammy that Nina didn't understand. It just sat there inside her, pulsing and swelling and seeping.

And here she was, sitting in the grandstands, watching it happen and wondering what on earth she should do to help. Or whether she truly wanted to help if it meant being Tammy's occasional punching bag.

Then Nina remembered that on that awful night, Tammy had tried to stop her from going off with Steve. How had Nina responded? She'd refused to listen to her. How had Tammy reacted? She'd texted Ryan. Her friend hadn't given up on her that night.

Nina's head pounded, her thoughts circling each other confusedly. It was too late in the evening, and she was too deep into the bottle for all this angst and analysis.

"We were having such a great night, and then I go and mess it up," Tammy said in a subdued tone. "I'm sorry. I'm feeling prickly. I need a little something to take the edge off. Want to join me?"

Quietly, Nina said, "I don't do drugs, Tammy."

"Doesn't hurt to ask. Come on, don't stay mad at me."

Sighing, Nina put a conciliatory arm around Tammy's shoulders. "I'm not mad."

Hurt, yes. A little shocked, maybe. But she could never stay mad for long.

"Forgive me?"

"Yes."

Until the next time. Because there was always a next time.

Chapter Fifteen

Nina clutched her head in her hands, Friday's midday sun spearing through sloppily closed blinds and piercing her eyeballs. Her back was a checkerboard of knots. The price you pay for spending the night on the couch, she thought, kneading away a spasm in her neck. Why hadn't she stopped at the grown-up number of two glasses? Instead, between her and Tammy, they'd enthusiastically knocked back two *bottles*. Another bleary glance at her wristwatch confirmed she'd slept away the morning.

You'll be sleeping on the street corner if you keep this up, she predicted darkly, wincing as her gaze took in the carnage atop the coffee table, the empty bottles and glasses, the encrusted plates, the congealed...*ugh*...that last item she couldn't even identify.

She did, however, recognize Tammy's spiky scrawl on a wine-stained note.

You passed out, and I had to leave to pick up my pick-me-up.
Thanks for the fun evening.
Love, T

Nina crumpled up the note, popped an aspirin, and shuffled her hangover to the shower, the hot water easing the throbbing in her head. After finishing her shower, she pulled on baggy tracksuit pants and a worn gray Adidas sweater and padded to the living room to tackle the mess. She swept leftover food and bottles into a trash bag and soaked the plates and cutlery in hot, soapy water.

Taking a cup of tea to the couch, she sipped it while checking her phone. A missed call from her mother (that conversation so wasn't happening today) and two missed calls from Ryan, both no doubt eager to know the outcome of her interview.

Just to brighten up her afternoon even more, the sun disappeared, the wind picked up, and the rain lashed her building with a ferocity that caused water to seep under her balcony sliding door and into her living room. Nina grabbed old towels and wedged them against the bottom of the door. This wasn't the first time this had happened. Her slick-talking landlord kept promising to send someone around to have a look, but Nina was still waiting.

She was mopping up the water that had collected on her living room tiles when her phone rang, loud in the silent apartment. She checked caller ID, debated whether or not to answer and finally caved. "Lucas."

"Whoa, you sound grim."

"I feel grim."

"Flu?"

"Yeah, a new strain named Merlot."

He laughed. "No sympathy from me."

"Not asking for any."

"Drinking alone, Nina? Should I be worried?"

"Relax, I'm not going all Howard Hughes on you." She settled on the couch and swapped the phone to her other ear. "I caught up with Tammy last night."

"Tammy." He said her name the way someone might say *homicidal maniac*. He'd never forgiven Tammy for duping Ryan and persuading Nina to accompany her to that house party.

"Yes, Lucas—Tammy. You know, the friend of mine who's a regular on *Crime Stoppers*?" She blew out an exasperated breath. "You really have the wrong impression of her. She's—"

What, Nina? Supportive? *Sometimes.* Kind? *Strike that.* Ready to drop everything for you in a time of crisis? *Untested.*

"—not all that bad," she finished lamely.

After a pause, clearly weighing his words with care, Lucas said, "I worry when you're with her. I worry about her influence on you."

The irony wasn't lost on Nina: Lucas warning her to be wary of Tammy and Tammy advising her to cut her ties with Lucas. Yes, Tammy's partying lifestyle was a concern, and yes, Nina suspected she used alcohol and drugs as memory wipes, but then again, Lucas jumped in front of bullets for a living.

She said, "Lucas, I don't have too many influences in my life at the moment. Let me hold on to the ones I have."

"I hear violins," he said lightly.

"Oh, get stuffed."

Laughter took his voice again. "That's the spirit. Anyway, you know I'll always be an influence in your life."

Yeah, Lucas Wilson, you're the slow-drip poison of false hope. Stretching out her legs, Nina said, "You can ease up on the worry because Tammy's leaving for Italy tomorrow."

"Permanently?" he asked, a note of hope in his voice.

"Paragliding holiday."

He made a noise that could mean anything.

She asked, "When did you get back?"

"Last night."

"The assignment went well?"

"Yep."

"Don't bowl me over with all the details."

"I'm sure your head can't handle too many details right now," he said, and she could hear the smile in his voice.

"No argument there."

"How'd the job interview go?" he asked.

She almost dropped the phone in surprise. How had he remembered? "Job interview," she repeated stupidly, not ready to answer that question just yet.

"Yeah, didn't you have one this week? At some fancy restaurant?"

Security specialists and their inconvenient memories, she thought. "Oh, yes, that job interview."

"How'd it go?" he asked again, impatience leaking out.

"Not too bad," she said vaguely. "They're still deciding." Should she tell him she'd have to move out of the apartment soon? Lucas would probably launch into operational mode and she wasn't in the mood. "So to what do I owe the honor of this call?"

And Lucas said, "I've met someone."

Three words that hit her like a wrecking ball to the chest. He'd always gone on dates, but he'd never said those words before. And in that tone. A distant part of her had known that one day she'd hear them from Lucas, and here they were, in all their brutal glory.

She should have mentioned the move. It would have delayed this awful moment for at least a couple of minutes.

"Wow," she croaked out, curling up on the couch. "Really?"

"Really." A second of silence. "Man, you sound bad."

"I sound worse than I feel." A whopper of a lie. She was becoming alarmingly adept at dishing them out. "I'll stay inside today, though, just in case."

"Yeah, the rain doesn't look like it's easing up anytime soon."

"So much for my grocery shop."

"Anything in the fridge?" Lucas asked.

"Enough for peanut butter on toast." Nina drew patterns on the throw cushion with a fingertip. If only she could hide indefinitely in this comfortable cave of small talk. That brought on a grimace. Her life was a long depressing list of *if onlys*. Her chin went up defiantly. Time to cross one off. "You've met someone. Where did you meet her?"

"On assignment. Tahlia was up there for work."

"Oh. But...weren't you on duty?"

"I'd organized another team to take the evening shift."

And he told her how Tahlia had literally bumped into him in the hotel restaurant, sending his drink flying, how she'd offered to buy him a replacement drink, and they'd sat and chatted late into the night, instantly hitting it off.

Lucas didn't go into too much detail, but he didn't have to. Nina could easily picture the two of them swapping life stories as they gazed deeply into each other's eyes, fingers grazing, knees touching, lips... No, no, her mind galloped away from that image.

According to Lucas, they'd enjoyed their time together so much, they'd arranged to meet up for dinner every evening after that.

Nina threw the cushion at the wall. She grabbed another one and hurled it at the sliding door where her imagination conjured up Tammy's I-told-you-so smirk.

"Nina?"

She'd been silent too long, she realized. "I'm here. I, um, thought someone was at the door. So you've only known, uh..." Let Lucas think every consonant and vowel of Tahlia's name wasn't imprinted on her brain.

"Tahlia."

"Right, Tahlia. You've only known her a couple of days?"

"Yeah," he confirmed, the note of wonder in his voice causing a sickening lurch in her stomach. "But it feels a whole lot longer. In a good way."

"Wow." The stupid exclamation kept plummeting out of her mouth, witless and inadequate and false. "This doesn't sound like one of your typical hookups," she said at last, probing a little despite herself.

Although those not-quite relationships had been difficult to endure, she'd always known they'd had an expiration date. Whatever this was with Tahlia sounded like it could end in a wedding date.

"This doesn't feel casual," he agreed. "There's something different about Tahlia. I don't know, I think I could get pretty serious about her."

Nina closed her eyes. Tammy was right. How many wake-up calls did she need?

"There's one complication, though," Lucas said. "Tahlia lives out of state."

Nina perked up. That was an excellent complication. "Any chance of her moving here?"

"I doubt it. Her family and her work is over there."

"Hmm. And your extremely successful business is here."

"Yeah," said Lucas reflectively. "I guess, for now at least, we'll have to confine ourselves to weekend visits, take it in turns to do the whole flying-back-and-forth thing."

"Sounds like a lot of trouble."

"We'll work something out. Anyway, Tahlia's heading back Sunday night," Lucas said. "I'd like you to meet her before she leaves. Nothing big, just coffee and snacks at my place."

"Your place?"

"Yes. Is Sunday afternoon good for you?"

"Sunday?" she asked, stalling. "I don't know."

"Ry and Liv will be there."

Oh, goody. Another madly in love couple to show up the conspicuously single person there.

"It's late notice, I know," Lucas said, "but I'm hoping you're free."

Anger charged through her bloodstream. *I've been free for eleven years, Lucas, you nitwit.*

"You know what, yes, I'll be there."

She'd go because she was consumed by curiosity to see for herself this woman Lucas was so taken with. A curious mind is a positive thing, she reassured herself. How else would inventions come about? Inventions like an interdimensional portal to shove certain females into so they can go live happily in another parallel Lucas-less world.

"Mind if I bring someone along?" she asked, the question spilling out of her before she even knew it was there.

"Someone?" Lucas asked after a brief silence. "A friend?"

"A date."

"A date?" he echoed, sounding taken aback.

"Yep. It seems we're both full of surprises today."

"You've certainly surprised me. How long have you been seeing him?"

"Oh, not long. It's still early days."

"How come I haven't met him?"

Such annoyingly good questions, she thought, wishing he would stop asking them. Scrambling for an answer, she said, "Well, I wanted to be sure of him first."

"And you're sure of him now?"

"As sure as I can be."

"Does Ry know about your date?"

Nina managed a laugh. "No way. You know how merciless Ry can be. But if you're there with"—*that woman*—"uh, Tahlia, hopefully that'll take some of the pressure off me."

"Glad to help," he said, sounding anything but glad. "What's his name?"

Her heart rate picked up. Name? Why would Lucas ask for a name? Why was that important?

"You know, it's a really weird-sounding name that's difficult to pronounce," she improvised. "I don't want to say too much about him. Wouldn't want to spoil the surprise."

After a moment, Lucas said, "Okay, bring him along, your mysterious man with the unpronounceable name." Another pause. "I look forward to meeting him."

That makes two of us, Nina thought.

#

Nina dialed Tammy the instant her call with Lucas ended.

"What's up?" Tammy answered.

"Your cousin of a friend," she said, wasting no time on preliminaries. "The one you wanted to set me up with."

"Yeah," Tammy said. "Brian. What about him?"

Nina groaned. "What did you say his name was again?"

"Brian."

"Are you sure?"

"What do you mean, am I sure?"

"Are you sure that's his name?"

"Of course I'm sure." Suspicion laced Tammy's voice. "Nina, have you been hitting the wine again?"

"What? No!"

"Then what's this about?"

Too keyed up to sit still, Nina pushed herself to her feet and paced the living room. "I've been thinking about what you said, about how I should start dating again."

"Uh-huh."

"Well, I might give Brian a go."

"That's quite a turnaround from last night."

"You know what they say... Everything looks different in the morning."

"Hmm. You know what they also say... You're not the only one who can smell your own crap." Nina heard the sound of laughter, the murmur of background conversation. "All right, I'm sitting in a Starbucks confessional. Spill to Aunt Tammy."

Sighing, knowing it was useless to try to bluff her way-too-astute friend, Nina filled Tammy in on the details of Lucas's phone call.

"Let me get this straight," Tammy said when she'd finished. "You want to use Brian to make Lucas jealous?"

"You know, 'use' is such a strong word."

"I'd say a fairly accurate word, in this case."

"All right, yes, I'm using Brian, but hey, you never know what might happen. I might just fall for him."

Tammy didn't answer immediately. "You say that flippantly, my friend, but you could really click with him. Just give Brian a fair chance, okay?"

"Okay," Nina agreed, feeling gently reprimanded. "I'll keep an open mind, I promise."

"Brian knows who you are, by the way. I've mentioned my very attractive, very single and vivacious friend to him a few times."

"Great, at least I'm covered," Nina joked. "How about sharing some details about Brian?"

"Hold on a sec, they're calling my name." Nina waited while Tammy went to collect her drink. Caramel macchiato, Nina guessed, her go-to Starbucks drug. There was the sound of sipping and then an appreciative sigh. "Ah, magnificent life-giving nectar. What do you want to know about Brian?"

"Well, for starters, how old is he?"

"Thirty-two. Wait, maybe thirty-three."

"Is he good-looking? I mean, *really* good-looking."

Tammy snorted. "It's reassuring to know you're not into the superficial."

"Just tell me he's not a troll."

"Brian is not a troll. Objectively, he's quite hot."

Nina absently straightened a dining room chair. "So why is he not married?"

"Last I checked, you're not married either," Tammy countered. "Neither am I. And there's nothing serial-killer wrong with either of us." She took another sip of her drink. "Maybe Brian's waiting for his...let me try to say this without throwing up...soul mate."

Nina frowned. "Tell me Brian's not living with his mother!"

"He's not." A tiny beat of a pause. "Anymore."

"Tammy!"

"Relax. Brian's sane, sweet, and employed. He's a disgustingly good guy."

"Does Brian know about Lucas?"

"No, I haven't mentioned your secret stalker-like crush on your other best friend."

"Good," Nina said, relieved. "All right, give Brian my number. Let's set this up."

#

Four hours later, her living room all tidied and vacuumed, throw cushions returned to the sofa, plates and glasses washed and put away, Nina sat in front of her laptop, a mug of ginger tea warming her palms, chewing her lip as she reread the specs for what sounded like a promising restaurant manager role. The position ticked all the right boxes except one: location. The restaurant, with the captivating name of Soul Fare, was situated in the main street of Barracat, a satellite suburb she hadn't heard of until five minutes ago. According to Google Maps, Barracat was over an hour's drive southeast from the city. If she took the train, it would be, door-to-door, an hour-and-a-half commute. Three hours every day. Could she do it? The answer came quickly: nope. Such a lengthy daily commute would suck the life out of her. She could move to Barracat, she supposed. She had to leave her apartment anyway, but she had no desire to move out of the city. The city was her home.

Nina was about to close the tab when her buzzer rang. She frowned, tearing her gaze away from the screen. She wasn't expecting anyone. Maybe someone had forgotten their key fob and wanted her to buzz them into the building. Her seventy-year-old neighbor, Mr. Hanley, was notorious for misplacing his fob. And other items. He'd once left his hemorrhoid cream outside her door, and she'd had the unfortunate task of returning it and obsessively scrubbing her hands for days afterward.

Nina picked up the entry phone. "Hello?"

"Nina Abrahams?" That wasn't Mr. Hanley's querulous and demanding voice on the other side of the intercom.

"Yes."

"Delivery for you."

Delivery? She couldn't remember ordering anything. "What kind of delivery?"

"Pizza," he said, naming an upmarket pizzeria and wine bar.

"But I didn't—"

"There's a note with the food." Nina heard what sounded like the rustle of paper over the intercom. "It says, 'Surprise dinner for a special friend. Can't have you eating peanut butter toast tonight.'" There was the sound of a throat being cleared. "The note also says to check the peephole before you let me in."

Lucas.

What?

On the rising rush of disbelief, Nina buzzed the delivery guy into her building, dutifully checked the peephole when she heard the knock, and opened her door to encounter an acne-ravaged teenager holding a gigantic pizza box.

He thrust the box into her hands. "This is for you."

"Thank you." Nina fumbled in her purse for a tip, shut the door, and deposited the box on the kitchen counter, the tantalizing smell causing her stomach to growl in anticipation. She hadn't realized until now just how hungry she was.

She opened the box, unable to hold back a gasp of delight. It was the most magnificent pizza she'd ever laid eyes on. The bubbly, slightly charred crust could barely contain the gourmet pile of toppings: chargrilled eggplant and zucchini, prosciutto strips, gooey buffalo mozzarella, swirls of pesto, and pine nuts and chili flakes scattered like fairy dust over the whole lot.

Nina smiled. Even when sending her what purists would label junk food, Lucas couldn't stop himself from ensuring as many vegetables as possible were piled onto the pizza.

Her chest tightened. *Blast it, Lucas, why do you do this to me? Just when I'm steamrolling ahead toward a bland but tolerable future where I'm not Mrs. Nina Wilson, you go and lasso my heart again and yank me back.*

Nina retrieved her phone from the coffee table. She wouldn't phone him. She was too afraid that the sound of his voice would trigger an embarrassing emotional outpouring. Instead, she sent him a text: *You just blew my mind.*

Lucas's reply came back swiftly: *A small explosion, then?*

She smiled, clicked on a laughing emoji, and followed it up with: *You didn't have to. Thank you.*

Can't let you starve. How was the pizza?

Haven't tasted it yet. About to take a bite.

She was hovering on the dangerous edge of inviting him over. There was more than enough pizza here, but she clamped down on the urge. A key part of her whole transformative process was getting used to doing things without him. Besides, Lucas was probably with Tahlia, and her heart could do without that confirmation.

Picking up a pizza slice, Nina took a bite, closing her eyes and chewing slowly. Wow. There was simply no other word for all the flavor combinations filling her mouth. She took her time polishing off the pizza slice, then grabbed her phone and typed:

Dinner is beyond delicious. Love it so much. Thanks again. Night.

She reread her message before sending it. Frowning, she deleted "love it so much." When it came to all things Lucas, it was safer to avoid any mention of love.

Nina powered down her phone, poured herself a glass of water, and carted the entire pizza box to the living room. Tonight, she wouldn't eat alone. Catherine Zeta-Jones and Aaron Eckhart would be joining her impromptu pizza party. Switching on the TV, she located *No Reservations* on Netflix, a feel-good favorite. This is bliss, she told herself firmly, almost convincingly.

Nina couldn't remember at what point in the movie she fell asleep, but she woke up with a start as the music for the closing credits blared through her speakers. This falling asleep on the couch was turning into a worrying habit. Yawning, she switched off the TV and popped what was left of the pizza into the fridge.

She was heading for bed when, clumsy with exhaustion, she bumped her laptop mouse, bringing her screen to life and revealing the web page she hadn't managed to close before her buzzer had sounded. There, glowing like the North Star in her darkened apartment, was the restaurant manager job in Barracat. Nina couldn't move, staring at the page.

She didn't know what it was about this job offer that was so appealing, but she had to be practical here. The restaurant was out in the suburbs, the pay probably less than she was used to. There were other positions in the city she could apply for. Yes, she wanted change in her life, but not this sort of radical, drastic change.

Close the tab, she told herself. But her hand remained frozen at her side.

She should apply. Just for the heck of it. She didn't have to accept the job, but at least she'd be able to satisfy her curiosity. What did she have to lose?

Before she could second-guess herself, Nina sent off her résumé.

Chapter Sixteen

Standing on the sidewalk, Nina grimaced as she considered the botched result of her effort to parallel park. She should slink back into her Prius and try again, but she'd already circled the block twice in a hopeful bid to find a parking space she could simply drive straight into. No such luck. Not on a Saturday afternoon with everyone out shopping.

Turning away from her car (fortunately, this time it had started with no trouble), Nina fought a bitterly cold wind to feed the parking meter and make her way to the café where she was meeting Ryan and Olivia for lunch. The café, newly opened in an affluent suburb hugging the outskirts of the city, was creating a buzz in restaurant circles, and Nina had been dying to eat there.

She was still in the dark as to why her brother had invited her to lunch today. Apparently, he and Liv had something important to tell her, but he wouldn't elaborate on the phone. *Tell me tomorrow at Lucas's place*, she'd said, but Ry didn't want to bring up the subject in front of Tahlia. So although it meant two days in a row of her brother, Nina wasn't feeling too put out. Not when Ry had offered to pay for her meal today.

She checked her watch. She was five minutes late. Martin Feenstra's words echoed like an uninvited guest in her head. *You wouldn't go to my wallet and steal five dollars, would you? But you're stealing five minutes of my time when you're late like this.*

Nina hunched her shoulders at the memory. Like the obviously unreformed thief she was, she pushed open the door to the café and stepped inside, scanning the interior in a brisk, professional sweep. Good lighting, rustic décor, clean floor.

She caught sight of Olivia seated at a corner table near the window, brow furrowed as she studied the menu with the same meticulous attention she gave to appliance manuals.

"I'm sorry I'm late," Nina said when she reached her. "Parallel parking was involved."

"No worries, I get it," Olivia said, which was a blatant lie. This was a woman spoon-fed military punctuality from birth and who parallel parked first try, every time.

Nina sat, shrugged off her jacket. "Where's Ry?"

"Bathroom." Olivia tilted her head in the direction of the funky signage on the café's exposed brick wall. "I'm starting to suspect that words like *tofu* and *kale* act as bowel triggers for him."

Nina winced. "I can't imagine this place was Ry's choice."

"It wasn't." Olivia looked smug. "I played the pregnancy card."

"Might as well wield it while you can," Nina said approvingly. "How's the nausea?"

"Up and down." Olivia patted her stomach. "Baby's behaving today."

Nina chuckled. "Still haven't settled on a name yet?"

Olivia grimaced. "Ryan favors Clorinda if it's a girl."

"What?" Nina could feel her jaw slacken with righteous auntie outrage. "Clorinda? Sounds like a toilet cleaner. Why would he do that to his daughter?"

"Do what?" Ryan asked from behind her, planting a quick kiss on her cheek in greeting.

"Call my unborn niece Clorinda."

"It's genius, really," Ryan maintained, sitting down. "With a nerdy name like that, she's less likely to take drugs or drink or pierce parts of her body that should never be pierced."

Olivia crossed her arms. "If it's a boy, he wants to call him Humphrey."

"Same logic applies," Ryan added.

Nina whacked her brother on the shoulder. "I'd smack you on the head if I thought for one second there was a working brain in there." She picked up a menu with calm finality, noticing Olivia struggling not to laugh. "My niece or nephew will not be called Clorinda or Humphrey."

"Is this why you accepted my invitation to lunch?" Ryan grumbled, rubbing his shoulder. "You wanted a bash-your-brother opportunity?"

"No, although that's always a gratifying bonus." She held up the menu. "Lunch on my brother at a cool new restaurant. How could I say no?"

"You are such a food floozie," Ryan accused.

"Unashamedly so. You wanted to share some news?" she prompted.

Ryan waved that away. "Not yet. What about you? You got the job at Ariadne?"

So far, she'd managed to fob off her inquisitive family with the excuse—all right, lie—that she was still waiting to hear from Martin Feenstra. She wasn't ready to tell them just yet. Not before she'd had a coffee to fortify herself.

To her relief, a dreadlocked server appeared at their table just then, iPad poised. "Are you guys ready to order?"

"No," said Ry.

"Yes," said Nina at the same time.

The server divided a weary look between the two of them. "How about I take your drinks order for now?"

"That'll be great," Nina said quickly.

Ryan shot her a look. "Fine." He turned to Olivia, and Nina could see him bracing himself. "Liv?"

So pregnancy hadn't tranquilized that...unique aspect of her sister-in-law's personality. Nina returned her menu to the table. She wouldn't be ordering anytime soon.

"A large golden latte, please," Olivia said.

The server nodded, stabbed at the screen with an index finger.

"I'll have it with almond milk. Are the almonds in your milk activated?"

The server blinked. "Uh, I'll have to check on that."

"Please do. Could you make the latte extra hot?"

The server nodded, typed away.

"But please don't burn the milk."

Another nod.

"What sort of turmeric blend do you use?" Olivia asked.

"We have our own house-made blend."

"Is sugar one of the first ingredients in that blend?"

"I don't think so. Yeah, I'm pretty sure it isn't."

Olivia leveled him a look.

"Ah, how about I check on that for you?"

"That would be helpful," Olivia said.

"I'll be right back," he muttered.

Ryan sighed as he watched the man's retreat. "I wonder if he'll return. There've been a few who never came back."

"You know," Nina said to Olivia, "you're one of those diners I hate having in the restaurant."

"I know what I want," Olivia said, wide-eyed and uncomprehending. "What's wrong with that?"

Ryan patted her hand. "What's wrong, love, is that the civilian workforce doesn't operate like a military unit."

"That man could do with some basic training. What employee doesn't know his own stock?"

"He does, Liv," Ryan said. "He just doesn't know it to the degree that you're asking of him."

"Those were fairly standard questions, Ry."

"Activated almonds? That's not standard, love. Next you'll be asking him what type of soil they grow the turmeric in."

Olivia's eyes widened. "I never thought of that. Why didn't I think of that?"

Ryan groaned. "C'mon, Liv."

Nina stared idly at the drinks menu, absently tuning out their argument that wasn't quite an argument. It seemed to be a habit among long-standing couples, the borderline friendly, back-and-forth squabble that obliviously excluded everyone around them.

A menu item caught her eye. She straightened in her seat, skin tingling with excitement. Payback time for Ryan's exhibitionist display of her photo in the dining room. She thought longingly of the cappuccino she'd been looking forward to, but Ryan's reaction would be worth the forfeiture of her coffee.

The server returned in less than five minutes, surprising them all, and armed with the information Olivia needed for her golden latte.

Ryan turned to Nina when Olivia was finished. "Your usual, sis?"

"Not this time." Nina glanced up at the server and said conversationally, "I see you offer a blue algae latte."

Out of the corner of her eye, she saw Ryan stiffen.

The server nodded. "Yeah, our 'smurf' latte is pretty popular. It's our most photographed drink."

"I'm not surprised. What gives it its blue color?"

"Please say food coloring," Ryan muttered.

The server shook his head. "The blue comes from the live blue algae in the drink."

"How about that?" Nina said over Ryan's groan.

"It's an acquired taste," the server added.

"I'll bet it is. Well, I'm game for a blue algae latte," Nina said breezily. "What about you, Ry?"

He paled. "Ah, come on. You know Saturdays are my favorite day of the week. Don't ruin that for me."

She arched an eyebrow at him. *You know the deal,* her eyebrow said. *You break a childhood pact and you'll hold the title of wimp forever.*

"Make that two," Ryan managed to choke out.

After the server left, Olivia said, "I keep waiting for the two of you to grow out of this drink-dare thing."

"Hey, don't forget Lucas is a part of this too," Ryan protested.

"Ry, mentioning a commitment-phobic bachelor who still plays with guns in no way helps your case."

Nina choked back a laugh. Ryan narrowed his eyes at her and said, "Speaking of our *esteemed* friend, he's joining us for lunch."

"He is?" Nina jerked slightly at the news. Her heart wasn't prepared to cope with Lucas just yet. His words were still fresh in her mind, jolting her awake at night, a bleak whisper in her ear during the day. *There's something different about Tahlia. I don't know, I think I could get pretty serious about her.*

"Where is he?" Olivia asked.

"He said he'd be a little late."

Their drinks arrived. Ryan stared in dismay at his blue latte. Looking at her drink, Nina began to experience the first stirrings of regret for her impulsive decision. She knew there were drawbacks to her competitive nature, and there sat one of them in all its bright blue glory on the table in front of her.

The server shifted from one foot to the other, his neck stiff from the monumental effort he was making not to look in Olivia's direction. He eventually worked up the courage to ask, "Will you be ordering food?"

There was sympathy in Ryan's clear blue eyes as he glanced up at the man, a fraternal *feeling your pain, buddy.* "Yes, we'll be eating."

The server's shoulders slumped, but he brightened when Ryan said, "We'll need a few more minutes, though. We're still waiting on someone."

After the server left, Nina lifted up her latte glass. A faint whiff of seaweed hit her nostrils, and her stomach lurched.

Ryan looked around the café in disappointment. "There's never a potted plant around when you need one."

"Chickening out?" Nina asked.

"When have you known me to cry *fowl*?"

She gave a small smile. "On the count of three."

They both took a gulp. Nina could pick up hints of coconut milk, lemon, and ginger. "It's not as revolting as I imagined it would be," she said after another tentative sip.

Ryan swallowed and shuddered. "That depends. My imagination seems to be more active than yours."

Olivia licked her lips and brandished her half-empty mug. "Well, mine's yummy. Proof that maturity has its advantages." Her eyes lit up. "Lucas has arrived." She waved a manic yoo-hoo, we're-over-here hand.

Heart thumping, Nina glanced up to see Lucas walking over to them. Blast it, it was criminal how good he looked. He slapped Ryan on the back and hugged Olivia, joking that he'd better get his hugs in now before her stomach got in the way.

"I've managed with your ego all these years, so my belly shouldn't be a problem," Olivia joked in return, earning a high five from Ryan.

Lucas smiled, eyes crinkling at the corners. "The food better be worth all this ragging." He leaned down to kiss Nina's cheek. "Good to see you, Nina," he murmured. The cool brush of his lips against her skin sent a shiver skimming through her.

Tilting her head back, she stared into his green eyes and resorted to a half-truth. "I'm glad you could join us."

"So am I." Lucas folded his tall form into a chair, his knee touching hers under the table.

She flinched. *Calm down, hormones, it's just a knee. It's about as attractive as an elbow.*

Ryan turned to Lucas. "Good assignment?"

"Yeah, no one was compromised or killed, so I'd call it a success." Lucas picked up a menu. "Have you ordered?"

"Just drinks," Olivia said.

Humor quirked Lucas's lips as he stared at the blue foam that coated the two glasses. "Looks like I timed my arrival perfectly."

"Blue algae, buddy," Ryan said, his face reliving the horror.

Nina stretched her arms above her head in satisfaction. "One of life's most rewarding moments, watching Ry drink that blue latte."

"Someone obviously needs more of a life," Ryan shot back absently.

Nina dropped her eyes to her menu, feeling the impact of his offhand comment like an unexpected blow to the stomach. Her brother had never spoken truer words, she thought, which was exactly why she was contemplating some serious changes to her obviously inadequate life.

She couldn't get mad at Ryan, though. When sarcasm was your family's second language, everyone took turns being the target. She sensed rather than saw Lucas looking at her, picking up on her feelings with an intuition born from years of friendship. He slipped a hand under the table and squeezed her knee. *Whoa.* She took back her earlier assertion. A knee was nothing like an elbow. Not with all those unexpected erogenous zones hidden there. Her startled eyes flew up to his.

Lucas winked at her, a I've-got-your-back wink. He turned to Ryan. "Hey, Ry," he said, pointing to the menu, "they have sprouted breads here."

Ryan reared back in his seat in revulsion. "What the heck, Lucas! You've seen what's sprouting on my great-aunt's chin. You know I can't eat anything with the word 'sprouted' in it."

"Lucas," Olivia gently admonished him.

Lucas tried to look appropriately chastised. "Sorry, Ry, slipped my mind."

Nina bit the inside of her lip to stop herself from smiling and knee-bumped Lucas in thanks. The knee had just graduated to the top of her list of favorite body parts.

"What'll you have to drink?" Olivia asked Lucas.

He did a quick scan of the menu. "I'll go for the bulletproof coffee."

Ryan let out a laugh. "Is that a joke?"

"No, it's the latest health craze," Nina said. "Black coffee with butter and coconut oil."

"Better you than me." Ryan opened the menu and frowned. "It's like they've invented a new language," he complained. "What the heck is ashwagandha and Lakanto and freekeh? Where are words I understand, like steak and fries and burger?"

"Ry, your cholesterol doesn't like those words," Olivia pointed out.

"But my taste buds like them," he said, in the mournful tone of a man knowing the argument was already lost.

Nina said, "Ashwagandha is a medicinal herb, Lakanto's a natural sweetener, and freekeh is roasted green grains."

"Thanks, sis, but my taste buds are still not convinced." Ryan tried to catch the eye of their server, but the man was steering well clear of them. He sighed. "Looks like you've scared him away, Liv." He attempted to flag down another server, but it appeared word had spread and everyone was doing a remarkable job of avoiding their table.

Lucas got to his feet and managed to commandeer a lanky young server who dragged his Doc Martens reluctantly to their table. This time, Ryan took it upon himself to keep a tight rein on his wife, and Nina breathed a sigh of relief when it took no more than five minutes to take down Liv's superfood acai bowl order.

They made small talk about Lucas's recent assignment and the scary situation his team had found themselves in on the third day when a crowd protesting climate change had surrounded their vehicle with their high-profile client inside, banging on the windows and trying to tip the car over. They'd had to extricate themselves from that delicate situation without flooring it and flattening a protestor, creating a PR nightmare for their client, while also ensuring that the vehicle didn't stop long enough to allow the protestors to drag their diplomat client out of the car and beat into him a revised environmental policy.

Their food arrived. Nina had eaten two forkfuls of her surprisingly delicious raw pizza when Ryan suddenly asked, "So give us your news, sis. You got the job at Ariadne?"

She finished chewing, the food souring in her mouth. "I was offered the job, but I turned it down."

Her words hung in the air.

"You did WHAT?" Ryan demanded.

Lucas stared at her. "I thought it was always your dream to work at a fine-dining restaurant."

"It was," Nina admitted, swallowing past the unexpected lump in her throat because, yes, it had been her dream for as long as she could remember, and she'd thought—hoped, really—that in the last day or so, she'd moved past that dream, but the knot of regret sitting in her throat told her she hadn't. Not completely.

Ryan said slowly, "Just to be clear, you were offered the job?"

"Pretty much."

"And you turned it down? Turned down a well-paying position at a prestigious restaurant?"

"Yes."

Ryan shook his head in bewilderment. "It's bad enough I have to eat cauliflower rice"—he gestured reproachfully at his plate of chickpea korma—"but now I have to learn that my sister has made a decision that makes no sense to me."

Throughout Ryan's tirade, Lucas hadn't taken his eyes off her. When Ryan eventually ran out of steam, Lucas asked, "Why?"

A sigh escaped her. How to explain her decision in a way that her self-appointed guardians would understand? "If I'd accepted the job at Ariadne," she said carefully, "I'd be the puppet at the end of Martin Feenstra's strings, and he'd be holding on to those strings so tightly, I'd simply be jerking in whatever direction he pulled. I can't work like that anymore. More importantly, I don't want to."

"What are you saying?" asked Lucas, frowning. "Are you thinking of getting out of hospitality?"

"No," she said emphatically. "Not at all. I love the industry, despite its imperfections." She lowered her eyes to her pizza, keeping them there so they wouldn't see the evasion in her eyes. "I'll set up more interviews this week."

Now was not the time to tell them about the e-mail she'd received this morning from Edith, the owner of Soul Fare in Barracat, asking if she could come in Monday for an interview. And the fact that she'd inexplicably said yes.

"I still don't get it," Ryan said. "I don't get why you would say no to working at Ariadne."

"I'm sure Nina knows what she's doing," said Lucas, finishing his Moroccan stew.

Nina threw him a grateful glance.

The look on his face said, *Tell me you know what you're doing.*

She gave a small nod. *Of course I do.* She could bluff with the best of them. She was still deciding whether or not to tell them about her landlord's e-mail, but then Olivia nudged Ryan and said, "Sweetheart, you want to share the news with Lucas and Nina now?"

"Okay." Ryan put down his knife and fork. "If anything happens to Liv and I, we'd like you and Lucas to be our baby's legal guardians."

Shock made it difficult for Nina to get the words out. "Legal guardians? Both of us?"

Ryan beamed. "Yep."

"That's quite an honor, Ry," Lucas said.

Nina's mind was whirling. *It's a terrible idea. Terrible! Were the two of them on strong medication when they came up with it? What were they thinking?*

Ryan lurched to his feet. "Blast it, I have to go to the bathroom again."

Ryan hurried off, and Olivia turned to Lucas. "Could you check on him for me, please? See that he's okay?"

Lucas's eyes widened. "I'm sure he's fine. His system's probably in shock, trying to process the health hit."

Olivia sighed. "I see I need to spell it out." She leaned forward, resting her arms on the table. "Lucas, I'd like a girly-girl chat with Nina, and your presence is getting in the way."

Lucas did an impressive eye roll. "Well, I'm not joining Ry in the bathroom, because there are certain noises I never want to hear from a friend." He got to his feet. "I'll wait outside. I need to make a call anyway."

As soon as he was gone, Nina swiveled in her seat to face Olivia. "Liv? What on earth?"

Olivia grimaced. "Sorry we sprang it on you like that."

"Wouldn't it make more sense to choose a couple as legal guardians?"

"You and Lucas are our closest friends."

"Yeah, but logistically, how would it work?" Nina asked. "If anything were to happen to you and Ry, then your baby would...what? Be split between Lucas and me?"

Olivia shifted in her chair. "Well, obviously, we'll try our best not to die."

"Liv."

"Okay, confession time. I'm hoping this announcement will be the smack over the head Lucas needs to open his eyes to the possibility of the two of you as a couple."

Nina closed her eyes against the pain of her statement. "Don't," was all she could say.

"But if Lucas—"

Nina held up a hand. "I'm moving on, Liv. I have to, for my own sanity. Lucas seems to be getting serious with this Tahlia—"

Olivia made a snorting, dismissive noise.

"—and I have to get on with my life. I have to stop waiting and hoping for Lucas to wake up. And you can't...you can't do things like this, because it makes it so much harder to move on."

A devastated look came over Olivia's face. "Oh, Nina, I'm sorry! You're right, I wasn't thinking. I thought I was helping." She bit her lip. "We've put the whole guardian thing out there. Now what do I do?"

Nina gave a small, strangled laugh. "Well, like you said, don't die."

Ryan returned to the table, touching Olivia's arm as he gingerly lowered himself onto his chair. "Who's dying?"

Nina dug up a smile. "The poor unfortunate in the bathroom stall next to yours."

Ryan pointed an unforgiving finger at her. "No discussing my toiletry habits. You remember the ban, don't you?"

"The one you made me swear to when I was *seven*?" Nina asked incredulously.

"The same one."

"You don't think we're past that by now?"

"No, I don't."

Olivia, struggling against a grin, said, "Oh, Ry, something you ate must not be agreeing with you."

Lucas, back from his phone call, clapped Ryan on the shoulder. "Don't worry, buddy. There'll be no seeds and sprouts served tomorrow. Your system will feel right at home."

"So we're still on for tomorrow?" Nina asked casually as Lucas slid into his seat.

"Still on," Lucas confirmed.

"And Tahlia will be there?"

"That she will."

"Great."

"What about you?" Lucas asked. "You still coming?"

"Wouldn't miss it."

"And you're still bringing...?" Lucas left a pause for her to jump right in there with a name, but Nina excelled at waiting out pauses. Years and years of training, courtesy of her mother.

Ryan turned a startled gaze on her. "What? Who are you bringing?"

"My date," she said, narrowing her eyes at Lucas, who leaned back in his seat with the satisfied look of a man who'd successfully uncaged the tiger.

"Date?" Ryan demanded, ignoring Olivia's squeal of delight.

"Yes, overprotective brother, my date."

Brian had called her early this morning, sounding courteous and friendly, exactly as Tammy had described him. To her intense relief, he was free Sunday and didn't mind accompanying her to Lucas's little gathering. They'd agreed to meet at a coffee shop beforehand and go together to Lucas's place.

"Is this a first date?" Ryan asked suspiciously.

"First date? No. Of course not."

"A date!" Olivia beamed at her. "Good on you."

"How is this good?" Ryan asked with a frown. "We haven't met him. He could have four wives stashed away and be on the prowl for a fifth, and along comes my sister and she's all 'Pick me, Mister Polygamist, pick me!'"

"Only your twisted brain could think that," Nina muttered.

"My eternally optimistic husband," Olivia agreed, squeezing his hand. "We'll meet him tomorrow and you can interrogate him then."

Oh, joy, Nina thought, already feeling sick with dread at how it could all blow up in her face tomorrow.

The arrival of the server spared her further interrogation. Everyone was too full for dessert, and Ryan, accompanied by Lucas, ambled up to the register to pay the bill.

Olivia stared fondly after them. "Ry's protectiveness toward you is kind of cute."

Nina turned on her. "Seriously?"

"Relax," Olivia said. "In six months, he'll be so busy being a father, he'll ease up on you."

Her sister-in-law had a point, Nina thought. All she had to do was ride out six months of her brother's hovering and micromanaging.

As they left the restaurant, heading to their respective vehicles, Ryan said, "Mom's waiting to hear from you about Ariadne. Don't forget to give her your news."

Nina mimed strangling herself.

"Try your best to tell her tactfully."

She opened her car door. "I'm in hospitality, Ry. Tactful's my middle name."

"Not when it comes to Mom," he called, claiming the parting shot.

#

Nina sent her mom a coward's text at one in the morning, New York time, when Cheryl Abrahams would be fast asleep.

ALL THE LOST PIECES

Hi Mom. Not pursuing Ariadne position. Looking at other options. C u when u get back.

Chapter Seventeen

Nina could feel her phone buzzing in her handbag. She didn't bother checking the screen. It was no doubt another death-by-a-thousand-cuts message from her mother wanting to analyze Nina's decision not to take the job at Ariadne. That was the last thing she needed right now. She was carefully nurturing this resurgent feeling of confidence brought on by the new balance in her bank account and the good-looking man who just happened to be her date walking alongside her on a Sunday afternoon, the sky a hopeful bright blue above them.

The instant Nina had spotted Brian in the coffee shop, her ego had done a fist pump. Tammy hadn't lied. Brian's tousled blond hair, vivid blue eyes, and muscular body had many of the female customers sneaking second looks. He was also a couple of inches taller than her, which was a bonus. She possessed the unfortunate tendency to turn all managerial when her dates were shorter than her.

From the flicker of admiration in his eyes when he stood to greet her, Nina guessed that Brian too liked what he saw. She'd spent some time agonizing over her outfit choice this morning. After discarding at least five options, she'd finally settled on a fitted midnight-blue dress, finishing it off with tights, boots, and a colorful scarf. She'd treated and straightened her hair so it fell like a waterfall of dark silk down her back.

Brian deposited her latte in front of her, and she murmured her thanks. He was a piccolo latte man, she noted with approval. It almost excused his limp handshake. Their conversation stumbled a bit at the start, but they soon found common ground discussing Tammy and some of her more dangerous stunts. Nina obligingly filled Brian in on the mix of family and friends he'd encounter today at Lucas's place. She managed to drop in a casual hint that he should probably avoid any mention that this was their first date because her brother would no doubt up the interrogation level. Brian nodded agreeably. Nina liked that he listened intently when she spoke. She liked it even more when a quick nibble of his thumb cuticle showed he was as nervous as she was. In nearly twenty minutes of small talk, she hadn't heard one crude or smarmy remark from him. All in all, Brian seemed like the kind of wholesome guy parents begged you to marry.

So *why* was he still single? Could the reason really be as simple as not yet finding *the one*? Or was there another underlying, more worrying reason? He's either a player, Nina thought, or there were issues. Specifically, mommy issues (the man was thirty-three and had been living with his mother up until a year ago).

Nina could almost feel Tammy skewering her with a withering look. Admittedly, Nina had no right to point a preachy finger. She might not have *major* mother issues, but she certainly had Lucas issues, which, yes, were the reason for her single status. So let's not get all judgy, she scolded herself as she and Brian finished up their coffees and began walking the short distance to Lucas's apartment building. Perhaps Brian was also secretly in love with someone (please, not his mom).

"Great building," Brian said admiringly when they reached the showstopping, glass-fronted entrance to Lucas's sleek residential tower.

"Yeah, it's pretty impressive," Nina admitted. She pressed Lucas's apartment number, and he let them into the building. The sumptuous lobby smelled of leather and lavender. Surrealistic artwork lined the walls at cleverly placed intervals.

"This is one of the city's hottest addresses," Brian said as they took the elevator to the eleventh floor. "Your friend's done well for himself."

Nina nodded in agreement, feeling a pinch of pride in all that Lucas had achieved. "He's worked really hard to get to where he is today."

The elevator stopped, and they stepped into the hallway. She'd hopefully timed their arrival so they wouldn't be the first ones there. She needed Ryan and Olivia acting as buffers when the moment came for Lucas to introduce her to Tahlia.

Buzzed by caffeine and Brian's reassuringly male presence, Nina made an effort not to overthink this. All she wanted was to enjoy the experience of a handsome man on her arm. It felt a bit like showing off a glamorous new handbag. Of course, it would help if she wasn't also thinking about the shiny new accessory that would be attached to Lucas's arm.

The door opened just as she was about to knock. Lucas stood there, his lips curving into a smile when he saw her. Ignoring Brian, he pulled her in for a hug. Nina breathed in the scent of him and closed her eyes at the familiar press of his strong body against hers, the comforting feel of his arms around her. She could happily stay in this position for the rest of her life.

Brian cleared his throat, and Nina's eyes flew open. Oh, crappity crap! Brian! Her date! She quickly disentangled herself and stepped out of Lucas's hold.

"Lucas, this is...uh...Brian. Brian—Lucas, an old friend of mine."

Brian held out his hand. "Pleased to meet you."

Lucas shook his hand. "Likewise. Just to be clear, it's...Brian, is it?" he asked, casting a meaningful look in Nina's direction.

Nina stiffened. Trust Lucas not to forget a single word of what she'd said on the phone Friday.

"Yeah, Brian."

"Good name," Lucas said. "Easy on the tongue."

Brian frowned. "I guess so."

Nina dug her nails into her palms. Why, oh why, did she get herself into these situations?

"Lucas!" Olivia's voice echoed from inside his apartment. "Where do you keep your serving platters?"

When Lucas turned away to answer her, Brian whispered in her ear, "What's up with your friend?"

Thinking furiously, Nina whispered back, "He's a name connoisseur. It's a thing with him. Best to ignore it."

Lucas faced them again, and they both fell silent.

Brian asked, "Mind if I use your bathroom?"

Lucas pointed down the hallway. "First door on the right."

"Thanks." Brian hurried off.

Nina tried to sidestep Lucas and follow Brian inside, but Lucas lightly grasped her elbow, halting her in her tracks. She reluctantly raised her eyes to his.

"Brian?"

She gave him her best wide-eyed look. "He's great, isn't he?"

His eyes narrowed. "I don't get it. 'Brian' is not difficult to pronounce. Why the secrecy?"

"Now's really not the time to talk about this."

Lucas stared her down. "Now's exactly the time."

She lowered her voice. "If you must know, Brian's real name is...uh...Brychekov."

"Brychekov?" Lucas repeated carefully.

Nina nodded. "His family call him that, but he's embarrassed by his name, so I agreed to call him Brian today. I also promised to keep his real name a secret. Please, Lucas, don't say anything to him."

Skepticism clouded Lucas's face. "Nina, this sounds reality-TV weird."

She gave a what-can-you-do shrug. "You know what they say, you don't choose your family."

"Hey, sis, you planning on coming in, or are we moving this get-together to the entrance hall?"

She'd never been so pleased to hear Ryan's voice.

"Coming," she called, slipping past Lucas, who let her go. She was feeling all unsettled. This afternoon was going to be difficult enough to get through without her having to keep track of all the lies that kept tumbling out of her.

Brian stepped out of the bathroom, and she caught up to him. "Everything okay?" she asked.

He patted his midsection. "Bit of a nervous stomach."

She wasn't surprised, especially when she saw Ryan bearing down on them, no doubt wanting to cross-examine her date before Olivia could stop him.

Sighing, she said, "Brian, meet my ridiculously overprotective brother, Ryan."

Smiling gamely, Brian held out his hand.

Ryan let it hang in the air a moment longer than was necessary before reaching out to grip it. "You married, Brian?"

Brian's eyes widened. "Married? No."

"What about Utah?" Ryan asked. "You ever been there?"

"Ryan!" Nina protested.

"Utah?" Brian's face flashed confusion. "Uh, no, I don't believe I have."

Ryan crossed his arms. "My only sister's about to become an aunt. It's a massively important role, and I can't have her hurt in any way."

"All right, that's enough," she said, her cheeks burning with embarrassment. Where was an earthquake when you needed one? It would be a miracle if Brian ever wanted to see her again after this afternoon.

"It's okay," Brian said, his smile looking more like a grimace. "I have a sister, and I can also be pretty protective of her."

Nina felt Lucas come up behind them. He put a hand on Ryan's shoulder. "Let's move to the living room," he said easily. "I want to introduce Nina to Tahlia."

Of course, Nina thought, her chest constricting. Tahlia. For a few merciful seconds, she'd forgotten that Lucas's new girlfriend was the reason they were all gathered in his apartment.

They headed down the hallway to the living room, Lucas thankfully leading Ryan ahead of them.

Nina snuck in a glance at Brian, who was looking a little shell-shocked. "Sorry about my brother," she said. "He obviously missed his calling as a mob enforcer."

"Is he always this intense?" Brian asked.

"Only when it comes to the three females in his life."

"Well, if the other two ladies are as pretty as you, then I can understand his intensity."

Aw, how sweet, she thought, but unfortunately also creepy since her mother happened to be one of the three. Nina had no problem being lumped in with her sister-in-law, but her own mother? That was a definite libido slayer.

"Oh, man, what a view," Brian blurted out on an awed breath as his gaze swept over Lucas's showpiece living room, where floor-to-ceiling windows overlooked the city's jagged concrete skyline.

Yes, what a view, her mind echoed as she caught sight of Olivia chatting to a tall woman rocking a classic monochrome look in black leather pants and a white silk top, her espresso-colored hair caught in a gleaming ponytail. Tahlia's elegant look perfectly suited the stylish aesthetic of Lucas's apartment with its slick black shelves, stainless steel appliances, and cream-colored couches.

Nina, in her blue dress and yellow scarf, felt like a garish splash of color disturbing the soothing neutral palette Lucas had going for him.

While Ryan stationed himself at Olivia's side, Lucas wrapped an arm around Tahlia's waist and pulled her close. The gesture was so intimate, Nina couldn't breathe through the hundreds of glass shards that had taken up residence in her throat.

Even with Brian at her side, this afternoon was going to be pure torture, she thought as she crossed the vast expanse of Lucas's living room toward the treacledom of happy couples.

"Nina, I'd like you to meet Tahlia," Lucas said.

Tahlia smiled warmly at her. "Lucas has told me so much about you."

Nina took a second to assess Tahlia's lithe figure, gorgeous bone structure, and penetrating black eyes. Sucking up her jealousy and insecurity and pain, stowing it away to be dealt with later, Nina hauled out a smile of her own. "Good things, I hope."

"He's been singing your praises." Tahlia placed a proprietary hand on Lucas's chest. "In fact, he makes you sound close to perfect."

"Oh." Nina snuck a peek at Lucas, but he wasn't looking at her. His attention was wholly fixed on Tahlia. Right. Her smile wavered a little. "Well, that's obviously untrue, but thanks for the compliment." Redirecting her attention to Brian, she touched his arm and introduced him to the rest of the group.

Taking in Brian's game ranger looks, Olivia's eyes widened, and she lunged for his hand. "It's an absolute pleasure to meet you," she gushed.

Nina winced, discreetly motioning for Olivia to tone it down a couple of notches.

"The pleasure is all mine," Brian replied. "Congratulations on the pregnancy." He gave her an eye-crinkling smile, and Nina watched Olivia mentally design her bridesmaid's dress.

If Olivia seemed deliriously happy for her, Ryan and Lucas—judging by the scowls on both their faces—were not. Irritation flared. It was time Ryan stopped thinking he was her father.

And Lucas? She didn't know what was up with him, but he had no reason to feel out of sorts, not with a woman who looked like that at his side. Speaking of which, Nina glanced up to find Tahlia staring at her with an expression of something like confusion on her face. When Nina caught her eye, she looked away.

Into the awkward silence that followed, Brian said to Lucas, "My mother's name is Shawna. S-H-A-W-N-A."

Lucas looked at Brian in incomprehension. Finally, he said, "Unusual name."

"Yeah, it is," Brian said, beaming. "You heard that name before?"

"No, I haven't," Lucas said warily.

Ryan was trying without success to keep a straight face. Nina knew that if she didn't change the subject, not even an elbow jab from Olivia would be enough to stop her brother from saying something wildly inappropriate. In desperation, she turned to Tahlia. "What is it you do for a living, Tahlia?"

"I work as one of the media advisors for the Human Rights Commission."

Of course she did. No menial data-capturing job for her. Nina fought the urge to close her eyes. Could the scales really be so unbalanced? Beauty *and* intelligence.

As Tahlia spoke about being part of a national inquiry into children in immigration detention, Nina could practically see Lucas's chest swelling with pride as his girlfriend described her meaningful, life-changing work. And then the question couldn't be helped: besides possible changes to belly fat and cholesterol levels, what meaningful impact did her work in hospitality have?

Nina tried to come up with an answer that wasn't soul destroying, but was distracted by platters of mouthwatering canapés arranged on the coffee table. Lucas had an upscale catering company on speed dial, and their food was consistently delicious. She popped a vodka-infused salmon tartlet into her mouth, almost moaning out loud in pleasure. There was her answer, she thought on a rush of relief. Her work brought pleasure to people.

Following her lead, the others tucked into the food, talking in between mouthfuls, the men dissecting the latest football game, Olivia continuing to quiz Tahlia on her work. The thing was, Tahlia seemed so depressingly *nice*. Listening to her talk, Nina waited for a gratifying hint of vanity or prejudice, some scrap of ugliness, to slip through, but Tahlia was overwhelmingly gracious, steering the conversation to Olivia's pregnancy and asking Nina about the various restaurants she'd worked at.

The alcohol came out. Ryan went for his usual beer, and Brian joined him. When Lucas and Tahlia both opted for wine, Nina, a diehard oenophile, snagged herself a cider, just to be contrary.

Lucas's brow creased. "What gives?"

She shrugged. "I'm in the mood for something different."

For a moment, he just looked at her, his brow still creased, like he was trying to work something out.

Brian took a couple of sips of beer before excusing himself and disappearing into the bathroom again. She frowned. The man must have the tiniest bladder.

"How did you two meet?" Lucas asked once Brian was out of sight.

Panic skidded through Nina as she felt the weight of their expectant gazes. Selecting a chicken and coriander ball, she said vaguely, "He's a friend of Tammy's."

Ryan groaned. "Tell me he's not planning on performing some death-defying stunt on the dining room table."

Nina knew Ryan was remembering the time Tammy had enthusiastically thrown herself across the hood of his precious Golf GTI to demonstrate the mechanics of her latest stunt.

Without thinking, Nina said, "Brian's not a stuntman."

"So what does he do, then?" Ryan asked.

Nina stared blankly at her brother. Do? She had no idea. In all her discussions with Brian, his occupation had never come up. Why hadn't she asked him? She noticed Lucas looking at her with interest. Her panic spiked. No way could he find out that Brian was a retaliatory first date. "Brian's, uh, he's a..."

Olivia, bless her sister-in-law's intuitive heart, swiftly interjected, "Don't tell us!"

Ryan frowned at his wife. "Why not?"

"Let's wait for Brian to tell us himself."

"Why?" Ryan asked.

"Liv's right," Nina said. "I don't want to steal Brian's thunder."

Tahlia tilted her head. "His job sounds intriguing and mysterious."

"It's not," Nina said hastily. "Not at all. It's...you know...a job." She threw a desperate glance in the direction of the bathroom. *Come on, Brian, what are you doing in there? Giving birth to your small intestine?*

When Olivia absentmindedly rested a hand on her stomach, Nina seized the opportunity to ask, "Any improvement on the nausea, Liv?"

"Looks like it's gone for good. Actually, I feel I'm back to my normal self."

Ryan's eyebrows shot up. "You don't think you're more...emotional than usual, love?" he asked cautiously.

"Emotional?" Olivia paused, then shook her head. "No, I don't think so."

"You cried in *Jurassic World*."

Olivia's eyes filled with tears. "That poor raptor lost all his brothers and sisters," she sobbed. "He was left all alone."

Alarmed, Ryan grabbed her hand. "I'm sorry, love, I shouldn't have brought it up." He made a frantic signal for Lucas to change the subject.

Before Lucas could come up with something, Brian returned from the bathroom, took one look at a tear-streaked Olivia, and said, "Oh, yeah, pregnancy hormones. They're a killer. A customer of mine had it really bad when she was pregnant."

Ryan curled an arm around Olivia and pressed a repentant kiss to her temple. "That reminds me, what is it you do for a living, Brian?"

Brian popped a stuffed mushroom into his mouth and spoke around it. "I'm the store manager at a nut shop."

Silence fell on all of them.

Nina glared at Ryan. *You asked the question! Say something!*

"So, ah, you're an expert on nuts?" Ryan asked.

"Yeah, pretty much," Brian said, eying out another canapé. "They're so important for the body, you know."

Ryan made some sort of strangled noise in his throat.

"I love nuts," Nina said quickly. "Cashews, almonds, walnuts, macadamias..."

Olivia gave her a funny look. She was babbling. *Shut up. Shut up. Shut up.*

Smiling to himself, Brian said, "My mom's also crazy about nuts. Actually, she was the one who got me the job."

Nina's stomach dropped. He'd brought out the Mother Card. She didn't miss the expression that flashed across Ryan's face before he ducked his head. That last comment would be the proverbial straw for her brother.

"I need another beer," Ryan mumbled before escaping to the kitchen.

Olivia hurried after him. "I'll bring out some more platters."

Nina could see the two of them huddled together in the open-plan kitchen, their shoulders shaking in silent laughter. She suppressed a sigh. This was going to be a long afternoon.

While Lucas engaged Brian in a discussion of his work at the shop, Nina stuffed canapés into her mouth so she wouldn't have to make polite small talk with Tahlia, who was stuck like an irritating burr to Lucas's side. Nina nibbled her way through half a platter of canapés in the time it took for Lucas and Tahlia to exhaust the topic of Brian's work benefits.

"I hear you own a bodyguard business," Brian said to Lucas.

Lucas leveled Nina an is-this-seriously-what-you-told-him look. Unperturbed, she responded with an all-out grin. *Hey,* her grin said, *I get my kicks where I can.*

Nina could feel Tahlia's gaze ping-ponging between them.

Lucas turned to Brian. "My company specializes in security, yes."

"Cool," Brian said. "Why a bodyguard?"

"A desire to protect and serve," Lucas said smoothly.

"C'mon, I'm sure there's more to it than that." Brian pointed his beer bottle at Lucas. "I bet you watched Kevin Costner in *The Bodyguard*. I bet you wanted to look cool with your earpiece and have your female clients fall for you."

Nina tried not to cringe. She knew Brian wasn't being deliberately obnoxious, that he was trying to connect with Lucas in a jokey, man-to-man way, but his clumsy attempt was failing miserably.

"Looks like you got me all figured out," Lucas said, knocking back the last bit of wine in his glass. "Anyone for a top-up?" When they shook their heads, Lucas left to retrieve another bottle from the kitchen, which was fast becoming the refuge to escape uncomfortable conversations.

Brian, oblivious to Lucas's irritation, headed to the bathroom again.

Spotting the confusion on Tahlia's face, Nina said, "Lucas hates it when people stereotype his security work. Christina's always teasing him about it."

"Christina?" Tahlia asked.

"Lucas's mom," Nina said after a pause. "You haven't met her yet?"

"No."

"Oh."

Lucas hadn't introduced Tahlia to his mom. He hadn't even mentioned her name to Tahlia. Despite their obvious early-days infatuation, their relationship hadn't yet developed to that level.

Hiding a smile, Nina took a sip of her cider. The afternoon was looking infinitesimally better.

"Another cider?" Brian asked when he returned.

"I'll have wine this time," Nina said, smiling her thanks and newfound contentment at him. "My turn for the bathroom."

Tahlia stayed her with a hand on her arm. "Shall I show you where it is?"

Nina's smile slipped a little. "Thanks, but I know where Lucas's bathroom is."

Tahlia put a hand to her chest, as if to say *silly me*. "Of course you do. I imagine you've been here many times."

"Many, many times," Nina said pointedly.

"You and Lucas have known each other quite a while."

"Since Grade One."

"A long time to be...friends." She held Nina's gaze, her meaning clear: *here I am, and there you are, still stranded on the wrong side of the Great Wall of Friendship.*

Nina carefully placed her cider bottle on the table. Resentment flared toward Tahlia, but she couldn't blame her. If the situation were reversed and she stood in those sexy Louboutins, expecting Lucas to return any minute to her side, she'd fight just as slyly to hold on to him.

In the bathroom, Nina splashed water on the back of her neck and confronted her pale reflection in the mirror. Her chest held that all too familiar ache she associated with Lucas. The only way she could think to escape this level of hurt was to kick him out of her life.

Could she do it? While it was unbearable to think that Lucas, whom she'd known nearly all her life, would no longer be *in* her life, it was equally unbearable to watch him live life with someone else.

Don't do anything drastic, she told herself, gripping the basin. No life-changing decisions next to a toilet.

Olivia grabbed her arm the moment she opened the door, causing her to jump in fright. "Liv! What on earth? Why are you skulking outside the bathroom?"

"Please, I stalk, I don't skulk." She tugged Nina into the quiet shadows of Lucas's bedroom. "Okay, spill. Is this your first date with Brian?"

"Uh..."

"Don't even think of lying to me."

"Okay, yes, first date."

"Nina," was all her sister-in-law said.

"I know, I know." Nina let out an unhappy laugh. "Brian's a knee-jerk reaction to Lucas telling me about Tahlia. I didn't want to appear desperate and pathetic."

Olivia gave her a meaningful look.

"Don't say it."

Olivia pressed her lips together. There was a pause while they stared at one another, then Olivia said, "You know, Tahlia reminds me of someone."

Nina gratefully went with the change of subject. "Who?"

"I can't put my finger on it. It's going to bug me the rest of the afternoon."

"Hey, why the private conference?" Ryan asked, sauntering into the room.

"Sweetheart, does Tahlia remind you of someone?"

"Yeah, she looks a little like Nina."

Olivia's eyes widened. "That's it!"

"I don't look anything like Tahlia," Nina said with feeling.

"There's definitely a resemblance," Olivia murmured thoughtfully. "Interesting."

"She's Tahlia minus the smoking-hot factor," Ryan added, glancing over at Nina. "No offense, but you're my sister, and I can't think of you in terms of smoking hot."

When Olivia gave an exaggerated clearing of her throat, Ryan's body went rigid. He said slowly, "And I have my pregnant wife next to me, so I shouldn't be thinking of any woman as smoking hot."

"No, Ryan Abrahams, you shouldn't be."

Ryan swallowed. "Hard to believe, but I'm wishing now I'd stayed to listen to Brian go into raptures about chocolate macadamias."

"Speaking of Brian," Nina said, "I better get back to him." Not that she wanted to. She was far more interested in watching her brother try to talk himself out of this one.

She left them in the bedroom and headed to the living room, coming to an abrupt stop when she glimpsed the odd tableau in front of her: Lucas and Tahlia hovering over Brian, who was doubled over and clutching his stomach.

Alarmed, she hurried over. "What's going on?" she asked Lucas, who looked relieved to see her. "Did you...punch him?"

"What?" Lucas looked appalled. "Of course I didn't punch him."

"Oh. Okay." She gathered herself and stared at Brian. "What's wrong with him, then?"

"Stomach cramps, apparently," Lucas said.

"Stomach cramps?" She put a tentative hand on Brian's shoulder. "Brian, was it something you ate? Are you allergic to anything?"

Brian shook his head, grimacing.

"What can we do to help?"

She noticed Lucas frown at her use of the word *we*.

Brian let out an agonized groan. "I just have to ride the cramps out."

ALL THE LOST PIECES

Nina watched in mute fascination as this gorgeous-looking man (admittedly, the contorted look on his face dropped the gorgeous factor down a level) wrapped his arms around his middle and slowly collapsed onto Lucas's beautiful thick shag rug.

"What the heck? You all right, Brian?"

At the sound of Ryan's stunned voice, Nina looked up from Brian's writhing form to see her brother and Olivia standing there holding hands, having clearly made up.

"Stomach cramps," Nina explained. "We're not sure what to do."

"Brian, has this happened before?" Tahlia asked calmly.

"Yes," Brian managed to gasp out. "When I'm nervous or stressed, like before an exam or sometimes on a date, my stomach goes into knots and I get horrible spasms."

Like a hundred-watt bulb exploding in her head, the reason for Brian's single status became suddenly, horribly clear.

Olivia shot her an urgent look. "Do something," she whispered.

Do something? Nina thought. You mean, something other than leaping up and running out of the apartment?

Nina knelt on the rug beside Brian. "Breathe," she instructed. "Slowly, in through your nose, out through your mouth." She'd recently watched a medical drama where that advice had worked remarkably well, but Brian wasn't calming down like the well-behaved patient in that particular episode. He was, in point of fact, becoming more and more agitated.

"Aargh," Brian moaned, rolling to one side.

"Soccer player," Ryan coughed out.

Nina glared up at her brother, and Olivia dutifully elbowed him in the ribs.

Brian said through clenched teeth, "When I get these pains, my mom presses my knees to my chest and that sometimes helps."

Nina flinched. *Wait, what? His mom did what?*

She threw a desperate glance at Lucas. He responded with an adamant head shake. *Your date, your problem,* his expression said. She didn't bother looking Ryan's way. Her brother would be of no use in this situation.

Maybe she should call Brian's mother, Nina thought wildly. Maybe she could come over and help.

Tahlia took a step forward, her work-honed conscience no doubt urging her to do something. If Tahlia came rushing to Brian's aid, that would only elevate Lucas's feelings for his girlfriend. *Look how practical she is! How caring!*

Nina gritted her teeth. She couldn't let that happen, not right in front of her. Gesturing for Tahlia not to worry, Nina turned to Brian and drew in a breath. She could handle this. She could help a suffering fellow human. She no longer wanted to date that human, but she could certainly do whatever was needed to alleviate his discomfort.

"So I just have to press your knees to your chest?" Nina clarified, staring down at Brian, who was on his back, knees already partially lifted.

"Yes!" Brian said on a gasp.

Lucas said softly, "Nina, I don't think you want to do that."

She held up a hand in what she hoped was a practical, caring manner. "It's okay, Lucas." She leaned over Brian, grasped his knees, and pushed them down toward his chest.

"Harder!" Brian directed. "Press harder."

Shifting position to gain better leverage, Nina applied more of her weight to his legs. Suddenly, there was the loud, protracted sound of what could only be an explosive release of gas.

Nina scrambled back in horror. Lucas, the traitor, fell back on the couch, covering his face with an arm in an effort to muffle his laughter. Olivia was already dragging a nearly hysterical Ryan to the kitchen, while a wide-eyed Tahlia stood rooted to the spot.

Brian sat up, a little pink in the cheeks, but looking immensely relieved, his mother's technique appearing to do the trick. "Thanks for that," he said to Nina, and she managed a nod back, unable to look him in the eyes.

Nina waited until the excruciatingly long round of "Glad you're feeling better," had passed before announcing that she and Brian would be leaving early. No one showed much surprise, except Ryan, who pulled her aside and begged her not to leave, saying that the last hour had been more entertaining than anything Netflix could offer.

In the lobby, Brian turned to look at her. "I don't think I'll be as nervous on the second date."

She chewed her lip. "Brian..."

He stared at his shoes. "No second date, I'm guessing."

"No second date," she confirmed as gently as she could. "But how about a lunch one day, as friends?"

"I guess that would be okay." Brian's face suddenly lit up. "Hey, would you mind if I bring my mom?"

Chapter Eighteen

Wanting no repeat of the Ariadne debacle, Nina arrived in Barracat twenty minutes early for her interview. Following the GPS directions to the town center, she couldn't stop yawning. She hadn't had the best night's sleep. She'd tossed and turned for ages, Brian and Tahlia taking it in turns to hijack her dreams. It had been horrible. Tahlia kept hiding Lucas's bathroom in different locations throughout the city, taunting her to try to find it. And Brian kept screaming "Push! Push!" right before his face exploded into thousands of tiny canapés.

She needed a coffee. A double shot, she decided, remembering Tammy's text message—*How'd it go with Brian? Details!*—that had woken her up at a hideous hour this morning. Nina hadn't replied to Tammy because a) the details were too embarrassing to recount, and b) surely Tammy had known of Brian's mother fixation, as well as his "nervous stomach," but had elected not to tell her. Why had Tammy set her up with someone so unsuitable? As a result, Nina wasn't feeling too happy with her friend right now, particularly when she pictured that friend blissfully enjoying the Italian Alps, far away from the fallout of her recommendation.

Nina's phone hadn't known what had hit it last night as it attempted to cope with the flurry of texts. There had been texts from her mother, demanding an answer as to why she'd turned down Ariadne (old news, Mom, more scandalous developments had transpired since then). Lots of weird texts from Ryan with lines and lines of exclamation marks and emojis of... *Really, Ry?* Her brother's infantile self was so easily activated. After Ryan's texts had come Olivia's. She'd instructed Nina to ignore all Ry's messages and then she'd sent her links to online dating apps and web sites: Tinder, eHarmony, Match, Plenty of Fish, OkCupid, Oasis... How many were there? It was like stumbling onto a hidden civilization.

There had been no messages from Lucas. He was most likely too busy saying goodbye to Tahlia, and Nina didn't want to think of all the ways one said goodbye.

Sighing, Nina turned up the volume on the radio so Zendaya could drown out the thoughts in her head. From what she'd glimpsed so far of Barracat, she was surprised. And impressed. Yes, it was out in the sticks, as the city slickers would say, away from everything hip and happening, but it seemed Barracat wasn't so much cattle country now, not with the rash of housing developments and the decent-sized mall that had sprung up.

She'd always loved living in the city, but the rush and racket of traffic and people, the drab grayness of all that concrete was simply no match for Barracat's wide expanse of blue sky and explosions of green. The only rush here seemed to be the succession of jacketed dog walkers and children heading to school.

Nina parked in the town center and walked down the main street on the hunt for coffee. She felt dull-witted with fatigue and knew she'd be no good in the interview if she didn't get a caffeine fix. Ten minutes later, sipping her so-so coffee (they could learn a thing or two from the baristas in the city), Nina tracked down Soul Fare. Great location on the main street, she noted, affording the restaurant the advantage of high foot and car traffic. Plenty of parking, eye-catching signage, and an elegant black and glossy wood storefront. All good drawcards for curious walk-ins.

Finishing her coffee with a few minutes to spare, Nina pushed open the glass door to Soul Fare and stepped inside. The timber flooring and wooden tables and chairs lent a slightly farmhouse feel to the restaurant. The lighting inside was also dimmer than she expected. A wall of windows overlooked the street, but evenly spaced panels of heavy, old-fashioned curtains obscured most of the view. Only three tables were occupied.

"Nina Abrahams?" A woman Nina guessed to be somewhere in her sixties popped up from behind the hostess stand, her brown eyes alight with engaging warmth.

"Yes, hi, I'm Nina."

"Edith," she said in self-introduction, and Nina shook her hand, taking an immediate shine to the owner of Soul Fare with her wide smile and laughing eyes. Her short white hair was styled in a bob and she wore a vibrant shade of red lipstick. The lipstick should have looked out of place on her lined face, but didn't. It felt like a bit of her personality—*this is me, vivacious and spirited and loving life*—had snuck through in the red.

"Come meet some friends of mine," Edith invited.

Nina tried to keep the surprise off her face. This was as far from her Ariadne interview as she could get. She followed Edith to a table where three elderly ladies sporting thick glasses, pastel cardigans, and eighties-style perms were clustered around mugs of coffee. They looked like three short, round, gray-haired gnomes, Nina thought.

"Nina, this is Claire, Angela, and Bianca," Edith said. "Ladies, I'd like you to meet Nina."

Before Nina could utter a word of greeting, Claire said, "Natalie Portman."

Angela squinted at Nina. "No, no, that actress from *The Light Between Oceans*, the one with the strange name—Alicia something or other."

"Alicia Vikander," Bianca supplied. Peering at Nina, she shook her head. "I disagree. There's a Jessica Alba look to her."

Nina tried not to fidget uncomfortably under their scrutiny. She'd experienced many odd conversations in her life, but this certainly counted as one of the strangest. She felt the weight of Edith's eyes on her, the realization settling in that, unlike Martin Feenstra's cerebral ambushes, this was a let's-see-her-in-action test.

Straightening her shoulders, Nina made sure her smile encompassed all of them. "I'm flattered, ladies, thank you. Let me say in turn that this has all the makings of a Meryl Streep, Judi Dench, and Helen Mirren reunion."

"Ooooh, I like her," Angela cackled, slapping the table with a liver-spotted hand. "I like her a lot."

Bianca and Clare nodded, echoing Angela's statement.

Under Edith's friendly yet watchful gaze, Nina made an effort to draw the three ladies out in conversation. Not that it required much effort. They were so eager to talk, she could hardly get a word in. After one or two questions, she found out that the three of them had formed a movie club and met at Soul Fare every Monday and Thursday to discuss and rate whatever movie they'd selected.

"We thought of a book club," Bianca said, "but it takes days, sometimes weeks, to read a book."

Angela nodded. "At our age, one of us could drop dead before the week's up."

"A movie's about an hour and a half, give or take, so this way, we get to meet twice a week," Bianca said.

"We only stay home if the arthritis is playing up."

"Or the bunions."

"We toyed with the idea of a strip club," Angela said. "Our motto was going to be 'let it all hang out,' but we thought people might object."

"I didn't mind so much," Clare said, her bosom taking up an impressive amount of table space. "Everything's hanging down, so why not out?"

The easy, steady patter of their conversation swirled around Nina. A part of her wondered if her interview challenge lay in how gracefully she could extricate herself from the conversation. Every restaurant manager had to possess that fairy godmother ability to engage with guests so they got their I-feel-so-special sprinkling, while also working the room and ensuring that none of the other diners felt neglected.

"What's the deal?" Angela asked bluntly. "Is she going to work here?"

"Nina's applying for the position of restaurant manager," Edith informed them.

The three ladies shared a look Nina couldn't read, but the back of her neck tingled in warning.

"She might last, this one," Angela said speculatively. "I hope so, anyway. The last one you hired, Edith, was useless. The man hadn't watched any of the *Mad Max* movies."

"And the lady before that had no clue who Ryan Gosling was," Claire said, her round face pink with disbelief. "I can't trust someone with my food if they haven't heard of RG."

"There were other things too," Bianca said, but before she could elaborate, a dark-haired server, who looked to be in her early thirties, appeared at the table with their food. She wore blue denims and a white top, overlaid with a full-body gray apron displaying the Soul Fare logo.

"Wonderful timing, Jeena!" Edith declared as plates of scrambled eggs, bacon, and toast were deposited onto the table.

"Ladies, that looks delicious," Nina said, hoping she was reading the situation—and Edith's expectations—correctly. "We'll leave you to enjoy your food before it gets cold."

Edith nodded, and the approving smile lines at the corners of her mouth told Nina she'd got it right. "Please let Jeena know if you need anything else."

"Don't you worry, Edith," Angela said. "Jeena always takes care of us."

Jeena favored them with a dry smile. Nina thought she seemed a little sullen for a server, but her movements were quick and efficient as she cleared the table of empty mugs.

"Who's your screen doppelgänger?" Nina asked Edith as she followed her to a table at the back of the restaurant.

"According to them, I'm a dead ringer for Jessica Tandy. It's a rare occurrence, though, for the three of them to be in agreement."

Nina laughed. "They certainly seem interesting."

"Oh, they keep me on my toes." Edith took a seat at the table. "And contrary to what they might think, I don't hire a front-of-house manager based on his or her movie knowledge."

Sitting opposite her, Nina pretended relief. "Whew."

They exchanged small talk about the weather and what it was like living in Barracat (minimal traffic, tons of parks, reasonable house prices, and only a small number of reputable restaurants struggling to stand out amid the marketing avalanche of fast food chains). Edith seemed in no hurry to get to the actual interview questions, or perhaps this was all part of her interview technique.

At last they drifted into work-related conversation. Edith asked about some of the ways she'd dealt with customer complaints, what she liked most about working in hospitality, and her management style.

Edith explained that she and her husband, Bill, had been operating Soul Fare for close to five years, with Bill working as head chef and Edith running the front of house. "The early days were crazy," she murmured. "We were working so hard, doing small renovations to the restaurant ourselves after hours. There were times we were too tired to drive home, and we took to keeping sleeping bags at the restaurant and crashing here. Oh, the fun we had." She blinked back tears. "The best part about it all is that we were together."

Jeena appeared and placed a pot of tea in front of Edith.

"Thank you, Jeena," Edith said, her voice still thick with emotion. "A strong cup of tea is just what I need right now."

Jeena's brown eyes widened and she flashed Nina an accusing look, as if she were the one responsible for Edith's distress.

Great, Nina thought. Only ten minutes into her unorthodox interview and already she'd made an enemy. It should bother her more, but one thing she'd learned over the years was that you couldn't control what other people thought of you. They were entitled to the ignorance of their opinions.

"What about you, my dear?" Edith asked Nina. "Can I offer you anything?"

"A cappuccino would be lovely." Nina glanced up into Jeena's delicate features and made an effort to smile. "Thank you."

There was no return smile. "Cappuccino coming up," Jeena said flatly. She turned to leave, her shoulders stiff with hostility, her long braid resting like a black snake against her spine.

Alarm kicked in. Nina noticed two other servers, one whippet-thin, artsy-looking young man and another brown-haired, middle-aged lady, shooting busybody, unfriendly glances in her direction. What was going on here? Had one of them hoped for the role of restaurant manager?

Edith, sipping her tea, appeared oblivious to the tension.

She was being paranoid, Nina told herself. The servers were probably showing harmless curiosity and nerves were causing her to read too much into their attitude.

"Bill was diagnosed with Alzheimer's early last year," Edith said. "He's in a nursing home now, and I want to spend as much time as I can with him before he's lost to me forever."

Nina nodded in understanding, a lump forming in her throat as she thought of the enduring strength of that kind of love.

"What about you?" Edith asked. "If you're living in the city, why are you applying for work here in Barracat? With your experience"—she gestured to Nina's résumé lying on the table—"I'm sure you could have your pick of restaurants in the city."

Edith looked so sympathetic and interested that Nina found an alarming amount of detail spilling out of her: the interview at Ariadne and her realization that she no longer wanted to work herself to death simply to show off a fine-dining restaurant on her résumé. She told Edith about her landlord giving her notice, but managed to clamp down on the urge to tell Edith about Lucas. Some rational part of her brain warned her she would appear more psycho than tragic in that particular segment of her life story.

Jeena delivered the cappuccino, and Nina smiled her thanks, praying no one had spat in it. She added her guilty teaspoon of sugar and took a sip. It was a good cup of coffee.

"I'm looking for a restaurant manager I can trust to run Soul Fare, someone with integrity and expertise," Edith said. "I believe you might be that manager."

Nina blinked, startled. She hadn't expected Edith's verdict so soon. She'd expected the usual handshake and a "You'll hear from me in a couple of days."

Edith must have seen her surprise, because she said, "I trust my feelings, and I have a good feeling about you. You're qualified and capable, but what I like most about you is you're attentive. When I told you about Bill, you listened. You showed empathy. Most applicants who sit opposite me talk my head off. In fact, they spend so much time telling me how great they are, they have no idea what's going on with me. That frustrates me, and it'll frustrate diners. I don't want frustrated diners, I want satisfied ones, and a manager who listens to them, who anticipates and meets their needs, will make all the difference."

Pleasure blossomed inside Nina at Edith's words. That was high praise from someone she'd just met. Nina felt her confidence, always so fragile, go up a notch.

"I like you," Edith said. "I feel we have a connection."

"I feel that too," Nina said, jumping right in there, shrugging off Lucas's urgent voice in her ear warning her not to make a decision where emotion trumped logic.

"So what do you think?" Edith asked. "Would you like to be the restaurant manager here?"

Yes! every instinct inside her screamed. She wanted to be that manager. She liked Edith. She liked the look of Soul Fare. Her only niggle of worry? The unpleasant sardine commute. All those additional hours she'd hoped to have to claw back a life for herself would be lost in travel.

"I want to say yes..." Nina began, and stopped.

"But you have reservations," Edith concluded. "Why don't you tell me what they are and let's see if we can deal with them?"

"It's really only one reservation," Nina said. "First off, let me say that I would love to work here, I really would, but the commute..." She grimaced. "Whether I drive or take the train, it's over an hour to get here. All that traveling would eventually get to me."

"I can see how that would be a problem," Edith said, looking thoughtful. "Well, what about moving to Barracat?"

Nina almost laughed out loud. "What?"

"You have to move anyway. Isn't that what you said? So why not Barracat?"

Nina fell silent. She couldn't move here. For starters, the city was her home. She loved the vibe and convenience of city life, loved being in the center of things. Her family and friends were all in the city. Abruptly, she revisited that statement. Her mother lived on the outskirts of the city, in the same upmarket suburb as Lucas's parents, but when Nina thought hard about it, she realized regular visits to her mother were on neither of their agendas. And Ryan and Olivia had settled in a suburb that was a forty-minute drive from the city, but only fifteen minutes from Barracat.

And friends? Unsociable work hours and neglect on her part had caused most of her school and college friends to meander into distant acquaintances. Only Tammy still counted as a close friend, and although she had an apartment in the city, she was rarely there. When Tammy was home, weekends often turned into wild parties where Nina could be called upon at any inconvenient hour of the night to urgently come over, which she always did, despite always vowing that this would be the last time. Invariably, she'd find Tammy passed out, with the expectation that Nina would clean her up like a good friend. So perhaps it wasn't a good idea to be so physically near to Tammy.

The only person tethering her to the city was Lucas.

Suddenly, her decision became so much easier.

"You know what? Yes, I could move here," she found herself saying, a mix of terror and excitement coursing through her.

Edith looked delighted. "I'm sure you'll love living in Barracat. In fact, if you're not opposed to the idea, I could help you find an apartment. I have a few friends with investment properties."

"Thank you," Nina said, touched by Edith's offer. "I'd like that very much."

Never mind what everyone would say, this decision *felt* right. It felt like a fresh start. And if Lucas wanted logic, she'd serve up some: Soul Fare opened at seven, closed at five. Give or take an hour to close up, she'd be home by six thirty. All those evenings free to catch up with family, find a hobby, make new friends. Start dating.

All the pieces of herself she'd lost along the way, well, it was time to start recapturing them.

Chapter Nineteen

The day after her Soul Fare interview, Nina decided to eat her frog. According to the bestselling book (which she'd reread last year in a bid to stave off her default practice of procrastination), this was best done first thing in the morning so you could get on with the day knowing your most challenging and stressful task (your frog) was over and done with. That was the theory, anyway.

Nina's frog, however, didn't do first thing in the morning, so Nina made arrangements to join her mother later that afternoon for a walk around the lake.

"Barra—what?" Cheryl asked now without breaking her stride.

Nina tried to catch her breath. She'd anticipated a leisurely walk around the lake, but this was what her mom termed a *power walk*. "Barracat, Mom."

"Never heard of it."

Nina tried not to sigh. Someone had been spending too much time in New York. "Population of fifty thousand. In one of the fastest growth corridors in the southeast. Barracat even has its own public toilets."

"You know what they say about sarcasm, Nina."

"That it isn't an attitude, but an art?"

"I was leaning more toward 'sarcasm is the lowest form of wit.'"

Nina bit back the profusion of responses (all sarcastic) that rushed to her tongue. "You're right. Apologies. No more witless sarcasm." She could feel sweat beading her forehead, and they were only halfway around the lake, the sun beating down on them. "Oh, look, there's a bench. Talk about fate. We could sit for a while and watch the swans."

Without breaking her inhuman stride, Cheryl Abrahams marched past the bench, arms pumping. Not even jet lag could subdue her mother. "Push through the pain. You know what I say, The Only Real Barrier To Achieving Your Goal Is In Your Mind."

Au contraire, Mother. It was definitely in her burning lungs and throbbing calves, but, deprived of her mother tongue, Nina could only nod mutely and try to keep up.

"What I want to know," her mother continued, "is why you said no to working at Ariadne and yes to this unheard-of Soul Fare place? It makes no sense."

"Great restaurant with loads of potential, lovely owner, a change of pace and scenery," Nina said, feeling a bit like a telemarketer. "What's not to understand?"

"Perhaps you could go back to Martin, tell him you made a mistake."

"I haven't made a mistake."

"I could put in a word for you, if you like. I've eaten at Ariadne enough times."

"Mom, are you even listening to me? I don't want to work at Ariadne." Nina caught sight of another bench and came to a halt. She sat down and watched as her mother continued to stride ahead, her lycra-clad figure getting smaller and smaller. Not the worst outcome, Nina thought on a tide of resentment, looking away from her oblivious mother to take in the sight of black swans gliding across the water.

The peaceful scene was broken two minutes later when Cheryl returned and said huffily, "Really, Nina, you could have told me you were stopping."

Nina didn't take her eyes off the lake. "Would you have listened?"

"There's no need to get defensive," her mother said, using the break to get in some squats. "I was simply trying to help."

"No, you were trying to interfere."

"I am at a loss as to how you want me to respond."

"How about 'Congratulations, Nina, on your new job.'"

"Congratulations?" Cheryl asked incredulously, pausing midsquat. "On what? On turning down a well-paying position at a prestigious restaurant? On moving to no-namesville?"

"Now look who's being sarcastic."

That was the thing with her mom, Nina thought. Nothing was ever really good enough. At school, if she got an A in math, her mother's typical response was "Perhaps if you'd completed more worksheets, you could have achieved an A plus."

If she didn't make the team for cross-country? "Well, Nina, you obviously didn't practice enough."

Lucas's family was so different. Christina wasn't afraid to speak her mind, but she was always her children's cheerleader. When Lucas or Francesca messed up, she never shielded them from the consequences of their actions, but always sought to highlight the good.

"Okay, Francesca, you came last in the race, but at least you finished. I'm proud of you."

And when Lucas got a disappointing B for a history test he'd studied hard for: "You did your best, Lukie. That's all I can ask of you."

What she would give to have a mother who was a cheerleader rather than a judge.

"Why?" Cheryl asked now. "Why would you choose to work in this place?"

"It's a change. Isn't that what you encourage people to do in your talks—to embrace change?"

"A forward-looking change. Not a backward one."

"That's the thing with change, Mom. You never really know if it's a change for better or worse until you take that step, but at least you have the hope of something better."

There was a moment's pause where her mother simply stared at her. Then she straightened, whipped out her phone, and started tapping away.

It took Nina a second to find her voice. "Are you writing that down?"

"It's a good sentiment, darling," she said. "I might tinker with it a bit, see what emerges."

Nina opened her mouth. She should tell her mother she'd probably picked it up from some article in a gossip magazine, but she let it go.

Close to the end of their walk, Cheryl unexpectedly suggested they go out for dinner. Nina hastily came up with an excuse. Whenever possible, she tried to avoid dining with her mother, not wanting her favorite pastime marred by a woman who calorie counted even the garnish on her plate.

After the usual awkward goodbye, Nina headed home and got straight into the shower, but not even twenty minutes of near-scalding water could wash away the sting of her mother's words. Why did every talk have to feel like a confrontation? She hated this bruised feeling, this vague sense of worthlessness that stayed with her whenever she interacted with her mom.

Nina switched on the TV and surfed channels, but there was nothing there that caught her interest. She picked up her phone. A Facebook scroll revealed plenty of photos of Tammy holding on to oversized cocktails and a variety of good-looking men, but seeing her friend partying it up simply depressed her and Nina tossed her phone aside. She opened the pantry cupboard, hoping a dinner idea would jump out at her, but the only item that grabbed her attention was a bottle of Kahlua. Oh, the temptation. She reached for the bottle, but, after a second's hesitation, dropped her arm to her side. If she resorted to alcohol after every encounter with her mother, she'd be in rehab in no time. She needed another kind of soothing. She picked up her phone again.

"Christina, hi," Nina said as soon as Lucas's mother answered.

"Nina, I was just thinking of you," Christina said fondly, and that ache inside Nina eased a little as Christina's warm voice washed over her.

"What are you up to?" she asked, making herself comfortable on the couch.

Christina, seeming to sense exactly what she needed, regaled her with stories of Colton and his sweet tooth. Nina felt the tension slowly seep from her, replaced by a welcome feeling of serenity.

And then Christina said, "Can you believe I found an empty box of Turkish delight in the trash the other week?"

"Um, Turkish delight?"

"Yes, a whole box! I can't imagine how Colton got hold of one."

Nina was *not* going to lose that lovely feeling of serenity. She asked hurriedly, "Any new recipes?"

"Oh, yes," Christina said, taking the bait. "You'll love this one."

Nina took mental notes as Christina launched into a detailed description of a new Alfredo sauce she was experimenting with, replacing the cream with cauliflower, parmesan, and mozzarella, and how it tasted so good, Colton was unable to tell the difference.

A little while later, Christina asked, "You okay now, Nina?"

"More than okay. Thank you for the recipe."

After promising to visit soon, Nina hung up and made her way to the grocery store, where she purchased all the items Christina had listed in the recipe. Returning to her apartment, she cranked up the *Game of Thrones* soundtrack and started chopping up ingredients. While her mom might be allergic to the kitchen, her dad would have loved working alongside her to recreate Christina's pasta dish. When she'd finished, Nina spooned herself a generous bowlful and ate it alone at the kitchen counter. It was as delicious as Christina had promised.

#

On Wednesday, Nina drove to Barracat to pick up Edith and look at a couple of apartments Edith had earmarked for her. The awkward tension Nina had anticipated at being cooped up in a car with her new boss didn't materialize as Edith's natural friendliness quickly put her at ease. As they visited the apartments, conversation flowed easily, with Edith filling her in on the staff at Soul Fare and the behind-the-scenes workings of the restaurant. Edith displayed an unexpectedly dry sense of humor, and Nina found herself laughing more than she had in a long time.

Nina treated Edith to lunch at a local café (Edith wanted to scope out the competition) and they had a riotous time picking out all the flaws in the place. After lunch, Edith directed Nina to a two-bedroom apartment only a ten-minute drive from Soul Fare. The previous tenants had done a runner, so the apartment was currently empty. It was modern, close to the shops and even boasted a small garden. Nina immediately fell in love with it. Best of all, the landlord (a friend of Edith's) offered a reasonable rent and was happy for Nina to move in as early as next week.

After signing the lease, Nina dropped Edith off at her house and texted Olivia to see if she was up for a visit. She was, so Nina spent the rest of the afternoon helping Liv wash baby clothes and assemble a fancy-looking cot. When Ry arrived home from work, Nina broke the news of her move, and their delight that she'd be so much closer to them was gratifying confirmation of her attempt to reboot her life.

The one person she hadn't told was Lucas. Nina wanted to break the news to him before he heard it from someone else, and she intended to call him, she really did, but for some reason, she kept finding excuses to delay speaking to him.

The next two days were taken up with packing. On Friday, she tackled her bedroom drawers. Unbelievable how much junk she'd collected. More pathetic and disturbing were all the mementoes from Lucas—handwritten notes, fortune cookies, concert ticket stubs—that she'd kept over the years. She struggled for only the briefest second before making up her mind and tossing the whole lot into the trash.

Staring at their dumped history, Nina reached for her phone to call him, but then remembered Lucas had flown out this morning to spend the weekend with Tahlia. She didn't want to speak to him when he was with Tahlia. That just felt...icky.

Sunday afternoon, her back aching from hefting heavy boxes all weekend, Nina was lying on the couch watching a news snippet on a platypus rescue (yes, she was scraping the bottom of the TV barrel) and contemplating dinner (a bowl of muesli because that was all she had energy for) when her phone rang. Lucas.

"Hey," she answered.

"Is Ry pranking me?" Lucas asked. "Or are you really moving to Barracat?"

Oh, blast it. She exhaled heavily. "I'm really moving."

"When were you going to tell me?"

His voice was flat, but she knew him well enough to catch the hurt there. "You were away," she said lamely.

He was silent for so long, Nina thought he'd hung up. "Lucas?"

"Have you started packing?" he asked abruptly.

"I've made a start."

"I'm coming over to help," he said, and hung up.

Nina levered herself up and looked around. The apartment was a mess, boxes everywhere, kitchen utensils on the counter, waiting to be packed away, piles of books on the floor, half a slab of dark chocolate on a table, waiting to be eaten. It took every ounce of willpower to leave everything in its current state. She'd moved past the phase of rushing around trying to make everything look perfect for Lucas.

But while she was brave enough to leave her apartment as is, she didn't have the courage to leave herself as is: covered in a fine layer of dust, wearing the baggiest tracksuit pants and top, and taking bed hair to a whole new level. With a groan, she jumped into the shower, changed into clean clothes, and was in the middle of blow-drying her hair when Lucas rang the buzzer.

A week had passed since they'd last seen one another, and Nina was hit with the hot and achy realization of just how much she'd missed him during that time. There'd been no checking-in-on-you phone calls or impromptu visits or late-night texts. He was caught in Tahlia's tractor beam, and there was nothing she could do about it.

At his knock, she opened the door. In jeans and a sweatshirt and weekend stubble, he looked good. Her heart dipped, though, when she took in his unsmiling face. It was a measure of just how thrown he was by news of her move that he didn't immediately berate her for not checking the peephole.

"I shouldn't have to hear it from Ry," he said, not moving from the hallway.

"I'm sorry," she whispered. "I should have made more of an effort to tell you."

"Yes, you should have."

They stared at one another in silence. Then Lucas sighed and folded her into a hug. "Why Barracat?" he asked softly into her hair.

Because I need to put physical distance between us. Because I need to step out on a path that perhaps makes no sense on the surface, but which feels right to me, even when it also feels terrifying.

"It's a change," she said. "They need a manager with fresh ideas, a new take on things. I think I'd really make a difference there."

His body stiffened against hers, and she didn't need to look at him to read the large-print thought lighting up his brain: *there she goes crusading again, taking on another underdog at her own expense.*

To his credit, Lucas didn't say any of that. He simply held her for a few seconds longer and then let her go.

Inside the apartment, Lucas stood in the living room and silently took in the evidence of her decision. "Looks like you've already made quite a dent packing," he said at last.

Nina straightened a barstool that didn't need straightening. "The moving van's coming Thursday, so I thought I'd better get started."

Lucas nodded. "I guess I'll have to find someone else to look after my plants."

Her throat was tight. "I guess you will."

It was such a harmless, innocuous exchange, but Nina knew with a kind of awful clarity that they'd crossed some sort of Rubicon in their friendship. Judging from the shadow clouding his face, Lucas seemed to sense it too.

"How about an espresso martini?" Nina asked suddenly, because it was that kind of week and she was at her happiest in the kitchen. She could use a dose of happy right now.

"Sounds good," he said, making himself comfortable on a barstool.

She told him about Edith and Soul Fare while she moved about the kitchen gathering vodka, Kahlua, and an espresso shot and pouring them into a cocktail shaker. She added ice, shook it up, and strained the creamy mixture into two martini glasses. A sprinkle of coffee beans on top finished it off.

She raised her glass. "To not jumping in front of a bullet."

He narrowed his eyes at her. "To staying employed for at least six months."

"To finally dating someone whose IQ is double digits."

"To dating men with normal bowel function."

A laugh burst out of her. "You win."

"I expected to," Lucas said, smiling. "I did have a whopper of a trump card."

"I was wondering when you'd bring it up," Nina said as they clinked glasses. "You've shown unusual restraint this past week."

"Only because I needed a week to recover."

"Big baby," she said. "What'll you do when you have your own children?"

As soon as the words were out of her mouth, she wanted to kick herself. No bringing up the subject of children with Lucas. She didn't want to jump-start his daddy hormones. Not with Tahlia and her genetically blessed womb waiting in the wings. She hastily gestured to his martini. "How's your drink?"

"Delicious."

Nina took a sip of her martini. Delicious and decadent, she thought as the caffeine and alcohol flooded her bloodstream.

Lucas ran his thumb along the rim of his glass. "You planning on seeing him again?"

"Who?"

"Brian."

She shook her head. "No. We, uh, called it quits."

Lucas nodded, his face unreadable.

"How's it going with Tahlia?"

"Good," Lucas said. "Yeah, pretty good."

When she skewered him with a look, he rolled his eyes. "You and your need for details." He cleared his throat. "I met her family."

"You did?" Nina swallowed. Or tried to. There was a monstrous lump in her throat all of a sudden. "Wow, looks like the relationship is progressing."

"Looks like it."

"So how did it go, the whole meeting-the-family thing?"

Lucas was silent for a moment. "On the one hand, really well. Pretty much the entire family was there on Saturday."

"By entire family, you mean...?"

"Tahlia's parents, two sisters, a brother, grandparents. A few aunts showed up as well." Her face must have shown her shock, because Lucas gave a rueful nod. "Yeah, it was like the entire family tree had planted itself in the backyard."

"Just to meet you?" she asked faintly.

"No. It was her brother's thirtieth, and Tahlia wanted me to join in the celebration."

Nina took a large swallow of her drink. "You got along with everyone?" *Please say there was a huge blowup, the parents hate you, the sisters hit on you, the brother thinks you're an idiot, and Tahlia never wants to see you again.*

"Yeah, I got along with everyone. What I found interesting is that every member of Tahlia's family is in some or other high-powered occupation. Even her grandparents, both ex-lawyers, serve on the board of a major economic forum."

Nina deflated in her seat. "A high-achieving family. That's...interesting."

"Actually, it was pretty irritating."

She perked up. "Irritating?" What a beautiful-sounding word. "Irritating, how?"

"They couldn't leave their phones alone," Lucas explained, frowning. "Throughout the afternoon, everyone was either taking calls, checking messages, or responding to e-mails. The whole family was in permanent work mode. It was irritating," he said again.

Nina took an oh-so-casual sip of her drink. "Even Tahlia?"

"Not so much," Lucas said, then added reluctantly, "but yeah, she was also on her phone."

Oh, the unveiling of a tiny, irritating flaw! May it grow and multiply! Nina gave a faintly judgmental "Hmm," while nonchalantly nudging a utility bill over her own phone charging on the counter.

Draining the last of his martini, Lucas got to his feet and rolled up his sleeves. "Right, where do you want me to start?"

Her eyes flew up to meet his. "You're serious about helping me pack?"

"Of course."

Joyous relief rose up inside her. She hadn't realized just how alone she was feeling until this very instant. Now there was the reassurance that for the next couple of hours she wouldn't have to face packing up her life on her own.

"The kitchen," she said with a smile. "Let's tackle it together."

Chapter Twenty

"Cody, table four has no water," Nina said.

Cody shot her a sullen look and hauled his skinny frame off to the water station to collect a jug and glasses and carry them over to table four, whose occupants fell on the water like tourists lost in the desert.

Fuming silently, Nina gave a welcoming smile to a young couple who looked like they were on a first date. The poor man appeared drenched in nerves. At the rate he was going (he'd forgotten to hold open Soul Fare's heavy door for his date and it had swung back to knock her in the shoulder), Nina didn't hold out much hope for him.

While she got them settled at their table and handed out menus, she did a quick and discreet scan of the dining room, searching for other neglected diners. It didn't take long. Table two appeared to be building their own mini version of a border wall with all the plates that had stacked up there.

Anger flared again, clear and bright. A busy Friday lunch trade was coming up, and the staff were dragging their feet and fighting her every step of the way. After two weeks of working at Soul Fare, Nina was ready to fire the lot of them and start afresh.

Unfortunately, there was no time to daydream about a mass ousting. She had to rescue this man from his nerves before he completely botched his chances. Smiling, she threw out an easy-to-catch joke and a compliment on his shirt, watching with satisfaction as he laughed and visibly straightened in his seat. Amazing what an injection of humor and confidence could do to change a person's appearance. When Nina saw the young lady looking at him with renewed interest flaring in her heart-shaped face, she quietly congratulated herself. *It's up to you now, buddy*.

As she left them to get to know one another better, Nina noted with disbelief that table two still hadn't been cleared. She signaled to

Camille. The brown-haired, middle-aged server had so far proved to be the least hostile of all the Soul Fare staff, but Nina noticed her lips still tightening in resentment as she set about cleaning the table.

As the minutes crept closer to lunch hour and guests continued to trickle in, Nina worked the room. Her role was deceptively simple: she had to ensure the food they served was first rate, her guests were content, staff were doing their jobs properly, and the restaurant was turning a profit. It all sounded straightforward, but she was at the end of her second week at Soul Fare, and most of her time had been wasted chasing and cajoling staff who shouldn't need babysitting.

Nina knew from painful experience that starting a new job was difficult as you struggled to find your feet. The restaurant industry, in particular, was rife with power plays and hierarchies of ego, so she'd anticipated a certain level of acrimony when she took on the role of restaurant manager, but she hadn't been prepared for this level of antipathy.

In truth, Nina was convinced that most of the staff were on a collaborative mission to make her working conditions unbearable in order to force her to quit. At first, it had seemed like an unfortunate series of mishaps: Cody brushing past her with a sizzle platter of prawns that seared her forearm, Ano, the head chef, giving her the wrong specials and then insinuating she'd misheard, Jeena serving her an oversalted staff meal, and personal items from her handbag showing up in the cooler or ladies' bathroom. But after two weeks of incidents like these, Nina knew they weren't accidents.

Edith didn't seem to notice anything amiss. She'd been in and out of the restaurant, going over the books with Nina, introducing her to everyone, and showing her how things worked, but she'd also been distracted, only staying for an hour or so at a time before hurrying back to the nursing home to be with her husband, whose Alzheimer's had spiraled.

Before she'd left yesterday, Edith had let slip one telling comment. "The staff here, they're like family, and protective of me," she'd murmured. "Give them time."

How much time? Nina had wanted to ask. Time enough for them to inflict some serious sabotage while they got over themselves? Although she'd heard some of the industry horror stories—employees locked in cooler rooms, strung up on meat hooks, burned with hot knives—this was behavior on a scale she'd never encountered before. Any attempt to talk to her staff about their behavior was met with either blank stares or surly silence. It was clear to her now why Soul Fare went through restaurant managers at an alarming rate.

Every morning, Nina had to go to work and feel the staff watching her. Watching and waiting. Waiting to see if she would run babbling to Edith. If she would collapse into a tearful, broken huddle in the middle of service. If she would crack and lose her temper in a spectacular fashion.

They didn't know her very well. If she was going to cry, she'd do it at home. Alone. It was a pride thing. And there was no way she'd run to Edith. Edith had enough worries of her own. She wasn't going to add to them. Anyway, Edith had hired her to do a job, and Nina wasn't going to let a bunch of staff behaving like recalcitrant children stop her from doing it. Pride again. She hadn't decided if it was a strength or a weakness. Maybe it was both.

Anger, though, that was her Achilles' heel. There was an overwhelming part of her that whispered she didn't have to take this crap. She had a degree behind her and years of practical experience. She was tempted to get rid of all of them (or at least the main troublemakers) and gather a new team around her, despite what it would cost in terms of time and effort. Edith, however, from day one, had been oddly adamant that Nina had to work with the current staff for at least six months.

Right now, six months seemed like an eternity.

Nina had just finished showing a family to a table when Camille hurried up to her. "There's trouble in the kitchen," she said in a low voice.

Nina's heart sank. Friday lunch service, often the busiest time in a restaurant, was looming. "What kind of trouble?"

Camille's brown eyes were unreadable. "The kind that needs your intervention."

Suppressing her irritation, Nina nodded. "All right, I'll sort it out."

Camille drifted away, and Nina hoped it was to do her job and not sneak away for another extended smoke break.

Before she headed to the kitchen, Nina took a quick look around the dining area, which was buzzing with animated conversations and diners tucking into their food. Jeena was working the cash register, and Nina noticed with a jolt the smile transforming her pretty face as she interacted with departing guests. Where was the sourness which seeped from her whenever Nina had to deal with her?

Cody was busy with a new table, and Frankie was churning through coffee orders. The thirty-six-year-old barista had been a teenager when his family moved here from Australia, but his accent was still strong and charming. He caught her eye and gave her a friendly wink. She smiled back. The short, plump barista had a kind face and showed no qualms answering all her work-related questions. She was grateful for his warm response and the fact that he showed no interest in restaurant politics. Frankie lived and breathed coffee.

Satisfied that everything seemed to be under control, Nina pushed through the swinging doors into the windowless kitchen. The heat hit her first, followed by an incredible wave of smells: basil, onions, garlic, something roasting in the oven, probably Ano's buttery Hasselback potatoes, one of Edith's favorite dishes.

And then the unfolding drama hit her: Ano's tall body looming over the line cook...what was his name? She normally had a good head for names, it was an integral part of her job, but his had slipped her mind.

The nameless line cook looked terrified, and no wonder. Ano, even in a benign mood, was an intimidating sight. But Ano in a bad mood, which seemed to be the current case, judging by the wooden spoon he was brandishing and the fierce scowl on his handsome ebony face, was a truly terrifying spectacle. She remembered the first time she'd accompanied Edith into the kitchen to witness the head chef in front of a stockpot barking out orders, how the sheer physical presence of him—his barrel chest, long legs and block-out-the-sun shoulders—had dominated the kitchen.

"A rookie mistake!" Ano growled now. "You should know better!"

"Yes, Chef."

"You don't deserve to be in my kitchen if you forget such a simple thing."

"Yes, Chef."

Nina frowned. The line cook's face was swollen, his eyes red rimmed and streaming. He looked like he was in agony.

"Everything okay in here?" she asked carefully.

When Ano stiffened, she knew it wasn't surprise at her presence. She had the feeling he'd known the exact instant she'd stepped into his domain. Slowly he turned to face her. Wearing a white chef's jacket and a black bandana to keep the sweat out of his eyes, he regarded her with barely disguised contempt.

The urge to take an instinctive step back came over her. She batted it away. She'd been fighting that urge ever since Edith had first introduced her to the thirty-something head chef, saying, "Nina, I'd like you to meet Ano, our genius on the stove."

"The name's Anotidaishe," he'd said, his bottomless dark eyes daring her to pronounce it properly.

"He's just teasing," Edith had said fondly. "Everyone calls him Ano."

Everyone but you, his eyes had communicated, and because Ano had that whole kiss-the-ring-of-Caesar vibe going for him, the rest of the staff had followed his lead like brainless lemmings.

From snippets of staff gossip, Nina had found out that Ano had been a teenager when he'd emigrated here from Zimbabwe. He'd worked at a butcher's shop after school, then washed dishes in the kitchen of a four-star hotel. From there, he'd climbed the ladder from line cook to sauté chef to sous chef. And now, here he was, head chef at Soul Fare, and a thorn in her side.

"Everything's fine," Ano said to her now. She didn't miss his subtext, *your cue to get out of my kitchen.*

The puffy-faced line cook—Stefan, that was his name!—flicked a pleading glance in her direction.

Nina hesitated. She stole a quick look at his station, glimpsed the chilies on the cutting board, and realized what he'd done: touched his eyes before washing his hands. A definite rookie mistake.

She opened her mouth to step in, all guns blazing with sympathy and advice, when she noticed Sunan, the kitchen assistant, a small-boned, quiet man from Thailand, who was nearly eclipsed by the towering pile of pots in the sink in front of him, hunch his shoulders as though bracing for an explosion.

In an instant, Nina understood what had happened to all the previous front-of-house managers who'd dared to encroach on Ano's territory. If she sided with Stefan, she'd be heading down that path, and none of the kitchen crew, no matter how well she got along with them, no matter how she championed their rights, would stand up for her. Not if they wanted to keep their jobs. In the kitchen, there was no such thing as democracy. The chef was the culinary dictator.

And right now, this dictator had his huge arms folded across his chest, waiting for her response.

Nina swallowed, trapped between pragmatism and her conscience. While she couldn't fault Ano's work ethic or skill or his preternaturally calm head for service, there still hung a serious question mark over his empathy level.

Then on the counter behind Ano, she spotted the milk carton. Relief unfurled inside her. Behind all the bluster, this giant of a man was hiding a small soft spot. The kitchen crew was his family, and a good chef took care of his family.

Keeping her tone casual, she said, "Looks like you've got everything under control, Ano. If you need eye drops, I have some."

Ano lowered his arms to his sides. "That'll be good," he said tersely.

"I'll send Camille in with them." She'd send Camille because she was the one who'd set her up, Nina realized now as she headed out to the dining area. Camille had worked here long enough to know Ano would have everything under control in the kitchen, but she'd no doubt hoped Nina's interference would put her at odds with the chef.

And here she'd assumed Camille was the least antagonistic of all the staff. Live and learn, Nina thought with a tinge of bitterness.

At least she had the satisfaction of knowing that Ano would direct Stefan to press a milk-soaked paper towel to his eyes to ease the burn and remove any last vestiges of chili oil. She hoped she'd read the situation correctly and somehow achieved the delicate balance of showing sympathy with the offer of the eye drops, yet still acknowledging Ano's authority and competence in the kitchen.

She had in no way won the war, but at least she'd managed to avert a nasty skirmish.

The moment she entered the dining room, Nina looked for Camille. She spotted her lurking at the water station and called her over, giving her the eye drops, but not saying anything else. Let her stew for a bit wondering what had happened, Nina thought. She'd wait until the end of the day to inform Camille that for the next two weeks, she'd be scraping off gum under the tables and cleaning the toilets.

#

"I'm thinking of quitting," Nina announced that evening.

"Don't you dare," Olivia said.

Nina glared at her phone, which was propped up on her stomach as she lay horizontal on her couch. What a shame her sister-in-law's voice carried so clearly on speaker. "It's been a nightmare two weeks, Liv."

"The first couple of weeks in any new job are horrid. You know that."

"I do." Nina sighed, staring out the window. "The thing is, I get along so well with Edith, the restaurant is great, and I can see so much potential there, but I can't realize that potential if the people who are supposed to be on my side are fighting me at every turn." She swallowed. "I wonder if it was a mistake taking on this role."

Olivia's voice was gentle. "You need to go the distance, Nina."

Nina felt color climb into her cheeks. There was a disquieting ring of truth to Olivia's words. She stared at all the boxes she hadn't yet unpacked. Was there a subconscious part of her that had anticipated, even planned, on not staying long in this position?

When she remained silent, Olivia said, "There's a reason you phoned me and not Cheryl or Ry or Lucas. You expected me to talk you off the ledge."

Nina closed her eyes. It was scary sometimes how well her sister-in-law could read her. Only with Olivia could she bare herself like this, knowing Liv would understand and sympathize, but also dish out whatever tough love was needed.

With everyone else, in response to all their messages regarding her new job, Nina had simply fired off generic texts:

Working hard and finding my way!

Enjoying the challenge!

Staff are keeping me on my toes!

Lots of smiley emojis and thumbs-up signs. Lots of fake, fake, fake.

Everyone appeared to accept her texts at face value. Lucas worried her since his emotional radar was more finely tuned than most, but he was too busy with work and Tahlia to pick up anything amiss. There was some consolation in that. She couldn't face his reaction, couldn't face the I-told-you-so expression he would be unable to hide. She was barely coping with her own disappointment and still trying to forget Tammy's reaction when she heard the news. "What the heck, Nina! I go to Italy for a couple of weeks and you end up in Fartsville! Were you snorting something when you made that decision? I thought you were going to move in with me. Well, don't expect me to visit the back end of nowhere anytime soon."

Nina confessed, "I'm emotionally exhausted, Liv."

"I know."

"It feels like the staff are all out to get me."

"Then get to them first."

"How? Fire the lot of them? If Edith gave me carte blanche in that area, I would."

"No," Olivia said thoughtfully, "dismissing them would be admitting defeat. In *The Art of War*, the key is to subdue the enemy without fighting."

Nina could hear Ryan's aggrieved voice in the background. "C'mon, Liv, not *The Art of War*! I'm starving. What about dinner? What does Sun Tzu say about feeding the forces?"

Her brother clearly didn't know his wife, Nina thought. Olivia had landed on her favorite subject, and Ryan and his bottomless stomach stood no chance.

"You need to know your enemy, in this case your staff," Olivia said, her voice taking on a determined note. "Knowing something important about them will be critical in turning them into allies. Right now, your staff are so busy protecting themselves from change, they're missing an opportunity for growth."

"You're saying I'm the change they fear?" Nina asked dubiously. For the life of her, she couldn't imagine inspiring any kind of fear in Ano. Contempt, yes. Hostility, absolutely. But fear? The notion was laughable.

"Only because you represent change," Olivia explained. "All you have to do is persuade your staff that change is a good thing."

"You make it sound so easy."

"Unfortunately, people are hardwired to resist change, so you have a tough task ahead of you. But I bet it's easier than telling your mom and Lucas that you quit after two weeks."

Chapter Twenty-One

At precisely 10:00 a.m. Monday morning, Soul Fare's door opened and in shuffled Angela, Claire, and Bianca in a potent cloud of rose water and lavender powder. At the sight of the three elderly ladies, Nina's mood instantly lifted, the near-permanent tangle of knots in her stomach easing a little. Their quirky movie club gatherings every Monday and Thursday were fast becoming the high points of her week.

"Hello, ladies," she said with a smile, collecting three menus from the hostess stand.

Angela squinted at her. "You're looking a little Anne Hathaway this morning."

"Hathaway in *Les Mis* or *Valentine's Day*?" Nina asked.

Angela cackled. "The latter."

"In that case, thank you for the compliment, Angela."

The weekend had achieved its purpose, then, Nina thought with satisfaction. After Friday's soul-stripping chat with Olivia, she'd decided to implement some changes. First change, a reasonable bedtime. She'd read somewhere that tiredness was linked to feelings of despair and hopelessness, so no more binge-watching late into the night to escape thoughts of work.

Second change, healthy eating habits. After weeks of emotional eating and feeling worse than ever, she had a pantry purge, secretly mortified at how many items she was forced to throw away. Her fridge and pantry were currently stocked with fresh fruit, salad kits, wholegrain bread, and yogurt. Also, she was determined to ease up on her drinking. While she didn't believe she had a drinking problem, she was astute enough to realize she tended to use alcohol as a coping mechanism.

Third change, prompted by Olivia's advice: going the distance. She couldn't keep living in a holding pattern, waiting for a better version of life to come along. With that in mind, she'd spent the weekend unpacking all her boxes, putting up her pictures, and buying a pretty and heavily discounted comforter on a lunch break. All in an effort to make the apartment look like a home.

The result of the weekend changes? Nina had arrived at work this morning feeling positive and energized. Not even Jeena's sullen demeanor as she completed her preshift setup could drag her down. Neither could Camille's displeasure that she was still on bathroom duty. The fact that Angela had also noticed a visible difference in her further boosted her confidence. She had a hopeful feeling this week would turn out better than the previous ones.

"Your usual drinks?" she asked when the ladies were seated at their corner table.

They nodded. Although Nina knew their preferences by heart, she obediently wrote down their order—decaf vanilla latte (Claire), extra hot flat white (Bianca), and half-strength skinny cappuccino (Angela)—because on her first day working here, Angela had bluntly informed her they didn't trust other people's memories when their own were so faulty.

"Excuse me," Claire burst out, and she made a beeline for the bathroom.

Angela said, "The prune juice obviously worked."

"Claire's been struggling for a while," Bianca confided to Nina.

"Constipation, thy name is old age," declared Angela.

Bianca let out a hoot of laughter, and her dentures fell out of her mouth.

Nina gasped, and they all stared at the yellow-stained teeth on the table.

Finally, Angela said, "Told you the lining was wearing out."

Angela and Bianca started giggling and couldn't stop. Nina was suddenly grateful the restaurant had no liquor license. She shuddered to think what might happen if the ladies had alcohol flowing through their bloodstream.

Bianca retrieved her dentures and popped them back into her mouth. A relieved-looking Claire returned to the table and wanted to know if there were any prune dishes on the menu (there weren't).

On her way to give Frankie their drinks order, Nina passed Cody escorting a woman in unflattering gym clothes to table three and asking, "Are you waiting for someone?"

Nina winced. Surely that question hadn't come out of Cody's mouth. Surely he'd been trained in the basics.

"No, I'm not waiting for anyone," the woman replied, looking irritated.

Squelching the urge to intervene, Nina chatted to Frankie while she waited for Cody to finish taking her order. As soon as he was done, she took him aside and said quietly, "Never ask a person dining alone if they're waiting for someone."

Cody frowned. "Why not?"

"The implication is that the dining experience isn't complete if you're on your own."

"But I didn't mean it like that," he protested, face flushing.

"I know you didn't, but it could be interpreted that way."

"Okay, yeah, I get it. Won't ask the question again."

At least he was teachable and generally amiable, Nina thought. Unlike a certain temperamental chef, currently in the foulest of moods. Ano's supply delivery had been an hour late this morning, and his disgruntlement still lingered, infecting everyone. The temptation to take one of the Japanese knives Ano was so fond of and prick the part of him that ought to contain a conscience was almost overwhelming. Big baby, she couldn't help thinking as she exited the kitchen, almost bumping into Camille.

"Everything okay?" she asked the server.

"Everything's fine," Camille replied, avoiding eye contact.

Nina opened her mouth to pursue it because Camille was obviously not fine, but she'd already disappeared into the kitchen. Nina knew there was no point in following her and trying to discuss anything in Ano's domain, not when the chef's territory felt like the lion's den.

Her phone beeped, and she checked the screen. A text from Lucas asking if he could come over tonight. Her pulse jumped with excitement. She'd last seen him over two weeks ago when he'd helped her box up all her kitchen gadgets. Yes, she'd informed his raised eyebrows, she was very much aware of her stockpile. While some women collected shoes (Olivia) or jewelry (Mom) or men (Tammy), Nina had a weakness for kitchen gadgets.

Lucas hadn't visited her new place, or chatted to her about her new job. Knowing his compulsion for interrogation, Nina had mixed feelings about having him over, but she craved a friendly face after two weeks of unfriendly ones.

She texted back: *Are you expecting dinner?*

Hoping but not expecting, Lucas replied.

Soup okay?

Sounds perfect.

Great. She had a tasty tomato pasta soup she could whip up in no time. Suddenly, the day looked so much brighter. Humming under her breath, Nina put her phone away, made her way to the hostess stand, and glanced around the restaurant. Her humming abruptly stopped. Only a quarter of the tables were occupied. At this time of the morning, it should be more full. With offices, shops, and a school close by, Soul Fare ought to be inundated with office workers conducting meetings over breakfast, shop staff making a quick coffee run, and parents catching up after dropping off their kids.

The thought crossed Nina's mind that she might have to sit down with Edith and talk about possible changes to Soul Fare. Perhaps if the restaurant boasted a more modern and fresh approach, it would attract new customers. She couldn't shake the uneasy feeling that Soul Fare would fold in less than a year if it didn't improve in the three critical areas of food, ambience, and service. But the timing wasn't right for this kind of conversation with Edith. Edith was so worried about Bill, spending more and more time at the nursing home so she could hold on to whatever fragments of memory her husband still retained, that she had no head space for the restaurant right now. Ironically, Nina knew Edith was trusting her to take care of things.

Throughout the weekend, Nina had reflected on Olivia's words, thinking of ways she could reach her staff. Olivia had said she needed to know her enemy. With that in mind, Nina decided to take every opportunity to study them, to try to pick up on clues that would give her an insight into each of them, a chink in their change-averse armor.

She watched as Jeena delivered drinks to Angela, Claire, and Bianca, effortlessly drawing smiles from the three ladies as she took down their food order. Jeena definitely had a knack for elevating a diner's experience. She was attentive without being intrusive, and diners asked for her by name. Nina suspected that if she could get Jeena to warm to her, that would go a long way toward winning over the rest of the staff.

A short time later, with her new objective in mind, Nina caught Jeena in a quiet moment and gestured to the small sketchbook poking out of her apron. "I often see you doodling."

"I don't do it on work time," Jeena said defensively.

"I didn't say you did."

"I only draw on my breaks."

"Right," Nina said, digging for patience, "I'm agreeing with you here."

"Do you want me to stop? Is that what you want?"

"What? No, of course not." Confusion bubbled up. She'd started this conversation in an attempt to connect with Jeena, and it was slowly careening into a multicar pileup. "Okay, Jeena, let's press Pause here," she said. "Firstly, I have no issue with you working on your sketchbook. I'm simply interested in what you draw in there."

Jeena regarded her skeptically for a moment, then she said, "Okay."

Nina gritted her teeth. "So what do you draw in there?"

Jeena shrugged. "Stuff."

Nina breathed out hard. Where was a toothpick so she could stab herself in the eye? It had to be less painful than this. "Right, well, great chatting with you. I'll let you get on with your *stuff*."

She walked away, muttering to herself to stay the course. Olivia had warned her it wouldn't be easy.

Ten minutes later, Nina spotted Cody taking a mini break at one of the back tables. Although she'd crashed and burned with Jeena, she might have better luck with Cody. He was scrolling through his phone and glanced up when she sat opposite him.

She ignored the expression of discomfort on his face. "Hey, Cody."

"Hey."

She gestured to his phone. "Catching up with friends?"

"Actually, I'm searching for new songs."

She nodded, doing her best to project interest. "You obviously like music."

"Yeah."

She knew he'd recently turned twenty (everyone but her had been invited to his birthday celebration at the local pub), but she didn't know much else about him. "Are you studying anything?"

"No."

"Okay." Nina cleared her throat into the awkward pause. "Is there anything in particular you're passionate about?"

He shrugged. "Not really."

She tried not to sound desperate. "Nothing?"

He thought for a second. "I'm into music."

"So you said." With relief, Nina noticed the arrival of several more patrons, and she got to her feet. "I better get back to work. Thanks for the chat, Cody."

"Yeah, anytime," he said cheerfully, oblivious to her sarcasm.

Nina headed toward a mother and son sitting at table five. Hopefully, her diners wouldn't give her as much grief as her staff. Parents loved it when others noticed and complimented their children and Nina had become adept at finding something positive to say for even the brattiest of offspring.

"Your son has beautiful eyes," she said now to the tired-looking mother, despite the fact that those beautiful eyes were currently slits of sullen rage because an iPad had run out of battery.

The mother perked up slightly. "Thank you."

The son glared at Nina. "You have a booster pack in this place?"

"No, we don't."

"What a dump," he muttered.

"But we have plenty to eat and drink," Nina said, forcing a smile. "What can I get you?"

"Coke."

The urge to whack a *please* into him engulfed her. She kept her smile in place. "Coke coming up."

Nina caught sight of Angela signaling to her. Excusing herself, she made her way to their table.

"We can't make up our minds," Angela said.

"No, we can't," agreed Bianca. "We'd like your opinion."

"About the food?" Nina asked, confused. "I'm sure Jeena—"

"Not the food," Claire cut in. "Today's movie under discussion."

"Sure, I'm happy to give my opinion. What's the movie?"

"*The Secret Life of Walter Mitty*," Bianca said.

"Oh, I love that movie!" Nina said. She'd watched it years ago with Lucas. He'd been going through a rough patch with his business at the time, and she'd just broken up with the handsome but shallow bartender she'd been casually seeing for a couple of months. The feel-good nature of the film had gone a long way toward boosting their spirits. Eager to contribute, Nina pulled up a chair.

"I don't get it," Claire began.

Nina jumped right in. "The movie is all about Walter escaping his monotonous life through daydreams where he's the hero on these wild adventures. The best part is when he embarks on a real-life adventure and it's about him finding his true self and embracing life." She sighed. "It's incredibly inspirational."

The three ladies stared at her blankly.

"Yes, thank you for that," Angela said, "but what we want to know is, why did Walter choose the red car?"

Nina was silent for a few seconds. "I'm not sure I understand."

Bianca said, "You know the scene where Walter lands in Greenland and he's at the car rental place and there are only two choices—the red or the blue car—and he chooses the red car. Well, why did he choose the red one?"

"He should have picked the blue car," Claire said. "I like blue. It's a soothing color."

"I like blue too," Bianca said. "Blue was the better choice."

Angela shook her head. "Walter was right to choose the red car. Red goes better with his dark hair."

"What do you think, Nina?" Bianca asked, and all three ladies looked at her expectantly.

I think I've tumbled into the rabbit hole, Nina thought. She cleared her throat. "Actually, I like both colors."

Angela waved an imperious hand. "But you must have a favorite of the two."

"Not really."

"I didn't take you for a fence-sitter," said Angela pointedly.

Nina swallowed. "Well, red is seen as a bold, adventurous color, and it's probably fitting that Walter chooses the red car because he's stepped out of his comfort zone."

Claire and Bianca let out disappointed sighs.

Angela gave a satisfied nod. "Told you red goes better with Walter's coloring."

#

In the quiet period after the lunch rush, Nina slipped out into the alley behind the restaurant to fill her lungs with fresh air and her stomach with Ano's chicken schnitzel burger. She was methodically making her way through all the dishes on the menu, and today was the turn of Ano's burger, popular with business people wanting a fast and tasty lunch option. So far, she was reasonably satisfied with most of the menu offerings. They were classic dishes and done well, but Nina couldn't help the nagging feeling that they lacked something. She couldn't communicate this to Ano, not until she'd determined what that elusive something was, but she did make it a point to provide feedback on a dish she'd tasted. The first time she'd done this, complimented Ano on his smashed avo offering, he'd shot her an incredulous look, as though she'd broken royal culinary protocol. Nina hadn't let that deter her. Instead, she'd persevered in letting him know what she thought in the hope that honest feedback would break down Ano's barriers. Soon, Nina noticed that Ano had exchanged his incredulous looks for brusque nods. Progress of sorts, she'd thought. Then yesterday, she'd been caught up in such a steady stream of disasters—a diner throwing up on his table and another attempting to do a runner—that she had no opportunity to give Ano feedback on his wild mushroom arancini balls, which she'd managed to wolf down in a micro break. When Ano had sought her out at the end of the day to gruffly ask her what she'd thought of them, Nina had nearly fallen off her feet in surprise. Acting casual, like it was no big deal the head chef was soliciting her opinion, she'd told him truthfully that she'd found them very flavorsome. Ano had nodded and walked away, not saying anything, but for hours afterward, Nina had nurtured the buoyant feeling that Ano had valued her opinion enough to seek it out. That was something. A small something, but she could work with it.

Keeping a steady grip on her chicken schnitzel burger, Nina stepped outside and stopped short when she spotted Frankie sitting on a milk crate, soaking up the sun as he stared at the screen on his phone.

"Oh, hey, Frankie. I didn't know you were out here."

"No worries. You're welcome to join me if you don't mind the economy seating."

"I don't mind." She plonked herself on a crate next to him. "At least there's legroom."

She stretched out her legs and balanced her plate on her lap. While she ate her burger—sharing half with Frankie and both of them of the opinion that while the schnitzel had a delicious crunch, the tomato relish was ho-hum—Frankie told her about his dream to one day open his own roastery. He spoke about coffee the way a wine lover would rhapsodize about wine. His Australian accent was so appealing, Nina decided he could be discussing toilet paper and she could still listen to him for hours.

"What about you?" Frankie asked. "You settling in okay?"

"Getting there slowly."

"Uh-huh. Staff still giving you trouble?"

So it was that obvious. She wiped her mouth with a napkin and nodded, unable to speak.

"Give them time. They'll come round."

The same unhelpful narrative as Edith's, Nina thought. Frankie's expression, however, was so sympathetic, she was tempted to offload onto him, but she knew how dangerous that could be. Restaurants were hotbeds of gossip, and Frankie, as sweet as he seemed, gulped down gossip like an espresso shot. She didn't want her words to one day come back to bite her. But she couldn't help admitting, "They're certainly a tough lot."

"Yeah, they are. I won't deny it." He blew out a stream of smoke. "They warmed to me quickly enough, but I'm not their manager."

"Yeah, I'm evil incarnate at the moment."

"Be patient with them," Frankie said. "They've had a rough time of it."

Nina focused on brushing crumbs off her lap, all the while thinking, *Poor things, did they lose all their steak knives in the backs of unsuspecting managers?*

"Any other advice on how to get the staff to warm to me?" Nina asked.

"Empower them," Frankie answered. "Give them leeway to be innovative."

She nodded, her interest stirred.

"I believe they're bored," he continued. "They're doing the same thing in the same way with the same set of tools. They need to be challenged."

Hmm, staff who were averse to change, but still wanting to be challenged. On impulse, she asked, "What about you, Frankie?"

His eyes lit up. "I'm keen to introduce more varied items on the drinks menu. Matcha lattes. Golden lattes. Wet chais. We're seeing an increase in health-conscious diners, and our menu should cater to this."

Nina nodded slowly, mulling over what he'd said, which was uncannily along the lines of what she'd been thinking. "I like your ideas," she said. "I'll talk to Edith, run some suggestions past her, see if I can get her approval on them."

Frankie's face fell. "Edith's not big on change," he said after a moment. "She and Bill have been running Soul Fare pretty much the same way since it first opened. There've been a few improvements, but nothing big."

Nina frowned. "So other restaurant managers have tried to introduce changes?"

"Tried and failed," Frankie confirmed grimly.

\#

It had to happen sooner or later. Nina had experienced the Tripadvisor trap in nearly every restaurant she'd worked in. This particular episode occurred after lunch in the form of a twenty-something, denim-wearing solo diner who'd polished off his fish pie and then called her over to ask if she could comp his meal because he was writing a review for Tripadvisor. Nina struggled to keep her expression neutral. Did he really think he was the first diner to try this? She informed him politely that she was sorry, but she couldn't do that. What she really wanted to say was *seriously, could you be any more cheap?* It didn't matter, though, how pleasantly she let him down, because she could tell from his offended exit that they'd be receiving a bad review.

Knowing there was frustratingly little she could do about it, Nina retreated to the tiny office tucked away at the back of the restaurant to catch up on paperwork. She was making changes to the staff rota when her phone beeped with a text from Tammy asking if they could meet up tonight in the city. Nina tapped her pen on the desk. She hadn't seen her friend since her return from Italy. It would be good to catch up, to hear all about her trip and try to repair the damage caused by her announcement that she'd moved out of the city. Unfortunately, she'd already committed the evening to Lucas.

She typed: *Sorry, busy tonight.*

Someone's finally got herself a social life, Tammy replied.

Nina frowned at the dig. The frown deepened when Tammy's follow-up message came through: *Giving Brian a second chance?*

Nice try, Nina thought. She'd messaged Tammy a brief rundown on what had happened with Brian and how she was never, ever going to listen to her recommendations again.

But she was not above her own little payback dig. Knowing how Tammy felt about Lucas, she texted back: *Seeing Lucas tonight.*

Less than five seconds later, Tammy answered: *So still no social life.*

Nina shook her head at herself. What was she thinking? She was crazy to spar verbally with Tammy. The woman had no boundaries. Honestly, she had enough people crap at work to deal with. She didn't want whatever broken sewage pipe Tammy was carrying around to overflow onto her day as well.

Gritting her teeth, she dug around for her nice gene and messaged: *What about another day this week?*

Let's see, was Tammy's sulky response.

#

Leaving her office twenty minutes later, Nina bumped into Camille, who was standing outside her door, holding a cup of coffee.

"Everything okay, Camille?" Nina asked.

Camille offered her the coffee. "This is for you."

Nina was momentarily lost for words. "Me?"

"I know you like a latte late in the afternoon. One sugar, right?"

"One sugar," Nina confirmed, touched that Camille had gone out of her way to extend an olive branch. "Thank you, Camille."

The server nodded and made an effort to smile. Nina sipped her coffee (whoa, way too sweet, but she wasn't about to complain and ruin the moment) and asked about Camille's family. They had an actual two-minute conversation about Camille's rebellious teenage son before the server excused herself.

Hope flared inside Nina. Olivia was right. Sometimes people simply needed time, and sometimes they needed you to act in a consistently fair and friendly manner. Maybe she'd take Camille off bathroom duty sooner than planned, Nina mused as she headed to the dining area.

The room was only half-full, and Nina immediately noticed the large, ruddy-faced male diner sitting alone and scrolling through his phone at one of Jeena's tables. His face looked familiar. She did what she usually did whenever she wanted to know anything Soul Fare related, she went straight to her source. "He a regular?" she asked Frankie, tilting her head in the direction of the man.

"Yeah, he comes in twice a week," Frankie said over the hissing of the steam wand. "Always sits at one of Jeena's tables."

Hmm, it wasn't uncommon for diners to prefer particular servers, Nina thought, but she couldn't help wondering if it was Jeena's service he favored or if the man had a thing for her.

"Any other details about him?" Nina asked.

Frankie poured the heated milk into a mug. "He's a mocha man."

"Seriously, Frankie?"

"It's how my brain works," he said with a shrug. "Look, I think his name's Brandon and I think he works in sales, but I *know* he likes mochas."

There was a simple way to solve this. Nina went over to maybe-Brandon and introduced herself. She found out his name was Brayden, not Brandon, and although he seemed polite and friendly, there was something in his flat-eyed expression that made her uneasy.

After Brayden left, she asked Jeena, "Have you had any problems with him?"

Jeena frowned. "Who? Brayden?"

"Yes."

"No, no problems."

Jeena's hesitation was minute, but Nina caught it. "I hear he comes in quite regularly."

"Yeah, he's a big tipper."

Nina framed her next words carefully. "If there are any problems with any patron, you know you can come to me."

Jeena gave her a you've-got-to-be-kidding-me look. Nina wanted to continue the conversation, sensing there was a whole lot more Jeena wasn't saying, but it was obvious she wasn't ready to open up. Maybe she'd never be ready, but Nina consoled herself with the thought that if Camille had come around, hopefully Jeena would too.

#

Nina switched off the last of the lights and locked up the restaurant. She wasn't feeling too well. In fact, for the last hour or so, she'd been feeling a little off, like she was coming down with something. Standing on the dark street, she leaned against Soul Fare's door, feeling sweat break out on her forehead. She didn't know if she could drive in this condition. She debated calling Olivia, who lived fifteen minutes away, but her pregnancy nausea had returned on the weekend with a vengeance, and Nina didn't want to drag her out when Liv was feeling so awful. She closed her eyes. Ryan worked late on Mondays, and she couldn't think of anyone else to call.

Taking a shaky breath, telling herself her apartment was only ten minutes away, Nina pushed off the door and staggered to her car. The drive home was a nightmarish blur of hanging on to the steering wheel and desperately fighting the nausea that battered her in one terrible wave after another.

The instant she pulled into her parking space, Nina flung open her car door and threw up onto the grass. As far as she could tell, there was no one around to witness her humiliation. Like a drunk, she stumbled to her first-floor apartment, unlocked her door, and barely managed to crawl to the bathroom before retching into the toilet. Spasms shook her body, and she could feel her vision wavering. Vaguely, she was aware of darkness rolling over her and her body falling onto the hard bathroom tiles.

Chapter Twenty-Two

"Nina, wake up. I need you to open your eyes." Lucas's deep voice was threaded through with worry. "Come on, honey, you're scaring the life out of me here. Please wake up."

Don't want to, Nina wanted to whisper. All her muscles ached. And her head... Her poor head throbbed unbearably. The thought of opening her eyes seemed like way too much effort, but Lucas wouldn't leave her alone. His voice kept urging her to wake up and talk to him.

Finally, just to shut him up, Nina opened her eyes. The first thing she saw was Lucas's face hovering over her.

"There you are," he said with a relieved smile.

"What happened?" She tried to lift her head, but dizziness swamped her.

"Take it easy." Lucas's hand was warm and comforting on her shoulder. "I imagine you're still pretty weak."

"Water," she croaked out.

Helping her sit up, Lucas carefully held a glass of water to her lips. "Small sips," he cautioned. "Let's not go through another round."

Nina cringed. Playing in her head like a disjointed film were hazy flashes of Lucas rubbing her back and murmuring indistinguishable words as over and over again, she emptied herself of everything inside her.

Staring down at her comforter, she whispered, "I'm so embarrassed you had to see me like that."

"Hey." He waited until her eyes met his. "Come on, it's me."

Exactly, she thought dismally. She looked down at herself. She was in her bed, in her pajamas, which meant that at some point, Lucas must have undressed her. Oh, the list of humiliations kept growing.

"Stop overthinking this," Lucas said firmly. "Remember when I ate that dodgy chicken and had to camp out in your apartment with its one bathroom and paper-thin walls?"

That got a small smile out of her. "I remember."

"So we're even," Lucas said easily.

"Uh-huh," she said, too worn out to disagree. "What time is it?"

"Nearly midnight."

"What?" Shocked, Nina sat up straighter. She'd closed up the restaurant just before six and had arrived home soon after. How long had she lain on the bathroom floor after passing out? She remembered waking up at one point and throwing up so violently, she couldn't draw a breath, feeling so awful and panicky, there was a part of her that was afraid she was going to die. But then Lucas was there, and he was holding her and saying, "It's all right, everything will be okay, just breathe for me."

She remembered bursting into grateful tears that she no longer had to endure this alone. Lucas had cleaned up after her, made sure she stayed hydrated, and carried her to bed when she was too weak to walk on her own.

It was mortifying.

It was amazing.

"How did you know I was sick?" she asked Lucas now.

He handed her a mug of ginger tea, and she sipped it while he filled her in on the last five hours, telling her how he'd knocked on her door at six thirty to no response. He'd tried calling her phone, but when she hadn't answered, he'd become seriously worried and had entered her apartment to find her semiconscious on the bathroom floor.

She had enough energy left to frown. "You entered my apartment? Please tell me you didn't break down my door."

He looked offended. "That's in the movies. I have tools for that sort of thing."

"Don't ever get rid of those tools."

"I don't plan to."

"Lucas." She looked into his clear green eyes. "Thank you for breaking into my apartment. And for staying despite all the...ugh, you know...vomiting."

Lucas took the empty mug from her hands and placed it on the bedside table. Locked in a staring contest with the mug, he said quietly, "It took years off my life seeing you like that. It's not a sight I ever want to see again."

Nina shuddered. "It's not something I ever want to go through again."

She stole a glimpse of his profile, jaw set tight, wishing she could pry open that impenetrable brain of his and see what was going on in there.

"Any more nausea?" he asked.

She shook her head. "I'm hoping I got it all out."

Lucas nodded. He looked tired. There were shadows under his eyes and his face was drawn. He'd unbuttoned his work shirt, and she caught sight of his jacket draped over her dressing room chair.

"Did you come straight from work?" she asked.

"Yeah."

"I didn't get to make you soup." It made her inexpressibly sad that the evening she'd been looking forward to had been ruined by a stupid bout of vomiting.

A smile flickered over his face. "I'm not too hungry right now anyway."

She gave a weak smile in return. "I'm not surprised."

He yawned, rubbed his eyes. "What a day."

Reluctantly she said, "It's late. You should go."

"I'm not going anywhere," he said. "You have me for the night."

She drew in a surprised breath. "Really?"

"Really."

Relief swept through her. "I'm glad you're staying."

"So am I."

She bit her lip. "I'll feel awful, though, if you catch what I've got."

"What you've got looks more like food poisoning than a gastro bug."

"How do you know?"

"Your symptoms came on pretty fast and they're easing already. What did you have to eat today?" Lucas asked.

"Coffee for breakfast—oh, don't give me that look, it was a busy morning—and for lunch, a chicken burger."

"Could it have been the burger?"

"I don't know." Her eyes widened in horror. "Lucas, tons of diners ordered the burger!" She spiraled for a few seconds into a grim place before remembering that she'd shared half the burger with Frankie. It was absurdly late to text someone, but Frankie had mentioned he was a night owl. She typed up a quick message, and Frankie replied almost immediately.

"He's fine," Nina said after reading his message. "So it's not the burger. That's a relief!"

"Anything else you ate or drank?"

She shook her head, too tired to methodically think through everything she'd consumed today.

"Let's leave it for now," he said. "Do you want to eat something? I could make toast."

She shook her head. "I don't think I can eat. But I'd love a shower." She *needed* a shower. She smelled...well, there were no words for how she smelled.

She was so unsteady on her feet, Lucas had to help her to the bathroom. She drew the line, however, at him standing guard over her in case she fainted. To placate him, she left the bathroom door slightly ajar. Every few minutes, Lucas would yell through the opening to check she was still standing. It should have been irritating, but Nina discovered she quite liked being fussed over. She took her time in the shower, letting the hot spray work its magic.

When she was finished in the bathroom, Lucas hopped into the shower. She was changing into clean pajamas when she noticed he'd changed all the bedding. She swallowed, warmth flooding her belly. How was she ever going to view him with platonic eyes if he continued bombarding her with such extraordinarily kind gestures? Her heart had no defense against that.

When Lucas emerged from the bathroom, he was wearing an old T-shirt of Ryan's that Nina had found for him earlier. She couldn't help chuckling at the tight fit.

"Laugh it up," Lucas said.

"Oh, I am."

When she hid a yawn behind her hand, he said, "Looks like someone needs to crash. I'll sleep on the couch."

"You sure?" she asked doubtfully. It was a three-seater couch, but his six-foot frame would still struggle to find a comfortable fit.

"Yeah, I'm good."

She located spare bedding in the linen cupboard and handed it to him. She could smell her soap on his skin, which did weird things to her insides. "You sure you had no plans for tonight?"

He shook his head. "Just pounding my boxing bag to take out my frustrations."

"Well, you can pound my pillow a few times before you fall asleep. Next best thing."

Lucas cleared his throat. Nina's cheeks flamed.

All this talk of pounding.

She was abruptly conscious that all she had on was a pajama top and shorts. And that Lucas was struggling to keep his eyes off her bare legs.

Her fatigue vanished as awareness flared between them, the air thrumming with tension.

Typically, this would be the moment she'd offer up a lighthearted comment to ease the awkwardness, but suddenly, she'd had enough of hiding her feelings. Right here, right now, she didn't care if Lucas saw how she felt about him. She didn't care if this ruined their friendship. She wanted to live forever in this moment and let the future fade away.

They continued staring at one another, neither of them saying a word.

And then Nina saw it. A flare of interest in Lucas's face. The taut, dark look in his eyes.

That wasn't the look of a friend. That was the look of a man who was, without a doubt, attracted to her.

Her heart soared. She was no longer good old Nina, sister of his best friend, the Ghost of Braces Past.

Please, Lucas, drop the stupid bedding you're still holding and hold me instead.

Her entire body throbbed with her need for him. It was like she'd been holding her breath for years, and suddenly, there was this great and overwhelming desire to let it all out.

She supposed if she were a better person, she'd feel guilty about Tahlia, but Tahlia, Shmalia. The woman would find another man in a heartbeat. Nina, however, had loved Lucas since what felt like forever.

Before she could think about it too much, she whispered, "I have a double bed. You're welcome to share it."

Unfortunately, thanks to her big, brainless mouth, the spell was broken.

As if coming out of a daze, Lucas straightened, blinking.

"Lucas..."

"Nina, no." He made a gesture of frustration, his expression torn. "I can't."

"You can't? Or you won't?" she asked, throwing it out there.

He let out a long, slow breath. "I won't do anything to jeopardize our friendship."

She frowned. Was Lucas buying into the absurd notion that a friendship was better than a romantic relationship? Her head hurt as she tried to think of a way to persuade him to take a chance on them.

But then Lucas said, "You and I, we can't happen... I'm with Tahlia."

The throbbing in her head grew worse. Right. Tahlia. A woman who looked fabulous in designer clothes, who boasted a high-profile career and an intellectually pedigreed family...and who'd captured the heart of the man she loved.

Her skin burning with humiliation, Nina looked away from Lucas, her gaze landing on her bed...no, no, definitely the wrong place for her eyes to land...ah, the vomit bucket, that was fitting...yes, focus on that.

Lucas's rejection stung, but there was one small comfort: he'd wanted her. He just hadn't wanted her enough. Or he'd wanted Tahlia more.

Lucas touched her face. The gesture was so tender, she wanted to cry. All too soon, he withdrew his hand to hold it tightfisted at his side. "Good night, Nina."

And that was that.

Chapter Twenty-Three

The next day, despite Lucas's protests, Nina decided to go in to work. She was feeling much better, she told him as he took over her kitchen and whipped up a breakfast of toast and scrambled eggs with a side serve of disapproval.

"I'm not hungry," she said.

He pointed to the barstool. "Sit. Eat."

"Fine!" she said grumpily. She picked up a slice of dry toast and nibbled on it, which seemed to appease him.

Lucas sat opposite her. Just looking at the pile of scrambled eggs on his plate caused her stomach to lurch in protest.

"About last night," he began.

"Don't want to talk about it."

Lucas cocked his head to one side. "You really are *not* a morning person."

She narrowed her eyes at him.

Lucas said, "Look, I'd rather not talk about it either, but I think we should."

She put down her toast. "Lucas, I was sick as a dog last night, and there you were, my knight in shining armor." She gave a shrug. "My defenses were low, and I happened to, um, latch on to you."

Lucas regarded her with an inscrutable expression, saying nothing.

"It was a moment of weakness," she continued.

Obviously, she'd had a lot of time to think through what she'd say to Lucas. When you're staring up at a dark ceiling, unable to sleep because The Scene of Your Mortification keeps playing in your head, you're likely to come up with a reasonable, if lukewarm, explanation.

She took a bite of her toast to stop herself from blurting out too much.

"You were pretty sick last night," Lucas said at last. "It's obvious you weren't yourself."

Nina offered a cautious nod. What must have been obvious to Lucas was the fact that vomiting doesn't eject your personality along with your stomach contents, but he was going along with her story, probably as eager as she was to slot the whole episode into the never-to-be-mentioned-again category.

"So we're going to forget all about last night?" she asked.

"Forgotten already," Lucas said.

The morning had warmed up considerably by the time Nina climbed into her Prius. Unfortunately, Lucas still hadn't warmed up to the reality of her going to work today. She understood his concern. Under any other circumstances, she'd stay at home to recover her strength, but she'd only just started working there. Who took a sick day after only two weeks?

Also, she had no desire to stay at home and torture herself playing the what-if game. Work would keep her mind busy. And she needed to keep her mind occupied more than she needed to give her body the rest it wanted.

The moment she walked into Soul Fare, Frankie abandoned his beloved espresso machine to fly to her side.

"How are you feeling?" he demanded.

"I'm okay, Frankie," she said, moved by his concern. "It looks like whatever I had is out of my system."

"That's good to hear, but you should be in bed. Why are you at work?"

He and Lucas should form a club, Nina thought. "I'm here to keep you out of mischief," she said lightly.

His eyes twinkled. "Well, I'm making you a latte to speed up your recovery."

Nina suppressed a smile. In Frankie's world, coffee was the tonic for all ailments. Caffeine and dairy were probably not the wisest choices after food poisoning, but it seemed to be a habit of hers to make choices that weren't always good for her. Case in point, loving an unattainable Lucas.

Sipping her latte a few minutes later—Frankie was right, this was *exactly* what she needed—Nina checked in with Cody, Camille, and Jeena to see if they had everything in hand for service in an hour. They did. Cody was busy setting tables, Jeena was stocking the display window with desserts, and Camille, looking unusually haggard, was wiping down and refilling the items on the condiments table.

"You all right, Camille?" Nina asked her.

"I'm fine," she mumbled.

Nina stared at her puffy eyes and the lank tendrils of hair falling in her face. "You don't look fine."

"I'm just tired," Camille said defensively. "I didn't sleep well."

Nina raised her eyebrows. "Why don't you freshen up in the bathroom? I'll finish up here."

Camille nodded. Nina watched Camille's wide-hipped figure trudge to the bathroom. She picked up a salt shaker. She wouldn't offer to let Camille go home. If she could be here after vomiting most of the night, Camille could grow a backbone and work through her fatigue.

A short time later, Nina called everyone together for their preshift meeting. Camille, she noted with horror, had scraped back her hair into a tight bun and put on some eye makeup. Lots of it. As though she were auditioning for a part as a streetwalker.

Someone cleared their throat. Nina snapped out of her appalled trance and faced the rest of her staff. From the moment she'd come into work, she'd noticed the sidelong glances shot her way and guessed that Frankie must have spread the word of her vomiting bout. But apart from Frankie, no one asked her how she was feeling.

She forced a smile. Time to exude positive energy in an effort to motivate everyone to offer exceptional service so guests could enjoy exceptional dining experiences. It was difficult, though, to summon up positive energy when the only vibe exuding from the group was along the lines of *why are you here stealing our oxygen?*

"Morning, everyone," she said brightly. "Let's start off the meeting with a shout-out to Jeena. Yesterday, I received feedback from a family at her table who were so impressed with her service that they made a large group booking for next week."

A blush blossomed on Jeena's cheeks at the scattered applause.

"Today, I want to focus on upselling," Nina said. "Who has any tips they'd like to share?"

Silence.

Nina knew from previous experience that drawing employees out in these preshift meetings was difficult, but today, it was as if they'd all collapsed into a collective coma.

"Surely one of you would like to share something?" she asked, trying not to sound like she was begging.

They stared at her in silence. Frankie, her only ally, was gazing into the middle distance, as though he couldn't bear to watch.

Turning to the head chef, she said, "Ano, would you like to tell us the lunch specials?"

She could sense everyone's surprise. The regular meeting format dictated that Ano present his specials only after she'd done her spiel. At least now she had their attention.

"All right." Ano's voice was a low rumble as he gestured to one of the bowls on the table in front of him. "Lemon garlic linguini with shrimp."

Ano described the dish in detail, the buttery white wine sauce, the plump sautéed shrimp, the lemon verbena garnish. He listed the allergens, then handed out forks so everyone could taste.

"Yum," said Cody.

Mindful of her still-sensitive stomach, Nina only had a small taste, but she agreed with Cody. Delicious. Ano's culinary talent seemed to especially shine whenever he came up with one of his chef's specials. This prompted a spark of an idea, one she wanted to explore further, but she was distracted by the fact that Ano was staring at Jeena as though waiting for her reaction.

Thinking back, Nina realized that Jeena rarely commented on Ano's dishes. Curious to test a theory, she asked, "What do you think, Jeena?"

Jeena started. After slicing a quick look Ano's way, she murmured, "It's delicious."

Ano beamed, his teeth flashing white against his smooth, dark skin, his eyes still watching her.

Jeena gave him a tentative smile in return, her cheeks a bright red.

Oh. How very interesting. Also, how inconvenient not to be able to explore this...development further since she had a meeting to run.

"Cody," Nina said, "what are some of the ways you could upsell the shrimp linguine?"

Caught off guard, Cody stammered, "Yeah...not sure."

"Give it a go," she urged.

"Um, okay." He cleared his throat. "I could ask a diner if they'd like, maybe, *two* bowls of the linguine."

You could, but only if the diner was, let's see, a sumo wrestler. "Cody, your average diner is not going to consume and pay for two helpings of the same dish."

Cody nodded slowly. "Okay, yeah, I see your point."

"Jeena?" Nina asked.

Jeena hesitated, and Nina thought for one horribly long second that she would simply revert to the shrug-and-stay-silent approach that had characterized all the other meetings. *Come on, Jeena,* Nina pleaded silently, *work with me here.* All she needed was one person to turn the must-hate-Nina tide.

To Nina's enormous relief, Jeena's competitive spirit won out. And perhaps the desire to show off a little in front of Ano. "I'd recommend that garlic bread or a side salad would go well with the linguine."

Nina smiled. "A great suggestion, Jeena. Thank you."

Frankie chimed in with "What about using the FOMO principle?"

Good old Frankie, he'd come through. She could hug him. "Excellent idea! The Fear of Missing Out is a strong selling tactic. Camille, any ideas how you could employ it here?"

Camille, clearly not wanting to be left out of the action, thought for a moment. "I guess you could say something like 'I'm not sure if we've run out of our shrimp linguine special. I could check for you.'"

Nodding her agreement, Nina complimented Camille on not coming across as too pushy or salesy. "The last thing we want is to annoy our diners into leaving," she said, and made a mental note to take Camille off bathroom duty.

After the meeting, Ano and his crew retreated to the kitchen and Nina dealt with a few housekeeping duties for the front-of-house staff. The meeting had gone better than she'd hoped. Today was shaping up to be a good day.

Customers poured in throughout the morning. Most of the diners were in a good mood, looking forward to their meal, and Nina found their enthusiasm infectious.

An hour after the lunch shift ended, Nina was standing at the hostess stand when a wave of dizziness came over her. She clutched the podium, waiting for the dizziness to pass. She'd pushed herself too hard, she realized. Trying to keep it together, thankful that the crowd of diners had thinned, she managed to make it to her office, where she sat down hard in her chair.

She closed her eyes. *If you faint at work, Nina Sarah Abrahams, I will never forgive you.*

She was taking slow, measured breaths and still lecturing herself when her door opened and Ano, wearing his chef's jacket and trademark black bandana, stepped into her office.

Great. Just great.

She could feel him staring down at her, no doubt taking it all in. "Frankie told me you were pretty sick last night," he said gruffly. "Guess you're still feeling the aftereffects."

She simply nodded, afraid that if she spoke, what would emerge wouldn't be words and it wouldn't be pretty.

Ano narrowed his eyes at her and shook his head. Nina didn't have it in her to pretend she was doing okay right now. "I just need to rest for a while," she managed.

"No, you need to go home."

She looked up at him, at the face so many people found intimidating, but beneath the stern demeanor, she could glimpse his concern. "You're right." She could see she'd surprised him. Actually, she'd surprised herself, but she'd had enough of being stupid. She needed to rest. "I'm going home."

"Good." He deposited a flask and a takeaway container on her desk. "Coconut water to get your electrolytes up and chicken soup to restore your strength. It's what my Gogo always gave me, and she was the best doctor I knew."

In the two weeks she'd worked here, this was the first truly kind act someone had shown her. Tears pricked her eyes. "Thank you, Ano."

He shrugged off her thanks. "It's nothing."

"Gogo?" Nina asked.

"My grandmother."

"She sounds like quite a woman."

"She was. Do you need someone to drive you home?"

"I'll be fine. Jeena can supervise front of house while I'm away."

Ano nodded. "If there are any problems, she can come to me."

Here's hoping for a few minor problems, Nina thought.

A couple of hours later, she was lying on her couch, dozing off and on, when Lucas called. "Hey, just checking in. How are you feeling?"

She cleared the sleep from her voice. "Not too bad." There was no need to mention she had to leave early. He didn't have to know everything.

"You taking it easy?" he asked.

"Of course."

He gave a derisive snort. He knew her too well. "Anything you need?"

She could hear background noises, people talking, a phone ringing. He was clearly busy. "I'm all sorted," she said, thinking of Ano's chicken soup. "Thanks for checking in, Lucas."

"Anytime. Just...take care, okay?"

After promising she would, Nina ended the call. She still didn't feel a hundred percent, but remembering Ano's gesture and the pleasure on Jeena's face when she'd told her she was in charge for the rest of the afternoon, Nina also felt more hopeful than she had in a long while.

#

Ano's grandmother was a wise woman, Nina decided the next morning as she got ready for work, pulling on no-nonsense denims and a white shirt. She was feeling so much stronger after a good night's sleep and Ano's recommended diet of coconut water and chicken soup. Her mouth watered at the thought of the flavorsome soup. She'd had another two helpings for breakfast, along with the disloyal thought that Ano's recipe might even nudge Christina's chicken noodle soup from top spot.

Driving to work, still thinking about Ano's soup, that was when it suddenly hit her. Whenever Ano came up with one of his own dishes, whether it was a chef's special or his chicken soup, the dish was bursting with flavor and inventiveness, showcasing his creativity far more than the dishes he served up from Soul Fare's standard menu. She had no idea what to do with this revelation, but it was something to think about.

As soon as she arrived at the restaurant, Nina touched base with Jeena, who was looking particularly pretty today, her glossy dark hair caught up in a soft ponytail, her brown eyes sparkling. According to Jeena, yesterday afternoon had gone well. The only hiccup had been a toddler upending her spaghetti on the floor. Nina complimented Jeena on a job well done, and Jeena even managed to reciprocate with a movement of her lips that Nina decided to interpret as a smile.

Nina entered the kitchen to return Ano's flask and thank him again for his kindness, but all she received in return was a terse nod. She exited the kitchen on a sigh.

Just then, Brayden, Jeena's flat-eyed admirer, walked into the restaurant. After greeting him, Nina offered him a seat in Camille's section, wanting to see how he'd react. As she'd anticipated, he politely declined, saying it wasn't suitable, and went straight to one of Jeena's tables. It seemed Ano had himself a bit of competition, Nina thought.

A middle-aged couple, Andy and Matilda, scrambled-egg-on-toast regulars, stepped through the door, and Nina seated them in their usual spot by the window.

Matilda looked up at Nina. "Guess what we're planning to do in our retirement years?"

"Couch surfing," Andy said.

"Traveling from country to country," Matilda said dreamily, "staying in strangers' homes, opening ourselves up to new adventures."

"Couch surfing?" Nina asked. "Really?"

"Oh, yes," Andy confirmed.

"Sounds great," Nina said. Then she couldn't resist asking, "Would you like to look at the menu? Perhaps try something different for breakfast this morning?"

They both looked shocked. "Oh, no, dear, nothing new," Matilda said. "Just our usual scrambled eggs on toast."

"Of course," Nina said, concealing a smile.

Out of the corner of her eye, she noticed Jeena delivering Brayden's coffee, Brayden pointing to something on the menu, and Jeena leaning in to see what he was pointing at. In the next instant, Jeena jerked back, her brown eyes wide. Nina straightened, feeling a prickle of alarm. Matilda was saying something, but Nina tuned her out, distracted by what was going on. Actually, what *was* going on? Jeena's face was flushed and Brayden was staring up at her, frowning. Something wasn't right.

Then a smile spread across Brayden's face. A smile that made Nina want to jump into the shower.

"Excuse me," she said hastily to Andy and Matilda, making her way as fast as she could to Brayden and Jeena. "Is everything all right?" she asked them.

"Everything's fine," Brayden said.

"Jeena?" Nina asked, glancing at her.

Jeena looked unsure for a moment, then she said, "It's all okay."

Brayden smirked. "Like I said, everything's fine."

Ignoring him, Nina stared hard at Jeena, who was avoiding her gaze.

Brayden held up the menu. "Since you're the restaurant manager, what do you recommend?"

Nina found a smile of her own. "I recommend you try another restaurant."

She heard Jeena give a little gasp.

Brayden gaped at her. "What did you say?"

"You heard me."

"No, I don't think I did. Maybe you should rephrase it. Or maybe you're also in the habit of overreacting, like Jeena here."

"Nina," Jeena whispered, "it's okay."

Nina held Brayden's gaze. "The coffee's on the house. Please leave."

Brayden looked from her to Jeena, an ugly shade of red creeping up his neck and suffusing his face. Good. She was pleased he was feeling a little of what he'd made Jeena feel. Humiliation. Helplessness. The thick choke of rage.

"Do you realize the terrible review I can give this restaurant?" Brayden asked. "Is that what you want? Are you thinking carefully enough here?"

The little weasel, Nina thought. Did he honestly think he could bully her? She tried to keep her tone level. "You'd better leave."

Temper entered his eyes. He got to his feet and took a threatening step toward her, a sneer twisting his lips. "I'm not going anywhere."

Beside her, Jeena went rigid. Nina stood her ground, despite the fear welling inside her. The only diners were a mother with a baby, and Andy and Matilda. She couldn't rely on them to help her. Cody was nowhere in sight, and neither was Camille. She could hear activity behind the espresso machine and guessed Frankie was making a move to intervene, but while she appreciated his heart, she knew if it came down to a fight, a rotund Frankie wouldn't stand much of a chance against Brayden's solid build.

"Jeena," Brayden said, "let's talk outside."

Nina stepped in front of her shaking server. "You're not talking to her, or to anyone else. In fact, you're no longer welcome here. Please leave."

Then Ano came out of the kitchen, trailed by Cody. Wearing a scowl and his black bandana, Ano looked gloriously imposing as he paused to take in the scene.

Thank goodness, Nina thought, relief surging through her.

Brayden's face paled at the sheer scale of the man bearing down on him.

"There a problem here?" Ano growled.

"No, no problem," Brayden stammered.

Ano narrowed his eyes. "Looks like you're the problem."

Pointedly, Nina said, "Brayden was just leaving."

And he did, in a satisfying, undignified scramble. Suddenly, everyone was talking at once. Andy and Matilda were animatedly dissecting the whole episode, and Nina knew they'd be riding this wave of excitement for weeks on end. Perhaps they'd end up couch surfing, after all.

Frankie had stopped by the table of the mother with the baby. She looked a little shaken, and he was caught up soothing her. Nina knew she needed to go over there and do damage control, but she first had to get her pounding heart under control. Anger and adrenaline had carried her through the confrontation with Brayden, but now they were starting to wear off and she needed a moment.

"I didn't overreact." Jeena's voice was so soft, Nina almost didn't hear her.

Nina turned to look at her, sympathy stirring when she saw how white her face was. "I know you didn't," she replied gently. "I bet his hand just happened to brush your breast. And I can guess this isn't the first time something like this has happened with him."

Before Jeena could respond, Ano demanded, "How long has this scumbag been harassing you?"

Okay, Ano, Nina thought, don't turn your scare factor onto Jeena. The woman you so obviously fancy needs comfort, not a lecture.

"I should have said something," Jeena whispered. "When it first started, I thought I was mistaken. I told myself they were only accidents. Then...I don't know, I just kept making excuses."

Ano's jaw worked. "You should have come to me."

Jeena blinked rapidly. Nina could see she was trying to get herself under control, trying not to break down in front of them. Ano wasn't helping matters. Still riding the aftermath of his concern, he was doing everything wrong while trying to do it all right.

Throwing Ano a meaningful look, Nina said, "I'm sure Jeena could do with a cup of strong tea right now."

Ano didn't pick up the hint. He was still quietly raging. "I should have given that scumbag some of his own medicine."

Nina sighed. *All right, Ano, you had your chance.* "Come on, Jeena," she said. "Let's get you that tea."

Nina settled Jeena down with a sympathetic Frankie and his tea-making skills, knowing she'd be in good hands.

She was about to check on the young mother when Cody came up to her wearing an anxious expression. "I was right to get Ano, yeah?"

She nodded. "It was a good call, Cody. Thank you."

He beamed and hurried over to Camille, who'd just stepped into the dining area, to fill her in on all that had happened. Nina felt a surge of irritation. Camille had taken one heck of an extended smoke break, but she decided not to tackle her. She'd had her share of confrontation for today.

Half an hour later, Nina was finishing up some paperwork in her office when there was a tap on her door. She looked up to see Jeena standing there.

"Oh, hi, Jeena," Nina said, surprised she was still here. "I thought you'd gone home early."

Jeena closed the door. "I need to speak to you."

"Okay." With a sinking feeling, Nina braced herself to hear the news that Jeena was quitting.

Instead, Jeena said, "I want to thank you for what you did. I can't remember the last time someone stood up for me like you did, confronting Brayden like that. And he was a regular here."

Nina opened her mouth, but Jeena shook her head. "Please don't say anything. Let me get out what I came to say before I change my mind." She took a deep breath. "Camille put some kind of syrup in your coffee. That's why you were so sick."

Chapter Twenty-Four

Nina waited until the end of the day before calling Camille into her office. Camille stepped inside, took one look at her face, and burst into tears.

Unmoved, Nina gestured to the chair in front of her desk. "Take a seat."

Still crying, Camille sagged into the chair.

Relenting slightly, Nina pushed a box of tissues across the desk in her direction.

Camille grabbed a tissue and dabbed her eyes. "How did you find out?"

"Really?" Nina asked. "That's what you want to open with?" She wasn't about to tell Camille that Jeena had overheard her boasting on the phone to a friend about a plan to scare the restaurant manager into quitting. Nina hadn't asked Jeena how long she'd known about the conversation before approaching her. She told herself it was enough that Jeena had even come to her.

"Why did you do it?" Nina asked.

"I was hoping that if you quit, Edith would give me your job. I didn't mean to give you that much," Camille admitted. "I had no idea it would hit you so hard."

"Well, it did," Nina said. "I threw up for hours. What if I'd had an accident driving home because I was so sick?" Just thinking about the terrible night she'd endured whipped up feelings of anger and resentment. She'd even thanked Camille for the coffee! "That was a really crappy thing to do, Camille."

Camille burst into fresh sobs. "I know! I'm sorry. If it's any consolation, I couldn't sleep thinking of what I'd done to you."

Nina stared at her in disbelief. "Of course it's no consolation."

"What happens now?"

"You can't stay here, Camille."

"Please give me another chance," she begged. "Please let me stay."

Nina shook her head. "You broke my trust in a huge way. There's no recovery from that."

Camille lowered her head and sobbed quietly into her lap.

Nina looked away from the sight, trying not to think about the fact that Camille was a single mother caring for a teenage son on bare-bones child support from a deadbeat ex-husband. What Camille had done was beyond petty politics and gunning for her job. The woman had literally poisoned her.

"There's no way I can let you stay," Nina said. "But against my better judgment, I'll give you a good reference letter. You'll have to settle for that."

Camille lifted up red-rimmed eyes. "Thank you. I know I don't deserve it."

"No, you don't."

Camille got to her feet. "I know this won't make up for what I did, but keep an eye on Ano."

Nina narrowed her eyes. "What are you doing, Camille? Stirring up more trouble?"

"No, it's not like that. It's just... I know of a number of restaurants who are trying to poach Ano, and let's just say he's not refusing their calls."

After Camille left, Nina buried her face in her hands, her anger fading and worry taking its place. In one day, she had to kick out a customer, fire an employee, and face the awful prospect that she might lose her head chef. It was hard to imagine how her day could get any worse.

#

Later that evening, Nina had just finished brushing her teeth when her phone chimed with a text from Ryan: *Hey, everyone's coming Saturday to check out your new restaurant.*

Nina frowned at her screen. *Define everyone.*

Your one and only awesome brother. Liv. Lucas. Tahlia.

Lucas. Nina knew that sooner or later she'd have to see him. She'd been hoping for later, but maybe the more time that passed, the more awkward it would be between them.

Breakfast or lunch? she texted back.

Lunch.

Okay. Will reserve a table.

Just got confirmation. Mom's also joining us.

Nina's stomach bottomed out. *You're not serious.*

Totally am.

Nina tossed her phone onto the bed and closed her eyes.

So she couldn't imagine her day getting any worse? It only went to show just how limited her imagination was.

#

Nina had a restless night debating whether she should confront Ano. She woke up with a dull headache and no great revelation. She didn't want to ask Ano straight out if he was looking for another job, so for the next two days, Nina covertly watched her chef. People typically slacked off if they were unhappy in their job, but Ano arrived on time for work, the food he served was still consistently good, and he remained meticulous about the cleanliness of his kitchen, ensuring that the floor was regularly mopped and the oven scrubbed every night.

Perhaps it was Jeena keeping him here, judging by the longing looks he directed at her when he thought no one was watching. Nina knew that Ano was also close to Edith, but were romantic attraction and loyalty enough to motivate him to remain at Soul Fare?

Late Friday afternoon, when the restaurant was quiet and they were getting ready to close, she sought out Ano in the kitchen. Stefan was taking the trash out to the dumpster, and Sunan was stacking the dishwasher.

"How's everything going, Ano?" she asked.

Ano paused in the middle of mopping his face with his bandana. "Fine."

"Fine?"

"That's what I said."

"I heard you might be a little...unhappy here?"

He leveled her a look. "I'm unhappy you're in my kitchen asking ridiculous questions."

Defiantly, her chin went up. As if rudeness would deter her. Thanks to her brother, she rocked *stubborn*. She framed her next question carefully. "If you could pick something you'd like to change here, what would it be?"

He stared at her suspiciously. "I can't think of anything."

"What about additional kitchen staff?"

Nothing changed in his face. Okay, so she was off base there. "What about the menu?"

"What about it?"

"Well, would you like to make changes to the menu?"

"It's Bill's menu," he said shortly.

Nina dug for patience. "I know, but would you like more creative freedom with the menu?"

For the tiniest instant, so tiny she might have imagined it, Ano's eyes lit up with excitement, but it was quickly masked. "The menu is what it is. I work with what I've got."

#

Saturday came around way too quickly. Nina dressed in the outfit she'd laid out the night before (bold red blouse and black denims) and took extra care with her hair and makeup, her stomach a ball of nerves. She was silly to feel nervous, she told herself as her hair sizzled under the ruthless heat of the straightener. She loved her family, loved her work (or at least she was starting to), but the two together were an unholy mix.

When she walked into Soul Fare an hour later, Nina couldn't help seeing the restaurant through the eyes of her family—the dark interior, the drab furnishings, the outdated artwork on the walls, the menu that hadn't had a revamp in eons. She knew all this, of course. It was one of the reasons she'd taken on the role of restaurant manager, for the challenge of helping Soul Fare reach its potential. But it was still early days, and she hadn't yet had the opportunity to implement any of the changes bouncing around in her head. Besides, you weren't supposed to go into a new job all guns blazing, alienating everyone with drastic changes. Never mind that even weaponless, she'd still somehow managed to alienate everyone.

Today, they were still short one server, and Saturdays were typically one of their busiest days. At the moment, though, the atmosphere was calm, staff quietly going about their preparations for the upcoming shift. Since Camille's departure, Cody was working harder than she'd ever seen him, and Jeena had taken to at least greeting her and participating more in preshift meetings.

After Nina touched base with Ano on today's specials, she went through a mental checklist on everything that needed to be done before Soul Fare opened its doors at seven and her family descended upon her in all their sarcastic chaos at twelve.

"Looks like you need a coffee," Frankie declared.

Nina gratefully accepted the latte Frankie held out. "I'd ask you to marry me if I weren't already in love."

Frankie raised his eyebrows. "That's news. When do I get to meet the lucky bloke?"

"He doesn't know. It's complicated and a bit of a mess."

Frankie gave a sympathetic shrug. "When is love not complicated and messy?"

\#

Cheryl Abrahams swept through the front door of Soul Fare like she was stepping onto a stage, her trim figure perfectly outlined in a tasteful skirt and sweater, makeup subtly done. You would never guess she was approaching sixty. You would also never dare mention it.

"Nina, darling." Her mother's blue eyes did a slow scan of the restaurant's interior. "So this is the little place where you work."

"A little place with big potential," Nina couldn't resist saying.

"Hmm."

"How was the drive?"

"Long."

"Anyway, Mom, welcome to Soul Fare."

"Hmm. Anyone else here yet?"

"Ry and Liv are already seated." She gestured to their table, where her sister-in-law was engrossed in the menu. "You know, Liv. Military punctuality."

"A marvelous trait," Cheryl said. "You should adopt it."

"Hmm," Nina murmured, not above adopting her mother's tactic. "Your schedule's usually so busy. I'm surprised you were able to make it today."

"So am I. You simply cannot imagine how hectic life is at the moment."

No imagination needed, Mom. Not when you insist on providing all the details. "Let's get you seated." *Translation: let's palm you off to Ry.*

At their approach, Ryan got to his feet. "Mom, you look younger every time I see you. What's your secret?"

"Having a charming son like yourself," Cheryl replied, patting her blonde hair and looking pleased at the compliment.

When Cheryl turned to greet Liv, Nina whispered in her brother's ear, "Still aiming to be the sole beneficiary in her will?"

"Ah, sis, jealousy doesn't become you."

"Brownnosing's not a good look on you either."

Ryan laughed. "It makes a brother proud to see his little sister so quick on her feet."

"Sibling survival training," Nina replied absently, noticing Cheryl's gaze straying to Liv's cute little bump before darting away. She told herself not to say anything, but then she remembered that since starting her new job, her mother hadn't once contacted her to see how she was coping. She let the words spill out. "You're going to be a *grandmother*, Mom." She exaggerated the title for impact. "Isn't that exciting?"

Cheryl offered a tight smile. "Very exciting. A new chapter in my life."

Nina knew her mother had a conflicted response when it came to Liv's pregnancy. On the one hand, she was over the moon at the idea of her first grandchild; on the other hand, she wasn't too keen on heading into grandmother territory, where the scenery was mostly crêpe skin and liver spots.

Ryan shot her a look that said, *why do you make it so easy for me to be the favorite child?*

Cheryl took the empty seat next to Ryan. Nina had just handed her mother a menu when she felt the charge in the air and looked up to see Lucas arrive with Tahlia. They were holding hands. Nina couldn't tear her gaze away from the arresting picture they made. It was like her lungs were filling up with water and she couldn't breathe.

Lucas's eyes found hers. It might have been her imagination, but he seemed to hesitate for a breathless second, squaring his shoulders before heading her way. The fact that he was sporting her favorite look—jeans, white shirt, blue blazer, and sexy stubble—knocked even more air from her lungs.

255

"Nina, hi." He let go of Tahlia's hand to greet her with a hug. She hated the slightly cautious way he held himself, the troubled look in his eyes that was in all likelihood mirrored in her own.

"Hello, Lucas." She gave his back a friendly pat and moved out of his arms. "Welcome to Soul Fare." Oh, good grief, she sounded like a flight attendant.

She glanced away from Lucas to see Ryan watching the two of them with a frown.

"Nice place," Lucas murmured. "I can see you achieving great things here."

"That's the goal."

He handed her a bottle of vitamin water. "To keep you going today. With everything and everyone"—a meaningful look at her mother—"here."

A lump formed in her throat. *Hold it together.* "Exactly what I need. Thank you."

He nodded slightly, then moved away to greet the others and Nina found herself facing Tahlia in all her sleek, gleaming racehorse beauty.

"Tahlia. Good to see you again."

"Nina. What a treat to see you at work."

Tahlia smiled at her. And Nina read in her smile, *What a treat that you'll be seeing to my needs for the next hour or so while I sit next to the man I suspect you love and enjoy the food you serve to us.*

"So you're down for the weekend?" Nina asked.

Tahlia nodded. "I'm staying at Lucas's place."

"Great," Nina said. "Great." She waved a hand around the restaurant. "Well, enjoy."

"Thank you." Tahlia drifted away to attach herself to Lucas, and there followed the usual exchange of hellos and cheek kisses. Nina watched her mother shrewdly appraise Tahlia, her face showing nothing of what she was thinking. At last, everyone was seated. With

Ryan and Lucas on either side of her, Cheryl looked in her element. Nina's heart softened a little. Who was she to judge her mother? She was as much a failure as a daughter as Cheryl was as a mother.

"A pretty tame drinks menu," Ryan commented, his scornful tone contradicted by the relief on his face.

It was too tempting. "We're looking to spice it up a bit," Nina said. "Maybe with the addition of a blue algae latte to the menu." Not that Barracat, with all the timid trappings of suburbia, was willing to embrace quirky beverage trends just yet.

"Yeah, well, take your time," Ryan muttered.

Knowing Olivia's fanatical attention to detail when it came to ordering menu items, Nina had arranged to look after their table, leaving Jeena and Cody to handle the rest of the diners. After taking everyone's drink order, and managing to field Olivia's ridiculous barrage of questions, Nina completed a circuit of the dining area, making it a point to visit every table. The air was alive with conversation, the kitchen was churning through food orders, and diners looked happy.

Nina delivered the drinks to her family. This was the nerve-racking part. Lucas and her family loved their coffee. Would Frankie's coffee meet their high standards? The praise at the table, however, was unanimous, and Nina let out a relieved breath. Frankie was an undisputed barista superstar.

"We have news," Olivia announced, reaching for Ryan's hand. "We're having a girl."

Everyone offered their congratulations, and Cheryl asked, "Have you picked a name yet?"

"It's a surprise," Olivia said.

Cheryl's eyes widened. "Even from me?"

"From everyone," Ryan said.

Good call, Nina thought, feeling tears prick her eyes. A girl. She was so happy for them. And so looking forward to being an aunt.

"My only son, about to become a father," Cheryl said, a proud wobble in her voice. "And my only daughter, not even dating anyone."

Of course, she had to spoil it. Plastering on her best attempt at a smile, Nina said, "Shall I take everyone's order?"

Ryan flashed her a sympathetic smile. "Yes, please, I'm starving." In obvious retaliation for Olivia's last health outing, he went for the chicken schnitzel burger and chips.

"Ry, your cholesterol!" Olivia protested.

"My cholesterol's been in charge for too long," Ryan said. "It's about time my happiness took over."

Lucas and Tahlia both opted for the grilled salmon and steamed vegetables.

"Soon the two of you will have matching T-shirts," Nina said, trying to sound casual, but unable to stop the ooze of sarcasm.

Lucas's head jerked back in surprise at her comment. Olivia looked up from her study of the menu, her eyes conveying an urgent tone-it-down message. Even Ryan was staring at her in astonishment.

"Matching T-shirts?" Tahlia's mouth was a thin, offended line. "As if we would be so crass."

"Ignore me," Nina said quickly. "I was just joking."

Cheryl piped up, "You know what I say, Nina... In Every Little Joke, There Lies A Kernel Of Serious Truth."

And you know what I say, Mom, Nina wanted to retort. *Blood Is Supposed To Be Thicker Than Water.*

She dug a nail into her thumb tip. This day could only get worse if the movie club ladies unexpectedly showed up and loudly and uninhibitedly started discussing *Fifty Shades of Grey.*

"So, Cheryl, what'll you have to eat?" Olivia asked, winking Nina's way.

Man, she loved her sister-in-law. She made a mental note to gift Olivia with the biggest jar of pregnancy-craving pickles she could find.

"I'm in the mood for a salad." Cheryl tapped a finger on the menu. "Do you have any more salad options, Nina?"

"Only what's on the menu."

"Hmm, a rather limited choice. I suppose I'll have the Greek salad, then. Dressing on the side. On second thought, skip the dressing. Fresh lemon juice should do the trick. And no feta in the salad either. You won't believe the high fat content of cheese."

Nina nodded, committing her mother's order to memory and feeling sorry for Stefan who would have the task of putting together such a sorry plate of food.

And because she couldn't help herself, Nina dug her hole a little deeper. "Hey, Mom, I was wondering, would you prefer to be called Nana Cheryl or Granny Cheryl?"

Ryan shook his head. *Why?* he mouthed.

"I haven't given it much thought," Cheryl replied, all huffy. "But let's not go on and on about it, Nina."

"Sure," Nina said, gathering up the menus and jerking her head at Ry. He understood her meaning and followed her to a quiet area next to the kitchen.

"What the heck's wrong with you?" he asked, frowning.

"Genes," she muttered, taking a big gulp of vitamin water.

"Stop poking at Mom. You're making it worse."

"She riles me up," Nina said. "Please, Ry, keep her in line."

He yawned. "Too much effort."

She narrowed her eyes at him. "Keep Mom under control, or I'll sneak a fat, juicy tomato slice into your burger."

Ryan blanched. "You wouldn't!"

"I would too!"

In the next instant, Lucas had joined their huddle. "Everything okay, Nina? You seem...tense."

Really, Lucas? How very perceptive of you. "I'm always tense when my mother is around."

He stared at her, giving away nothing of his thoughts. "You sure that's all it is?"

"I'm sure," she lied.

Ryan frowned, looking between the two of them. "Is something else going on here?"

"No," Nina said. "I just need Mom to...not be Mom."

Then Lucas said, "Will it help if I draw Cheryl's attention away from you?"

Ryan snorted. "Good luck with that."

"You forget what I'm capable of." Lucas gave her shoulder a warm, reassuring squeeze. "I'll take care of Cheryl."

He was true to his word. Every time her mother looked at her and opened her mouth, Lucas jumped in with a question or an amusing anecdote. With Cheryl's attention diverted, Nina could feel some of the tension slowly seeping from her.

In the middle of looking after their table, Nina noticed an oh-so-interesting dynamic emerge. She'd assumed that Cheryl would get on with Tahlia. They were both intelligent, career-driven, high-profile (any more adjectives and she'd throw up) women. Instead, there seemed to be this low hum of animosity between the two of them. It was like a verbal UFC fight over whose job was more important. Talk orbited around deadlines and prominent people they'd interacted with, then it devolved into which e-mail or text message had to be answered right away.

Of course, this meant that whenever Nina approached their table, Tahlia was on her phone. She could see the irritation on Lucas's face, which he was trying his best to hide.

ALL THE LOST PIECES

Here's a self-evident truth, Nina thought. If something's a problem when you're dating, it's only going to get worse after you're married. She hoped Lucas was smart enough to realize that.

Chapter Twenty-Five

Three weeks later, eight o'clock on a Friday night, Nina sat in a booth in a diner, her stomach a curdling mix of nerves and excitement. She tried to distract herself from the upcoming meeting by doing a critical evaluation of the place—the table water smelled too heavily of chlorine, the lighting was too dim, the pies looked too gravy soaked—but her heart wasn't into it. Besides, it was a diner, chosen for its proximity to the nursing home, not for its fine dining experience.

It had been a busy three weeks since her family's visit to Soul Fare. Ano and Jeena were still hovering around one another, neither of them acting on the obvious attraction between them. It was painful to watch.

Angela, Claire, and Bianca were on a Tarantino/Scorsese binge. It was unnerving listening to these sweet ladies with their gnomish faces and mothball-smelling cardigans review gruesome acts of violence while they tucked into their eggs and bacon. Nina had to perform intricate seating gymnastics to keep families with small children away from their table.

On the family front, Olivia was in first-time-mother mode and obsessed about being fully prepared for the baby's arrival. Only last week, she'd dragged Nina on a three-hour shopping spree for a bewildering assortment of baby items, including a salt lamp for late-night feedings and slip-proof baby kneepads.

Lucas was still doing the commute thing with Tahlia, but sounding more and more exhausted the few times she'd spoken to him. She wanted to ask if Tahlia was worth all this effort, but she stayed silent because she was afraid of his answer. It still felt strained between them, but they were both trying to small talk away the awkwardness.

Interestingly, two days ago, Ryan had let slip that all was not exactly rosy between Lucas and Tahlia. Apparently, they were arguing over something and had been for a while. Olivia had attempted to grill Lucas about it, but he was his usual tight-lipped self, saying only that they were trying to sort it out.

Sort what out? Nina couldn't help wondering. It was all very mysterious. And it was killing her not to know.

Edith entered the diner, pulling Nina out of her thoughts. As Edith headed toward her, Nina could see the physical toll that Bill's illness was taking on her. Edith's small frame appeared even frailer, and worry lines had carved themselves into her face. Even her red lipstick seemed muted.

They exchanged hellos, ordered drinks, and shared a smile over a comfortable silence.

Staring into Edith's tired, sad eyes, Nina skipped the weather talk and took a chance. "How's Bill doing?"

An expression of relief came over Edith's face. It was Nina's guess that most people would avoid bringing up the topic of Bill for fear of upsetting her, but Nina also knew that those treading the waters of grief and hardship often craved the lifeboat of talking out their pain and fear to a sympathetic listener. So Nina gave Edith her full attention and just listened as she described Bill's confusion and bouts of paranoia, his brief periods of stability, followed by agonizing downward turns as the disease took its toll on an already-weakened immune system.

According to Edith, the most painful aspect of Alzheimer's was watching the man she loved slowly disappear in front of her as more and more of his memory fell away. Nina squeezed Edith's hand in sympathy. She'd never met Bill, but what an awful thing to endure.

Their drinks arrived.

Composing herself, Edith clasped her tea in both hands. "You know, my dear, I said in our interview that what I appreciated most about you was your ability to listen. I'm pleased to see that it still holds true."

Nina was touched. "Anytime you'd like to talk, I'm happy to meet up."

"I'll remember that." She sipped her tea. "Have you settled in at Soul Fare?"

"I have," Nina said, surprised to find it was true.

"You mentioned that Camille wanted to move on?"

Nina chose her words with care. "Yes. It wasn't working out for her." *Not with her trying to poison the manager.*

"What a pity," Edith said.

Nina made a noncommittal noise.

"Are you looking for another server?" Edith asked.

Nina shook her head. She explained to Edith that over the past couple of weeks, she'd seen that two servers were enough, particularly if they were both hardworking and competent (interestingly, after Camille's firing, both Jeena and Cody had risen to the challenge).

"What about the weekends?" Edith asked. "When it's so busy?"

"I hired an extra server for the weekends."

Edith set down her tea. "I trust your judgment. So do Ano and Jeena. They both speak highly of you."

Nina nearly toppled off her chair. "They do?"

"Ano tells me you keep out of his way, which is high praise from him."

After giving their order to the server (a pie of the day for Edith, while Nina took a chance on the beer-battered fish), Nina had to keep her hands clasped together in her lap to stop herself from nervously rearranging the cutlery on the table. Now was the moment to talk about the real reason she'd been pushing for this meeting.

"Who came up with Soul Fare's menu?" Nina asked during a lull in the conversation.

"Bill. He's a self-taught cook, you know."

Nina smiled. "He's very talented."

"Yes, he is."

"Edith, I've been wondering, have there been any changes to the menu?"

Edith's eyes grew distant as she considered the question. "Six months after we opened, Bill removed a few dishes that weren't selling too well. He replaced them with classic comfort food, and these were well received. I don't believe the menu has changed much since then."

"And when did Ano start working with you?"

"About two years after we opened," Edith said. "Bill was head chef, then he hired Ano to assist him. When Bill couldn't cook anymore, Ano took over the position of head chef."

"Has Ano introduced any changes to the menu?"

Edith shook her head. "Ano wouldn't interfere with Bill's menu."

The server arrived with the food. Nina poked at her fish and waited until Edith had eaten half her pie before taking a fortifying breath. "Edith, how would you feel if I asked Ano to make a few changes to the menu?"

"Changes?" Edith put down her knife and fork. "You'll have to clarify, Nina."

"Just, you know, tweaking a few dishes, maybe introducing some new ones."

Edith looked horrified. "You're talking about changing Bill's menu."

"Not changing it," Nina said quickly. "More like updating it."

"But it's Bill's menu."

"And it will always be Bill's menu," Nina tried to assure her.

"No, it won't. Not if you change it."

"I think Ano especially would benefit from playing around with some of the dishes."

A quizzical frown appeared on Edith's face. "Ano?"

How to say this? *Bluntly,* she decided. "Edith, I believe we might lose Ano if we don't give him scope to be more creative with the menu."

"But Ano's fine. He's happy. He's been doing these dishes for years." Even as Edith said the words, a note of uncertainty crept into her voice.

"Exactly my point," Nina said.

"What about the daily specials?" Edith asked. "Ano has room to be as creative as he wishes with the specials."

"I don't know if that's enough, Edith."

What Nina didn't say was that she believed Soul Fare was suffering from menu fatigue. And if they didn't update the menu, they'd lose not only their head chef, but their diners too.

"Bill came up with every single one of those dishes," Edith said. "He spent years getting them right."

Trying not to show her frustration, Nina said, "I understand, but—"

"Enough, my dear," Edith said with a catch in her voice. "I realize Bill's mind is going and in all likelihood he'd never know if we changed his menu, but I'd know. And I don't want to betray him like that."

Taking a ragged breath, Edith picked up her knife and fork, signaling the end of the discussion.

Nina held back a defeated sigh. She'd given it her best shot, but it hadn't been enough. There was probably something more she could say to persuade Edith, but nothing came to mind. And it would be insensitive to push her any further. The galling truth was, she'd tried and failed.

#

Despite her failure to secure any changes to the food menu, Nina did manage to wrangle a few concessions from Edith with regard to the drinks menu. When Nina gave Frankie the news Monday morning, the barista was close to hyperventilating from happiness. They brainstormed a few ideas, then Nina gave Frankie a budget and left it all in his capable hands.

Edith had also given Nina the go-ahead to refresh some of Soul Fare's interior features. Putting aside her disappointment over the menu, Nina spent her evenings scouring online home décor stores, researching design options, and jotting down ideas. She loved every minute of it. In fact, she was so busy, she rarely thought of Lucas.

Her first project was to get rid of the plastic flowers on every table and replace them with rustic wooden planters holding artificial plants. Yes, they were still fake, but they were green, and the restaurant needed greenery. It was about optics.

After the planters, Nina stayed late one evening and took down the heavy curtains she'd secretly hated. She worked late into the night, cleaning the glass and varnishing the wooden frames. She didn't get to bed until well after midnight, but the look on everyone's faces the next morning when they walked into Soul Fare made all the hard work worthwhile.

"I can't believe what a difference it makes," murmured Jeena, staring at the gleaming wall of windows overlooking the street.

"The place looks bigger," said Cody.

It was true, Nina thought, pleased with herself. Removing the old-fashioned curtains opened up the interior, giving the restaurant a fresh, modern look.

Jeena gestured to the windows. "Did you do this all yourself?"

"I did."

"It must have taken you a long time," said Cody.

Nina said vaguely, "Not too long."

Cody frowned. "You didn't ask us to help."

Taken aback by his statement, Nina said, "I didn't want to impose. It would have meant a lot of after-hours work."

"You should have given us the choice," Jeena said.

Nina stared at the two of them as they drifted off to slip on their aprons and prepare for the upcoming shift. They both looked a little put out. She'd assumed she was doing them a favor by not asking them to stay behind on their own personal time to help. Now as she headed to her office to pay bills, she wondered if she'd gotten it completely wrong. Maybe they wanted to be involved. Maybe they wanted to feel that sense of accomplishment she was feeling. She sat at her desk and stared unseeingly at the wall. It was a bitter truth to realize that she could make all the improvements in the world to the appearance of the restaurant, but if she didn't have the support of her staff, Soul Fare wouldn't survive.

Chapter Twenty-Six

Nina adjusted her blouse and looked at her watch again. Tammy was fifteen minutes late. She sighed. Fifteen minutes felt like fifty when you were sitting alone in a cocktail bar.

"What's a pretty girl like you—"

"Don't bother," Nina said without turning around.

She heard the man mutter something and move away. Honestly, this was the last place she wanted to be right now. Her head was throbbing and her legs ached from standing all day. When Tammy had messaged her yesterday asking if they could meet up at a trendy cocktail bar in the city, she'd immediately agreed. After all, it had been over two months since she'd last seen her. They were definitely overdue for a catchup.

"Nina!"

At the sound of Tammy's voice, Nina stood up to greet her friend, trying to disguise her shock at Tammy's appearance. She'd lost weight, her skin was pale, and her normally beautiful red hair looked lank and dull.

"Long time no see," Nina said, kissing her on the cheek.

"You moved to the other end of the earth, that's why."

Ignoring the dig, Nina drained the orange juice she'd been nursing and waited while Tammy worked her usual magic and secured them a sought-after booth in the quieter section of the bar. Tammy slid into the seat opposite her and they regarded each other in silence.

"I missed you," Tammy said abruptly.

"I missed you too," Nina responded automatically, but she was surprised to realize she hadn't thought about Tammy much at all.

When the server appeared, Tammy ordered a martini and raised her eyebrows when Nina asked for a virgin daiquiri.

She didn't owe Tammy an explanation, but she said, "I'm driving."

"Why don't you stay over at my place?"

"Thanks, but I have an early start tomorrow."

Tammy shrugged. "Your loss."

While they waited for their drinks, Nina brought Tammy up to date on all the goings-on at the restaurant. She was careful not to mention Lucas since she didn't want to set Tammy off, but Tammy was already edgy and distracted, full of boasting about her sexual exploits in Italy. There was something going on with her friend, and Nina wasn't sure what it was.

When Tammy ordered another martini and then another, the evening went downhill from there, because an alcohol-fueled Tammy was all sarcasm and scorn and over-the-top flirting with anyone possessing a heartbeat.

Eventually, after stifling yet another yawn, Nina said, "It's late. I should go."

"Don't be such a killjoy."

"Tammy—"

"One more drink," Tammy pleaded.

"All right, one more," Nina agreed tiredly.

Tammy grabbed her hand. "I'm proud of you, Nina. I can't remember if I've ever told you that, but I'm truly so proud of you and so thankful for our friendship."

Nina felt her heart soften. If only she could experience more of *this* Tammy. It was these glimpses of charm and sweetness that kept her hanging in there, hoping for more moments like this.

For the next few minutes, they reminisced about some of the funnier times they'd shared, then Tammy excused herself to head to the ladies' room. When Nina saw her emerge wiping her nose, disappointment flooded her, followed by anger. That was it. She'd had enough. Tammy could do coke on her own time.

She picked up her handbag and got to her feet. "I'm leaving."

Tammy didn't bother trying to persuade her to stay. She simply offered a contemptuous farewell wave. "Call me when you decide to leave the nunnery."

Nina fumed the whole drive home. Why did she put up with Tammy? Was their friendship too toxic? Should she end it? What was the right thing to do here?

Her head hurt from questions with no clear answers. She knew without a doubt what Lucas would advise, and there was a part of her that longed to follow his advice, but she couldn't help the nagging feeling that Tammy, on some level, relied on her to help keep the darkness at bay.

The next morning, Tammy texted her usual apologies.

Not good enough, Nina texted back. *Not this time. What's going on?*

Her chest tightened when she read Tammy's reply: *Battling demons.* It was her most honest answer to date.

Nina took a few seconds to think, finally typing: *In a battle, it helps to have someone at your side.*

And then Tammy's response: *You want to return to my past and help me fight an uncle who couldn't keep his hands to himself?*

There it was, at last. Tammy's demon. Or one of them, at least.

Oh, Tammy, I'm sorry.

So am I. No one believed me. He's dead now. No justice for the wicked.

I believe you.

Nina waited, but there was no reply. She let out a defeated sigh, knowing Tammy was no longer reachable.

#

The only way to push Tammy from her mind, Nina decided, was to throw herself into work. For weeks now, she'd been searching for ways to empower her staff, but to her frustration, she'd come up empty. A feeling of failure plagued her. Her personal life sucked, and it wasn't much better at work either. If only she could get one area of her life right.

She had the first germ of an idea during one of Cody's breaks as she watched him sit outside the restaurant with his earbuds in, listening to music and swaying to whatever beat was playing. She kept thinking about the fact that Cody's favorite topic of conversation was music. He knew the names of an impressive number of artists, even the obscure ones, and you could hum a few bars of a tune and most of the time Cody could name the song straight away.

After wrestling with the issue back and forth in her head, Nina decided to take a chance. Part of empowering her team was loosening the reins, she told herself.

At the end of a busy Wednesday shift, she called Cody aside. "How would you like to be in charge of Soul Fare's music?"

A mix of hope and excitement crossed his face. "You mean it?"

"I wouldn't be offering it to you if I didn't."

"Okay, yeah, I'd love to do the music! That would be awesome!"

She put a warning note in her next words. "Cody, you know our clientele, so you know what music will best reflect the personality of the restaurant."

He nodded vigorously. "Totally. I'm thinking chill, intimate music. Nothing intrusive."

"You have a week to put together a fifty-song playlist. Let's see how it goes from there."

"A week is cool. I got this, Nina."

"I hope so."

Ten minutes after Cody left, Nina was checking that everything was in place for the next day when Jeena stalked in from the kitchen. "You've got to be kidding me. You put *Cody* in charge of the music?"

"I'm giving him a trial run."

The appalled expression on Jeena's face whittled away some of Nina's certainty.

"A trial run! You want Eminem blaring from the speakers?"

"Let's give him a chance, Jeena."

Jeena stared at her for a moment, then nodded and left without a word. Before she turned away, however, Nina had seen the look on Jeena's face, a look that said, *okay, so you're giving him a chance, but what about me?*

#

Cody's big day rolled around surprisingly quickly. Although Nina had dropped hints throughout the week for a preview of his playlist, Cody had cheerfully ignored them all, keeping his music choices close to his skinny chest.

On Wednesday, jittery with nerves, Nina let Cody loose on the iPod. The first song filtered through the speakers, smooth and soothing, like that first velvety sip of coffee. The next song followed and then the next, the tempo and genre of the music changing just enough to keep things interesting. Nina slowly relaxed. Cody had done it. He'd managed to put together an eclectic playlist of nostalgia-heavy tunes, as well as upbeat songs and easy-listening music that would appeal to both the older and younger crowd.

She could feel Cody's expectant eyes on her throughout the morning, but she waited until the lunchtime shift had ended before connecting with him in her office. "How are you feeling?"

"Nervous."

"No need to be." She smiled at him. "Well done, Cody."

"I nailed it?"

"You did."

A wide grin broke out. "Yeah!"

"The music hit just the right mood for every meal service. How did you manage that?"

Bouncing on the balls of his feet, Cody looked eager to share. "I read on a restaurant blog that it's better to play faster-paced music during lunch rushes to turn tables quicker. And when it's quiet, like late afternoon, slower-tempo music will persuade customers to hang around and spend more on drinks and desserts."

Her chest swelled with pride. Cody had exceeded her expectations. "You did your research and put a lot of thought into this. I'm proud of you."

His smile stretched further. "Thanks, Nina."

"Can you put together another two or three playlists?" she asked, making a mental note to check with Edith that they were fully compliant with copyright law.

He nodded. "Oh, yeah, absolutely. I had a lot of fun doing this."

She watched him walk away with a spring in his step, then she sought out Jeena, who was over at the server station sorting out cutlery. "So. No rave club music. No top-forty hits. No elevator music."

Jeena shot her a sideways glance. "Are you gloating?"

"A little."

Her lips twitched. She was fighting a smile. "I suppose you deserve to gloat just a little." She was silent for a few seconds. "You took a chance on Cody, and it worked out."

"I took a chance on him, but he was the one who came through."

Jeena nodded. "It's good to see him so motivated."

"It is," Nina agreed, picking up on the wistful note in Jeena's voice.

Your turn's coming, she wanted to say, but she kept quiet. The truth was, Nina didn't know what skills Jeena possessed that could be employed and nurtured so she too could feel a sense of ownership in Soul Fare. Honestly, she was at a loss.

ALL THE LOST PIECES

#

Nina stood nervously next to Edith as she slowly scanned Soul Fare's dining area, her eyes widening as she took in the exposed windows and light-filled spaces and splashes of greenery.

At length she said, "You've made some changes."

Nina held her breath. "What do you think?"

"I like it," Edith said finally. "You've done well, my dear."

Taking advantage of the goodwill wave she was currently riding, Nina asked, "How about a fresh coat of paint for the interior walls?"

"What color are you thinking?"

"White. It's clean and crisp, and it'll make the area look more spacious."

A couple of seconds ticked by while Edith considered this, then she gave a nod of approval.

Elation surged through Nina. "It's going to look amazing," she assured her.

Half an hour later, as Edith was getting ready to leave, she murmured, "I wish Bill could see what you're doing here."

For the rest of the day, Nina couldn't shake off Edith's words and the look of regret on her face.

The next morning, Nina took photos of the windows, as well as the wooden planters, and sent them to Edith. Edith called her later that day to say she'd shown the photos to Bill, and, for a magical second, there'd been a glimmer of recognition and excitement in his eyes.

"Thank you," she said to Nina in a tremulous voice.

And Nina promised that once the walls were painted and more decorations put up, she'd send her photos of those changes as well.

Chapter Twenty-Seven

Two days after the conversation with Edith, before Soul Fare opened its doors for the day, Nina was making her way to her office when she noticed Jeena's sketchbook lying all by its lonesome on a table at the back of the restaurant. She walked slowly toward the table and looked around. Jeena was nowhere in sight.

She couldn't stop staring at the sketchbook.

Don't do it, she told herself. It had taken ages for her to build up a fragile bond with Jeena, and she could destroy it in an instant if she went snooping around.

But the sketchbook was like the eye of Sauron. She couldn't take her eyes off it.

Of course, because Jeena went out of her way to ensure that no one caught a glimpse of whatever it was she scribbled in those pages, that just made Nina all the more curious to know exactly what was in there.

Pretending to stumble, Nina reached out a hand to balance herself.

Oops, look at what she'd done, she'd flipped open the book and...

Her mind went blank, and she stared in astonishment at the page in front of her, her surroundings fading away.

On the page, Jeena had drawn an accurate caricature of Bianca, one of the movie club ladies. The caption was *If your dentures give you trouble, there's always soup.* It was sharp and funny and showcased some serious talent.

"What the heck are you doing?"

Nina guiltily snatched her hand back.

Jeena grabbed the sketchbook and held it close to her chest. "How dare you! That's private property."

Nina winced. "I'm sorry, I was just curious—"

"Your curiosity doesn't give you the right to pry into my business."

"You're right." She held Jeena's gaze. "Look, I apologize, but from the small glimpse I had, you are really good."

Surprise flickered across Jeena's face. "Thanks," she said finally. And then, as if she couldn't help herself, she added, "Not that you're an expert."

"Not that I am," Nina admitted, heaving a massive internal sigh. *Honestly, reaching her is like trying to scale Everest.*

#

The rest of the day didn't get any better. A family with a toddler came in, and from the moment they sat down, the child started screaming like her parents were scalping her. A bowl of fries was quickly ordered, but the demon-possessed toddler simply lobbed the fries at surrounding diners. Eventually, the beleaguered parents left, and everyone, staff and diners alike, breathed a sigh of relief.

At one point in the morning, there was a glitch in Cody's playlist, and heavy metal screeched through the speakers, startling an elderly lady into thinking she was having a heart attack. It took a couple of panic-stricken seconds before she realized that the pain in her chest was actually heartburn caused by the raw onions in the salad she'd just eaten. Yes, she admitted sheepishly, her doctor had advised her to no longer eat onions for exactly that reason. Still, Nina comped her meal and then had to listen to a lecture from the onion lady on the benefits of classical music.

#

When Nina got home later that evening, her intention was to have a shower and head straight to bed because lousy days like this only got worse. Instead, she ended up making herself a cheese and tomato sandwich and settling on the couch in front of the TV. Two hours later, she was still there, fighting to stay awake while zombies attacked anyone who crossed their path. When her phone rang, she answered it without registering the ringtone.

"Nina, darling."

Nina's heart sank. She should've gone to bed. "Mom, hi."

"You sound awful."

"Just tired."

"You should be in bed, then."

"That's what I keep telling myself." Nina sat up and made a halfhearted attempt to tidy up around her. "How's everything going?"

"Darryl and I aren't together anymore," Cheryl said, a catch in her voice. "He broke it off."

Not unexpected news, but Nina could hear how upset she was. "I'm sorry to hear that."

"I really liked him."

"I know."

"Anyway," her mother said briskly, "Nothing To Gain By Dwelling On The Past."

Finally, a Capitalized Saying she agreed with, Nina thought. "Have you dived into a box of chocolates yet?"

There was a sharp intake of breath on the other end of the line. "Nina, no man will ever drive me to chocolate."

Hastily she said, "Of course not."

"Hopefully, Daughter of My Womb, you're not that weak."

In all likelihood, she kept the chocolate industry in business. Now was a good time to close off the conversation. "I'm feeling pretty tired, Mom, so—"

Then Cheryl asked, "How are *you* doing, Nina?"

"Me?"

"Yes. How's it going at the restaurant?"

It's going well was what Nina planned to say, but instead what tumbled out of her was "I haven't had the best day. Actually, there haven't been many good days there."

She half expected Cheryl to launch into her I-did-warn-you speech, but to Nina's astonishment, she said, "Tell me what's going on."

And Nina, surprising herself, let it all spill out: the difficulties she was having with the staff and how they still treated her like an outsider. She told her mother about Edith and Bill, and her disappointment at not being able to change the menu, but how reluctant she was to push Edith.

When Nina finished, Cheryl simply asked, "Do you want to continue working there?"

Nina considered the question. "Yes," she said at last, because, in the end, despite all the frustrations she'd listed, her work was still challenging. And, on very rare occasions, thinking of her recent breakthrough with Cody, rewarding.

"Then listen to me," her mother said. "You can do this. You are more capable than you realize."

Shock briefly stole Nina's voice. "You've never said that to me before."

"It sounds like you need the truth," Cheryl said. "And the truth is, you are good at what you do."

"I don't understand," Nina said helplessly. "You've always put down my work. In fact, you've repeatedly encouraged me to look for another occupation."

Cheryl sighed. "Yes, I have."

"Why?"

"Because I know the terrible toll the restaurant business takes on your health and your family. Your father loved working in the restaurant, but the job demanded that he be there all day and night. When he did have a day off, he was so exhausted, he slept the hours away." She sighed again. "I didn't want that for you. I didn't want you to be in an occupation where you're not there for your family, or you're up pacing for most of the night because your legs are throbbing from the varicose veins you never had time to deal with."

Nina's throat closed, and she leaned back against the sofa. She had a sudden glimpse into what it must have been like for her mother. It was a different picture from the one she remembered—cooking alongside her dad in the kitchen, his Saturday visits to her restaurant cubby—but now she was flooded with the realization that her picture had huge chunks missing...all those birthdays and bedtimes and school events where her father had been absent.

"Why haven't you told me this before?"

"I didn't want to spoil your memories of your dad. You idolized him so much."

Regret tore through Nina. She had the sense this was something Cheryl had wanted to say to her for a long time. "I thought you were ashamed of me."

"I could never be ashamed of you," Cheryl said. "I can be irritated and angry with you, I can want what I think is best for you and push you toward that, but that's just me being a parent. Ashamed of you? Never."

Nina was struggling to sort through all the emotions coming at her like an out-of-control truck. How could she feel such relief, as if a crushing weight had been lifted, but also feel like bursting into tears? Everything was so mixed up. All those wasted years of miscommunication and resentment. "I'm sorry I got it so wrong, Mom."

"I didn't exactly get it right either. And I'm sorry too. I should have told you this earlier."

Nina was silent for a bit. "My job at Soul Fare looks nothing like the one Dad had. That's why I took it. I can have a life outside work."

"Are you certain you don't want to explore—?"

"Mom," Nina warned.

"All right, I won't mention it again."

She would, but Nina found she wasn't filled with resentment at the thought. She'd lost sight of the reality that most families were made up of personalities you typically might not choose to associate with, but blood ties meant that no matter how much you sniped at one another, you were and always would be irrevocably connected. Maybe the only way for her to achieve any kind of peace was to simply accept her family as they were, with all their peculiarities and foibles.

They spoke for another fifteen minutes, but by unspoken agreement, they kept it light, with Cheryl sharing highlights from her seminar and Nina describing some of the funnier antics of her diners. For the first time in as long as she could remember, Nina wasn't in a hurry to get off the phone with her mother.

But when Cheryl tried to set her up on a blind date with a "darling man, tons of money and ever so amusing," Nina decided now was a good time to say goodbye, before they ruined this fragile new understanding between them.

#

Over the next couple of days, Nina arranged for the inside walls of Soul Fare to be painted. The result was incredible. The whole interior of the restaurant was transformed into a clean white space. Nina took photos and sent them to Edith, who loved the look.

Now she just needed to soften the starkness of the walls, and she had a couple of ideas. On one wall, Nina hung artificial plants on a timber pegboard, transforming that section into a wall of greenery that complemented the tabletop planters and added to the eco feel. She found some old shop signs in a secondhand store and positioned them around the pegboard, and the result was a quirky, slightly bohemian vibe.

"Nice," Jeena murmured when she was done.

"Thank you." Nina caught her sneaking a look at the other walls, blank canvases begging for a concept. "Any ideas, Jeena?"

Jeena's lips tightened. "No."

"You sure?"

"Yes." Abruptly she turned away and headed for the kitchen.

For the rest of the day, Nina couldn't forget that look of longing on Jeena's face. She was obviously interested in decorating the walls, but she'd also flat-out refused to contribute. Nina chewed her bottom lip. What on earth was she supposed to do with that contradiction? She didn't have a degree in decoding whatever weird thought processes were playing out in Jeena's head.

Stuff it, she thought, stacking the menus into the hostess stand. Forget Jeena. The woman was just too much hard work.

After locking up the restaurant, Nina shopped for groceries, grabbed herself a pampering bouquet of tulips, and decided to extend the self-love when she arrived home. Unfortunately, not even a long soak in a bath filled with Epsom salts and lavender oil could eject Jeena's face from her thoughts.

The next morning, with everyone involved in prep before service, Nina approached Jeena. She was curious to test out an idea she'd woken up with after a fitful night's sleep.

"Jeena, yesterday I asked if you had any ideas for Soul Fare's walls," she began.

Jeena crossed her arms. "I remember."

That, Nina realized, noting Jeena's defensive posture, had been her mistake. She'd asked her for ideas that she, and not Jeena, could implement. Nina tried to live by two buzzwords at work—trust and empowerment—and she'd neglected to apply either of them in this situation. "Well, now I'm thinking that I'd like you to take charge of decorating the rest of the wall space."

Interest stirred on Jeena's face. "You're putting me in charge?"

"Yes."

"Why the change of mind?"

"I remembered your sketchbook and the talent on those pages." She smiled at Jeena. "And if I can trust Cody with the music, I can trust you with the walls." At least she hoped so. She was taking such a chance here, but her gut told her that this decision felt right. "What do you think?"

Jeena swallowed. "I'd love to work on the walls."

"Great." Nina was already walking away when Jeena blurted out, "Nina, wait!"

Nina turned to face her. "Yes?"

Jeena's voice was hesitant at first, but picked up in confidence as she spoke. "What about a large chalkboard on the wall next to Frankie's station for Ano's daily specials? We could purchase one with a rich wooden frame to match the window frames."

Nina wanted to hug her! She would if she thought for one minute Jeena wouldn't react by pushing her away. "That's an excellent idea."

"It will save on printing costs," Jeena said, "and I can do a bit of artwork around the specials."

Nina tilted her head to one side, studying her. "You've obviously been thinking about this?"

Jeena colored. "Yes, I have."

Nina gestured to a chair. "Let's sit." When Jeena had taken a seat, Nina said, "Why don't we extend that concept outside? We could have a blackboard on an easel outside the front entrance."

Jeena straightened in her seat, excitement rolling off her. "Something fun and playful to attract passersby."

"Exactly. Let your creativity go wild. It could be a witty saying, an inspirational message, a comical drawing. I think diners will appreciate the fun aspect of it."

They bounced a few more ideas around, then Jeena cleared her throat and said, "Thank you, Nina, for this opportunity."

A lump formed in Nina's throat. It was her turn to simply nod because she didn't trust herself to speak.

It had been a good day, Nina thought as she closed up the restaurant and headed home. She'd made huge inroads with Jeena, who'd run another idea past her about putting up local artists' work on the remaining walls and giving diners the option to buy them. It would be a sort of rotating art exhibition, she explained.

It was a superb idea. Nina liked the fact that they would be supporting the local art community, not to mention the added benefit of Soul Fare receiving beautiful wall art that could turn into conversation pieces. Her confidence in Jeena hadn't been misplaced.

Yep, a really good day, Nina concluded, turning into her street.

And then she spotted Lucas's car parked outside her apartment building.

Chapter Twenty-Eight

Heart hammering, Nina pulled into her usual spot and hurried out to meet him. "What's wrong?" she asked as Lucas climbed out of his car. "Is everything okay with Liv?"

"Liv's fine."

Relief whirled through Nina. "Oh, thank goodness."

As her heart rate slowly returned to normal, she took a closer look at him. He seemed...out of sorts. Shadows darkened his green eyes, and his brown hair was disheveled, as though he'd been raking his fingers through it. He appeared to have come straight from work. He wore a dark suit, jacket and tie abandoned on the back seat, white shirtsleeves rolled up to his elbows, top button undone.

He looked achingly handsome, and her hungry eyes consumed him.

"This is a surprise," she said at last, when Lucas didn't say anything.

"I took a chance you would be home." His eyes met hers, but only briefly, before flicking away again. She frowned, puzzled. He was acting so strangely. What on earth was going on? A sense of trepidation lodged in her chest.

"You're in luck," she said lightly, in a bid to ease the curious tension surrounding him. "This is my one and only evening free on my busy social calendar."

A corner of his mouth lifted, but he didn't respond in a similar lighthearted manner. Instead, he asked abruptly, "Can I come inside?"

"Yes, of course." Still feeling off-balance, she made her way to her apartment, Lucas walking silently beside her. They were so very careful not to touch one another.

In the entrance hall, Nina shed her coat and keys and handbag. "Make yourself at home. I need to change out of my work clothes."

She also needed time to compose herself. She had no idea why Lucas was here, but she couldn't shake this peculiar awareness that things were shifting between them. Telling herself she was overreacting, Nina dumped her clothes into the laundry hamper and pulled on black leggings and a loose-fitting T-shirt. After gathering her hair into a messy bun, she took a deep, bracing breath and headed down the hallway to find Lucas in the kitchen, pouring himself a glass of water.

She joined him, hoisting herself onto the countertop to give her legs a welcome break.

"Busy day?" he asked, taking a sip of his water.

"Busy enough."

He looked out onto her living room. "You've settled in nicely."

She nodded. "There are a few things I'd still like to get to make the place more of a home, but I'm not in a hurry." Nina twisted her fingers together. She was prone to babbling when she was drowning in nerves. "You hungry?"

He shook his head. "I'm not sure I can stomach anything right now."

Neither could she. There were all kinds of flutterings taking place in her belly. But why would Lucas be nervous? She waited a few beats, then asked, "Lucas, why are you here?"

"Look, can we not do this in the kitchen?" he asked, his voice gruff.

Confusion filled her. *Do what?* "You want to move to the living room?"

At his nod, they settled on the couch, Lucas on one end, Nina facing him stiffly on the other end, as far away from him as she could get without falling off the couch.

Without preamble, he said, "Tahlia and I are no longer together. We broke it off."

Nina kept still, trying to wrap her head around what Lucas had told her. For so long, she'd been filled with an awful kind of certainty that the two of them would end up with a mortgage, kids, a scruffy dog—the whole happy family scene.

She couldn't say she was sorry, because she wasn't. Not one bit.

"Why did you break up?" she asked, wishing she'd poured herself a glass of water just for something to do with her hands.

He ran a hand over his jaw. "We were arguing all the time."

"You were?" she asked, pretending ignorance.

"Yes."

"Oh."

He seemed in no hurry to elaborate. All right, she was going to have to pry it out of him. "What were you arguing about?"

His eyes held hers. "You."

"Me?" It came out as a stunned squeak.

He nodded, his expression unreadable.

She swallowed. "I don't understand."

"Tahlia accused me of having feelings for you. She was convinced there was something between us."

Nina's mouth was so dry, she had trouble forming the words. "Well, there is something between us," she said. "Friendship."

Lucas said slowly, "According to her, there was something more than friendship between us."

Her heart crawled up into her throat. She wasn't prepared for this moment. The terror of saying or doing the wrong thing paralyzed her.

Lucas watched her intently. Nina didn't know what he was searching for. A fervent denial? Confirmation that Tahlia was correct in her suspicions? More to the point, what was he *hoping* to see written on her face?

To survive in her industry, however, Nina had become a pro at presenting her neutral hospitality face. He wouldn't see anything she didn't want him to see.

"Nina?" Lucas prodded.

Choosing her words with care, she asked, "Why would Tahlia think that?"

The question seemed to throw him. Good. It was now his turn to be on his guard, to tiptoe around what they weren't saying here.

"I don't know," he said at last. "Do you think there might be...something more between us?"

She felt a swell of disappointment. Really? He was leaving it all in her court?

She folded her arms. Let him pick up on that message. "Lucas, when I was sick that one night and you came over, I put myself out there and said you could share my bed. Do you remember what you said?"

The deep frown on his face suggested that that was the last thing in the world he wanted to remember.

Nina didn't wait for him to respond. "You told me you wouldn't do anything to jeopardize our friendship. Do you remember that?"

He winced, as though any reminder of that night was painful. "Of course I remember," he said, his voice low. "But—"

She made a frustrated gesture, anger building up inside her. "You made your feelings very clear that night. And now you've broken up with Tahlia, and you're...I don't know...lonely and confused...and I just... I can't have this conversation with you. A lot's happening at work, and I don't...I don't have the head space for this."

After a pause, he gave a stiff nod. "Okay."

"All right, then," she said, equally stiff.

They sat there staring at one another, neither of them making a move to stand.

Finally, Lucas said, "I should probably go."

"Okay."

Her throat was tight as she walked him to the door, the air as heavy as her heart with all the unsaid things between them.

"Goodbye, then," Lucas said thickly.

"Bye," she said in a small voice.

In the next instant, she was caught up in his arms and his lips were on hers. Shock gave way to relief, and then heat filled every part of her.

At last, her soul sighed. All these years of wondering and waiting, and now the reality was that Lucas's hands were sliding to the back of her head, his fingers twisting in her hair, his mouth moving urgently on hers, as though he too had been waiting and waiting for this moment.

She curled her fingers into his shirt and pulled him closer, thrilling at the strength and power of his body pressed against her. Her skin felt alive, sensitive to his every touch, her stomach free-falling down the longest, steepest cliff.

Suddenly, Lucas pulled away. "I'm not lonely or confused," he said roughly. "That night, you were the sickest I'd ever seen you, and I wasn't going to take advantage of that. Also, I was with Tahlia. I'm not a cheater. That's not who I am." He framed her face in his hands and his eyes never left hers. "But I am madly, crazily in love with you, Nina Abrahams. And I'm all kinds of stupid for not realizing it earlier."

His words made her dizzy. And scared. And wonderfully, indescribably happy. "Lucas..." She couldn't speak. She'd waited so long to hear those words from him.

He kissed her again. Softly at first, but it didn't take long for the kiss to deepen. Pleasure hummed through her. Her mind emptied of reason and only sensation consumed her.

With obvious reluctance, Lucas broke off the kiss and rested his forehead against hers. "Nina, honey, we need to talk and if we stay here another minute, talking is the last thing we'll be doing."

"Talking's overrated," she murmured against his lips, and he laughed softly.

"I agree, but maybe if we'd talked more about us, we could've reached this moment sooner." He drew back slightly, giving her a questioning look.

Nina realized what he was asking for. It was now or never, she decided. "I love you too," she said on a shaky breath. "I've been in love with you since I was eighteen. Since the night of the house party."

She registered the astonishment widening his eyes. The strained tightening of his lips. His stunned silence.

Well. Either she'd done an excellent job of concealing her feelings, or Lucas possessed a spectacularly defective emotional radar.

He laced his fingers through hers and tugged her back toward the living room. "We definitely need to talk."

They sat together on the couch, Lucas keeping her close to him, still holding her hand, as though he couldn't bear any more distance between them.

"All those years," he said, a disbelieving note in his voice, "you really felt that way about me?"

She nodded. "What about you? I mean, when did your...you know...feelings for me change?"

"The night of the charity gala," he replied without hesitation. "When I saw you in that dress, my first reaction was to rip it off and—" He cleared his throat, color flaring delightfully on his cheekbones. "Let's not go into all the things I wanted to do to you."

So her eye-wateringly expensive dress *had* achieved its intended effect, Nina reflected with satisfaction.

"My reaction shook me up," Lucas continued, "because, heck, that's not the way a friend would feel. Then, when you were up on that stage, I couldn't take my eyes off you. I kept thinking how brave you were and how much I wanted you."

Nina remembered the way he'd looked at her that night. She remembered his words: *You would've been my first choice.* "You should have said something."

"Maybe. But you and Ryan and Liv are my closest friends. I didn't want to do or say anything that might damage our friendship, so I just shrugged those feelings off. At the time, all I could think about was how much I'd lose if we stopped being friends. I never allowed myself to think how much I'd gain."

She struggled to take it all in, dazed by everything Lucas had confessed to her.

"Then when you brought Brian as your date, I was so jealous, I wanted to toss him out the window. I should have been happy for you, but I wasn't. And that was when Tahlia started to pick up on my feelings for you."

Nina had to ask the question burning like acid inside her. "If you were feeling this way about me, why were you with Tahlia?"

Lucas didn't flinch from the question. "Tahlia's a lovely woman. Yes, I was attracted to her, I enjoyed being with her, but there was always this niggle that something wasn't right. One day, Olivia pointed out that Tahlia bears a strong resemblance to you. It hit me then that I no longer wanted to settle for replicas of you. I wanted the real deal."

Nina felt a rush of gratitude toward Olivia. Who needed a sister when you could lay claim to the greatest sister-in-law in the world?

"I still don't understand why you waited so long to tell me how you feel."

His mouth twisted. "Tammy made it very clear you weren't interested in a serious relationship with anyone."

Nina's mouth dropped open. "What? When did Tammy say this?"

"About three years after the house party. It was at your twenty-first. Remember, your mom had rented out the community hall to celebrate?"

She remembered. She also remembered how much she and everyone else had to drink that night.

"Tell me exactly what she said."

His forehead creased as he thought back. "She said that because of what happened that night at the house party, you always find excuses to cut short your relationships, that dating just brings back memories of the attack."

Nina frowned. "I don't remember saying anything like that to her."

"According to Tammy, the reason you feel comfortable with me is because I'd never make a sexual advance toward you."

"Why would you believe anything Tammy told you?" Nina asked. "You detest her."

"Nina, your life lived out her words," Lucas said quietly. "I don't trust Tammy, but your relationships never lasted more than three months."

Lucas's statement left her flabbergasted. "Those relationships didn't last because I was in love with you! Not because of some hang-up from the past!"

"So Tammy lied." His voice held a slight edge.

Nina bit her lip. "She must have misinterpreted something I said. I'll speak to her."

Lucas pulled her closer. "Let's not talk about Tammy anymore. Let's just savor the fact that we're together now."

"I still can't believe we got it so wrong."

Lucas gave her that slow smile of his, the one that always took out her knees. "Now's our chance to get it right."

Chapter Twenty-Nine

The following two weeks were among the happiest of Nina's life. She saw Lucas every day after work. During the week, he drove down to Barracat, and they would spend the evenings walking hand in hand around the lake (Lucas tried to cajole her into going for a run, but she told him she'd spent enough time chasing after him, and her running days were over). In a quiet spot under the willow trees, they'd eat baguettes stuffed full of mozzarella, tomato, and basil, and make out. When they were in the mood for company, they played pool or darts at the local sports bar (she couldn't beat him, no matter how she cheated).

On the weekends, Nina drove to his apartment in the city, where neither of them had any desire to venture out. Lucas would order up the most exquisite sushi, and they'd snuggle on the couch and watch romantic comedies. He cooked her waffles every morning while she attempted to coax his herb plants back to life. There was a lot of laughing and teasing and wrestling that usually ended up with Lucas pinning her beneath him (a not-altogether-unfavorable outcome).

On Wednesday afternoon, Lucas surprised her by popping in to Soul Fare to have lunch.

"Hey," he greeted her, giving her an outrageously flirty look.

"Hello, Lucas." She offered him a brisk, professional nod in return. As she showed him to his table, handed him a menu, and took over serving him, she tried to channel her cool, calm hostess self, but she fooled no one.

"That your bloke, yeah?" Frankie asked with a teasing grin, while Cody and Jeena shot surreptitious glances Lucas's way every couple of minutes.

What probably gave her away was the smile she couldn't keep contained. Nina felt as though happiness radiated like sunbeams from her every pore.

"That's my bloke," she confirmed in a soft voice.

Even Ano, sensing a disturbance in the Force, emerged from his empire to see what was up with his subjects. Lucas charmed the giant chef with the right mix of compliments and questions, and soon the two of them were deep in conversation. Nina shook her head in disbelief. It had taken her months to rouse even a glimmer of a smile from the man!

Although everyone at work now knew about her and Lucas, they both agreed not to say anything to their respective families just yet. Nina didn't anticipate problems. After all, her mom adored Lucas, Olivia had been rooting for them to get together for ages, and Lucas's family already viewed her as part of their clan. Ryan would initially be dumbfounded, but after that...elation? Horror?...she wasn't sure.

Having everyone know, they both agreed, would no doubt add complexity to their relationship, with all the questions they'd face, the explanations they'd have to give. Right now, neither of them wanted complicated. They wanted *this* to be their secret a little while longer.

The person Nina dreaded telling was Tammy. She knew how Tammy felt about Lucas. She'd called Tammy to confront her about what she'd said to Lucas all those years ago. Tammy was surprised Lucas had told her, but her friend maintained that Nina had definitely said to her she wasn't—and never would be—interested in any sort of serious relationship after the attack.

"But I don't remember ever telling you that," Nina said, confused and uneasy.

"You don't remember because you were drunk," Tammy insisted.

Nina let it go. Perhaps she'd subconsciously felt that way and alcohol had let loose those feelings that night. And Tammy, for whatever reason, had passed the information along to Lucas.

It was done. In the past, and Nina had no desire to dwell there. Not when she had a future to look forward to.

#

On Monday, half an hour before the preshift meeting, Nina sat at one of the tables in the dining area checking her e-mail. She noticed Ano wander in from the kitchen, looking smart in his crisp chef's jacket and black pants.

"Ano," she called, indicating the seat opposite her. "Will you join me? Please," she added when he hesitated.

He pulled out a chair and sat. They chatted for a few minutes about food trends, and then the conversation turned to his back pain and sore knees, chronic complaints from chefs. Nina listened sympathetically, but wasn't foolish enough to offer advice.

In a pause in the conversation, she asked, "What's the special today, Ano?"

His face brightened. The man loved talking about food. "Onion and goat cheese tart."

"Any chance of a sneak taste?"

"Sure." He retrieved one from the kitchen and set it down on a plate in front of her.

The tart looked gorgeous. She took a bite, nearly moaning in ecstasy. The caramelized red onion with hints of thyme, butter, and vinegar perfectly brought out the smoothness of the cheese, and the pastry just about crumbled in her mouth.

"This is delicious! One of the best tarts I've tasted."

"Goat cheese is a favorite of Bill's," Ano said. "Edith's coming in later this afternoon, and I wanted to create something special that she could take to Bill."

"That's really sweet."

He shrugged off the praise. "Apparently, Bill's favorite foods can sometimes trigger memories for him. Edith likes it that she's able to connect with him through food."

Nina stared at him, feeling her skin prickle with excitement.

Ano shifted uncomfortably under her scrutiny. "Okay, what's with the serial killer eyes?"

"Ano, you've done it!" she whispered.

He frowned. "What have I done?"

She jumped to her feet. "You've solved my problem!"

"I didn't know you had a problem," he muttered. "Where are you going?"

"To jot down some notes before I forget," she said over her shoulder as she hurried to her office.

"Notes for what?"

"My new plan."

#

Absently, Nina picked at her cuticles as she watched Edith taste the goat cheese tart. When Ano gave her a pointed look, she stopped, linking her hands in her lap. Yes, it was a horrible habit she'd picked up and one she was trying to break.

Finishing the tart, Edith smiled her approval at Ano sitting across the table from her. "You've outdone yourself." As Edith continued to compliment him, Nina sat silently, formulating her argument.

When Ano kissed Edith's cheek and headed back to the kitchen, after leaving her with a tart to take to Bill, Nina said, "Edith, could I have a minute to discuss the menu with you?"

Edith's face clouded over. "We've already discussed this. I'm not changing Bill's menu."

Pumped full of enthusiasm and nerves, Nina said, "Please hear me out. It's not about changing the menu. It's about creating a menu that will honor Bill's legacy."

Nina presented her idea to Edith, explaining that Ano would come up with a menu where each dish would have one of Bill's favorite ingredients as the hero component. Basically, the whole menu would be about Bill, she went on. It would be a celebration of Bill's love of food.

Nina could see that Edith was intrigued enough not to outright dismiss her idea as she'd done previously.

"Best of all," Nina continued, after taking a deep breath, "whenever Bill tastes one of his favorite foods, hopefully it'll evoke good memories for him. And for you."

Nina didn't say anything more, knowing instinctively not to push it. Instead, she sipped the latte Frankie had brought over and let Edith mull over what had been said.

"You mentioned before that you think Ano is feeling stifled here," Edith said at length. "Do you still believe that?"

"Yes, I do."

"I don't want to lose him. He's been such a huge part of our journey here."

"I don't want to lose him either," Nina said. "He's a talented chef, and he loves his work."

Edith's perceptive eyes searched her face. "You've put a lot of thought into this, my dear."

"I know how important it is to you to keep the memory of Bill alive in Soul Fare."

Edith touched her wedding ring. "Your notion that Bill's legacy will live on in the menu, but in a different way, appeals to me." She bit her lip. "I don't know."

Softly, Nina said, "You can trust me."

Edith's delicate fingers encircled her teacup, as though she needed something to hold on to. "I keep reminding myself that you've managed to win over the staff, as well as change the look and feel of the restaurant for the better." She swallowed. "If I can trust you with all that, then I believe I can trust you with the menu."

Relief surged through Nina. "Thank you, Edith. You won't regret your decision."

Edith's eyes shone with unshed tears. "I confess it's also a selfish decision," she said. "If through one of Ano's dishes I'm able to have a moment of connection with my husband, even for only a few minutes, then that alone makes it worthwhile."

Just thinking about the powerful love that Edith and Bill shared caused a lump to form in Nina's throat. This was what she wanted for her and Lucas (minus the Alzheimer's). She wanted to grow old with him and share a love that transcended even the ravages of time.

\#

Ano had finished his shift and changed into street clothes when Nina gave him the good news about the menu. He reacted as she'd anticipated: bristling at her interference, grumbling that he didn't need her going to bat for him, defensive at the unsaid implication that he would leave Soul Fare. She suspected a part of him needed to put on a show. After five minutes of nodding along to his token rant, she told him to get over himself, and the grin he'd been restraining broke free, excitement spilling out of him at the chance to take creative ownership of the menu.

For the next couple of days, Ano played with various recipes, working on flavor combinations, presentation, and portion sizes. Edith had given him a list of Bill's favorite foods—mushrooms, pork, seafood, chili, miso, sweet potato, cauliflower, among others—and Ano was like a man possessed, his eyes often taking on a faraway look in the middle of a conversation as he reworked a recipe in his head.

The best part about those days were the tastings. Every day, Ano would summon all the staff to sample his creations, listening with a ferocious frown to everyone's comments, then making whatever adjustments he decided were needed. It amused Nina that Ano paid close attention to what Jeena thought. Her feedback, Nina was pleased to discover, was honest and insightful.

It was clear Ano was having fun pushing the boundaries in the kitchen, and all that energy and exuberance was revealed on the plate: scrambled eggs taken to the next level with the playful addition of ginger chili sambal. A beef burger with lashings of miso mayo and oozing pimento cheese. A sweet potato rosti with a masterful sprinkling of nori dust. Wild mushrooms paired with carrot hummus and crispy prosciutto. The tossing of wasabi peas and smoky roasted cauliflower into a rocket and fennel salad. Nina found that Ano could make even a simple pasta dish of fresh tomatoes, garlic, chili, capers, and black olives look and taste delightful.

Once Ano was satisfied with a dish, they'd invite Edith over for a tasting. She loved every single one of his creations. When Nina told her they'd elected to keep Bill's chicken waffle recipe and have it on the menu as Uncle Bill's Famous Chicken Waffles, Edith was overcome with emotion.

Watching her trying to regain her composure, Nina felt like crying herself. Happy tears. They'd done a good thing here. Had it really been only a few weeks ago that she'd felt like such a failure, both personally and professionally? Now it looked as though her life was finally on track.

Chapter Thirty

Nina was being thoroughly kissed by Lucas when her phone rang. You had to hand it to the man, she thought on a hazy wave of desire. When Lucas applied himself to something, he did it one hundred percent. No holding back.

It was a cold and rainy Saturday evening. Lucas had cranked up the heat in his apartment and they were lying on his humongous couch, which was more comfortable than her own bed. They were supposed to be watching a movie, but the plot line was so banal, they'd found something more interesting to do instead.

"Ignore it," Lucas murmured against her lips.

She smiled. "I was planning to."

Her phone rang out. Two seconds later, it started ringing again.

Lucas growled in frustration.

She sat up. "It might be Ryan or Olivia."

Please let nothing be wrong with the baby, she prayed silently as she reached for her phone. Olivia had recently started spotting, which the doctor assured her was normal, but he'd instructed her to rest and keep monitoring the bleeding. Nina had popped in last week to check on her, relieved to note that mom (and baby) appeared to be ridiculously healthy. And ridiculously observant, as Nina had feared.

"Why are you glowing?" Olivia had asked suspiciously. "I'm the one who's supposed to be glowing here. What's going on?"

Nina was dying to tell her the news, but she and Lucas had agreed to inform Olivia and Ryan together. Instead, she'd given Liv an impulsive, distracting hug and said simply, "It's my auntie glow," which had seemed to allay her suspicions.

With a resigned sigh, Lucas sat up too. "I guess you'd better answer."

"Hello," she said into her phone.

"Nina, I need your help."

"Tammy?" A sinking feeling washed over her. Tammy's words were slurred. "What's wrong? Are you okay?"

Nina heard Lucas blow out an irritated breath.

"I need you to come to my place."

"You're scaring me. What's going on?" Nina listened in growing alarm as Tammy gave a whispered, disjointed account of her having invited some guy she used to work with to her apartment and how they'd ended up drinking and dabbling in a few drugs, but things were getting out of hand.

Out of hand. Nina's skin prickled with unease. "What do you mean?" she asked, but Tammy, flying on a cocktail of who knew what drugs, wouldn't elaborate. She simply kept repeating for Nina to please come to her apartment.

"Is the guy still there?" she asked, getting to her feet.

Lucas stood too, frowning, his eyes on her. He'd clearly picked up that it was serious.

"He's still here." Tammy's voice was low and scared.

"Call the police."

"I can't."

Of course she couldn't, Nina thought. Not with all the illegal drugs that were no doubt littered throughout her apartment.

"I'll be there as fast as I can." She hung up, frantically looking around for her shoes, coat, handbag... What else did she need? She couldn't think properly.

"Nina." Lucas stayed her with a hand on her arm. "Calm down. You can't help Tammy if you're all worked up."

She briefly closed her eyes. He was right. Panic only led to mistakes.

He grabbed his car keys. "Would you listen if I asked you to remain here?"

"I can't, Lucas. She called *me*."

"I don't want you anywhere near whatever this situation is."

"It's not my first choice of places to be either, but I have to help her."

"Let's go, then." His expression was grim. "You can fill me in while we head out."

She snatched up her coat and handbag. "I realize this isn't your problem. You don't have to come with me."

Opening his front door, Lucas shot her an incredulous look. "You think I'm letting you go there alone? Not a chance. I'm coming with you."

Of course he was, because what was she going to do? Knock the guy out with her handbag? "Thank you. I know how you feel about her."

He drew her in for a quick, hard hug. "I'm going because of how I feel about *you*."

In the elevator, as they descended, she gave him a rundown of Tammy's call.

"She's just trouble," he muttered as the doors opened to the underground parking garage.

She touched his arm. "Please, Lucas, not now."

They climbed into his Range Rover, and as he pulled out onto the dark street, driving as fast as he dared, Nina couldn't shake the cold feeling in the pit of her stomach. She was worried about Tammy, but the thought wouldn't leave her that she was also putting Lucas in danger. Yes, he had training for this sort of thing, but still...anything could go wrong.

Fifteen minutes later, Lucas parked in front of Tammy's apartment building. They hurried out of the car, and Nina used the key card Tammy had given her ages ago to gain entry. The elevator was too slow in coming, so they took the stairs two at a time to her apartment on the second floor. They exited the stairwell door, Tammy's apartment right in front of them. All at once, Nina heard a loud crash coming from inside. Her heart thundered in her chest. "Lucas," she said, her voice catching.

"It's okay," he said calmly. "Give me the key."

She hadn't realized how much her hands were shaking until Lucas took the key from her. He opened Tammy's door, stepping into the entrance hall, keeping her close to him.

Inside, they could see into the living room, and it was a mess. Chairs upended. Drawers open and pictures askew on the wall. Broken glass on the floor. A deep crack in Tammy's expensive flat-screen TV.

Nina couldn't spot Tammy anywhere.

But there was no missing the giant of a man who seemed intent on destroying Tammy's living room. In fact, he was so absorbed in his work, he didn't notice them at first, allowing Nina to get a good look at him. The guy's freakish size indicated a chronic steroid user. He was wearing a white tank top and was tattooed in so many places, there was barely a patch of clean skin left. His head was shaved, and he looked absolutely terrifying.

"Hey, big guy," Lucas called out. "Why don't you put down the vase?"

The guy stiffened and turned in their direction, still holding the vase. Then, with an enraged roar, he hurled it at them.

Lucas sidestepped and took Nina with him, angling his body so he remained in front of her. His face was hard and tight, and he didn't take his eyes off the guy. The vase shattered behind them.

"Let's calm down here," Lucas said, but that only infuriated the man even further.

"Don't tell me to calm down!" he screamed, spittle flying, the veins in his neck bulging. "Don't you tell me to calm down!"

They all heard a groan. It came from the kitchen, which looked out onto the living room. An island counter separated the two areas.

Another groan. Relief rolled through Nina. Tammy. She was alive, but Nina had no idea how hurt she was. She was desperate to check on her friend, but her path was blocked.

Then the man tilted his head toward the kitchen, and Nina's heart sank. He'd obviously heard Tammy's groan.

"You know steroids shrink your balls, buddy," Lucas said matter-of-factly.

What the heck is Lucas doing, goading him like that? But when the man's head whipped around to face them again, fury lighting up his face, Nina realized that Lucas was deliberately provoking him, keeping his attention off Tammy and focused on them.

With a roar, he charged in their direction. Lucas pushed Nina out of the way and used the man's momentum to slam him headfirst into the wall.

Her heart still thumping, Nina eyed the man now lying dazed on the floor. "I thought we'd need an elephant tranquilizer to take him down."

"Brain over brawn," Lucas said. "You want to check on Tammy while I tie him up?"

Nina nodded, resisting the temptation to kick the man in the ribs as she passed.

"Careful where you step," Lucas warned. "There's glass everywhere."

In the kitchen, Tammy was trying to sit up. Nina rushed over to her, her stomach plummeting at the sight of her beautiful face all bruised and swollen. "Hey."

Tammy winced. "Hey, yourself."

She helped Tammy maneuver so that her back rested against a kitchen cupboard. "Anything broken?" Nina asked, studying her friend.

"Don't think so."

Lucas appeared in the kitchen, running his eyes over Tammy. "You all right?"

"I've been better. Where's Blake?"

"I'm assuming he's the maniac who likes to beat up women?" At her nod, he said, "He's restrained. He won't bother you again."

"What are we going to do with him?" Nina asked.

"Don't call the cops," Tammy pleaded.

"I've called some of my men," Lucas said. "They're coming here to take care of him."

Nina's eyes widened. "You mean, take care of him...like the mob."

With only the slightest twitch to his lips, Lucas said patiently, "Take care of him so the police find him away from here with a drug stash and he goes to prison for a long time."

"Oh. Okay. That sounds...better."

Tammy dropped her gaze. "Appreciate your help, Lucas."

"Let's get you out of here," he said, supporting her as she got to her feet. "You can stay at my place tonight."

#

They put Tammy in Lucas's guest bedroom, gave her a painkiller and a sleeping tablet, and when Nina checked on her fifteen minutes later, she was fast asleep.

In the kitchen, Lucas leaned against the countertop and sipped his decaf coffee. He'd made her a frothy hot chocolate in a hug mug. Her heart swelled. Exactly what she needed right now. Although it was after one, they were both too wired to fall asleep just yet.

Nina went straight to him, slid her arms around his waist, and rested her cheek against his chest. "Thank you for helping Tammy."

"Nina." At the seriousness of his tone, she drew back to stare up at him. There was a look in his eyes she hoped she'd never see again. "Every time I think of you going into Tammy's apartment alone, I want to punch something."

"I wasn't alone." She picked up her hot chocolate and took a sip. "You were with me."

"This time," he said, his voice rough with emotion. "What about the next time Tammy calls you?"

She frowned. "Hopefully, there won't be a next time."

"With Tammy, there's always a next time."

"Well, maybe after tonight she's learned her lesson."

Lucas's stony, dubious expression said he doubted that.

She set down her mug and took both of his hands in hers. "I don't want to argue. Not tonight. We'll talk to Tammy in the morning, okay?"

He went silent for a few seconds, then nodded.

No doubt the same thought running through her mind was running through his. They'd both taken Sunday off in anticipation of a relaxing day together. But now, they wouldn't be strolling in the Botanical Gardens or trying out the new Asian fusion café food critics were raving about. Instead, what loomed ahead was a difficult conversation with Tammy, trying to persuade her to get the help she so obviously needed.

#

On Sunday, Tammy woke up at noon and came stumbling through to the living room. Nina was lying on the couch, her feet in Lucas's lap. They were watching an over-the-top disaster movie, the name of which Nina had already forgotten. To thank her for the magnificent breakfast she'd cooked this morning (scrambled eggs, bacon, mushrooms, wilted spinach and hash browns), Lucas was massaging her feet and calves, his thumbs working her pressure points. This, Nina thought, biting back a moan, had to be one of life's greatest pleasures.

"You and Lucas look pretty cozy," Tammy commented, easing herself onto the armchair opposite them.

Nina straightened, removing her feet from Lucas's lap, then felt guilty for her reaction and irritated at Tammy for triggering the guilt. She had nothing to be ashamed of. But her irritation vanished as she eyed Tammy. The bruises on her face had darkened, and she was clearly favoring her ribs. She also needed a shower.

"How are you feeling?"

Tammy grimaced. "Sore."

"You hungry? I saved you a plate of food."

Tammy shook her head. "I'm not hungry."

Apart from a brief hello to Tammy, Lucas remained silent, his face giving away nothing of his thoughts.

Nina took a moment to study her friend. "Tammy, what's going on?"

Tammy gave a shrug. "I just got carried away, you know. Overdid it a little."

That was one perspective. "How could you let some guy do this to you?" *How could you do this to yourself?* was more in line with what she wanted to ask, but it felt like she'd be kicking Tammy when she was down. Perhaps that was a conversation for another time.

"You have a problem," Lucas stated flatly. "You need to check yourself into rehab."

Okay, then, so they were having this conversation now, it seemed.

"Stay out of it, Lucas," Tammy snapped. "I appreciate you helping me out last night, but I called Nina, not you."

"I have clients who struggle with drug addiction," Lucas said, keeping his voice even. "I can give you the contact details of a good treatment center."

"It's none of your business," Tammy said. "This is between me and Nina."

Anger flickered across his face. "What happens to Nina *is* my business."

His words hung in the air. Slowly, Tammy said, "So you and Lucas are together now."

"We are," Nina confirmed, reaching for Lucas's hand and gripping it tightly. He gave her a reassuring squeeze back.

Tammy tried for a smirk, but it didn't take. "Here's hoping it lasts."

"Lucas is right," Nina said, ignoring her cynical comment. "You need help."

"Look, I know I need help." Tammy's frank admission startled her. She could sense even Lucas's surprise. "But I've tried a treatment program before. It didn't work."

"That was a short-term program," Nina said, remembering. "Maybe a longer one—"

"I can't afford to take the time off work," Tammy blurted out. "I need the money."

"It doesn't take a genius to guess where all your money went," Lucas muttered darkly.

Tammy shot him a dirty look, but didn't respond. Nina watched as Tammy folded her hands in her lap and straightened her shoulders, like she was preparing for something. Fear ballooned in Nina's chest. She suddenly didn't want to hear what Tammy was going to say next.

"My landlord is kicking me out, and I need a place to stay," Tammy said, keeping her eyes on the coffee table. "I was thinking I could live with you for a while."

Yup, it was as bad as she feared.

Lucas didn't bother to hide his burst of harsh laughter. "You've got to be kidding me! Are you insane?"

"Please hear me out," Tammy begged, ignoring Lucas and fixing her gaze on Nina. "Nobody else understands me like you do. I want to get better, I do, but I can't manage it without you."

"Tammy, I really don't think—" Nina began.

"Blake knows where I live. I don't feel safe in my apartment anymore."

Nina kept silent, Tammy's arguments closing in on her.

"I've done some research," Tammy continued in a rush. "There's a therapist who has a practice in your area. I promise I'll go two, three times a week, whatever you want. Please, Nina, I can do this, but only with your help."

Then Tammy started to cry. Shock lurched through Nina. In all the years she'd known her, she'd never seen her cry. Not once. And that told her more than anything else how desperate Tammy was.

"Okay...look...don't cry. We'll figure something out."

Lucas stared at her. "Tell me you're not seriously considering this."

Nina scrubbed a frustrated hand over her face. She honestly didn't know what she was considering. At this point, all she was certain of was the terrible feeling of being pulled in two different directions.

There was a long, uncomfortable pause as tension swept over the living room. Then Lucas directed a pointed look at Tammy.

To her credit, Tammy picked up on his signal, mumbled a vague excuse and hobbled off to take a long shower, leaving the two of them alone. "Coffee?" Lucas asked after a minute.

"Yes, please."

They were both silent as Lucas made the coffee and Nina tidied up his kitchen. When he finally handed her a mug of hot, strong coffee, she knew they could delay it no longer. By some unspoken agreement they remained in the kitchen, out of earshot of Tammy.

"Nina." The way Lucas said her name was a soft rebuke. "You know that whenever Tammy's around, there's drama and chaos."

"I know." She tightened her grip on her mug. "And, yes, I admit that sometimes I'm sick and tired of dealing with her messes, but we've been friends for eleven years."

His brows knitted together. "The friendship you have with her—it's not healthy or stable."

"She just has bad days."

"She has a bad life!" Lucas set down his coffee with a hard *click*. "You're excusing her destructive pattern of behavior."

"I'm not excusing it!" she retorted, anger stirring. "But you don't know her past. You don't know what's happened to her. She needs me."

"You can't change her. She has to do this on her own."

"I know that, but she wants to change, and I can help her."

He rubbed the back of his neck. She could see him striving for calm. Lucas had a blind spot when it came to Tammy. Ironically, he'd level the same accusation at her.

"I don't believe her," Lucas said bluntly. "I think she's lying, manipulating you, because Tammy is all about manipulation."

"And you're all about distrust." The mouthful of coffee she'd taken soured on her tongue. "Your job has made you too suspicious of people."

"And you're too trusting. Especially where Tammy is concerned."

"Maybe that's the crux of it," Nina said. "I do believe her, and I want to give her a chance."

"I understand you want to help her, but *living* with you? That's a step too far."

"You heard her, she can't stay in her apartment anymore and she doesn't have money at the moment for her own place."

"When Pablo fired you, I told you that some fights you need to let go. This is one of those fights."

"I don't let friends go, Lucas!"

"She'll poison you and she'll poison our relationship," he said, a hint of desperation in his tone. "She's had plenty of practice."

Nina felt sick to her stomach, stunned that they were fighting like this. Everything felt so tangled and complicated. A few days ago, it had seemed so simple—she loved Lucas and he loved her. Against all odds, after so many years, they'd finally gotten together. And now this.

"You can't expect perfection from friends." It terrified her that perhaps he expected perfection from her. "Everyone messes up now and again."

Frustration tightened his jaw. "This is not now and again. This happens way too often with her."

"She said she'll go to therapy. That's a good sign."

He released a fast, hard breath. "If you allow Tammy to live with you, she'll do her best to destroy our relationship. I can't watch that happen."

"Now you're exaggerating."

"Am I? You've got a soft heart, Nina, and a habit of taking on lost causes, even at the expense of your own happiness. Tammy is taking advantage of that. I don't trust her. Not for one second."

"But you trust me, right? Well, trust me to do the right thing here. Support me in this."

"I can't support you when I know in my gut you're doing the wrong thing."

She stared at him, at a loss for words, her eyes burning. He didn't say the words, but his message hung heavily in the air nonetheless: *It's either Tammy or me. It can't be both of us.*

Some small, angry part of her couldn't help asking, what if there was another friend Lucas disapproved of? Would he force her to dump that friend as well?

Then again, he was looking out for her. His arguments were reasoned. He was concerned. Justifiably so.

But, she argued, shouldn't he support her decisions—even if he didn't agree with them? He accused her of having an unhealthy dynamic with Tammy, but wasn't his intransigence creating an unhealthy dynamic with her?

At last, Nina said, "Lucas, if you can't support me, perhaps we need a break from one another."

It felt almost unbearable for her to say the words. It looked as though it was equally unbearable for Lucas to hear them.

"A break?"

"Just for a little while. Just until Tammy gets back on her feet. I can't help her if you're fighting me every step of the way."

Lucas looked stunned. "She won't get back on her feet. Not if it means us getting together. She'll do anything to keep us apart."

"Lucas—"

"Nina, I love you."

Her throat was suddenly too tight for her to speak. Lucas didn't understand. This could be her one chance to finally break through to Tammy, to help her friend cold-shoulder the demons she'd been battling all her life. "I love you too, with all my heart, but I can't abandon Tammy."

He looked devastated. Furious. And a whole assortment of other emotions she couldn't identify. "So that's it? You're choosing Tammy over our relationship?"

Her stomach twisted hearing him say the words, the finality of them. Yes, that seemed to be exactly what she was doing. What other option was there? She couldn't deal with both Tammy's desperate need for help and the pressure Lucas was putting on her. It was all too much. It was as though she was trapped in a rollercoaster with no brakes and hurtling toward a decision she couldn't avoid. She drew in a jagged breath. "You're the one who forced this choice."

"Fine," he said abruptly, the hurt rippling across his face. "If it's Tammy you want, that's who you'll get."

Chapter Thirty-One

When Nina dragged herself out of bed and walked into Soul Fare on Monday morning, Frankie looked up from where he was stacking milk cartons into the small refrigerator under the counter and did a double take when he saw her. He straightened, wiping his hands on a dish towel.

"Everything all right?"

"Everything's fine, Frankie." Her voice sounded high and strange.

"You look a bit...weird."

"I didn't have the best night." An understatement. She'd had possibly the worst night of her life, staring at the dark ceiling for hours, the memory of the shattered look on Lucas's face as she and Tammy left his apartment causing pain to swell in her chest until she thought it would tear open.

Tammy had spent last night at Nina's place. They'd both been too exhausted to do much talking, but Tammy had hugged her tightly, the relief visible in her eyes, when Nina had said she could live with her as long as she promised to go to therapy regularly. Tammy had tried to ask about Lucas, but Nina had shut her down. No way was she discussing Lucas with Tammy.

Today, Tammy and a male stuntman colleague were heading back to Tammy's place to put her stuff into storage. Tammy had told her not to wait up, that she'd only be back later tonight. It was hard not to feel suspicious, but Nina didn't have the time, the energy, or the desire to police her friend.

"If you're not feeling great, why don't you take the day off?" Frankie suggested now.

She shook her head. "It's better if I'm at work."

Frankie nodded and said nothing more, but she noticed he kept a careful eye on her and was kind enough to make her hot, strong lattes whenever he thought she needed them, which appeared to be fairly often, as though caffeine was the only thing keeping her upright and functioning.

Nina had no idea how she got through the day. She interacted with diners and staff, but everyone and everything felt so far away. It was like she was half functioning, dragging heartache around like a diseased limb she wanted to rip off her body. She spent most of the time in her office, trying not to think about the fact that she and Lucas were no longer together. Thinking about it at all sent her spiraling.

After the last customer left Soul Fare and they'd finished cleaning up, Frankie lingered while she locked up and offered to walk her to her car. She couldn't think of a gracious way to tell him she'd prefer to be alone.

With both of them bundled up against the cold wind tearing down the street, Frankie said, "I'm putting it out there that you can talk to me anytime."

"Thanks, Frankie."

"Whatever it is you're going through, I've got your back." His awkward kindness had her fighting tears as he gave her shoulder a brief pat before striding away.

After climbing into her car, Nina sat in the driver's seat, took out her phone, and gave in to an urge she'd managed to resist all day: checking for any messages or missed calls from Lucas. Nothing. She felt... She didn't know what she felt. Disappointment? Anger? Anguish? None of the above. It was like she was dead inside.

She carefully placed her phone in her cup holder and drove home.

When she spotted Ryan's car in the street outside her apartment building, panic shot through her. She parked behind him and threw open her door.

"Calm down, nothing's happened to Liv or the baby," he reassured her as he approached.

She sagged against the car in relief.

"I came to talk to you about Lucas."

She stiffened. "What about Lucas?"

"Look, can we go inside?" Ryan shoved his hands into the pockets of his jacket. "It's cold out here."

"It's been a long day, Ry," she began.

"C'mon, sis, have a heart."

"Fine." She led the way inside. Ryan took off his jacket and settled on a barstool at the kitchen counter while Nina busied herself putting the kettle on and taking out mugs and tea bags and asking questions about Olivia and the pregnancy.

Ryan finally had enough of her deflecting. "What the heck's going on between you and Lucas?"

"Nothing," she mumbled.

He gave her the look he'd perfected over the years, the how-stupid-do-you-think-I-am look. "I spoke to Lucas today. I invited him to a barbecue at our place this weekend, and he asked if you were coming. I said I planned to invite you later today, and you know what he said? He wouldn't be able to make it. When I asked why, he told me to speak to you. He sounded grumpy as all heck."

Avoiding his eyes, Nina poured boiling water into the mugs and frowned at the slowly darkening liquid swirling inside. Why had she made tea? She wasn't a tea drinker. She hated tea.

"What's going on? Have you two had a fight or something?"

"It's between us."

"Don't give me that line," Ryan retorted. "You're my sister and he's my best friend. Heck, he's your best friend too."

She lifted her eyes to meet his. "What if I never wanted him to be my friend?"

Confusion clouded Ryan's face. "I don't understand."

"You never figured it out?" she asked.

"Figured what out?"

"That I'm in love with Lucas!"

He gaped at her. "What?"

Nina told him how she'd fallen in love with Lucas at the house party and how she'd been in love with him ever since. The words poured out of her—how they'd finally gotten together, the incident with Tammy, and what she saw as Lucas's ultimatum.

Ryan's mouth opened and closed. It was rare seeing her brother at a loss for words. He typically had so much to say, and that was what she expected now, some lame joke meant to snap her out of it or a lecture on Tammy's bad influence.

Ryan, however, surprised her. He came around the counter and wrapped his arms around her.

And that numbness, that dead feeling that had encased her for all of today and kept her talking and breathing and going through the motions, melted away, and Nina cried. She cried like she couldn't stop. Ryan held her and didn't say anything, but his hug said it all.

#

Three days after Tammy moved in, Nina overheard her on the phone making an appointment with a therapist. The stab of relief she felt startled her. Only to herself could she admit she'd half expected Tammy not to keep her promise.

In the evenings, if Nina wasn't catching up on paperwork, she and Tammy would watch TV on the couch. Tammy favored reality shows and Nina didn't object. Other people's drama took her mind off her own. Tammy felt the need to cook most nights, and although cooking wasn't her strength (her meals were too oversauced and overspiced), Nina appreciated the effort she put in.

Tammy had work, but nothing too hectic. She was training with a B-list actor for a fight scene for a low-budget TV show. Since she wasn't needed all the time, she was gone for only a few days a week, allowing her to schedule visits with her therapist in between.

ALL THE LOST PIECES

Nina threw all her energy into work. A large chunk of her time was taken up with setting up Soul Fare's social media accounts. She'd discovered some time ago that the restaurant had an abysmal digital presence. She'd been meaning to rectify that for a while now, knowing they were missing out on a large customer base. With that in mind, she worked on making sure Soul Fare had a presence on Facebook, Twitter, and Instagram. She posted every day, hoping to build brand awareness and drive traffic to the restaurant.

Ryan was worried about the amount of time she was spending at work, but her brother didn't understand that the restaurant was a world Lucas didn't occupy, one where she didn't encounter memories of him around every corner.

It helped that she was getting along well with Jeena. The chalkboard outside Soul Fare was a huge hit. After only two weeks, Nina noticed an increase in walk-in diners, as well as more and more people stopping in their tracks to take selfies of whatever illustration or amusing saying Jeena had created for the day. The movie club ladies in particular enjoyed the chalkboard, especially as Jeena had taken to drawing a famous actor on Mondays and Thursdays and the ladies got a kick out of guessing who it was.

Nina invited Edith to lunch one day, and Edith expressed absolute delight at the changes. She kept staring at the wall displaying the paintings of various local artists. They hadn't yet managed to sell any, but a number of diners had expressed interest, and Nina was confident of a sale soon.

"Bill would love this." Edith blinked back tears. "He was all for supporting the local community."

Thinking it a perfect opportunity, Nina spoke to Edith about a pay raise for both Jeena and Cody. Edith was quick to agree, and Nina let her convey the good news to them.

When Edith left the restaurant an hour later, a beaming Cody rushed over to thank her and tell her he was thinking about saving his money to study sound engineering. A terrific idea, she told him.

Jeena waited until the end of the day before approaching her in her office. "You know, when you first arrived, I thought the absolute worst of you."

"I know." Curiosity prompted her to ask, "Why?"

Jeena gave a half shrug. "Almost all the restaurant managers I've worked with have claimed my ideas as their own."

"I'm sorry to hear that," Nina said. It was a relief to discover that Jeena's initial antagonism and distrust had little to do with her. Her mother was right when she'd said that all relationships are colored by the baggage everyone carries with them.

"I came to apologize," Jeena said, "and to thank you for speaking to Edith about a raise."

"Apology accepted." She held Jeena's gaze. "And your talent earned you that raise."

Jeena looked down at her clasped hands. "Maybe after work sometime, we could go for a drink or something."

It was a moment before Nina could speak. *Find joy and purpose in the small moments,* she'd read somewhere, and it was advice she was surviving on. She found a smile for Jeena. "I'd like that very much."

\#

Ryan and Olivia extended frequent invitations to hang out at their place, which Nina was happy to do since it gave her breathing space from Tammy, who was on her best behavior, but every time Nina looked at her, she was reminded of the choice she'd made. Ryan and Olivia tried to hide how worried they were, but concern was written all over them as they hovered over her, offering her endless plates of food as though she wasn't feeding herself, chatting in overbright voices about Olivia's voracious appetite and huge stomach. They spoke about nearly every subject under the sun except for the one that mattered to all of them. Nina watched a lot of movies at their place. By unspoken agreement, there were no romantic comedies or tragic love stories. Instead, they watched films with drawn-out car chases where everyone was double-crossing everyone else and where the body count was as high as the cleavage on display. Mindless stuff. Ryan was beside himself with excitement whenever the TV was switched on.

No one mentioned Lucas.

On her days off, she and Olivia went on slow, ambling walks exploring the countryside. They spoke about Cheryl and Liv's father and the baby, and Nina found these walks to be a sanity saver. Olivia's expression was often troubled whenever Nina mentioned Tammy. Nina knew her sister-in-law shared Lucas's opinion of Tammy, but Liv was tactful enough to simply listen and not say anything.

Nina tried her best to contain her thoughts to work and family, but sometimes, her attempt at self-censorship failed, and there'd be a cut-off-at-the-knees memory involving Lucas. Her head, it seemed, was filled with him. Right now, lying in bed and staring at a shadowy ceiling, she was torturing herself by reliving every exquisite sensation of Lucas's hands on her skin, the heat of his body pressed against hers, the smell and taste and feel of him.

The undertow of pain was fierce and fast. Nina went rigid with the savagery of it. She'd once heard that if you're caught in an undertow in the ocean, you're to hold your breath and eventually, you'll pop up to the surface. So she held herself perfectly still and waited it out, and finally, finally, she could breathe again.

Chapter Thirty-Two

Three weeks after her breakup with Lucas, Nina's alarm went off, and she opened her eyes to discover that the world no longer felt like one dark hole swallowing her up. She lay in bed and tested the feeling, tears pricking her eyes when she realized the desire to pull the covers over her head and sink into an endless sleep wasn't there anymore. The world still felt gray and dull, but it was no longer black. It was a start.

Tammy was still sleeping when Nina left for work. She called her mother from the car. They were speaking more often, tentative conversations where they were both discovering more about each other's lives and trying to listen without judgment and criticism. Ironically, Nina still hadn't told her mother about Lucas. Cheryl adored Lucas, calling him her second son, and Nina wasn't yet at the stage where she felt ready to test the dynamics of their newfound bond.

Arriving at work, she was depositing her handbag in her office when Frankie walked in and placed a large latte on her desk.

"Thanks, Frankie." She picked up the mug and took a sip. "Mmm, tastes heavenly."

Frankie's eyes widened in surprise, and he stared closely at her.

"What?" Nina asked.

He stumbled a bit over his words. "Uh, this is the first time in nearly three weeks that you've, well, complimented my coffee."

She waved away his words. "Don't be silly. I love your coffee. Of course I've complimented you."

Quietly, Frankie said, "No, you haven't."

"Really?" she asked, suddenly uncomfortable.

"Really. We've all been pretty worried."

In the face of her confusion, Frankie recounted how everyone at the restaurant had sensed she'd been hit hard by something and they'd all rallied around her. To her amazement, Nina learned that Jeena had stepped in to shield her whenever there was a difficult diner, Ano had made sure she ate by cooking some of her favorite meals, keeping the portions small when he realized she didn't have much of an appetite, Cody had put together playlists of upbeat music in an attempt to lift her spirits, and, most amazing of all, Stefan and Sunan had taken it in turns to follow her home every night, making sure she arrived safely.

A lump formed in her throat. Their small acts of kindness undid her. All at once, she remembered Frankie bringing her cups of coffee throughout the day, sitting with her while she ate so she wasn't alone. She said shakily, "Frankie, I had no idea."

"Good," he said, his voice gentle. "We didn't do it so you'd know. We did it because we care about you."

#

Nina soon had a chance to repay Ano for his kindness. She discovered that while her chef was a creative genius in the kitchen, he wasn't too imaginative when it came to writing up menu descriptions. In fact, his descriptions were so bland, Nina's taste buds couldn't even stir themselves. What diner was going to get excited reading a menu that was simply a sterile list of ingredients?

Nina was all ready to step in and help Ano write the menu, but as she watched Jeena compose a clever saying for today's chalkboard, she had an idea. Casually, Nina wandered over to Jeena to chat to her about working with Ano on the menu. Jeena played it cool, but Nina noticed her face light up with eagerness. Once she'd roped in Jeena, she crossed over to Ano's kingdom to talk to him, and he agreed before she'd even finished speaking.

At the end of the day, as a result of her shameless manipulations, Ano and Jeena were sitting at a table together, heads bent nice and close, smiling shyly at one another as they worked on descriptions for the various dishes.

"An awesome move of yours," Frankie commented, pausing in the cleaning of his barista station to observe the two of them.

"I have a gift," Nina acknowledged.

"Your matchmaking streak has achieved what we've been trying for ages to pull off."

"They make a cute couple," Nina said. "It's up to them now."

Frankie's eyes fixed on hers. "What about you, Nina?"

She stiffened. "I'm fine, Frankie."

Sympathy softened his gaze. He knew she was anything but fine. He offered her his arm. "How about we leave Ano and Jeena to lock up, and you and I go out for that long overdue drink?"

Gratitude welled up inside her, and she linked her arm in his. "Sounds like a marvelous idea."

#

Ano and Jeena became a couple after that evening. They suited one another, Nina thought. Jeena softened Ano's stern demeanor, the chef cracking a smile more often and more easily. And in the headlights of Ano's adoring gaze, Jeena glowed, her confidence blooming.

They were also formidable work partners. Ano's culinary skills and Jeena's flair for descriptive writing resulted in a menu that was an instant hit with diners, both regulars and newcomers. The adjectives were punchy and mouthwatering: charred lemon butter asparagus, orange-infused ricotta hot cake, wild mushroom medley, crispy pan-seared salmon, caramelized butternut. Some days, Soul Fare was so full, the queue was out the door.

Edith popped into the restaurant at least once a week, sipping her tea and soaking up the energy and enthusiasm around her. A couple of days ago, she'd casually mentioned that in the not-too-distant future she might be open to selling Soul Fare. Of course, she added with a smile, there was only one person she'd consider handing over her baby to. Every time Nina thought of that conversation, a lightness came over her. Maybe her dream of owning her own restaurant was closer than she'd ever dared to hope.

While work was satisfying and her relationship with her mother had improved to a level that left Ryan and Olivia at a loss for words, Nina was still wrestling with the crushing truth that she and Lucas hadn't communicated for over three weeks now. Yes, here she was, soldiering on in her life journey, carving her own path and so on, but how crappy and sad that all she could see was one set of footprints on this path.

"You know, you're better off without him," Tammy said one evening while they were cleaning up after a dinner of steak, baby potatoes, and roasted vegetables.

Nina knew exactly which *him* Tammy was referring to. "I'd say it's a conflict of interest, you giving me relationship advice with regard to Lucas," she said flatly.

"Yeah, so I'm biased, but you need to get on with your life."

That was rich, coming from someone who was living with Nina because her own lifestyle was so financially and emotionally destructive, she couldn't afford to live on her own, but Nina bit down on the sharp retort. She didn't want to provoke her, not when Tammy was having more good days than bad. On the good days, usually after her sessions with her therapist, Tammy would return all energized, making an effort to clean the apartment and asking after Nina's day. Watching Tammy slowly reclaim her life was a gratifying reminder that she'd made the right choice.

On the bad days, however, Nina would return home and Tammy would still be in bed, fast asleep, the room smelling stale and sour. Nina would bet she'd spent the whole day sleeping. She'd sigh and wake her up, and Tammy would be confused and disoriented, and

Nina prayed she wasn't doing drugs. When Tammy was in the shower, Nina pushed aside any qualms of conscience and searched her room, but she found no evidence that Tammy was using again.

Tammy visited Soul Fare only once, wanting to see where Nina worked. Nina joined her for lunch, and afterward introduced her to everyone. Cody, of course, was immediately captivated by Tammy, Jeena was polite but wary, and Ano was his usual taciturn self, immune to Tammy's charms.

And then, one Saturday evening, Nina returned home after dropping by Ryan and Olivia's place to find a strange man sprawled on her couch, Tammy sprawled all over him. Her coffee table was littered with dirty plates and glasses.

Anger rose up inside her, and she pulled Tammy aside. "You know our deal—no strange guys in my home."

Tammy smirked. "His name is Dillon, and he's not a stranger to me."

"My house, my rules."

"My parents spent my whole life suffocating me with their rules! Now you're doing the same thing!"

Nina silently counted to three. "Get rid of him, Tammy."

"What's your problem? We're not drinking or using."

"I'm taking a shower. He better be gone when I come out."

Brushing past her, Tammy muttered, "Your house has become the place where fun goes to die."

Nina didn't see the man again after that. Tammy sulked for a few days, then seemed to move on. Nina, however, found she was struggling with a sense of exhaustion as she constantly tried to guess what mood Tammy was in, what her reaction would be to some piece of news she shared with her. She started having headaches and a weird pain in her stomach. She went to the doctor and his first question was "Do you have any stress in your life right now?"

"This is not what friendship is supposed to look like," Olivia said with a worried furrow between her eyebrows, when Nina shared a little of her feelings with her. "I know you care about Tammy and you're trying to be a good friend here, but at what cost to yourself?"

"Funnily enough, that's what Lucas said."

"Companionship, enjoyment, support, upliftment. That's what you should get from friends."

"The good news is that Tammy's getting stronger. She's doing really well with her therapist."

"When will she be strong enough to move out and live on her own?" Olivia asked.

"I don't know."

"Nina —"

"How's Lucas?" Nina asked, changing the subject. "I assume you guys still see him?"

"Of course we do," Olivia said. "He looks as miserable as you."

"Thanks."

"He also asked after you," Olivia admitted on a sigh.

A swell of happiness and longing filled Nina's chest. "He did?"

Olivia shook her head unhappily. "The two of you. You're meant to be together, but you're both so unbelievably stubborn. And now you're both paying the price for your stubbornness."

Chapter Thirty-Three

On Wednesday, half an hour before the preshift meeting, Nina was sitting at one of the tables in Soul Fare's dining area, checking her e-mail, when Ano appeared in front of her, looking smart in his crisp chef's jacket and black pants.

"I need to talk to you," he said, looking uncomfortable.

She closed her laptop. "Okay."

He eased himself into the chair across from her. "I saw Tammy in town yesterday," he began, and then he told her that he'd listened to his gut and followed Tammy to a storefront on the town's outskirts, where she'd gone inside. "You should know that the owner of that store has a reputation as a drug dealer," he finished.

"How do you know that?" she asked around the bitter lump of disappointment in her throat.

"The info came from someone I trust."

Nina buried her face in her hands, her mood bottoming out. She took a long, uneven breath and glanced up. "What time was this?"

"Around four."

"Tammy was supposed to be visiting her therapist at that time."

Ano kept quiet.

Nina looked at the smart, kind face of her chef. There was Ano, on his day off, looking out for her. "Thank you for telling me."

He gave a brief nod and pushed to his feet. His arm lifted, and for a moment, she thought he might pat her shoulder, but then he turned away and disappeared into the kitchen.

It was impossible to concentrate after that. After making a phone call, Nina left work and drove to her apartment.

"You're home early," Tammy said in surprise, tucked under a blanket on the living room couch.

Nina picked up the remote and switched off the TV.

"Hey," Tammy protested, sitting up.

"Have you been seeing your therapist?"

A guarded look came over Tammy's face. "Of course."

Resentment burned in Nina's chest. She'd always told herself that this was a season for Tammy, that this wasn't her story, but now she wasn't so sure.

"I phoned him, Tammy. He said the last time you came to see him was weeks ago."

"What the heck is this?" Tammy exploded. "Are you sneaking around behind my back?"

Feeling her heart rate rise with her next words, Nina said, "Lucas was right. I want you to pack your bags and leave. You need to book yourself into rehab."

"You're Lucas's mouthpiece now?" She waved a disbelieving hand in the air. "I asked for your help, not for a lecture like you're my keeper. You're supposed to be my friend. Are you seriously kicking me out?"

Nina's stomach cramped as a sliver of doubt snuck in. Was she doing the right thing here? What if her actions pushed Tammy over the edge? She felt her resolve weakening, but then she remembered all Tammy's broken promises. All the lies. And her own sleepless nights and worry-filled days.

She was suddenly infused with strength. Yes, she was doing the right thing. At last.

"Tammy, you need help, and I realize now I can't give you that help. I've messaged you the contact details of a good treatment center. Please call them. Not for me. Do it for yourself."

Tammy's composure faltered for the first time. "I'm not an addict," she said. "I only use drugs to take the edge off, like everyone else in my circle."

Tears pricked Nina's eyes. She blinked them away. "I want you out by the end of the week."

A hardness came over Tammy's face. "You know what, I'll be glad to go, because you never really trusted me, anyway. Not when you had lover boy keeping tabs on me all this time."

Nina frowned. "What are you talking about?"

Tammy gave her a who-are-you-kidding look. "Why do you think Dillon never came around to your place again? It sure as heck wasn't because you laid down your petty house rules. Lover boy scared him away, that's why."

It took her a moment before it sank in. Lucas. Watching over her, despite what she'd said to him. She felt a painful tightening in her chest. She'd messed up. Spectacularly. Sometimes, she was her own worst enemy.

Without hesitation, she said to Tammy, "Please make sure you're out of my apartment by the end of the week."

There was nothing more she could do for her friend, Nina concluded, feeling a swirl of conflicting emotions. There was anger and despair, a great deal of sorrow, but also a glimmer of relief that she would no longer have to deal with Tammy and her erratic mood swings, her phone calls in the middle of the night. She would no longer have to deal with the worry, the endless worry over what Tammy was doing, what she would say next, and how much it was going to hurt.

She left Tammy alone in the living room and immediately called Olivia. "I need your help."

#

The front door opened. Nina heard Ry's voice, and then the deep rumble of Lucas answering him. A swell of nerves rolled through her stomach. She was surprised to discover she was trembling.

"Breathe," Olivia instructed, giving her arm a reassuring squeeze.

"This no longer feels like a good plan," Nina said.

"It's a *very* good plan."

"It's a desperate plan."

Olivia eyed her. "Well, yes, because you are desperate."

There was no denying that. She needed to fix what was broken between her and Lucas, mostly because she was the one who'd wielded the hammer to their relationship. The same self-destructive hammer she'd been swinging most of her life.

"Besides," Olivia said, "it's too late to back out now."

Yes, it was, since Nina heard Ryan and Lucas make their way toward the living room, where she was standing with Olivia, trying not to appear like the sad, desperate, hopeful person she was.

Right after she'd told Tammy to leave, Nina had enlisted Ryan and Olivia's help to cajole (Ry would insist *trick*) Lucas into coming to their house this Friday evening and to please not mention that she would be there. Nina wanted neutral territory and she didn't want to take the chance that Lucas would refuse to meet her if she approached him directly. Ry and Liv had eagerly agreed to help her, almost as keen as she was for her and Lucas to sort things out.

This morning, Tammy had packed up her stuff and was gone before Nina left for work. She didn't say where she was going and Nina didn't ask. As an extra precaution, Nina had organized for the locks to be changed to her apartment.

The moment Lucas walked into the living room, Nina felt the impact of his presence like a shock wave. Oh, how she'd missed him! Please, she prayed now, there had to be a way to come back from your mistakes.

As soon as Lucas saw her, he stopped dead, glancing over at Ryan with a frown.

"Surprise," Ryan said with a sheepish grin.

"What's going on?" Lucas asked, and Nina's heart ached at how tired and vulnerable he looked.

Olivia grabbed Ryan's arm, tugging him toward their bedroom. "Right, we're just going to leave you two alone."

"Don't disturb us!" Ryan called out, and Olivia gave his arm a playful swat, her cheeks reddening.

Once they'd gone, Nina locked eyes with Lucas. The silence stretched between them, the air swirling with all the awfulness of the past month. Nina had a whole speech prepared, but she was so overcome by the sight of him that the words wouldn't emerge. They somehow felt too small for such a huge moment.

"How are you?" she couldn't help asking, which, hats off to her, took the prize for the stupidest way to start this sort of conversation.

He took a long time before answering. "Not good."

"Neither am I," she said softly.

He simply nodded, and she didn't know if it was her imagination, but she thought his expression said, *And whose fault is that?*

"I've missed you," she confessed, her voice cracking a little at the admission.

She watched him swallow. "Why am I here, Nina?"

"You're here because you're the first person I think of when I wake up in the morning. I go to sleep and dream of you. Throughout the day, I'm wondering what you're doing and if you're okay." Her voice hitched. "I never want to give you a reason to leave me again."

"I never left you," Lucas said. "I might not have been physically at your side, but I never left you. I was always close."

His words floored her. For several stunned seconds, she couldn't speak as her mind struggled to comprehend the magnitude of what he was telling her, then she said, "Tammy said you scared away that guy friend of hers—Dillon, I think his name is?"

"We had a chat, yes. His criminal record didn't make for pleasant reading."

"Why would you do that?" she asked in a whisper. "I mean, I was the one who asked you for a break."

ALL THE LOST PIECES

"I gave you the space you wanted, but I didn't trust Tammy and I needed to make sure you would be okay. I couldn't let anything bad happen to you."

Nina's eyes widened as realization hit, and it was suddenly hard for her to breathe. "Wait a minute, were you Ano's *trusted source*?"

After the briefest hesitation, he nodded. "Ano didn't trust Tammy either. When he saw Tammy visit that storefront, he got hold of me. I did some digging and found out that Ano was right to be suspicious. The store owner is a drug dealer."

"You never left," she said in wonderment. "In spite of what I said."

"You can't get rid of me that easily," he said.

"Lucas, you were right about Tammy. You're here right now because I wanted to say how sorry I am. I'm sorry for not listening to you. All these weeks I've been so stubborn and stupid and I nearly threw away the most precious person in my life."

He was quiet for a moment, digesting her words. "I'm not entirely blameless here," he admitted. "I put you in a difficult position, making you ultimately choose between Tammy or me. It wasn't fair to you." She watched as the tension left his shoulders. "Come here." He pulled her urgently to him, his arms closing around her, as though he couldn't bear to be apart from her for one more second. Her only thought was how perfectly they fit together. Then he kissed her, and she stopped thinking, losing all awareness of reality and riding the exhilarating and intoxicating rush of being in Lucas's arms again.

When Lucas pulled back slightly, disappointment flickered through her, but his eyes met hers and he said, "I love you, Nina Sarah Abrahams." There was no hesitation in his voice, no conflict in his expression. He seemed absolutely, one hundred percent sure of this. Of them.

"I love you too," she whispered, her palm flat against his heart, feeling the strong, steady beat there.

Then he murmured against her lips, "Would you like to have dinner with me next Saturday?"

Her breath caught. "Which restaurant?"

His slow grin had her heart beating faster. "Belles Âmes."

Acknowledgments

I couldn't have written All the Lost Pieces without the following people:

My husband, Craig. You deserve the first mention because I absolutely couldn't have done this without you at my side. You are the love of my life. Your love and support mean the world to me.

My daughter, Paige, who loves books as much as I do. Thank you for reading this book with great enthusiasm and offering invaluable feedback.

My amazing editor, Linda Ingmanson. This is a much better story because of your insights.

Sarah Hansen from Okay Creations for my gorgeous front cover.

Huge thanks to my beta-readers for your feedback and support.

Lastly, thank you to my sister, Karina, for giving me the spark of an idea for this book. The most outlandish things seem to happen to you (in this case, that live auction you participated in), and I end up shamelessly inserting these incidents into my novels. Thanks, sis!

About the Author

Lara Martin writes books about imperfect people living messy lives, falling in love and getting their perfect happily-ever-after. She's lived in South Africa and Australia and now calls the UK her home. She's tried a variety of amazing and awful jobs: video game reviewer, graphic designer, insurance claims agent (she has no idea how she landed this one), proof reader, feature writer, and magazine editor. She lives with her husband (always the first reader of her novels), two slightly terrifying teenagers, and the requisite psychotic cat. When she's not writing, she can be found haunting local coffee shops.

You can find her online at laramartinauthor.com, @laramartinauthor on Instagram, or @Laramartin123 on Twitter.

Printed in Great Britain
by Amazon

21975456R00192